The Journey
(Beyond the Savage)

By

Susan Kaye Behm

One half of the royalties for this book go to support
the Ephesians Life Ministries.

Also by Susan Kaye Behm:

Civilized Savages

Secrets in Paradise

R.A.C.E.

"This is a powerful story of a ritual abuse survivor's struggle
        To be heard, believed, and accepted
        To learn what is normal and deal with questions of what is real
        To accept that she was not permanently damaged and not perma-
        nently separated into an alien world, a life apart, on the outside
        looking in.
This tells of a courageous journey
        From hiding her true self to being known
        From wanting to die to choosing life
        From being shaped by the past to living in the now
        From being disillusioned and disappointed to learning to trust
        God and people
This story can impact those who have experienced abusive treatment and
        those who want to help."

Eleanor Sloat, MS, MA, LCPC, RN, CS-P

"Susan Kaye Behm has done it again…a compelling must read…this is one sequel that can stand alone. We follow the story of Joey Benson and her struggle through acceptance, gang violence, and even more abuse.

Debbi Lawson, AASDP

"Through compassion, and an amazing thing God calls Grace, *The Journey*, illustrates that a life abused and nearly destroyed can be redeemed. The author seems to have that cherished 'seeing the forest through the trees' mentality that should motivate us all to press on and reach deeper and higher despite worldly trials."

Melissa Baker, B.S.

"A young girl's unrelenting search for freedom from obstacles is so great that they threaten to overwhelm and destroy her mind, body, and soul. It's the story of loving grandparents who prayed and a teacher who saw more than a rebellious girl, and who dared to reach out and care. For anyone longing for Hope in the midst of their own tiresome struggle, this book is a beacon of light in the dark world of abuse."

Patricia Best

"This book took me into a world I knew existed but otherwise would never have visited. It has had a powerful impact on my life and will do the same for you...Thank God for a survivor-turned-author who takes her horrible experiences and uses them to help others. She is an amazing inspiration to me and will be an amazing inspiration to you, too! There were times I wanted to put the book down because I felt as though I was experiencing the pain right along with the character, and I wanted it to stop...then I realized that if she could keep going, I needed to keep going. I wanted her to know that I supported her and was determined to walk this journey with her. I am so glad that I did, and you will be too."

Laura Poore

"An inspiring journey from abuse and shame to healing and hope."

Theresa Conrad, B.A.

In this moving sequel to *Civilized Savages,* author Susan K. Behm once again plunges us into the brutal, almost surreal world of abuse survivor Joey Benson. Using the first person narrator, Behm blends candid, insightful musings with detailed descriptions, so that even the most innocent of us understands the horror of coping with the aftermath of sexual abuse. In the end, Joey's prayers are answered when she finds one person who endeavors to rescue her, restore her faith and lead her to salvation, begging us to question what we can do to reach out to those who are broken and forced to live in silent shame. For too long the epidemic of ritual abuse has been ignored. Thanks to Susan Behm, the victims not only have an advocate, they have a voice.

Maria E. Hayner, B.S. Ed., B.S. Bible

Ephesians Life Ministries is a private, non-profit organization which provides faith-based counseling, support groups, and education to individuals, couples and families struggling with addictions, trauma or abuse, depression, anxiety, grief, relationship problems and other mental health issues. While the views expressed by the author do not necessarily reflect those of our ministry, we support her efforts to increase awareness of the horror of sexual abuse of children.

For further information, contact us at:

Ephesians Life Ministries
1620 Elton Road, #204
Silver Spring, MD 20903
301/439-7191
www.ephesians.org

For the Family's big
White Family, big
Our daily choices, big
and small, affect everyone
we contact. One choice we can
and should make is to love and
reach out to those who are hurting.
Awareness brings caring and caring brings
love and love brings action.

God bless you!

SK Behn
I Chron 28:20

June 10, 2006

651898

customer's order no.		phone		date 6/10/06

name The White Family

address

city, state, zip

sold by	cash ☐	charge ☐	shipping information
	c.o.d. ☐	on acct. ☐	

quantity	description	price	amount
1	Civilized Savages		15 00
2	Journey		16 00
3			31 00
4			
5			
6			
7			
8			
9			
10			
11			
12			
13			
14			

received by

a adams   keep this slip for reference   DC5808UV

Dedication

A special thank you to Debbi, who has seen me at my best and my
worst and is still there to prop me up on the leaning side.
And to Bob and Pat who find it in their hearts
to spend time praying for me and
they are special people to a lonely adult.
And to Connie and Tom, who always have an
encouraging word and are ready to pray with me
to help me keep on going.
And to Laura, who is always ready to push me a little
farther than I think I can go.
To Diane, who keeps me in her prayers to keep me
on the right path.
And to Maria, who is ready to give a listening ear when I need it.
To the ladies who make up my special support network, who pray
for me on a regular basis and are always there with an encouraging
word and a prayer.
To the members of Fellowship Baptist Church -- who have become
my family -- and to the rest of my support network; they
support me through the ups and downs of my healing journey.
And to Mrs. J and Mrs. B., the two Christian teachers who
influenced my life because they let Jesus' love flow through
them to a lonely suicidal teenager.
And to Sue, who is there to constantly uplift, encourage,
support, and have faith in me that I can do it.

Table of Contents

Author's Notes xiii
Prologue xv
Chapter – 1   Dumped off 17
Chapter – 2   Family Strangers 21
Chapter – 3   No Escape 29
Chapter – 4   The Misfit..................................33
Chapter – 5   Mirror Image 39
Chapter – 6   Prejudice in Action...................49
Chapter – 7   Us Against the World 55
Chapter – 8   Confused and Alone 67
Chapter – 9   Learning Prejudice 79
Chapter – 10   Plan of Doom 89
Chapter – 11   Unspeakable Lessons 99
Chapter – 12   A Special Friend.....................109
Chapter – 13   Don't Feel 117
Chapter – 14   Invitation for Trouble 131
Chapter – 15   Welcome to my World 139
Chapter – 16   Still Captive 149
Chapter – 17   Don't Tell 157
Chapter – 18   Revenge War 161
Chapter – 19   Flashbacks and Memories.......167
Chapter – 20   To Survive 179
Chapter – 21   Mistaken Plan..........................183
Chapter – 22   The New Order Lives on..........187
Chapter – 23   All Alone 197

Chapter – 24   Time to Die?.............................205
Chapter – 25   Don't Feel 213
Chapter – 26   Lost Opportunity.....................225
Chapter – 27   Nothing Left?..........................235
Chapter – 28   Pain of Feeling.......................239
Chapter – 29   One Makes a Difference 247
Chapter – 30   Emptiness Within....................255
Chapter – 31   Unsweet Sixteen......................263
Chapter – 32   Random Kindness....................271
Chapter – 33   The Sun Rises 275
Chapter – 34   Step Forward...........................285
Chapter – 35   Echoes of Darkness.................289
Chapter – 36   Wanted, One Childhood...........297
Chapter – 37   New Life?.................................299
Chapter – 38   New Hope?...............................305
Chapter – 39   Heart Changes.........................317
Chapter – 40   My Journey 321
Epilogue 323
Living Tapestry 325
Appendix – A   Definition of Terms...............335
Appendix – B   Helpful Websites for Support and
               Information 339

Author's Notes

The Journey is a work of fiction based on many of my own true-life events with certain things changed to protect the victims and the survivors. Life is never easy. For some, however, it is made even harder by the bad choices of others. It is only through the grace of God that these choices can be overcome and the individual can eventually acquire hope to keep moving forward through their life's journey.

You may ask, why I would choose to expose such personal and private matters? If the things shared here can help to raise the awareness of just one person, and through that awareness he or she begins to care about those who are hurting around them, then possibly we may be able to prevent another individual from becoming an innocent victim of abuse. If that can happen, then I can feel a sense of purpose to some of these things that have happened to me. In addition, the process of giving voice to one's experiences becomes an acceptance of that knowledge, and this is an important part of the healing process. By listening to our own voice, we can hear the voices of others. When we pay close enough attention, we hear our own pain; we validate our own struggle, and recognize our own strength. This is one way to become whole again.

I have been termed a "survivor" by most people who know me. Survivor is an interesting description. I define a survivor as one who goes through a number of trials, beats the odds of endurance, and emerges victoriously to talk about their experiences. If that is what a survivor is, perhaps I do qualify. To truly survive, however, we must have a purpose to our survival, or there is nothing to grab onto when the journey feels impossible and the odds insurmountable. My purpose, I suppose, for surviving was to reach beyond mere survival and existence and refusing to give into the pain and depression. I have continued to survive only because I am not one who gives her their circumstances. I refuse to let my abusers win.

Tori Ames said "Healing takes courage, and we all have courage, even if we have to dig a little to find it."

It is my prayer that your awareness will be raised so that you will care, and that through your caring you will seek out people, like me, who are hurting so badly inside, and you will let us know you accept and care about us. You may not understand what has happened to us, but what we need more than anything is a friend.

In writing *The Journey*, it is my purpose not only to give you a deeper understanding of my own experience, but also to sensitize you to those around you and the pain they may be facing. We do not know the potential hurts and horrors inside the people we meet every day of our lives, but we do know that we are commanded to care. We are God's arms and legs on this earth as we display the love of the compassionate heart of the Creator of the Universe. We can be the comforting hand that helps others over the rough spots, and the shoulder to lean on through the rough experiences of life. For those of us on this journey, we can use our own experiences to help others find peace in the love of their friends and family, and above all, in the family of God.

Prologue

In "*The Journey*", Susan Kaye Behm's intriguing sequel to "*Civilized Savages*" we continue to follow the perseverance of Josephine Benson. We see how Josephine Benson, a typical 11-year-old girl, is delightfully oblivious to the rampant unemployment, runaway inflation, and other problems plaguing the world of adults. Following a knock on the door of her grandparents' home, Josephine's childhood ends and her nightmare begins. The "New Order" is attempting to seize control of the country, and Josephine is one of the early and expendable pawns in this grab for power. The leaders of this group relentlessly and systematically use whatever means available to steal the childhood of these children-their dignity their humanity-until they become killing robots. These children endure many brainwashing techniques: drugs, torture, guilt, shame, fear, rage, and deprivation.

Somehow through all of this organized abuse, "Joey" is able to keep her world separated from theirs. The Underground movement rescues Joey and returns her to the outside world. Now, in *The Journey*, we walk side by side with Joey as she battles to overcome her programming to seek peace within herself. We journey with her as she deals with puberty, adjusting to her new life of living with her parents, endures even more abuse, and faces prejudice from the local towns people at every turn. We will walk with Joey as she moves from victim to survivor and from survivor to victor. We will struggle with her, cry with her, and become angry for her. Through all these emotions, we'll watch this preteen grow into a young woman and see one individual's struggle to overcome the abuse that was inflicted upon her.

Chapter - 1 - Dumped Off

T he old, broken down sedan coughed and wheezed its way down the nearly deserted street. Bumping to a stop, it hit the curb right in front of the dining hall, and I finally allowed myself to breathe. The anxiety slowly gave way to guarded relief as the realization that I had made it began to register … I was here! I was going to college!

I was anxious to exit the stuffy car and breathe the air of freedom.

"We'll let you out here," Mother snapped in her usual commanding and otherwise emotionless tone.

"Okay!" I replied.

All I wanted was to get out of the car before I discovered that perhaps this was all a dream and I would awaken back at home, once again a slave to Mother and all her whims.

She scooted her front seat forward slightly, and I tried to squeeze myself through the small opening. Though I didn't dare mutter it out loud for fear of being forced back in the car and driven home again, I couldn't help but wonder why she couldn't have just gotten out of the car? I suppose because that would've been the considerate thing to do, so Mother did the opposite. Instead, I struggled to force my eighteen-year-old body through the twelve-inch space, angry but unsurprised at Mother's all-to-usual behavior. I did manage to laugh to myself as I pictured the struggle an infant endures as it squeezes through the birth canal into a brand new life and wondered just how much I resembled that child at this moment!

My hand burned as it gripped the car's roof, hot from the southern August sun and trying to pull myself out. After much effort, I had both feet planted solidly on the concrete. I straightened my clothes and I reached back for the one remaining bag. I guess I should be grateful that at least Edward carried the other things up to my dorm room and deposited them in the middle of the floor.

I was looking forward to my new life. I was seven hundred miles from what I had been forced to call my home for so long. No one here that I know of had ever heard of the "New Order". This could be my fresh start. I would finally be able to leave all my horrific memories and sad feelings behind me and begin to know happiness. My heart was filling with thoughts of hope and new beginnings!

I barely touched ground when my thoughts were interrupted with the coughing of the car's engine as it began to drive away.

Was that it?

That moment, Mother issued her final uncompassionate blow to me by dumping me at the curb like nothing more than the morning trash at the corner receptacle.

Perhaps it was wishful thinking, but shouldn't there have been more? I'm not sure what I was expecting; I only knew that something important was missing.

The sun was shining brightly, so I held my hand above my eyes and tried to focus on the old car as it drove away. Before they'd gotten too far, Mother cranked the passenger window down and barked, "Don't forget to write," then she quickly turned forward again and they were gone. I stood in silence as I watched the car disappear into the distance.

What did she expect me to write about? We barely even spoke when we lived together! Why does she care if I write or not?

Without my consent, memories began to flood my mind...I wonder what she's going to do now? Who's going to do all the cooking? My heart began to beat harder as emotion began to well inside of me.

Who's going to clean for you now? What about the mending and the laundry? And who do you think is going to clean up after you? Who's going to be there to repair everything when you and your drunken friends finish your tirades? And after all that, no goodbye? No take care or even good luck! How about, "it's been nice knowing you?"

As I stood alone on the sidewalk, I began to chastise myself. I couldn't be surprised at her behavior. Why would today be any different than any other? Why had I even let myself hope for anything different? After all, any hope I'd had only led to more pain and disappointment. For weeks now I'd been looking forward to this day and she'd hardly said a word about it. Now it was here and she was gone.

The mixture of emotions inside of me weighed me down like a dog's wet coat, and I knew I needed to shake them off. I was finally free of the tyranny and torment I'd lived under for the past six years. Mother, Edward, and her drunken friends would not have control over me anymore. I was free...

It had been a long hard struggle to get this far. It had taken a great deal of courage and a lot of hard work to be here, I reminded myself. I was standing on the walkways of a real college campus! Neither of my parents had attended college; Mother hadn't even finished high school. Maybe they were jealous because I had a chance to make something of my life? There were a thousand maybes but one thing for sure – I had escaped from all of it

I couldn't decide whether to jump up and down and click my heels at the joy of my newfound freedom or to simply stand there and feel alone. Even though I had reached my goal, there was still a hollowness deep inside that I couldn't understand or even begin to explain

There was no disputing the fact that I was ecstatic to be away from those people, so why did I feel this way? It still felt like something was missing inside. There were people back home I would miss, like Mrs. Smith, but I don't think this was the answer to what was lacking. I couldn't understand what could be missing.

Why did I feel so empty inside?

Here I was in college! Me, Joey Benson, made it here on my own merit. I'd gotten the grades, made the honor society, and I'd worked hard to save the money. Now, I had the opportunity to show them all.

My given name is Josephine, but I was given the name of "Joey" at the age of eleven. I'd grown accustomed to being called Joey, and preferred it. The name fit the image I had of myself.

This place would be my sanctuary and my refuge. Here I could put to rest all the horror of the past. My nightmare was finally over! As I stood there, I pressed my fists deep into the pockets of my denim skirt and allowed a slight smile to cross my face. After all, my problems were over!

Weren't they?

I walked along the sidewalk and breathed in the sweet air of freedom. Before long, though, my mind wandered back to a similar place and time opening a floodgate of memories. They poured in overwhelming me. I closed my eyes and could see everything so clearly as my mind took me back to a place I had hoped to never visit again . . .

Chapter - 2 - Family Strangers

I had nobody. After being rescued from the New Order, a para-military group, I was so confused. Things got worse after my grandparents were killed. I didn't know who was on my side or and who was against me. I ran from every person that came near me. There was no one I could trust, so I spent a lot of time in the woods hiding.

I miss Grandmother and Grandfather so much.

Without thinking about it, one day as I was walking, I went to their old house. It was much the way I remembered it. That house had been my special place of refuge until the day the soldiers came to take me away. I stepped onto the porch and tried the doors, but they were locked. Finally, I sat down on the steps.

What will happen to me? The winter months would soon be here, and make it hard to live in the woods. I need to make a plan.

During the time I lived with my grandparents, they told me my parents were alcoholics, whatever that meant. Maybe it means losers who don't care about their kids; that'd describe my parents. I knew I never wanted to go live with them.

I feel truly alone.

A dark sedan pulled into the driveway, a very mean looking woman waved her hand for me to get off of the porch and get into the car.

I stood up, but didn't walk toward her.

"Get in the car!" she ordered.

"I don't know you, and I am certainly not going any place with you. You could be New Order spies sent here to take me back. Or you could be one of those crazy Underground sects who killed my grandparents while he tried to protect me. You just go back where you came from and leave me alone."

The lady glared at me.

"I'm a caseworker from Social Services. My job is to take children like you to live with the adults responsible for your welfare." She stated flatly.

She reached over the front seat and opened the back car door and jerked her head towards it.

Oh please! I fought people bigger than you before. Try and make me leave with you!

All of a sudden, the driver's door opened. I saw a man's head above the roof of the car. As he walked around the car, I saw he was a very tall, strong man with really nice clothes.

He moved so fast that he and was at my side before I could even realize what was happening. He grabbed my shirt collar and shoved me toward the car. I tripped as he dragged me to the car, and I had to fight to keep my balance. Before I was able to think about how to get away, he threw me head first into the open car door and slammed it behind me. I landed hard in the back seat, and it felt like the fabric was biting the skin of my face as I slid across the seat. I hurried to reach for the door handle, but it was locked. I was trapped.

I need to get out of this car.

I started getting really nervous and couldn't breathe very well.

The man got back into the car and neither of the strangers said a word. After they looked at each other for a second, the man started the car and backed out of the driveway. He shoved the car into drive and we were on our way.

Who do they think they are? I gotta find a way to get away from these creeps, but first I gotta figure out where they're taking me.

I sat up so that I could see out of the windows, and I watched my grandparents' house disappear, then the neighborhood was gone. The car just kept going until everything I recognized had vanished. When we started driving through places I'd never seen, I started to get really mad.

"Wait! Where are you going?" I demanded.

They just looked at me, and still wouldn't say anything. I wanted to strangle the lady, but the woman had slid a wall of thick wire bars to separate the back seat from the front seat. I was trapped. I threw myself against the back. I was really ticked off with these people.

I ran my fingers through my hair and tried to think.

I need a plan. I'll bide my time and watch for the opportunity to get away from them all. They have to stop this car at some point.

"Hey! Why won't you answer me?" I tried to muster my best commanding voice. "What are you going to do with me? I have rights you know, and you're violating them."

Neither of them even turned around, nor did they look in the rear view mirrors.

Then, the woman broke the silence.

"You're going to live with your parents," she said flatly, and retuned to ignoring me.

Instead of houses with big yards and nice trees and parks, we were driving through this nasty neighborhood with dead grass and broken trees. The houses didn't even have yards, and there was concrete everywhere.

I'd sure hate to live here.

I looked out the window at houses with boarded windows, broken screen doors hanging by only one hinge, and trash on the ground everywhere. Just looking at this neighborhood gave me the chills. Then the car stopped.

What? Here? You have got to be kidding me!

The man got out of the car, opened the trunk, and removed a paper bag. He moved to my door and opened it. Before I could slip under his arm and escape, he had hold of my collar again. I felt him lift me up so my feet barely touched the ground. The more I tried to fight him, the tighter he gripped my collar. I felt like I was choking so I held my throat, making it impossible to use my hands to fight him.

The lady started to come toward us. Her dark blue suit was so tight she could hardly walk. Her hair was pulled back and tied on the top of her head. It looked so tight it could almost pull the skin on her face right off her skull. Maybe she was really some type of an alien.

Everything about this lady was so tight; I thought she'd snap like a rubber band if anything were pulled tighter.

We walked up the sidewalk to a house with pukey green siding. It was one of the few houses that didn't have boards on the windows. I got this sick feeling, and my gut told me this was the place my parents lived. The man deposited me on the porch. He released my collar and handed me the paper bag.

"Don't move from this spot until instructed!" The alien hissed in my ear.

Then they turned to leave. Both moved quickly down the driveway and back into the car. They never told me why I was there.

Why did they bring me to my parents? I feel sick. Inside there's a weird scary feeling.

My guts kept me out of a lot of trouble in the New Order. It was kind of like a warning that helped me get ready and make a plan when I knew something bad was about to happen.

The caseworker and the big man sat in the car and waited. I think they wanted to be sure that I knocked on the door and went into the house instead of running away.

Why didn't they stay at the door and at least introduce me? Isn't that what people are supposed to do?

I remember Grandmother and Grandfather doing that.

It's not like I was expecting anything extra from them, but they could at least do their job.

I hadn't lived with my parents since I was a baby. They'd come to see Grandmother and Grandfather to borrow money, but they really never wanted to see me. I guess their expectation was that my grandparents would care for me and free them of the responsibility of a child. Now I was supposed to live with them and be one big happy family? We didn't even know each other. I had a very bad feeling about this whole thing.

I reluctantly knocked on the door and waited for someone to answer. While I waited on the porch, I peeked inside the bag. Someone must have gone inside my grandparents' home and gotten the things I had there. The only clothes were several pairs of rust colored fatigue pants, a couple of pairs of black uniform pants, some uniform shirts, and socks. It was pretty obvious; no one wanted to spend any money on buying me new clothes that wouldn't make me stick out like a sore thumb. The New Order issued all of these clothes. Any clothes that I had before the New Order were now too small. As I rummaged through the bag, I did a double take. There in the bottom of it was a small, stuffed bunny rabbit. It had been a birthday gift from Grandmother and Grandfather on my first birthday. A strange feeling choked my throat. I quickly covered the bunny with the clothes. I didn't want anyone else to see him. It was the only thing I had left from my grandparents and I was afraid someone would take him.

I ran my hands over my uniform, and tried to straighten any wrinkles. I licked my fingers and ran them through my short brown hair to keep some of the stray hairs in place. My boots were brown suede leather, so at least I didn't have to worry about them needing to be polished. Maybe I'd make a good impression.

But maybe it wouldn't make a difference.

One thing weighed heavily on my mind, "I was very much alone!"

Why would these people want me now when they didn't want me then?

My grandparents were the only ones that ever cared about me. I could still see them in my mind if I concentrated hard enough, but when I did, I felt that aching in my throat. So, maybe it wasn't a good idea to try to remember them.

I feel so alone!

It was a very chilly day for late August. Although, I shouldn't have been too surprised since I could remember snow coming as early as September. My hands were numb from the cold. I knocked on the door again, but still no answer. The knocking stung my fingers. I put my hands under my arms to try to warm a little them from the biting cold. I tilted my head from side to side trying to see through the openings between the curtain and the door, but I couldn't see any movement.

Were they sure someone lived here? Maybe they were hiding so they didn't have to be stuck with me. Why didn't the Underground or the people in the car or someone give me a coat or something warm to wear? I guess it was probably because I didn't matter to them.

It felt like forever before I finally saw movement through the curtain spaces. The door opened, and there stood one of the biggest people I'd ever seen. She was almost six feet tall and probably two hundred pounds. She reminded me of the New Order military leaders. She had short frizzy black hair and sharp brown eyes that looked right through me. Her face was caked with too much makeup and that made her look even more frightening.

"You're my kid, huh? They said we have to take you." Her voice was loud and forceful.

"Yes, Ma'am!" I answered with my best military response. She looked me up and down. This seemed worse than a New Order's inspection.

A frown crossed her face, making her down right terrifying.

"Don't just stand there so I have to heat the outside! Get in here! Move it!" She barked.

In the background, I heard the car drive away. With my paper bag in hand, I hurried into their house. I stopped inside the door and waited for further instructions. She closed the door behind me then walked in a circle around me, and she looked me over again.

"Let's get a few things straight right up front," the sound of her voice made me jump. "You're here because they said we had to take you. You will do exactly as you are told, or you will be declared an unruly minor and taken away by the police and *locked in jail.*"

Her words bit into my insides.

How could she have her own flesh and blood locked in a cage?

It normally would have hurt more, but I wouldn't let anyone hurt me inside. In order to survive in the New Order, you learned to be tough and not have feelings even if you did have them.

"Now that you are here, you will work for your keep. You will cook the meals, clean the house, wash the clothes, do the mending and ironing, and whatever else we tell you to do," she kept going. "You will keep your room clean. You will not bother either of us, or any of our guests. We're not into being a mommy and daddy. Your room is at the end of the hall. Go there now! I will call you when its time for you to cook dinner."

Mother pointed down the hallway. She walked over to her rocking chair and perched herself on it. I hadn't seen Father. I was left standing just inside the door overwhelmed by her orders.

What kind of a place is this?

I moved down the hallway in the direction she'd pointed. Somehow I felt like a new nightmare was beginning, a nightmare that I couldn't even begin to imagine at this point. I barely entered my room and put the paper bag on the bed when I heard Mother yelling.

"Josephine!"

I hated being called Josephine. Josephine was the innocent kid that lived with her Grandparents before the New Order took her. The New Order gave me a new name, Joey. In my opinion, Josephine ceased to exist that day and Joey took her place. I left the room and walked to the living room.

"You'll be starting school next week," she began. "I expect your grades to be perfect. I also do not want to hear so much as a rumor that you're causing trouble there. It's bad enough people knowing where you've come from. That New Order has a reputation. I don't need any further disgrace."

I bit my tongue to prevent myself from saying something I'd regret. Her threat of having me locked up echoed in my head.

"You'll come straight home from school. You'll still be expected to do the chores I told you about, and then you can do whatever homework you have. I know there are others from that New Order of yours that go to that school, but you are forbidden to hang around any of those hooligans." She stopped her speech.

I guess she was done. I went back to my room and I prayed that this new nightmare would end soon.

I don't want to be me.

Chapter - 3 - No Escape

As I stared at the barrel of a pistol only inches from my head, confusion flooded my brain while being forced to my knees. My mind refused to comprehend this scene. I'd seen it all too many times in the New Order's training films. Never once, though, did I think I would end up being the one to be shot. Someone grabbed my hair and yanked my head back forcing it to line up with the gun barrel. I was so scared that I couldn't think clearly. I wanted to die, but not like this.

Why am I being forced into this? These things were only supposed to happen to the enemy. The bloody endings of movies we were forced to watch flashed through my head. I kept staring down the gun barrel and couldn't believe that all this is real. Can this be happening? Will I really die this way?

Clenching my jaw, I bravely looked into the darkness of the barrel.

I wonder what it will feel like to be hit by a bullet? Will there be much pain? Why are my own people doing this to me?

I shoved all shadows of fear into their secret closet. The most important rule in the New Order was to show absolutely no emotion or it would be certain death.

I accepted the fact that I would die today. One good thing about all of this is that soon my pain inside would be gone. So, I waited to die.

Can we just get this over with?

The officer in charge, Major Doyle, pushed the cold steel of the gun against my skin. I forced my eyes to remain open. I bit the inside of my lip to help maintain my blank expression. I watched his finger begin to squeeze the trigger. I held my breath. Slowly, he pulled the trigger further and further back. Click! The chamber was empty.

My whole body shivered, but I hoped no one noticed it. My insides turned into jelly. I was really glad I hadn't wet my pants. That would have brought swift and immediate punishment. I had to make myself breathe again.

I was alive, but I had wanted to die! I had prayed to die. Death would have been better than this constant pain inside. God, why won't You let me out of this pain and torture? Why couldn't I just die and be free?

The people around me shoved me to the ground. As I hit the dirt, gravel bit into my face.

I sat up suddenly and blinked. Everyone had disappeared. Sweat covered my entire body. I looked around the room. I was in my bedroom having another nightmare. It seemed that I relived every horrible event from the New Order. I couldn't escape this hell I faced night after night. Each time was the same; I'd wake up afraid and wouldn't know where I was. I lived in the shadows of nightmares that would awaken me with silent screams tearing through my brain. I pleaded with the darkness to take away my fears. But the nightmares returned repeatedly. I couldn't run away from them.

Tossing and turning around in the bed, I began punching the mattress with my fist.

Why did I have to live this way?

I pounded the bed so hard that I scared myself. I felt out of control.

That is unacceptable. I could never allow myself to lose control. That was another major rule in being a good soldier in the New Order.

But the pain inside made me so angry that I kept punching the bed until I finally collapsed in exhaustion. Lying there with my face on the bare mattress, I swallowed hard and forced the pain to go away. I couldn't let it out. I didn't know how to deal with it.

Being out of control makes you weak! At least that is what the New Order's programming repeated in my brain.

I tried to calm myself down by breathing slowly and counting. Finally my heart was beating normally again. I rubbed my hands over my face and my fingers through my hair and I tried to shake the memories from my head, but my mind was stuck there. Rolling over onto my back, I tried to shift my mind onto another subject, but the New Order still controlled my thoughts.

I wonder how Major Doyle would have reacted if he had to face the same thing he put me through? I don't think he could even pass his own test.

I smiled as I thought about being the one to hold the gun and watch him sweat and squirm. I allowed my imagination to go one step further and guessed he'd probably have wet his pants. Now that would have been a funny sight. Him standing there in his fancy uniform with wet pants.

All of a sudden a sharp pain stabbed my stomach. I doubled up and rolled onto my side and faced the wall.

What a time for my conscience to kick in? It happened every time I let myself think about inflicting the same pain and torment on the New Order's leaders.

Pulling my arm across my stomach, I held it firmly in place trying to relieve the pain. This happened every time I had a nightmare. The stabbing pain grew more intense, and I felt like I was going to throw up. I forced myself to choke back the sensation. Using my free hand, I wiped the perspiration from my face. I hadn't gotten use to the smells and nuances of this house yet. Everything seemed wrong. Instead of the sterile barracks smell I had filled my lungs with in my earlier years I now had to deal with stale cigarette smoke, old alcohol and vomit. It added to the sensation to heave. Everything was knotted up inside. It felt like my head was coming apart.

Why am I here? I don't belong here. I don't fit in. I'm a misfit in any society. Why can't life be solid and unchanging?

Chapter - 4 - The Misfit

S till lying on the bed, my brain continued racing in a million directions.

I don't fit in here.

I thought life would be different now that I was out of the New Order. Wasn't living in freedom supposed to be more peaceful?

I don't know what to do to feel like I belong.

In the New Order, I didn't have to do anything. Their drugs and brainwashing took care of most of it. I thought I'd at least be able to live without the fear of some fanatic attacking me. Instead, I'd have to watch my back here as much as I did there.

The Underground rescued me from the New Order's torture chamber. They brought me to a new place, but the people here aren't prepared to deal with New Order refugees.

No one really understood what happened to me in the blink of an eye that day when the soldiers came. The play and pleasure of my life was changed to fear and mistrust while in the New Order. I'd once overheard Grandmother say that my youthful innocence was changed to a horrible nightmare.

I didn't understand what she meant at the time, but I think I was beginning to understand more.

The images that filled my brain from life in the New Order were more grotesque than most soldiers of war would ever see. Each day continues to be a battle for survival. Survival meant hiding your true self and never letting it out. At least that way you know your true identity is at least some place within you. Survival meant divorcing yourself from any possible feelings and emotions. Burying all of these things as deeply as possible and posting a sign saying, 'no digging here'.

Somehow I expected the horrible nightmares would end now that I was supposed to be living in freedom, but nothing changed.

Who am I, really? I'd hoped that someone would help me find my true self, but I can't trust those people.

The New Order's goal was to make us robotic soldiers. Maybe they succeeded.

Maybe I really wasn't a person any longer? Every day I continue to play a different part in life's mixed up drama. I wear a mask so no one will see inside. I even fool myself. Perhaps, I can't even trust myself. When I look in the mirror, who is the reflection of the person staring back at me? It is someone I don't know. Why had all this happened? Why must I pretend to be someone else each day in order to pass for being 'normal'? Who am I, really? I guess until I know these answers I must conceal the real me. I'm not the soldier the New Order tried to make me. But, I can't let myself act the way I feel inside, or I won't survive. There's only one option left, I can't risk anyone knowing the true me for fear of them trying to steal what's left of me.

I was twelve, and I already felt I'd lived too long. My life was knotted up like a ball of string. Living with my birth parents was worse than living with absolute strangers. Their only interest was in beer. They didn't care about their own kid. I don't know why they even bothered to have me. Mother had me nearly chained to the house. To keep my sanity, though, I found a way to sneak out and have time alone. I needed these solitary times away from there. It was especially needed after the awful nightmares. Neither Mother nor Father knew about the nightmares, or they didn't care. They never said anything to me about them. I suppose they didn't care as long as they had free slave labor to cook and clean.

I had to get up and out of this house. I needed fresh air to clear my head. I knew that staying in bed would only result in more nightmares.

I got out of bed and smoothed my clothes, put on my boots, and gently opened the bedroom door. I froze in place and listened. After straining to hear their snores coming from the room, I slowly took a step into the hallway. Hearing the expected sounds, I allowed myself to move forward. Creeping one step forward and stopping, I listened. I froze in my tracks at the creak of each floorboard. Then, I listened again. I slowly moved forward until I reached their bedroom door, which was left open a crack. I peeked inside.

The whole house smelled of stale cigarette smoke and vomit, but it was worse in their bedroom. Once they woke up from their unconsciousness, I'd have to clean whatever mess they'd made. They were lying across the bed without any clothes on. I turned away quickly; so I wouldn't see them. The scene nearly caused me to vomit with disgust. I had worked hard at not seeing the ways the New Order made the others undress as part of their punishment and now I didn't want to see this.

How could anyone forsake the protection of your clothes, especially in the presence of another person? Clothing was a barrier of protection and safety. It was also a means by which you could hide yourself. The scene in their bedroom would never have been permitted in the New Order.

My mind recalled some of Mother's words to me when I arrived. "There will be no coddling like you're used to from your grandparents, and I don't know what they taught you in that military school, but here, you obey me. Otherwise, I'll have you declared an unruly minor and made a ward of the state. They'll put you in jail."

If her intent was to scare me into submission, she was succeeding. I knew what it was like to be locked up. I had my fill of being locked in cages, dark rooms filled with bugs, and being in other places I didn't want to think about. I was determined never to be locked up again for any reason. I'd rather die first. Since Mother ruled the household, I had to step lightly around her. She had a nasty temper that she displayed whenever she didn't get her way.

Father hadn't said much to me since I moved in. I'd only seen him a few times. Most of the time he was sucking down a bottle of beer. He was a small man and appeared to be rather sickly, or maybe it was just the effect of the cigarettes and booze.

From the first time he saw me, he made no attempt to hide his disappointment that I was not the son he had always dreamed about.

As if I could control whether I was a girl or boy. Although since being in the New Order, I didn't feel like either one. The family name would die with me. On reflection, maybe that was a good thing.

I was no longer a part of the New Order; I didn't belong to this family, and I didn't fit into my new environment. It was an existence rather than a life.

In the few short days that I'd been here, I'd heard them blaming me for their money problems. That was confusing since I hadn't eaten much of their food, and they hadn't spent anything on me for clothes, personal items, toys, music or anything else. Overall, it seemed they were unhappy that they were now stuck with me and had no one to pawn me off on. They even blamed me for my father losing his job because he was drunk. I gathered he had a hard time holding down a job even before my arrival.

One thing they did to get a few dollars was to drive around the county passing checks on an account that had no money in it. This provided a few dollars for their booze. Somehow this didn't seem to be the right thing to do, but what did I know? They didn't have checks in the New Order.

Currently, the car was impounded because the police had stopped Father for drunk driving. In the few times I'd ridden with them, we'd nearly landed it in the river, hit the side of a bridge, and barely avoided driving off an overpass that was under construction. This was all within the few days that I'd been living here. At least for the time being there would be no more terrorizing rides. Let them go hitchhike to the bars alone. I was content to stay at the house without them. I could sit in my room or on the porch and bask in the peace and quiet.

I took every opportunity I could find to escape into my own little world even if it was only for a few hours. This morning there were still a couple of hours before I had to report to that school. I had some time to ride the bike that the caseworkers brought over the day after they left me here. I guess my grandparents had gotten it for me as a gift when I escaped the New Order, but they never had an opportunity to give it to me. Once I figured out how to ride it, the bike gave me a greater sense of freedom.

Reaching the front door, I gently removed the locks and opened the door. I held it against its hinges to prevent any squeaks. Most of my actions and reactions reflected my training, but in many cases this proved to be a good thing. Pulling it softly behind me, I took a deep breath of the early morning fresh air. It was the smell of freedom. At this hour it was only nature and me. I liked that. Mother and Father would be passed out for at least another few hours. They wouldn't even know I was out of the house.

I didn't have to worry about dealing with any of the townspeople, parents, or even spies from the New Order. They were still snuggled in their beds asleep. I was free to enjoy the deep blue skies and early morning sunrise.

Chapter - 5 - Mirror Image

The chilly fall air felt invigorating as I grabbed my bicycle. I swung my leg over the seat, sat down, and began to pedal. The autumn leaves were beginning to be dipped in nature's paint wells: the sun spread its blanket of warmth; the dew glistened on the grass; and the air was crisp and clean. It always seemed so sad when it was time for one season to leave and another to make its appearance. This year it was especially difficult for summer to wave goodbye and autumn to enter. There'd already been too many changes in my life. I wanted something to stay the same for a while, but in life nothing stays the same. Now I lived with people who hardly acknowledged that I existed. I lived in a town where people hated you because of where you were from. I was about to attend a strange school where I had no idea what the rules of survival were and I didn't have a clue how to fix any of it.

One positive note was that a few others that had escaped the New Order lived in this same town. I'd probably be in some of the same classes with them. That might be helpful. It wasn't like we were close or anything; the New Order would never have permitted that.

The thought of attending a school where the kids would hate you as much as their parents did gave me a sick sensation in the pit of my stomach. I shook it off and continued to pedal. The sky opened up and a fall shower began to cleanse the earth. I especially loved to ride in the rain. It made me feel clean, at least for the moment. I pedaled faster as I approached the puddles; I loved to see how high

I could make the water spray. My baseball cap kept the water out of my eyes and off of my head. I didn't care if the rest of me got wet. The shower quickly ended and the sky turned from eerie black to a warm blue. The sun's rays produced a beautiful rainbow.

Racing down the dirt road, I felt a certain freedom. I pedaled faster. I closed my eyes and felt like a bird gliding through the air. I was no longer earthbound with all of its pain. Unfortunately, this would be the closest that I could come to true freedom for a long time. But for now, I was free from everyone's rules. I was free of all the groups that sought to hurt me. I let my mind feel the excitement of it all and breathed it all in. It was very sweet.

In a split second the bicycle wheels locked bringing it to a sudden and an abrupt halt. My sensation of flying took on reality as I sailed over the handlebars. I did a somersault landing on my back with a thud. Fortunately, I landed in some soft dirt and grass on the side of the road. I couldn't breathe. I began to panic. Dazed and helpless, all I could do was lay there trying to suck air into my lungs. My body refused to move. I felt like a toppled turtle. As I lay there, I felt a sense of danger closing in on me.

What happened? What made the bike stop so abruptly? Why had the beauty of the day ended like this? No time to analyze this now. I need to gather my wits about me.

I saw a shadow of movement from the corner of my eye. I couldn't stay here like a helpless turtle, but my body refused to cooperate. I continued gasping. I was helpless. My mind raced through the various scenarios.

Who was out there? Who did this and why?

I caught sight of a rust colored uniform moving into a position to hover over me. As I lay there looking up at my captor, a flash of recognition sparked in my brain. Jesse Burrows!

Since the beginning of our training days with the New Order, Jesse had been a constant thorn in my side. The leaders had put me in command of the unit. He had done everything he could to undermine my authority. We trained side by side. Jesse was always more aggressive and ruthless. Yet, for some reason, I was given command. I was never sure why. One day I overheard the leaders discussing that they needed to adjust the drugs they were giving Jesse to better control him. The drugs were used to aide in their brainwashing, but also in their ability to control us. A tweak here or there could make us more aggressive killers or tamer soldiers.

Through the course of time, I moved up in rank faster than he did. He was frequently being busted in rank because of his disobedience to orders. I kept passing their tests and was promoted. When he was assigned to my unit, I wanted to ask the leaders to transfer him, but I knew this would only cause problems for me. So I constantly had to watch my every move knowing he was waiting for me to slip up. He wanted a reason to report me. He wanted my position and would've loved to punish me. He would disobey my orders to test me. This would result in my being forced to discipline him, which led to further humiliation for him. All of this made things worse.

"Well, well, well! Who do we have here?" Jesse smirked as he looked down at me. The tone of his voice sent shivers up and down my spine.

Why is he here? What is he planning? I doubt he left the New Order.

I swallowed back the rising fear inside and cursed myself for not staying on my guard. I shouldn't have allowed myself to feel the rain on my face and participate in all that folly. I worked at regaining my breath so that I would not be at his mercy. I shook my head to clear my thoughts; I knew there would be plenty of time to chastise myself later.

Finally, I managed to roll to my left, which reduced a bit of my vulnerability. His cockiness clouded his judgment. Ever since he was under my command in the New Order that been one of his weaknesses. Rolling put me out of his reach. I staggered to my feet and stood face to face with my mirror image, or was he my reflection? Were we truly opposites, or were we really the same? The burning in my lungs subsided and I felt my breath come easier.

Jesse's face was now within my full vision. His eyes were still filled with anger and hatred. I searched his features for some spark of humanity, but I couldn't see anything except the deadness of the New Order's programming. His savage expression betrayed their creation. Knowing the brutality of the New Order caused the hair on my neck to prickle. Fear wrestled for control of my senses.

What is the matter with me? Why am I feeling these weird sensations?

If I were going to survive this encounter, I would need to concentrate.

As I contemplated my options, Jesse leaped into the air, with his boots aimed high. He caught me square in the chest; knocking what little air I had managed to gain out as I hit the ground. This time he moved so that he was straddling over me. His frame towering above me. I wasn't sure how tall he was, but from this perspective he appeared to be a giant.

His green eyes were hungry for prey. He was figuring me for it. His sandy brown hair was still cut to regulation. His uniform had a few more decorations since I'd seen him last. I wonder how many more of his own family members he had killed to earn them.

"Don't try to get up on my account!" He said with a prideful grin. Resting his hands on his knees, he brought his face closer to me.

He was enjoying this far too much. After years of training with him, I knew this was one of his weaknesses. Jesse gloated too much over an opponent between bouts. It usually gave the person the advantage of recovering and ready for his next move.

"You've grown soft Benson. I took you down without even breaking a sweat. Your instincts are dull. In my opinion, they weren't all that sharp to begin with," he sneered. "I always suspected you never were the best or the brightest, even though the leaders thought you were."

His words stirred something primitive within me. I had to at least get to my feet, if I were to have any hope of coming out of this. Not wanting to telegraph anything to him, I kept my face neutral. He was well aware of many of the same tactics that I knew.

He stood back up to his full height and put his hands on his hips. He was assuming the posture of the New Order leader's when they were inspecting us.

"My, my, my! Benson, your hair is not regulation. Look at yourself! You're a mess! Perhaps you need to be reminded about the effectiveness of true discipline, New Order style. As I remember, you were quick to dish it out to those under your command. Especially to me."

He rocked back on his heels pleased with himself. That was my opening. In the blink of an eye, I swept my foot around, kicking him in the calf of his leg. The element of surprise knocked him off balance. That was all I needed to scoot out from under his stance, scramble to my feet, and move away a safer distance. He scrambled to his feet and crouched slightly. He glared at me. I had beaten him again.

There we stood, like two animals ready to fight to the death. I felt something warm trickling down my forehead and into my left eye. I instinctively swiped at it. Blood covered the back of my hand. I must have cut my head when I somersaulted over the bike handlebars and hit the ground.

"What are you doing here?" Now that I could breathe, it was my turn to demand some answers. I forced my voice into the command tone I used in the New Order.

"So you do bleed?" he chided, ignoring my question. "And here I thought you were so superior that you weren't even flesh and blood. Oh, my disappointment is that you are mere mortal like the rest of us poor slobs."

I stared at him. He shifted a step, and then I'd counter with a step of my own. To any onlooker we may have appeared to be doing some type of a dance. I couldn't afford to let him gain even a single step. I had been fortunate in catching him by surprise so I could get to my feet. I didn't want to push my luck.

"I'm glad that you're surprised to see me," he laughed, "I've been following you since you deserted, but you always managed to be a step ahead of me. Today I was lucky. I was here and there you come doodling along like you haven't got a brain in your head to keep your guard up. Deserters are punished, and I am here with my own patrol to bring you back to face justice," he gestured to the trees.

"You needn't have come on my account," I retorted trying to ignore the sting of being referred to as a deserter.

He smirked.

"If you have orders, I want to see them," I insisted. I wasn't sure what I'd do if he actually produced a paper with his orders on them. I knew regardless that I wouldn't go willingly with him. I felt safe in calling his bluff.

"No! You're the criminal here, and I don't have to do anything you say," he replied. "Besides, I'm in command now, not you."

He moved forward. I dodged to the side. We missed each other and remained in our dance formation.

"Major Doyle thinks that you're one of the important ones. The New Order has a price on your head. Why they'd want you back is beyond me. To make matters worse, they want you back in one piece. If it were up to me, I'd bring them your broken, bloody corpse after I had my fun. But I follow orders and I want the reward."

"Since when do you follow orders?" I challenged. I couldn't decide if he was lying about the price on my head or the orders, but somehow I doubted it.

"Don't start with me, Benson!" he growled.

I knew I'd struck a nerve. He never could disguise his anger. I knew I needed to tread carefully in angering him. I needed to make my strikes quick and precise. His anger made him as dangerous as a wounded animal.

"I am no longer a citizen of the New Order. Therefore, I am not a deserter. You have no legal rights to take any actions here. This is free territory," I added with authority. I remembered lesson one from the New Order's training manual: maintain eye contact and speak with authority. The enemy often announced their movements with their eyes.

"Personally, I don't care if this is the North Pole and Santa Claus himself has granted you refuge. My plan is to bring you back and cash in on the reward. Besides, this could mean a big promotion for me. Besides, it will give me great pleasure to watch tried for desertion, disobeying orders, helping the enemy, and whatever other charges they can dream up."

"Those people were not enemies. They were helpless elderly people, I said defensively. I needed to be careful not to allow my own anger to get out of control. He would surely take advantage of my mistakes.

He waved his hand dismissively.

As I watched him, I was quite certain I was seeing the epitome of the New Order's textbook soldier.

Is he one of their success stories? What makes me any different from him?

"I'm not the first to leave and probably won't be the last, so why go to all of this trouble?" I questioned.

"You don't get it, do you? For being declared the best and brightest, you sure are stupid!" he laughed.

I knew it irritated him to have to say that. He was always jealous of the fact that the leaders held me in such high esteem. I outranked him and had beaten him in every competition, which added insult to injury.

"The Major wants to make an example of you to discourage anyone else from considering escaping from the other groups."

"You're not taking me back," I replied firmly.

"What's wrong with you, Benson? You had the power of rank and all its privileges. You had what should have been mine! Don't you know that everything revolves around who has the power? You had it all! The leaders were falling all over themselves to give you promotions, privileges, and whatever else they could. What did you do? You threw it all away by leaving," Jesse chided me.

"Power is everything!" he continued. "Power lets you put your mark on the world. It lets people know that you've passed this way. Power lets you choose whatever path you desire, and let's you control your own destiny. Power lets you define your own world. No one can tell you what to do!"

How long did it take the leaders to program that into him?

"Wise up Burrows!" I snapped back at him, "The New Order has no real power. The power you think you have is all an illusion,"

"Shut up!" His eyes flashed with anger as he growled. His speech ignited something inside of him, something savage. He charged at me taking wild swings, but I easily dodged them. "You've been listening to the Underground propaganda too much. You don't remember the teachings."

"The only one listening to propaganda is you. You're the one that just gave the big power speech. At least my thoughts are my own," I countered.

He shook his head in disgust at me. "Shut up! Your fate is sealed. I'm taking you back! You're not cheating me of my reward or my promotion." Distracted by his own cockiness, he didn't see my side step. This put me in a perfect position. In a flash, I tackled him to the ground. We rolled over and over, both of us holding onto the other's forearms. Mud splashed around us. I tried to yank a hand free, but I couldn't break free of his grasp. He kept a strong grip on my wrists. Neither of us could throw a punch.

I rolled him over so that I was on top. I managed to force his wrists to the ground; I tried again to free a hand to hit him. I managed to do so, and my fist caught him on the side of the jaw. He didn't seem phased by the blow. With a sudden burst of strength, he shoved me backwards and he rolled clear. I hit the ground. Before he could jump on me, I was able to get to my feet and prepare for his next charge. I barely dodged his charging body. I stumbled as I side-stepped. Seeing I was off balance, he dove at me, connecting, we both fell to the ground. Now he was on top of me. He gripped my throat and began banging my head on the ground.

I clenched my jaw to resist the pain and prevent myself from biting my tongue. I dug my nails into his forearms as I gripped his wrists. Somehow I managed to shove him off of me. My fingernails drew blood as they scratched deep into the skin. I crawled away on all fours and used a log to push myself to my feet. Both of us staggered a little from exertion. Suddenly it was like a bell went off. We stood there glaring at each other and then began exchanging punches like a couple of boxers.

"Where are all of the reinforcements you were bragging about?" I hissed, as I landed a solid punch to his nose. I took a moment to wipe the blood from my own mouth with the back of my hand. Breathing hard, I taunted him in choppy sentences. I wanted him to forget his training and let his emotions control him.

"No one would trust you as their commander. You're here seeking glory for yourself. It's not even the reward is it?" I taunted.

He shrugged and took a deep breath. We stepped back for a moment.

I wonder who helped him find me.

Jesse growled something I couldn't understand. My presence always pushed his buttons. He began to move again, and I countered. Somehow, we managed to maintain a tie.

We circled around a few more times but it was obvious to both of us there was no way either of us would win. Jesse hated stalemates. He slowly backed away.

"I guess we are at a draw. I don't like draws," he said with disappointment. "I'll get you another day."

"Don't leave on my account," I taunted.

"Now is not the time," he nodded with a grin, "I will find you again, and you'll be even less of a soldier. Then, you'll be mine, and I'll savor the sweetness of seeing you beg me for mercy. I'll make you pay for every drop of blood you drew."

"Don't count on it!"

"See me in your nightmares," he said as he parted.

I kept him in view, not daring to take my eyes off of him. I knew this was not over by any means. It was clear; I needed to be even more alert from now on. I couldn't afford any surprises.

I watched him slink off into the shadows of the woods. I strained to listen; I heard his footsteps crackling through the brush. He wasn't making any attempt to be silent. I was quite sure there were no others hiding in the woods as he had boasted.

That liar!

As I sat down on the ground, I hugged my knees to my chest, and heaved a sigh. I pressed my hand to my eye and to my mouth. The blood had dried above my eye and on my mouth now. I was exhausted.

A feeling of vulnerability followed. I knew I needed to get away from this spot. I wasn't sure if Jesse would double back or not, but I wanted to be long gone if he did. I was convinced he had an ally some place close that informed him of my movements. A draw would eat at him until he could win. So, there was no question that there would be a rematch. The time and place just needed to be decided.

I pushed myself to my feet; I knew I needed to move on. I walked over to where my bicycle lay on the ground. Every step caused the muscles in my body to protest in pain. I took one look at the badly bent bicycle on the side of the road and shook my head. A feeling of sadness ached in my throat. My beautiful bike was broken. My gift from my grandparents had been taken away. One more thing stolen from me! My major source of freedom was lying there in ruins. I kicked the dirt in frustration.

Why did everything I enjoy end up being taken from me?

I had no choice but to leave it there.

Guess I'm walking home! I need a plan for the next time I encounter Jesse. When we meet again, I might not be so fortunate as to walk away from an encounter with him.

There was no doubt Jesse was still a savage. He was still ruthless. I wonder if the New Order thinks of him as their pride and joy now? Their brainwashing and drugs erased any childhood he may have had. For that matter, they took everything from all of us. What did we have while we were locked in those dark rooms? What do any of us have left? What do we have left if we no longer served them? Our humanity fled long ago in those dark rooms. Even if we have escaped their direct control, we still live the nightmare day after day.

Rubbing my hands through my hair, I allowed my mind to dwell on Jesse.

If I consider Jesse a savage, I wonder what I am?

The question took root in my mind. Those roots felt like they reached down from my head and painfully gripped my stomach. Unconsciously, I pushed my hand against my stomach hoping it would help ease the pain, but it didn't. Not only did I have to deal with the townspeople and my parents, now, I could now add Jesse to the list.

Chapter - 6 - Prejudice in Action

Once I was sure that Jesse was truly gone, I turned and began my long walk back to the house. I needed to get cleaned up before going to school this first day. I was very upset at the loss of my bike. It had been my major means of escape. Even though I'd only had it for a few days, it had proven its worth. Now it was gone.

Why is every good thing taken away from me? My grandparents said that their God would always take care of me. Where is He? Why is He letting these bad things continue to happen to me? What do I need to do?

I kicked at a rock to distract myself from those thoughts.

As I walked along the roadside, memories of my encounter with Jesse disturbed me. Not only did it bother me that I was now faced with a battle on another front, but seeing him reminded me too much of where I came from. He was everything I had been and possibly still was. It hurt too much to think about.

Why would anyone want to change a bunch of kids into soldiers? We spent years in the New Order growing up in an unpredictable and dangerous environment. The leaders used their torture, taunting, humiliation, lies, and drugs to create obedient, robotic soldiers. They could stir us into a murderous rage or have us calmly standing at attention, all at their whim. They could make us kill and not have our consciences bother us, and in some cases not even remember it. The leaders were experts at confounding our reality. Their goal was to destroy who we were and redefine us in their terms, this completely destroying our self-worth.

I remember Grandmother and Grandfather talking about what God thought of you as being more important that what others say about you. I never really understood what they meant. I wonder if I can ever find this God they talked so much about.

It was bad enough to have had to live through the New Orders' torture, but now to be supposedly free and not given a chance by anyone. The irony of it all is that I escaped from the New Order with great peril to everyone that aided me from the Underground and now that I'm in freedom, I'm looked upon as an enemy. The townspeople assumed we were all robotic animals like Jesse.

How unfair life is!

My identity was so locked in step with the New Order; I didn't know my true self. No assistance was offered by anyone to help us adjust. Maybe both the townspeople and the refugees could benefit from some help, but everyone was too lost in their own selfish prejudices to worry about helping others. In their minds, people who are different don't deserve to be accepted. At least that seemed to be their philosophy. No one cared that I continued to live in a personal nightmare because of all of it. Add in the deplorable living situation with Mother and Father, and I wondered why I was even born.

The media fed everyone in the area information about the New Order and their heinous activities. It was well known that the New Order bred killers. To them, this meant that none of us could ever change or be trusted. Was this truly what the Underground wanted for the refugees they rescued? I walked on, jamming my fists in my pockets; and I kicked at the rocks as I moved forward. An overwhelming feeling of sadness swept over me.

I wonder if anyone else ever feels alone. This certainly is not a good way to feel. I wouldn't want anyone else to feel this way. It all hurts so much inside. I hate life. I hate my heritage. My pain is so intense, and I don't even how to tell anyone about it! For that matter, there really isn't anyone that I trust enough to tell.

Would anyone miss me if I just disappeared or ended it all? I think everyone might be happier. Mother and Father wouldn't have to argue over spending money to feed me. The townspeople would have one less person to be afraid of, and most importantly I'd be free of the pain. Maybe those kids from the New Order that already committed suicide: Charlie, Bobby, and so many others -- had the best idea of all. At least they no longer have to deal with this programming stuck in their head and they're free of the pain.

If I have to continue living, then the only way to survive is to fortify a wall around my true self. Except now I find myself building a second wall within the first to protect me from this new world. Life is much too frightening not to. This seems to be the only way to continue to survive.

I wish I were someone else, someone who never experienced the New Order. I wish I had a life instead of a nightmare; a family instead of taskmasters; and a home instead of just a place to stay. Unfortunately, wishes are for idealists and fools.

Radiated from deep within a wave of pain choked my throat.

I didn't understand why these pains continually attacked me, but I was sure I needed to keep the cause of them buried deep inside the walls. It was dangerous to feel anything. To keep yourself numb inside meant you could continue to survive and cope. My insides felt tight and my throat hurt. I hated this because it kept happening and I didn't understand what was wrong with me. It was too scary to dwell on.

As I walked along in thought, I noticed a car slowing down near me. It stopped ahead of me. I instinctively stopped several yards behind the car. I was wary of its purpose. As I watched with curiosity, the car pulled onto the gravel shoulder of the road. I wasn't sure if I should continue walking or turn around and run but I didn't want to show any fear. The driver hit the gas pedal. The wheels spun, spraying dirt and stones at me as it roared away. I dove for the ground and covered my head as the gravel pelted me. When the rain of debris ended, I lifted my head to watch the car speed away. I shook my head in confusion. When I rose to my feet, I was covered with even more dirt. The grime felt caked on in layers. I tried to spit the muck out of my mouth and brush the mud from my hair and clothes. I wiped the grit off of my face and out of my eyes.

Why would the driver do that? What did I ever do to any of them? These people don't know us. All they knew is the horrific tales coming from the news media. I guess since I came from the New Order, they assumed I willingly engaged in these activities. Of course the news didn't mention we were held captive, tortured, and brainwashed. They're just as brainwashed as we are, only theirs is by their own news media. We're different, so that makes us people to be feared? They have no idea how much we lost because we had the misfortune of being abducted by the New Order. We lost our identity and we were robbed of our humanity. We're the ones who suffered torture, humiliation, and lived in constant fear. We're the ones who don't know how to fit in. We live in constant emotional pain, have nightmares every night, and live with flashbacks that relive the trauma over and over again. Where's the news regarding these topics? We're the victims! Why are they so prejudiced? I can't help what happened. What do I have to do to be accepted? Are they really that stupid or do they just not care?

I continued walking. Maybe if I could take them through the New Order experience for just one day, they'd understand a little of what it was like.

How else could they really understand what the brainwashing, the torture, and the drugs did to us? Somehow I don't believe they would even care. I guess it is not fair to expect them or anyone else to understand unless they experienced the whole thing.

Feeling a deep emptiness inside, I desperately wanted someone to understand. I felt so very alone.

"Maybe I don't belong in this world either," I said aloud to myself.

For a time, I almost wished I were back in the New Order. At least there, I knew the rules. I expected people to respond certain ways.

I guess I wanted this place to be different. I thought that life would be easier here, that there would be no more pain - there are no more training films - but the memories continue to play in my mind. There is no more brutality, but the townspeople exercise their own brand of it. I just want everything to be good. Maybe I don't deserve things to be good. Maybe I deserve to have lost everything including myself. I've had enough fighting, hatred, and bitterness to last my lifetime and beyond.

Rachel said that God could heal all of this Why doesn't He?

Rachel led the Underground group to rescue me. I repaid her by taking her hostage, but her words were permanently embedded in my mind. She seemed to have the answers on how to be free from this pain. Rachel had gotten beyond the turmoil and the pain. I needed to find her so she could tell me how. I could be free of the pain too.

Is there truly healing? Where are You, God? If I knew where to find You, I would see if You could be trusted. If You could, I would pour out my heart and soul, and scream out the pain that has been silent for so long. Would there be only silence to echo back to me? Would You show prejudice like these people? Where are You, God?

Chapter - 7 - Us Against the World

The incident with the car left me shaken, especially happening so closely after my fight with Jesse. I searched for a place to sit and let myself settle down. I found a large shade tree off to the side of the road. Anyone passing by would not be able to see me there. I needed to be able to let my guard drop slightly and let my tired body regain strength. This would be the perfect place to rest and think. I'd also be able to enjoy the wonderful colors of nature and feel the breeze wash over me. They always had a cleansing effect on my soul. I loved to watch the green leaves surrender to the spectrum of yellows, oranges, and reds. It was all so orderly. Order was a thing I longed for in my present state of chaos.

I'm not sure how much time passed while I was absorbed in admiring nature, but the crack of a twig started my heart thumping like a jackhammer. I scrambled to my feet. My head twisted in all directions as my eyes darted about searching for the cause of the sound. My fighting instincts primed quickly.

"It's just me!" a voice called from the woods.

I turned to face the sound and stared in that direction. I didn't recognize the voice, so my senses stayed on alert. A figure emerged from the tree line. The clothing identified her as a fellow refugee of the New Order. As she neared, I recognized her as Bert Fisher.

Her real name had been Roberta before the New Order took her. Genderless names were a part of the New Order's brainwashing us into robots. Bert stopped and waited for me to signal that it was okay for her to approach. I raised my hand to signal.

At least she remembered New Order protocol. Approaching unannounced or unbidden could get one killed.

Bert was one of the few refugees that I'd spoken to since I'd been here. I remembered her briefly from the New Order, even though she wasn't under my direct command. The Underground had rescued her and now she was living with an abusive aunt.

I guess no one bothered to check out the people they were sending us to live with.

Bert moved forward and took a seat next to me on the grass. She was built slightly smaller than me, but her rust colored jeans, suede leather boots, flannel shirt, and short hair cut clearly identified her as one of our own.

She began to rock back and forth as her eyes darted around the area. Bert clearly was not comfortable about being here. Our training kept us on alert for the threat of constant danger. Even outside of the New Order, the programming maintained a firm grip on us. We sat quietly. Suddenly she stopped rocking, turned to face me, and broke the silence.

"What are you doing here?" She asked.

"Just taking some time to think," I replied.

She stared at my face for a few moments then noticed the cuts and bruises. "What happened to you?"

Instinctively, I touched my face and winced slightly. "I had a fight."

"With whom?" She questioned, and then a look of panic began to creep across her face as she tried to guess.

I studied her expression to decide if she were a spy or a true refugee.

One can't be too careful.

She started rocking again and glancing around. Every stirring of the breeze through the leaves caused her to jump.

"Who did you fight?" she repeated adding more emphasis to her words.

"Jesse Burrows," I answered flatly.

She stopped rocking and stared at me with her mouth open. She moved her lips to speak, but no words came out.

Maybe she truly is a refugee. A spy wouldn't be as worried about Jesse.

She began rocking harder.

Why is she rocking like that?

"Don't you think we should leave this area before he comes back?" Bert questioned nervously. She was fighting to keep her voice steady. Any variation would betray her fear of Jesse. "It's not safe for us to be out here in the open. He could be watching."

"I met him back there," I said, motioning with my hand. "But you're right, we shouldn't stay out here too long. Besides Jesse, there's always the townspeople to be concerned about," I added remembering the incident with the car.

We got to our feet and moved back to the edge of the road. The terrain in the field was uneven and jarred my aching body. We walked and picked our way back to the road and headed toward Mother's. The sun was fully up now. I knew that I had better get back to the house before my parents woke up. They would be livid if they knew I had snuck out of the house in the early morning hours.

"I better head for home and get changed," I said to Bert.

"I'll walk with you part of the way," Bert offered. "If there's any more trouble, at least there will be two of us."

I opened my mouth to object but closed it. I decided that she had a point. I shoved my fists back into my pockets. I walked beside her in silence. Our path took us toward the soccer fields at the school. In a couple of hours, they would probably be bustling with activity. Though at this hour, the field was deserted. We were vigilant as we neared populated areas. We each scanned our surroundings. We didn't want any surprises.

"What's that over there on the ground?" Bert asked motioning to a small lump. My eyes followed the direction she was pointing. I squinted my eyes to discern what it could possibly be, but couldn't decide. I knew it was something that didn't belong, but I wasn't sure if it was road kill or something else. We walked warily towards it. As we moved closer it appeared be a piece of clothing. That didn't seem so unusual. There always seemed to be lost articles of clothing on the side of the road or sneakers hanging over electrical wires by their laces. Personally, I didn't understand how anyone could be so reckless with their things. Mother would have beaten me severely if those were any of my clothes. Arriving at the lump, Bert reached over and picked it up. Holding it with both hands, she held it up to examine.

A puzzled look crossed her face.

"What?" I asked.

"It looks like Casey's jean jacket," she concluded.

"Casey moved here, too?" I didn't know all of the refugees that had been relocated to this area. Even if I recognized them as refugees, I still wouldn't know all of them because some had been assigned to different camps in the New Order. I guess sooner or later we'd find each other. Perhaps they didn't introduce us to each other so we'd have time to adjust. If that was the case, it was a big joke. There's no such thing as randomly adjusting after our experiences. I recognized Casey's name, even though I didn't know much about him. He had not been directly under my command, but he had a good reputation.

"Yeah. The Underground helped Casey escape about six months ago. He was turned over to social services. The caseworkers insisted that he live with his father since he was the closest relative. It doesn't seem to matter to them that his father beats him all the time. The two of them live in a small apartment without much furniture. His father treats him like an animal. I went to visit Casey once when his father was out of the apartment. You wouldn't believe it. Casey sleeps on a small mattress on the floor in the corner of a bare room. The whole place smells like booze. They didn't even have food in the refrigerator," Bert informed me. "The place is a pig pen. I can't imagine placing a dog into those circumstances. Makes you wonder about those child welfare people. I wouldn't call what Casey deals with living in freedom.

"Seems like alcoholism is a common thing." I didn't come out and say that Mother and Father were also alcoholics, but somehow I think she understood.

"Casey only has this one jacket. I was with him when he got it from the local mission," Bert added. "I wonder why he would have dropped it on the side of the road?" She slung the jacket over her shoulder. "Next time I see him, I'll give it to him. His father would kill him if he knew."

I could imagine what Mother would do to me if someone found my jacket on the road. The list of possible punishments was endless. We began to walk again. Bert was a step or two ahead of me. Abruptly, I stopped in my tracks and stared at the jacket hanging over Bert's shoulder.

"Wait!" I ordered, I sounded more commanding then I intended to. "What's that on it?"

Bert wheeled around to face me. A confused expression crossed her face for a moment, and then she held the jacket out in front of her.

Taking the jacket in hand, I began to search for the thing that had caught my eye. Bert continued holding the other end of the jacket.

"There!" I said pointing at spots on the front of it. The stains were reddish in color like spilled ketchup.

"Blood!" we both said at the same time.

Blood is something I could easily recognize. I saw enough of it in the New Order.

Walking back the few steps to where we'd picked it up I knelt down. My body complained from the earlier fight. I checked the ground around where the jacket had been laying.

"It looks like drops of blood on the ground here too," I observed as I dabbed my fingers on the red sticky blades of grass. Bert bent down for a closer look.

Suddenly, she stood up and began scanning the area. Her face took on a stricken look. Somewhere in the distance we could hear a low moan.

Is that an animal or a person?

We moved cautiously in the direction of the sound, and continued our vigilance. Ambush was an ever-present thought. My heart was pounding so loudly it nearly drowned out every other sound. The closer we got to the school, the louder the noise became.

It definitely is not an animal.

As we neared the place where the school and the gate to the field met, I could just barely make out something on the ground. We broke into a run still trying to watch for a possible ambush. The dark lump became more visible. Drawing closer, I was able to make out the features more clearly.

"It looks like Casey!" Bert exclaimed.

The figure lay face down on the ground moaning. Bert arrived first and knelt beside him. She turned him over gently and instantly jumped to her feet in horror.

"Casey!" she gasped in shock.

I arrived and stared. The sight of him nearly caused me to throw up. It had been a while since I'd seen anyone beaten up so badly and wasn't quite prepared to see it here. I'd seen worse in the New Order, but seeing Casey so badly hurt caught me off guard.

I was definitely losing some of inhumanity that the New Order had programmed into me. I never would have come close to vomiting over such a sight while I was there.

Bert moved closer to him. Casey was barely conscious. He continued to moan in pain. I knelt next to Bert and examined Casey's injuries. His hands were cut up, probably from defending himself. His face was swelling and turning a deep purple and scarlet. His lips were cut and bloody. Blood was drying around his nose. The front of his flannel shirt was covered with blood. His brown wavy hair was matted from the blood trickling into it from a cut above his eye. The smell of blood was making me nauseated.

My mind flashed to the car that had stopped along side of the road and then sprayed me with dirt and gravel. Could they have been his attackers? The car would have been heading in this direction. Looking at him, my insides trembled. What would have escalated them to this much violence?

This could have been me. Maybe Grandmother was right when she said that Someone watched out for us. She called that Someone, God, but it didn't make sense to me. Yet, I couldn't escape the reality that the people that did this to Casey were probably the same ones in the car I had met earlier.

After seeing Casey so badly injured, I forgot my own pain and discomfort.

"Casey?" Bert gently turned his head to face her. She tried to rouse him to consciousness with her voice. She gave his body a slight shake. Still only moans

I watched his chest rise and fall.

At least he was breathing.

"Hey, Casey! Attention!" Bert modulated her voice to her best commanding tone. Her tone caused me to jump in alarm. I guess she was trying to reach down to his programming level with hopes that would rouse him. After Bert repeated the command several times, Casey finally tried to move his mouth.

"Bert?" He groaned in a whispered response.

His eyes were still closed. He moved his head slightly from side to side as he was fighting to become more alert.

"Yeah, it's me," Bert replied with a noticeable sigh of relief. "Just lay still. We're going to get you some help."

"There was six of them, I think," Casey began, telling us what happened. His voice was very low and strained. "I was so scared."

Casey tried to open his eyes, but they were so swollen, they would only open to form slits. I wasn't sure if he could even focus, but he nodded recognition. "I'm sorry, Chief," he said to me.

I guess he knew me by reputation from the New Order.

His voice dropped into a whine. "I couldn't fight them all off. There were too many of them." His face took on an expression of terror as his mind replayed the attack. It quickly changed to one of guilt.

Somebody had hurt him badly. I was quite sure it was that group from the car. I don't know why I was spared Casey's fate, but I was thankful. They had done something in a single act that it took the New Order drugs, torture, and mind control to do: they broke him. Otherwise, Casey would never have admitted to me or anyone else that he was scared.

Casey fought to control himself. He did not want us to see what they'd done to him inside, but he couldn't stop the tears from flowing through the swollen slits.

I felt my heart ache for him. I knew why he was fighting so hard for control. I would have done the same. I wouldn't want to appear weak before my compatriots, either.

My mouth felt like sandpaper. I cleared my throat. "It's okay! They're gone now!" I put an awkward hand on his shoulder. I'd seen other people do this as some type of symbol of comfort. I wasn't sure how that gesture was supposed to bring comfort, but it must do something if other people did it.

Finally, between swallows and choking back emotion, Casey managed to regain a measure of composure. He began to tell us more about the attack.

"I was out walking, trying to stay away from the house until my dad drank himself into oblivion. A car with a bunch of the town kids pulled up behind me. I kept on walking. Then I heard the car doors open and several sets of shoes crunch in the gravel. My instincts instantly sent off bells and whistles in my head. I began to run for it with hopes I had a good head start. I heard them shouting to each other as they chased me. I became confused when their footfalls were fading instead of closing in. I thought maybe they were giving up and going back to their car. They were.

The car doors slammed and tires spun dirt and gravel. They began chasing me with their car. I could hear the roar of the engine moving closer. One of them must have been perched on the hood. When the roar of the car got close, the guy did a flying tackle. He landed on my back and I lost my balance. I fell forward, eating gravel as I hit the ground. I tried to wrestle free; I managed to shove my attacker off by spinning around. He was left holding my jacket. I guess they tossed it aside. I started running again. The car started after me. Not knowing the area well, I ran into a dead end. They had me trapped against the fence. I started climbing it," Casey choked out, "Before I could top the fence, two of them had raced out of the car and were pulling at my feet. I lost my footing and slid down the fence. All six of them were on me. I fought with all I had." Casey's swollen face grimaced. "A couple of them held me down punching my face and another one kicked me repeatedly. Even outnumbering me, they still used weapons. They let me get to my feet while one of them took out a knife and started waving it in front of me. My eyes were swelling so I had trouble following the attacker's hands as he shifted the knife from left to right. I knew I was going to die. Then their leader heard something that spooked them."

"Let's get out of here!" the guy shouted.

"They ran back to the car and took off."

Casey stopped his tale. He lay in silence. His breathing was hard and labored.

"I'll go call an ambulance," Bert volunteered and ran off without waiting for my reply.

I sat on the ground next to Casey. I didn't know what to say to him. I knew he had suffered beatings in the New Order and from his father. What these town kids' did to him was not only despicable because of their ganging up on him, but they broke his spirit.

How do you rebuild a broken spirit?

Looking up at the sound of running footfalls, I saw Bert returning.

"Ambulance is on its way!" she said out of breath.

I nodded.

"We need to get out of here." Bert continued, still panting. I could hear a siren sounding in the distance. "If the cops find us here, they'll arrest us."

"I know, they will think we did this even though he's one of our own." I added. "The police are just as prejudiced as everyone else in this town. They're not interested in the truth; they just want scape-goats to blame."

"And another reason to hate us," Bert added. "We won't be far!" She said to Casey.

He nodded weakly. I'm sure he knew as well as we did the possible consequences of us even being seen in the area.

We scrambled to our feet and hustled off to the nearby shrub-bery. We could be hidden from view and still be close enough to see what was going on. Once the police saw his clothes, they won't even attempt to investigate the scene. They wouldn't search for any clues or even tape off of the area. They didn't see the purpose in it.

I saw the strobe lights and heard the ear splitting sirens. They didn't know it was a New Order refugee, or they wouldn't have hurried to the scene.

The police and the paramedics came to a screeching stop. They swung the car doors open, and grabbed the equipment. They all ran over to Casey. I watched them stop abruptly as they recognized he was a refugee, and they did just what I thought they would do. The stared at his New Order clothing and gave each other a knowing nod.

After their recognition, they cautiously moved toward him. Their duty demanded that they treat him, or at least administer the basic first aid. They were not required to transport him to the hospital. They knew we didn't have insurance so they didn't want to extend charity to us. That was saved for their own kind. A little smelling salts helped Casey back to a semi-conscious state.

"We can't transport you to the hospital, kid," one overweight paramedic said.

"School will be starting in a little more than an hour. Maybe some of your kind will come along and take you home," the other paramedic added as he glanced up at the cop standing nearby.

I saw the cop nod in agreement. The officer didn't bother to ask Casey any questions about what had happened. It didn't seem like he cared all that much. I gritted my teeth in disgust. I felt like jumping out of my hiding place and telling them all what I thought of their town, their parentage, and whatever else I could think of, but I knew better. I'd be arrested on the spot and placed in a cage. I couldn't let that happen.

The paramedics finished bandaging Casey's cuts and wrapped up the sprained joints. They packed up their gear. The police said something to the paramedics that made them laugh. They climbed into their respective vehicles and drove away. They disappeared, leaving Casey propped up against the fence. They didn't appear to care if he lived or died. The probably thought if he did die, that would be one less refugee they would have to deal with in the future.

The streets were once again quiet. Bert and I moved from our hiding places and returned to Casey.

Tears were flowing down his face. That group would pay for what they did to him.

"What should we do with him?" I asked. "We can't take Casey to his house. There's no telling what his father will do to him."

Bert nodded her agreement.

"He can't stay here. He's in danger. Besides he needs a place to rest," I added.

"I know a place we can take him," she said. "I found it one day when I was hiding from the townies. It's only a few blocks away from here."

Since that was the only plan we had, I skeptically nodded. I wondered where Bert was talking about. Bert and I put Casey's arms over our shoulders and grabbed his belt with our free hands. We hoisted him to his feet, and helped Casey stay balanced as the three of us made our way down the street. I wasn't sure about this place Bert was talking about, but didn't see any alternatives. We walked about four blocks. The streets were relatively deserted. Most people were probably just getting out of their warm, comfortable beds.

Bert stopped in front of an old abandoned house. The windows and doors were all boarded up, and looked like it desperately needed paint. From a distance, the house was scary looking.

"This is the place," Bert announced.

Bert pointed with her hand toward the back of the house where I saw a set of wooden doors angled into the foundation.

It reminded me of the cellar doors at my grandparents' farmhouse. My mind started to flash to memories from there, but I quickly shook them out of my head.

There's no time for that now.

As we arrived at the doors, Bert shifted Casey's weight to me. She lifted the latch and opened the doors. It was hard to see inside. The only light was from the outside as it crept down into the darkness through the opening. She grabbed hold of Casey and moved forward. We carefully ducked our heads and felt for the steps with one foot at a time. I wasn't sure what we were entering or what we would find inside. Bert appeared very confident with the place. Despite all of our attempts to be gentle, Casey still moaned in pain with each jostle of the steps.

Inside the room, I could feel the sand on the floor. I wonder why there was so much sand on the concrete floor, but there was no one to answer that question. I waited for my eyes to adjust to the dimly lit surroundings before I could see anything else. It took a few seconds but my eyes gradually grew accustomed enough to the little bit of light to make out the details of the room. To my surprise, there were pieces of furniture scattered around: a broken couch, an overstuffed chair, a table or two, and a footstool. Bert and I settled Casey onto the broken couch. He groaned as his aching body touched it.

I stood there staring at him helplessly lying on the couch. I clenched my jaw to keep from showing any type of reaction.

Every inch of him must be bruised. I'm glad it wasn't me... What am I saying?

Twinges of guilt hit me no sooner than the thoughts paraded through my mind.

I watched Casey drift off into a troubled sleep, leaving us to contemplate the events of the morning.

"Don't worry, I can take care of Casey," Bert assured me. "Besides, I don't think I will be alone for long. I think that other refugees will come after the first class or two, or they'll come after school. I'm skipping today so I can stay with him. Some of the others from the New Order congregate here when they need some place to go to get away from things."

"I guess I must be one of the last to know this place existed," I said.

"Only because we hadn't seen you alone to tell you about it," she said trying to be diplomatic.

I nodded. "I better get home before my parents realize that I'm gone. They expect me to be in school this morning." I looked at my watch. It had been several hours since I had left for my bike ride. "Then again, Mother and Father probably already know that I'm not there."

The picture of a badly beaten Casey was etched into my mind as I left the cellar. His fate could have been mine. There was nothing I could offer him in the way of comfort or encouragement. I had to leave him alone in his pain, both physical and emotional.

My mind shifted to Grandmother and the way she talked to this One she called God. I heard my name mentioned often to this One asking Him to protect me. I didn't understand the why then and I don't think I understand now, but possibly this God protected me today. With the exception of today, I think this God has abandoned me. Whoever He is! Maybe He only shows up in dire crises. Most of the time I don't feel Him near. Yet, Grandmother believed, so I guess I must hold on and hope her God finds me.

Chapter - 8 - Confused and Alone

Iarrived at Mother's house and I slipped in through the back door. I hoped they were still passed out so I could creep back to my room. Quietly opening the door, I eased it closed, and turned, coming face to face with Mother. The look on her face sent shivers up and down my spine.

"Where have you been?" Mother demanded. She was always cross when she had a hangover, which was almost all of the time.

"Out!" came my curt reply. I looked at my watch. I'd have to hurry. School would be starting shortly.

They both disgusted me to the point of nausea. I hated being accountable to such poor excuses of humanity. They knew nothing of self-control. Who did they think they were? Wanting to know where I'd been when they couldn't care less about me any other time. They send me into areas that are unsafe to gather bottles for their deposit so I could cash them in for them to take the money and buy booze. I do all the work so they can party. They go out and get bombed regularly and don't give a second thought about the fact that I'm in a house with no heat, and often no electricity because they didn't pay the bills.

Mother stared at me with hands on her hips. "What happened to your face?" She was, of course, referring to the discoloration on my cheeks and around my eyes, and the swelling lip. Her tone was far from caring; and it made me wonder why she even bothered to ask.

"If you must know, I fell off my bike," I snapped, "Like you care!"

I knew I shouldn't have added the last statement, but sometimes I just couldn't help it. Her very manner just beckoned for a smart answer. Mother's drinking, lack of caring and self-control irritated me beyond words.

I hate having to take care of them. I thought it was supposed to be the other way around.

I don't think she'd like it if I demanded where she'd been after they'd been out drinking all hours of the night.

"Watch your mouth! I'm still your mother," she barked her response.

Since when! Giving birth to me doesn't make you my mother.
I glared at her.

Mother could have been a fairly attractive woman except I think her constant drinking was prematurely aging her. Black mascara was smeared around her eyes, making her look a bit like a raccoon.

"What's all the racket? Can't a man have peace and quiet in his own home?" Father demanded as he staggered into the kitchen, and bumped into both doorposts. He fell into a chair near the place I was standing.

"Your daughter's been out roaming the streets again, God knows where, and comes back here, and starts mouthing off to me," Mother complained to him.

It's always interesting how she insist that I belong to him when she complains about me, and swear I was hers when he had a problem with me. Yet, neither of them ever wants to really claim me.

I didn't like standing so close to Father. I was afraid he might hit me. I tried to inch away. Faster than I'd ever seen him move his backhand smacked into the side of my head before I could brace myself. My already aching head exploded in pain.

Just what I need; more bruises to my head and face.

I wrestled my fighting instincts back into their place. My militia training and strengthening would have been more than enough to take them both on, but I knew better than to strike back. Losing control would have gotten me a trip to the nearest juvenile detention facility. They wouldn't give it a second thought. It was a very effective threat since the very thought of being locked in a cage sent waves of panic through my being. So, for the short term at least, I would have to put up with their abuse.

I stared at Father with a look that combined anger with one of a wounded animal. Wounded animals can be very dangerous. But for now, I would retreat and lick my wounds. I straightened my body in defiance. My jaw clenched and the pit of my stomach knotted, but I kept everything stuffed deep inside under control. They wouldn't see any response from me.

"Respect your mother!" He ordered.

Respect? Respect? Who is he kidding? What's there to respect about either one of them? Respect is earned! And in my opinion neither one has earned any respect.

"I would have thought they'd have taught you more respect in that military school," he added sarcastically as he opened another beer.

Military school? Is that all he thought it was?

I refrained from shaking my head outwardly in disgust, and I bit my tongue to prevent my mouth from letting any thoughts surge forward.

The words sneered in my brain. I turned to exit the kitchen without a word in an attempt to avoid further conflict.

"Bring me my purse!" Mother commanded as she sat down in the kitchen.

I'm a slave!....Josephine, fix me dinner....Josephine, give me more potatoes....Josephine, clean the house....Josephine, wash the dishes....Josephine, do this and Josephine, do that.

"Right," I replied coolly. I walked to their bedroom to retrieve it; I nearly gagged from the smell of sour alcohol that permeated the room. The bed was a mess. I had to wade through the clumps of dirty clothes covering the floor. I was afraid of stepping in something. It took me a few minutes to find the purse in the dishevelment. Once I located it, I quickly glanced around to be sure they weren't behind me. As I slipped her wallet out of its place, I quietly opened it and removed a few dollars and some change.

It is payback time. She never remembers how much she spent at the taverns. Besides I got some of this money for her, so I'm just taking some of what's mine. She won't miss it.

Efficiently replacing everything as I found it, I completed the errand. Returning to the kitchen, I handed the purse to her.

"I got to go to school," I said as I turned on my heels to leave. I didn't want her finding more things for me to do.

I exited the room successfully and left her counting her money. They were trying to determine if they had enough to finance another day of drinking. I retreated to my room and carefully hid the money in a special pouch I had attached to the bedsprings.

The bed was tempting me to stretch my aching body out on it. I craved rest, but knew that even if I could, the nightmares would return and rest would flee. A loud summons interrupted my longings.

"Josephine, get yourself to that school!" Mother ordered.

What did she think I was doing?

I sighed loudly. After quickly washing my face, changing clothes, and smoothing down my hair, I headed back to the kitchen. I was used to dressing quickly from the days in the New Order.

"You're not wearing that are you?" Mother questioned loudly, as she looked me over.

I wonder why every word she says needs to be decibels above what the normal person spoke in.

"Yes," I said with a sneer. "What am I supposed to wear?"

"Can't you wear something that looks decent? Those clothes look like you slept in them." She continued her assault. "Why don't you dress like the other kids around here?" Her voice held a note of sarcasm.

"I don't have anything like other kids," I said through gritted teeth.

You know, you could buy me clothes with that welfare money they pay you for my care.

"What I have are old lady hand me downs that you got from your aunt. She's in her sixties. The style of dress is not exactly that of a teenager. Those clothes would be worse than these. I refuse to even be caught dead in them!" I barked.

I moved to the door, opened it, stepped through, and slammed it shut before she could say another word. If she were still home when I returned from school, my actions would earn me several slaps or punches. I was subject to Mother's every whim. The amount of booze she consumed during the day would determine the severity of the beating later on.

For whatever reason, Mother seemed to be constantly filled with rage, and she made me the object of that rage. I don't know what I ever did to make her so angry all of the time. But it must have been really bad. Maybe just the fact that I'd been born was enough; perhaps she didn't like the idea of being saddled with the responsibility of raising me. Not that she did all that great of a job. Maybe she just liked being a bully. I know she liked fighting my father and anyone else she came in contact with. Since the moment I was deposited on her doorstep, she worked to make every day of my existence a living hell. Sometimes I wondered who was worse – her or Major Doyle from the New Order's militia. I am certain that she didn't consider me any more human than he did.

God, if You're really there, please get me out of this place.

At least I wasn't wearing my militia uniform; my clothes were what we'd wear when we were considered off duty. Actually, there wasn't much difference between our off duty clothes and our regular uniforms. The biggest difference was that the off-duty clothes didn't have the stripes and insignias on them. Dressed in my flannel shirt, rust colored jeans, and boots; I headed for the dreaded public school. I double-timed it to the school so I wouldn't be late. Being late in the New Order was severely punished; I wasn't sure what they'd do here, but I didn't want to find out. I passed several town kids on my way there. They stared and pointed. I glared back at them showing they weren't going to intimidate me despite what they did to Casey. I slowed my pace as I arrived at the school.

The building was a large, multilevel brick building. It was larger than almost any building that I'd ever seen before. Concrete steps led up to a set of huge wooden doors. The building was old and decrepit. It made me feel creepy standing in front of it. The cornerstone on the building dated it over a hundred years old. It didn't hide its age very well. I hadn't seen buildings this tall in the New Order. The school at the compound in the New Order was only one floor. I wondered how I would find my way around this huge maze.

This was truly a strange place. Some of the students had long hair and others had very short hair; some were even bald with only a strip of hair in the middle of their heads. Their clothes were equally as strange. Some had on jeans, mostly blue. Others wore some type of clothing that went only to the thigh and didn't have any legs in it.

As I watched the kids stream in the front doors, I nearly longed to go back to the New Order. This was the first time I'd seen more than a handful of town kids in one place.

I took a deep breath and walked toward the steps. Several kids bumped into me as I climbed. This put me on edge. I wasn't used to people touching me other than to hurt me. It was the law in the New Order that you were never allowed to let anyone touch you at any time. With each bump, the person uttered some sort of language that I didn't understand. I had heard Mother and Father use similar words, but I didn't know what they meant. I knew I'd handled worse things in the New Order and survived. I hoped my luck would continue.

I stepped into the building. I had no idea where to go as my ears were met with the commotion of slamming lockers, loud voices, and shuffling feet. I wandered down the hallway. Pressing against the wall, I tried to be as invisible as possible. I must have been going upstream since everyone else was going in the opposite direction. Everyone was bumping into me and shoving me aside.

No one offered assistance or direction. Mostly they just stared, pointed, and whispered. I wasn't going to lower myself to ask them for help. For all I knew, they'd attack me on the spot, just like they did Casey. No one tried to understand or even think about the refugees having trouble adjusting. We were just expected to comply.

I accepted the fact that I had no clue where I needed to go; I swallowed my pride and found my way to the school office. Opening the door, I stepped inside. Immediately the hustle and bustle of the room stopped. Everyone turned to look at me. I glanced over my shoulder to see if I had missed some great attraction that was worth staring at, but realized they were staring at me. I could read the expressions on their faces like open books. Most of them were hostile, not wanting "my kind" here. Others were confused, probably wondering why I was dressed oddly, and others were suspicious because they'd heard the media reports about the New Order.

I stepped cautiously up to the desk, keeping the room under surveillance. I didn't feel safe, and I wanted no surprises.

"May I speak to the secretary?" I asked no one in particular.

A middle-aged woman approached the desk warily. She wore wire-rimmed glasses and had shoulder-length brown hair that flicked from side to side as she walked. She was dressed in a well-tailored suit. I wondered what she thought I was going to do to her.

"Yes?" She said as she continued to stare at me.

"This is my first day here. I don't know what classes I'm supposed to attend or where they're located."

"You should have gotten a schedule of classes when you registered. Why don't you have one?" She asked.

"I don't know why I don't have one. I think the Social Service people registered me," I replied.

She gave me an apprehensive look.

"What's your last name?" She asked. There was a hint of alarm in her voice.

"Benson, Joey... I mean Josephine." I doubted that she'd go for my preferred name.

She took a noticeable deep breath, turned, and walked to the rear of the room. She opened a box on the counter and began thumbing through some cards. Pulling a card, she walked over to a copy machine and made a copy of the card, then returned to the place where I stood.

"This is your schedule." She explained to me as she handed me the copy. "Don't lose it!"

I stared at it dumbfounded. The abbreviations and odd room numbers didn't make any sense to me. I looked at her with a confused expression.

"I don't know my way around the building. The numbers and abbreviations on this paper don't mean anything to me."

"Are you stupid?" She asked as she studied my face, probably to figure out whether I was joking or not.

I guess it didn't matter if you were rude to the New Order refugees. Stupid was not a word that I was accustomed to being called by anyone other than Mother. I bit my tongue to stop a sharp retort that might try to sneak through my mouth. I guess she realized that I wasn't going to answer her question.

How do you answer that question?

"The first digit of the room number tells you the floor the remainder of the number is the location of the room on that corridor."

I nodded and waited for further explanation, but there was none. I turned around and departed without another word. Standing in front of the office, I stared at the piece of paper. It listed seven classes, the teachers' names and room numbers. I was no closer to knowing where to find the rooms than I had been when I entered the office.

While I stood there considering my options, other refugees walked up and joined me. It was a relief to see some non-hostile faces. The other refugees looked as confused as I felt. Another individual joined us. Her name was Jackie Swink; she'd escaped the New Order and had been dealing with this culture longer than the rest of us. She'd already attended this school for a year.

"You guys look like you could use a guide," she volunteered.

We gratefully nodded in unison.

She looked at each of our schedules and explained the "Up" staircase and the "Down" staircase, as well as the consequences of getting them mixed up. She also explained to us how to find our lockers, the bathrooms, and the cafeteria.

After her instructions, she also gave a parting word about what the bells meant. She was well aware of our New Order training to react at the sound of bells. She didn't want us diving for cover on the first day. Jackie pointed us in the correct direction and sent us on our way. Our little band moved toward the "Up" staircase and headed for a place they called "homeroom". After a little searching, we found the correct room. Several of us filed into one of the classrooms, and we found a cluster of empty seats. As we entered the room, we became the immediate center of attention. I tried to ignore the staring eyes, the whispers and the giggles as I took my seat. The metal desks were similar to the wooden ones we had in the New Order. At least something was a little familiar. With all of the stares they were giving us, you'd have thought we were some type of important people or something.

I looked around the room; this was indeed a very strange-looking place. There were strange curtains made out of aluminum slats that were held together with string. The walls were made out of rough cinder block. It was an ugly room. The classrooms in the New Order were much more attractive. We at least had posters of battle scenes, banners with slogans on them, and implements of war to decorate the walls.

As we sat waiting for the teacher to arrive, I was bothered that no one was assigned as a lookout. This person should have been at the door watching for the teacher. Once spotted, an alarm would sound so we could all be ready to jump to attention. There were severe penalties for being late to salute.

Why don't they seem worried about being disciplined?

I almost wanted to order one of the refugees to be the lookout but was afraid of overstepping my boundaries. Consequently the teacher entered the room without an announcement. My heart leaped into my throat as I saw him enter.

Suddenly, a familiar word echoed in the room: "Attention!" Billy shouted.

In the New Order, the teachers outranked all of the students. It didn't matter what your rank, everyone stood at attention for the teachers.

Reacting out of instinct, we jumped to our feet and snapped to attention. We were met with stares from the other class members. I didn't understand why no one else was standing. There was a few seconds of silence, then the other students burst into laughter.

Why are they laughing? Didn't these students respect their leaders? Why didn't the teacher reprimanding them for not showing the proper respect?

Still standing at attention, my eyes returned to the teacher. His expression was one of anger.

"What's going on here?" He demanded. "Why are you people standing at attention?"

Why are we the ones in trouble?

My face burned hot with embarrassment as the rest of the class continued to peal with laughter.

Why is showing proper respect something to mock us for? Why is the teacher angry at our sign of respect? Why is no one willing to help us instead of making fun of us?

"Sit down!" The teacher ordered, "and the rest of you settle down."

Reluctantly, I looked around at my compatriots. They were looking at me. Even though we hadn't all been in the same unit, they knew I outranked them. I nodded to them and we sat. The teacher gave us a stern look as he sat down at his desk to begin taking attendance. Almost immediately the class members began jumping up imitating us. Some were throwing sloppy salutes at each other and falling back into their chairs laughing themselves to tears.

"Enough!" Barked the teacher. "You six are not going to be a disruptive influence in my class. Perhaps a trip to Mr. Wilcox's office will teach you hooligans a lesson." He gestured toward the door.

Great! Our first day, and we've already been labeled hooligans. Why were we the ones getting in trouble when the rest of class is acting like a bunch of disrespectful idiots?

I felt my face burn. Biting my tongue, I stood to my feet, straightened myself to my full height and moved defiantly towards the door. I kept my head held high. The others fell into step behind me.

We marched back to the principal's office. Upon arrival, the secretary ushered us immediately into the principal's office. She gave us that same disgusted look she had when she gave me my schedule. It was almost as if we were expected. I came to a halt in front of the desk and each refugee stepped forward next to me to form a horizontal line across his office. We stood there facing him as he hung up the intercom phone. No doubt the teacher had already phoned him to relay his side of the story.

Mr. Wilcox appeared to be in his fifties. He was dressed in a dark suit with a dark bow tie. His narrow brown eyes were distorted through his thick-lensed glasses. Thin, graying brown hair was combed in strange ways trying to cover his balding areas. Mr. Wilcox stood but remained behind his desk. I guess he felt he needed a barrier between himself and us.

The six of us stood at parade rest as we stared at some mark on the wall above his head. We'd all been through dressing-downs in the past. Not to mention the humiliation that the New Order leaders would put you through. I wondered how this would compare.

"What did you think you were trying to pull up there? What kind of a stunt was that? What planet are you from? This is not the army any longer! Are you too stupid to recognize that fact?" His voice was nearly shouting.

What does he think the New Order is?

"We only accepted you into this school because the state said we had to, but mark my words, I don't have to keep troublemakers in my school. They have special schools for people like you."

People like us? Makes us sound like we have some kind of disease!

His face turned beet red as he lectured. "I'm sending you back upstairs lest you think that you can pull these stunts to get out of going to class. I want you to sit in your desks, pay attention, and don't cause any more trouble. I don't want to see you back in this office, or you'll force me to take some drastic measures. You're not in the New Order any longer, so fit in or leave!"

With that, he sent us back to class, as we walked back single file, with me leading the way, my mind erupted in angry thoughts against this man.

How dare he tell us to just fit in? Doesn't he think we would if we knew how? He can't understand that our actions are programmed into us.

What did he know about the New Order? I guess he only knew the things that the media reported. He knew nothing about what we had experienced or us for that matter. What was worse, he didn't care. That much was obvious. All he wanted from us was conformity. He didn't care if we learned anything in this stupid school. He didn't care about us.

He just wants to be sure there is no trouble and he assumes that we would be the origin of that trouble if it comes. Trouble is already here and it is not from us. Trouble is, the reason Casey is laying on a broken couch in an abandoned house recovering from a severe beating. If we were to start trouble, there would be no question about responsibility. If we were to start trouble, we'd be swift and deadly.

I ached inside. I longed to fit in. Couldn't anyone understand that? Isn't that some sort of basic human need? Even with other refugees, I still felt very alone. The New Order's training didn't allow us to form any friendships with each other. None of us had chosen to be part of the New Order. Why couldn't anyone understand that?

Why did our presence ignite such prejudice? I guess one thing was for certain – We were alone! We were alone and very different from everyone else, and no one cared.

We're alone!

Chapter - 9 - Learning Prejudice

Every day was a journey in torment. The teachers remained suspicious, expecting that our every action was some type of a coup to undermine their authority. The name-calling graduated to physical assaults. Usually, they'd get a group together and wait until one of us was alone before attacking. They knew they had to outnumber us in order to bully us. The teachers and staff looked the other way when these things happened. I guess it was their way of putting their stamp of approval on the students' actions. Just walking down the hallway could be a nightmare, because you never knew who was the next one to be shoved, tripped, or pushed.

The cafeteria usually was a free for all. We'd get our trays of food and before we could find a seat to eat, we'd be tripped or have the tray knocked out of our hands, scattering the food, dishes, and tray across the floor. The cafeteria monitors always made us clean up the mess. When we complained, they swore they didn't see anything. If we managed to get the tray to a table, before we could eat, someone would come along and dump it in our laps. Others would throw food at us.

I watched as the compatriots fought hard to suppress defensive instincts to retaliate. None of us wanted the possible alternative of being locked up some place. The state required that we go to school or we would be breaking the law, so we were stuck here. I could read my own frustrations and growing anger in the reflections of the faces of my compatriots. We were unable to walk around the school alone without being subject to attack.

Here we were, the finest trained soldiers of the New Order, and these puny towns kids were bullying us. This couldn't continue. Our instincts, our pride, our training, and our programming wouldn't allow it.

It seemed there was a selected group that appointed themselves to be our chief tormentors. To date, their boldest act had been to severely beat and humiliate Casey. They were looking for more ways to torture us. Bert was shoved into a locker and wasn't found for two hours. Having been confined in small dark places as part of her training, this sparked some horrific memories. Alex Redman, another one of the refugees, and a rather large young man, had his head flushed in a toilet. He was so humiliated that he cut school for nearly a week. The Sheriff found him and forced him to return.

For me, both school and home were houses of horror. When each school day ended, I raced for the exit doors trying to escape before anyone had an opportunity to attack me. At least the time between school and home offered some hope of escape, as long as I could stay invisible. One day as I raced outside, I ran into Jackie nearly knocking her over. Reaching out quickly, I grabbed her and steadied her on her feet. She was gathering the refugees together on a corner of the sidewalk. I was amazed that the group was gathering in the open. At least there was safety in numbers. Jackie motioned for me to join them.

"What's going on?" I asked. I kept my eyes looking above their heads, watching for anyone that might be trying to sneak up on us.

"I thought I'd gather us together to see what can be done about our current problem," Jackie stated. "When it was only me attending the school, most everyone ignored me. I guess they figured one person wasn't a threat to them. Now that there's more of us, I think they're feeling intimidated and want to strike before we have a chance to organize."

"I don't think it's a good idea for us to talk about this out here in the open," I cautioned.

Jackie gave me a look of disgust at my interference. She quickly changed her expression before anyone else noticed.

"Benson's right, I think we should go to the abandoned house and continue this discussion," Chris Mitchell added. Chris escaped from the New Order at the beginning of the summer.

"I agree!" Casey chimed in. His face was still swollen and was turning various shades of purple. He had missed the first three days of school because of the beating. When he returned, I watched several of the town kids snicker and point at his injuries. Casey served as a clear reminder to us of what these people were capable of doing, and none of us wanted to endure that humiliation.

Not wanting to run the risk of an outsider finding us: we paired off and dispersed in different directions. Bert and I joined up. The two of us walked away from the school, heading in the opposite direction of the house. After about three blocks, we switched directions. We made several more turns, changing directions each time before we headed for the house. I assumed this exercise was repeated by each of the groups as they headed in separate directions. Twenty minutes later, Bert and I arrived at the house. Jackie and Casey were already there.

Jackie was thirteen, a year older than me, but I would have been her superior officer in the New Order. She'd been out of the New Order for over a year. She lived with her mother, but rarely saw her. Jackie's mother spent a lot of time away from their tiny apartment in the company of men. I wasn't sure if she was in any type of an abusive situation like the majority of us were. Other than that, I didn't know much else about her. I had first met her briefly after my escape from the New Order. There was something about her that made me uncomfortable. I couldn't explain it then or now. She still gave me a weird feeling.

My former compatriot, Bobby Matthews, had told me just before he died that he thought Jackie was a Militia spy. He never said why he thought that. I wasn't sure if I believed Bobby or not.

Bobby and I had been through a lot together in the New Order. He had helped save my grandparents during our escape. Once we were out, he began using drugs to find relief from the constant internal pain. He was high on drugs when he shared that information with me.

I admit there is something about her that makes me suspicious, but I can't quite put my finger on what it is.

Soon, the other pairs began to arrive.

Entering the basement, I settled myself on the sandy floor against the wall.

I still don't understand why this house has so much sand on the floor. I'll admit it does make it warmer than sitting on the cold concrete.

I pulled my knees to my chest. Bert Fisher sat on the floor near the couch. Casey sprawled out on the couch. He was still recovering from the beating and took every chance he could to lay down. Bert leaned against the couch and watched over him like a sister. In school, she stuck with him making sure that he was not alone at any time. In his current state, he would have been easy prey for those that wanted to show how tough they were by attacking the former soldiers of the New Order.

Next entered Willie Hinson and Billy Schultz. Willie took a seat on a cushion near the door. His slim build and small size made it hard to believe he was twelve. His handsome face was framed by black hair. His steel gray eyes never betrayed what was going through his mind. Willie still dressed in our customary rust color jeans and flannel shirt. His only break with the New Order's dress code was that he rolled his shirtsleeves over once to make it more comfortable for his long arms. He arrived only a month ago. He tended to remain quiet and looked to the rest of us for leadership.

Billy Schultz moved to the farthest wall away from the group and sat down in the sand. He was twelve and tended to be even more of a loner than the rest of us. He didn't look around; instead, he sat drawing in the sand with his finger. His black eyes were like coal. Billy's face showed bruises from a beating he had received several days before from the town kids. After a big struggle, half a dozen of them managed to finally pin his arms and legs down, one of them sat on his chest and held a knife to his throat. While Billy was pinned helplessly, they punched him over and over. They didn't stop until his eyes had swollen shut, and he was bleeding from his nose, mouth, and eyes. No one knows for sure if these attackers would have stopped if Alex and Lindsey hadn't spotted the commotion and come to his rescue. The attackers scattered.

I think the town kids would kill us if they thought they could get away with it.

Alex Redman and Lindsey Kenton were the next pair to enter the basement. They moved over toward Billy and sat down on either side of him. Billy was clearly uncomfortable by their attention.

Alex was broad-shouldered and muscular. He escaped shortly after Jackie did. It had been almost a year. He let his dark brown hair begin to grow longer so that it covered his ears and pushed out over his collar. Swapping his Militia garb for blue jeans, sneakers, and a long-sleeved tee shirt, he nearly could pass as one of the town kids. His eyes were like two pieces of green ice, his expression remained flat. I considered Alex to be unpredictable. Between the rumors that I remember about his service in the New Order, and the things I've heard since made him a typical loose cannon. In many ways, he reminded me of Jesse Burrows. His pent up energy made him constantly ready for a fight.

Lindsey was Alex's shadow. She escaped around the same time he did. She and Alex had become quite friendly, especially after she had been grabbed by a group of townies and had her head flushed in the toilet. It must have taken a huge number of townies to subdue her. She was a very muscular twelve-year-old girl and quite capable of giving any one of us a fight we wouldn't soon forget. Her blue eyes showed warmth that was a new addition to her countenance. I wondered where that originated. She too was letting her hair grow longer. Both of them had too much energy and not enough ways to blow it off. They spent a lot of time together. I didn't know where they went, or what they did when they were not in school or at the abandoned house. The only thing we knew was that they spent a lot of time together. Speculation suggested that their activities would never have been accepted under the rules of the Militia.

The last pair to arrive was Gerry Kling and Chris Mitchell.

Gerry Kling, formerly known as Geraldine before the New Order took her, age thirteen, took a seat near Bert and Casey. She had bright brown eyes and a wide grin. She always had a grin on her face. I hadn't met her until I rescued her from a locker a couple of days ago. She was the second of the group to be stuffed in one. Gerry had been trapped for over two hours.

I wonder where she picked that grin up.

Smiles were not standard issue in the New Order. Even when she arrived at the meetinghouse with bruises from beatings that her aunt had given her, the smile never faded.

Chris Mitchell's black hair and dark features almost made him invisible in the shadows. His rust colored jeans and flannel shirt allowed me to see the outline of his figure. The Underground had helped him escape about six months before. The unfortunate thing for him and for the rest of us was that once the Underground brought us here, we were left to fend for ourselves. No one assisted us with adjusting to life in freedom.

It was hard to believe this was true freedom. Somehow I pictured it to be different from the New Order's terror. Yet, it was the same type of violence only with a different name and place.

I guess I felt a type of kinship with these refugees. We all lived through hell. I was quite sure that the others lived the nightmare over and over in their minds as I did. From the day we were taken by the New Order for their special "training", we lost nearly everything. We ceased to be children and were forced into being robotic soldiers. They stole our childhood. We were humiliated and violated by their programming, making us do things that we would never have done. Control over our own minds was taken from us. There were no such things as boundaries or protection. Since we were no longer considered human, there was no such thing as self-esteem or self-worth. They discouraged any attempt at forming relationships. All feelings and emotions were prohibited, even though they used fear as a motivating and controlling tool. Added to all of this, we were pumped full of drugs to make us easier to control and manipulate. They encouraged us to be suspicious of everything good, and there was no such thing as safety or trust. The leaders used all of this to remove every shred of humanity from us.

Since our rescue by the Underground, we each had the misfortune of being forced to live with parents or guardians. All of them turned out to be abusive. They didn't understand the things we'd been through and didn't know how to deal with us. They became frustrated and vented their anger on us. After being freed from the New Order, no one prepared us for the severity of the drug withdrawals. I thought for sure that I was going to die during those days.

From the shreds of statements I've heard from the others, I gather they too had similar experiences. The Underground didn't warn us of the differences that we would face in our new world.

Maybe they weren't fully aware either, or maybe they didn't know what to do to help us.

Nothing we did could help us escape the horror of the memories that we were left with as a result of our experiences.

What do we have left?

The ten of us sat in silence for a while, each lost in his or her thoughts. Sharing those intimate thoughts with each other would never happen since we were all too well trained for that.

"I'm sure that by now we've all experienced to an attack of some type from the town kids." Jackie began, breaking the silence.

In the dim light of the room, I could make out unanimous nods. Jackie paused.

"So, what can we do about it?" Billy Schultz asked. "I personally am getting fed up with all the crap that we are having to take. It's like living through some of the punishments of the New Order all over again. Give me a gun and I'll show them a thing or two."

"We could blow up this stinking school," Willie said, showing his impulsiveness.

Wasn't stopping the violence the whole reason we were removed from the New Order?

Lindsey quickly responded, "That would only prove to them that what they think of us is true."

"Lindsey's right! We don't need to do something that drastic," Jackie added. "We need to protect ourselves, but we also need to try and figure out how to cope in these new surroundings."

"How can we cope when we're constantly being attacked?" Alex growled. "Besides, what chance do we have of coping here?"

Other ideas were tossed about. I just sat and listened.

My thoughts shifted.

I hate this school! I hate these townspeople! I hate everyone! I hate me! I just want to die like the others and end the suffering.

Gerry asked. "Jackie, you've got a better understanding of what these people are like, since you've been around them the longest. What do you think we should do?"

All of the side conversations stopped, and everyone's attention turned to Jackie. I stopped my inner discussion with myself. I, too, turned to hear what she had to say.

"First, I think we need a definite plan." Jackie began.

That is rather profound! I probably shouldn't be so cynical since I am in the same boat with the rest of the group.

Hearing the snickers from those in the shadows, I assumed I wasn't the only one with that thought.

Jackie frowned and waited for the snickers to stop before continuing. "I think we need to unite."

"We're already doing that!" Gerry retorted in disgust. "We already can't even go to the toilet without someone accompanying us."

"I mean, we should be more organized," Jackie explained. "We make some ground rules that we all agree to follow. We apply the same discipline we learned in the New Order. Since we haven't figured out the rules here, we take the rules from what we know and make them work for us here."

The expressions that I could discern seemed confused.

"Rule number one, I think we shouldn't go any place alone. This was our number one rule in the New Order – always be with a compatriot," Jackie said. "Remember, we are superior to these people. We've been trained to be elite soldiers. There's no reason we should be losing to these cowards."

Her words were met with nods from the group. I could see that their responses spurred her forward.

"I think we should form what is known around here as a gang," Jackie announced. We looked at her quizzically as if she had just spoken in a foreign language.

After a long silence, Bert spoke and asked the question that we all were thinking. "What's a gang?"

I don't think any of us had heard that word before.

"A gang is a group of individuals who hang out together, work as a group, and defend each other against attacks. I saw this movie about gangs from a place called New York City. These gang members were tough and got a lot of respect. No one messed with them. They organized themselves, staked out their area, and then they didn't let anyone push them around. People cringed in fear whenever they were nearby. They attacked rather than waiting to be attacked," she explained.

Jackie's plan was met with much approval. Since we were all misfits in our new environment, there was no reason not to accept her plan. I think we were all sad, alone, and hurting, but no one would ever admit to it. I guess it was time that we learned to be prejudiced too.

"I know that most of our home lives are about as abusive as our school lives. This is another reason I think we need to band together even tighter. Since we have no one else, we can at least have each other. We'll have a place to belong."

I sat in silence suspicious of her motives for such a proposal but didn't let on. After all, what other choice did we have if we are going to survive here?

What is she thinking wanting a group of former super soldiers to unite together? Is she setting the stage for us to form our own militia group and go on the attack? This could be just the excuse that lands us all in jail. Why would she want us to cause trouble on purpose? Weren't we causing enough trouble by accident? What is she up to?

I knew something had to be done, but I wasn't sure that forming our own private army was the answer. Were we just reclaiming the only thing that we knew, rather than trying to adjust to our "New World"? Who's to say?

Chapter - 10 - Plan of Doom

The next day after school, we gathered back at the abandoned house to pick up the discussion of the night before. We had all decided we needed some time to think about Jackie's suggestion. To make matters worse, more fuel had been added to the fire. During gym class, some of the girls had cornered Bert in the gym locker room. I'm not sure how many girls attacked her, but I was quite sure there was a sizeable number. They stripped Bert and then threw her clothes all over the locker room. She was forced to roam around the locker room naked in search of her clothes. The girls sat around on the benches and threw out crude comments. Sometimes, just as Bert would find an article of clothing, it would be wrenched away from her and tossed to someone else in a game of keep away.

As I looked at Bert now I could still see the humiliation in her expression. She sat quietly on the floor next to the couch. She had her knees pulled up to her chest and her body positioned in a way to make her as small as she possibly could. I think she would have become invisible if she could. Pangs of guilt twisted in my stomach as I felt a sense of relief that it wasn't me.

In the New Order this was the way to ultimately humiliate an individual and punish them for even the smallest infraction of the rules. I had made it a point to follow the rules to the letter so that I would never have to face this punishment. I couldn't even watch when others were subject to that type of humiliation. In some ways, I had to admire Bert for being able to even sit with us after her ordeal.

The basement sounded like a swarm of bees had invaded with all the buzzing. I could hear determination in their voices I hadn't heard since our days in the New Order. I glanced at Jackie. She seemed to be waiting for the group to become stirred up, before she decided to speak further about forming this gang that she had mentioned yesterday. I guess she was waiting to see how serious we were about this plan of hers so that she could be assured of positive results.

One of the few things that I knew about Jackie was that she didn't like to fail. How did she get so much power over everyone?

Jackie stood to her feet and cleared her throat.

"According to the movie that I watched about gangs, they attempt to instill fear by intimidating rivals and citizens alike. The more fear and intimidation we can generate, the more power we will have. After all, isn't power what we all want?"

Her little talk about power reminded me of Jesse and that made me nervous. I saw firsthand what craving for power could do to someone. The fact that she was using the hunger for power as a motivator made me all the more suspicious of her and scared for all of us.

She had worked the group into such a frenzy that I would have been skinned alive if I'd offered any protest at this point. Rushing in now with an opposing opinion could be disastrous.

"Once we get established, people will fear us so much that they'll walk on the other side of the street from us. They won't enter the same parking lot where we're standing. They will learn to give us the proper respect that we deserve. All the while they'll remember they brought this on themselves. We will repay them for every attack they dared to initiate against any of us," Jackie spoke authoritatively.

Jackie sounded like many of the propaganda films we were stuck watching in the New Order. We were recreating the exact atmosphere that others had fought so hard to free us from. Somehow I didn't think this was the best way to say 'thank you' to them. On the other hand, we were left here without any help to adjust to this society.

The face of my grandparents appeared in my mind. Their expressions were sad. I knew in my heart this was not the right thing to do, but at the same time, I needed to find a way to protect myself from the attacks by the town kids. I couldn't bear any of the humiliation that the others already endured to this point.

After all, the teachers, students, and the townspeople were already united against us in an unannounced war. Our only crime - we were different. They were making it impossible for us to start the new life we were promised.

Even with all of its faults and possible disasters, I was leaning towards Jackie's idea. We needed to do something to create some type of safety for ourselves. We couldn't control our home environments. Our alternative was to create our own safety in school and on the streets. I suppose by banding together, we would also find a sense of belonging to something that promised security. One thing was certain the attacks and their severity were escalating. I was afraid of what they would do next.

When I thought of Bert's different traumas, I knew being locked in a locker or stripped in public were both fates worse than death to me. I thought about Casey's beating and how it broke his spirit. I remembered the vow I made while in the New Order; I knew that no one could ever be allowed to do that to me. Pictures flashed through my mind of what had happened to the others. I couldn't allow myself to be a victim of any of that. Continuing survival meant I had to do whatever I could until I could find a way out of this horrendous situation. I was especially afraid of being a victim of Bert's fate. I think I could have dealt with a beating better than what happened to her in the locker room.

With all of this in mind, I couldn't help but agree with Jackie. My pride shoved my suspicions to the side for the time being and I nodded my approval.

"Sounds good to me!" Billy shouted and waved his fist in the air. "Let's do it!"

"We'll get even with them for every bit of misery they've put us through," Lindsey added with a smirk on her face.

"We'll do it for Casey!" Bert announced.

"We'll do it for Bert!" Casey yelled in return.

"We'll do it for all of us!" Alex chimed in.

That was the turning point. Jackie had won them all over. For better or worse, she had won me over as well.

"Let's do it!" Everyone agreed as they moved toward the center of the room to slap each other's hands. The small basement echoed with loud excited voices.

Jackie let them carry on for a short period of time, letting them become further charged up.

After the noise had reached its peak and begun to get somewhat quiet, Chris asked the question that was probably on everyone's mind. "What's our first step?"

Silence quickly filled the air as Jackie let the anticipation hang in the room knowing that every eager eye was focused upon her.

It was obvious to me; she just liked the attention that it brought her. She learned the rules of how to control a group from the New Order, and she learned them very well. I leaned forward and rested my elbows on my knees to get a clearer view of her expression, but I couldn't read her face. She had created a detached look as to not give away her thoughts to the others.

What does she have up her sleeve? Why is she waiting so long before she answers Chris' question?

As I looked around the room, I could see the excited expressions on each face as they waited.

Finally, she spoke. "According to the movie, a gang needs a leader. So our first order of business should be to choose a leader," Jackie informed us. "I think we should pick someone who is already trained as a leader."

Jackie paused again and let the words sink into the group. The members looked from one to another as they replayed her words in their heads.

"The leader's job will be to plan out strategy. It won't be much different than planning battle strategy in the New Order. Think of one among us who excelled at that. Our leader should be someone that we look up to with respect. Who fits that description?"

Again, everyone looked from one person to the other.

Where was she going with this?

My wandering thoughts were stopped abruptly as she continued, "I believe Benson should be our leader. After all, the leaders of the New Order considered her to be the best and the brightest. Not to mention, she achieved the highest rank of all of us. As we all know, courage was the strongest factor to be promoted in the New Order." She paused and waited to see if there would be any objection. I thought I detected a look of satisfaction in her expression.

Is she setting me up for something? I am surprised to say the least. I hadn't hung around with the refugees much until lately. Jackie was the one who told us about gangs and what they did. Why didn't she want the leadership role?

All eyes focused on me. My face turned hot from everyone's stares.

"Benson was a second lieutenant in the New Order; that outranks any of us. She is therefore the ranking officer here. As the leader she can offer us the degree of discipline we're accustomed to," she continued. "We want to go about our tasks in true military fashion, none of this disorganized junk that the town kids have been partici-pating in. Our strikes will be quick and efficient as only a true mili-tary leader could command. I think Benson has proven that she can do this for us."

I shot Jackie a puzzled glance. Her expression was neutral.

Is she some type of New Order spy and setting me up for a fall so that I would be forced to go back to the New Order? Why didn't she want to be leader? Did she think she would be my second in command and actually pull my strings? If that is her thought, she is dead wrong... Why me? ... What is her plan? ... I don't even believe all the stuff she is saying about me. Does she really think that they're buying it? ... I'm in favor of forming the gang, but I'm not sure why she is nominating me as the leader.

I wasn't sure that I agreed with all of the philosophy that she had put forth to the members about gangs. My mind tried to imagine the type of strategic strikes she and the others had in mind.

Could I really follow through with their plans? Then again, if I am the leader, I might be able to control these activities.

My suspicions flowed through my mind. The thought of being the leader of this newly formed gang made my stomach hurt. There was something wrong with the whole plan, but I couldn't put my finger on it. It seemed the only way that I could truly be effective in controlling them was to be the leader.

Maybe if I'm in charge, I'll be able to keep them in line and maybe out of trouble.

This whole ordeal still made me very suspicious of Jackie. Was she setting me up for something?

I wonder if she is in league with Jesse Burrows or perhaps the Major?

Bobby Matthews' warning came to my mind about her possibly being a spy. Other thoughts fired through my brain one after another, faster than a machine gun. I had completely lost touch with what was going on in the basement.

I don't know how much time had passed when my attention was yanked away from my thoughts by a familiar voice.

"You okay?" I heard Bert's words. "Do you accept?"

I looked in her direction.

When she saw me look at her, her expression showed relief. I thought I detected a glint of pride in her eyes at my being chosen as the leader of the group.

"Huh?" I grunted. I wasn't sure what had been said while I'd been lost in my thoughts. "The vote is unanimous for you to be our leader. Do you accept?" Alex asked, looking at me with a pleading look.

Looking from face to face as they eagerly awaited my answer; I managed to stutter, "O-okay..." I probably should have given it more thought, but it all happened so quickly.

"The floor is yours," Jackie conceded.

I nodded and cleared my throat. Looking around the room, I saw that every eye was still fixed on me. Sweat trickled down my back as I faced them. I was afraid to stand. I didn't think my feet would hold me, so I remained seated.

"Before we do anything, we will need to plan. We will need to spend some time in observation. I don't want any of us running around unprepared. Planning will be what sets us apart from the town kids. This is the only way we will be able to successfully retaliate and to take the control we are setting out to gain."

Eager nods came from everyone around the room.

"So, I need volunteers to gather information about those who have already attacked us. They will be our first priority. We will repay them for what they did to us," I announced.

It amazed me how easily I could slip back into the role of being a unit leader. "I'll find out where some of those town kids live, and maybe we can pay them a little visit with some spray paint," Willie offered with a devilish grin.

"Henson, I said observation!" I barked at him.

The devilish grin faded, he nodded his compliance.

Suddenly, I realized that as uncomfortable as I was playing this role I'd been assigned, I had to convince them all to respect my authority and to trust my judgment if I were ever going to be able to turn things around for the good.

"We need to find the ones who beat up Casey and get revenge for him," Bert stated. "I think that should be our first order of business. The things that were done to the rest of us all deserve payback, but Casey's was by far the worst."

"I agree, but it will be done in a timely and orderly fashion. We are not going to blindly attack anyone," I reminded them.

"I know some places we should visit and cause the store owners some problems for throwing us out," Billy added.

"Schultz, there will be time to share ideas of future missions, but first we will plan our payback."

The room was alive with suggestion after suggestion. I couldn't tell for sure, but I thought everyone was speaking up. It was hard to understand some of the suggestions since they were all talking over one another.

"Enough!" I shouted. "There will be plenty of time for each of you to give your suggestions. This is not the time for it. We will maintain our priorities."

"As a gang we can establish our dominance over this town. Soon, we'll be able to do anything we want." Jackie continued to glamorize the idea of power to the rest of the group. "From the things that I saw on TV about gangs, we can make the citizens of this town prisoners in their own homes. We can use the very lessons that we learned at the feet of the military leaders in the New Order. These people thought we were dangerous for just moving into their cozy little town. Well, they're about to find out just who they're dealing with."

"Thank you, Swink, but that will be enough from you. I believe you had me appointed leader. So, let's just stick to the business at hand," I said flatly. I was trying hard not to sound too overbearing, lest they feel as though they'd made a mistake. On the other hand, though, our training demanded order and even though we didn't always want it that way. It was the only way we'd ever known.

Jackie glared at me but fell silent.

Gerry started to open her mouth but changed her mind and closed it quickly.

The whole group was silent. I couldn't put a name to their expressions, but they made me feel uncomfortable. I needed to do something to change them quickly.

"I assure you we will retaliate for every deed that was done to any one of us at least two-fold," I announced.

Their expressions then changed to a look of relief.

I wonder if any of them are having second thoughts about forming a gang like I am.

It wasn't uncommon for any of us to sit alone with our thoughts for hours, but at this point, no one would say anything against this decision. Our programming prohibited that.

I noticed that most of the members had begun staring at Casey. He had become our rallying point. After seeing what happened to him, the group members were constantly nervous and on edge. No one wanted to be broken down in that manner. Jackie's suggestion of forming a gang came at a time when we were all feeling vulnerable.

As I looked at each individual, I still felt uncomfortable about re-creating what I saw as just another version of the New Order. However, banding together seemed to be the logical thing to do for survival. We needed the support of being closer to our fellow compatriots. We needed the protection that we could give each other from those who sought to drive the "savages" away from their well-ordered town.

I had to admit that we all needed something. Perhaps forming this gang would be what we needed: belonging and protection, not just for us but also for those that had similar experiences. I guess we were all doing what we could to escape the pain we felt inside. Maybe being together more would help us.

One thing I knew for sure was that we needed to somehow re-discover our humanity and the things that most others took for granted things that would help identify us as humans in spite of all the inhumanity that was practiced around us. Maybe if we could convince ourselves that we were still human despite what was done to us, we could demonstrate that to others and make them believe it, too. Maybe being together in this gang would do that for us.

Then again it could all be part of the propaganda we were being sold by Jackie. During my time with the Underground, they had told me that individuals separated from their emotions were capable of some of the most inhuman acts imaginable. The New Order had programmed this separation of emotions into us, since being freed, most of us had been unable to make that connection again. If what the Underground said was true, then I was about to lead a group into committing more atrocities than we had done in the New Order. But how could we ever be able to put the pieces back together that the New Order had ripped apart? And were all the pieces even still inside of us?

I'm so alone and confused. Where is Grandmother's God? Why did He have to take them away? If they were here, I know everything would be all right.

But I truly am alone. I have to admit that us banding together will bring me a sense of belonging and maybe a feeling of not being so alone.

It didn't matter if we liked each other or not. We were pushed together for one reason and for one reason only -- protection. Because this was our only reason for sticking together, I was afraid that at some point the group would be beyond control no matter how much authority my rank dictated.

If we gain too much power through our activities, we will be no better than what the townspeople already think of us. We're playing with fire, and I know that someone will end up getting burnt. In this case, it will probably be us...why don't they see that?

Chapter - 11 - Unspeakable Lessons

After our newly formed gang dispersed from the abandoned house, it was time to return to reality. The weekend was here and that meant two very long days at the house with Mother and Father. My steps were heavy as I neared the house. I felt a sense of relief wash over me as I turned the corner. They weren't home. I walked around to the back door and entered. I always liked it when no one was home. If I had to be here, that was the best time.

Even though they weren't there, I knew I'd better fix dinner so that it would be ready whenever they returned. It was always a challenge to keep it warm yet not let it burn while waiting for Mother and Father. I decided to fix spaghetti. It was one of the few meals that was easy to fix and keep warm for them. Just as I finished making dinner, they arrived at the house.

I often wondered if they could even taste anything with all the beer they constantly drank. Mother entered first and immediately staggered over to her chair. As she fell into it, the chair rocked back against the wall. I often wondered if it would tip over with her weight falling into it, but somehow it always held.

"Where's dinner?" she demanded.

"It's coming!" I replied curtly.

When Father entered the house, he stopped to turn on the television and then staggered over to the couch. After serving Mother her dinner, I brought Father his. Both took their plates without a word of thanks.

"Where's the cheese?" Mother questioned. "And bring me another beer."

"I only have two hands. It's coming!" I snapped back. Some days I could hold my tongue better than others. Today, I had too much juggling around in my head to keep my tone in check.

"Watch your mouth!" Mother ordered.

I brought her the cheese and another beer. Finally, I was able to sit down on the floor to eat my dinner. By this time it was lukewarm, but I didn't mind. That meant I could eat it faster.

I sneaked a peek at my watch wondering how long it would take for the two of them to start picking at each other. It happened every night. I focused my attention on the television as I heard the early warning signs.

"Why do we have to watch the baseball games all of the time?" Mother began and then shoved her mouth full of spaghetti.

"Because I want to see my team play!" Father said through gritted teeth.

"It is so boring. There are plenty of other shows we could be watching. I'm missing some of my favorite programs," she complained.

I kept one ear on the TV and the other ear listened for the increase in pitch and intensity of their voices. This would be the signal for me to run so that I wouldn't be caught in the middle of their argument. Before I knew it, Mother had taken her plate of spaghetti and dumped it on Father's head. I grabbed my glass of Kool-Aid and my plate, ran for my bedroom. I was very well practiced at doing this. I could reach the bedroom and dive under the bed without spilling anything on my plate or from my glass. Fortunately, my bed was more like a cot and had a good two feet of clearance underneath it.

I'm not sure where I would've hid otherwise. Once under, it is very difficult for anyone to force you out from underneath.

The move was a little trickier with a bowl of soup, but I still was able to do it. There under the bed, I finished eating my dinner.

When I couldn't hear their raised voices any longer, I ventured back into the living room and glanced around the room. Mother was sitting in her chair as if nothing had happened. Father was sitting on the couch with two plates beside him. He had pulled the spaghetti noodles off of his head and put them on one of the plates. There was still sauce in his hair, but he didn't seem to mind.

Profanity was not something that I was well acquainted with. They didn't use it in the New Order and my grandparents certainly never used it. This was one of the things that I had to get used to since coming to live with Mother and Father. Most of the words I didn't understand. I really didn't care to learn much about it. It seemed the more they drank, the more often these words came out, so I knew they were words I would never want to use.

"Josephine, tell your father...." Mother ordered. The words that followed were ones that I didn't understand. I wasn't in the mood to try to dodge her beating tonight, so I repeated the words to Father as she instructed. In my innocence, I had no idea what I had just said to him.

Suddenly, he erupted into anger. His face turned redder than the spaghetti sauce in his hair. He lunged for me. I didn't know what I had done or why he was after me, but I didn't want to wait around to find out either. I ran for my room. My feet were running so fast, I don't remember them even touching the floor. I got to my room a couple of steps ahead of him and slammed the door shut.

I braced my body between the door and a section of the wall that jutted out.

What did I do wrong? Why is Mother having me say something to him that would make him so angry? Is this entertaining for her? She orders me to deliver a message to him, even though he is sitting next to her. I obey orders as I'd been taught to do.

Mother did absolutely nothing during all of this to help me. As far as I knew, she was still perched on her chair. Maybe she'd gotten up to change the channel so she could watch her programs.

Father pounded and kicked on the door with such force that several times I felt the door try to give. I was shaking. I'd never seen Father this angry before. Usually Mother was the one who got this angry. He banged and punched the door. I wasn't sure how much time had passed. I was concentrating on keeping my body stiff and rigid in order to keep the door closed. I was afraid that he would kill me if he got a hold of me. Whatever she had me say to him enraged him. It was like having a charging bull on the other side of the door.

Suddenly the pounding stopped. Silence fell on the house. I was too well trained to relax my vigilance. I didn't know what he had planned, but I had a feeling that it wasn't over. The silence was eerie. I didn't know that he had gone into their bedroom and into the closet. You could move from their room to mine through the closet to enter my room. His wrath must have sobered him some. He came charging through the closet door. Before I could react, he had me by the shirt collar and yanked me to my feet. He hit me across the back of the head a couple of times. The blows made me feel dizzy.

Father dragged me to the bathroom saying something about how vile and dirty a person I was. My head was spinning too much to understand his words.

"It's my responsibility to correct this," he continued.

He tore my clothes off and jammed a bar of soap in my mouth. I was humiliated to be standing there with him. I gagged as my saliva mixed with the soap. Father turned on the water in the shower and shoved me into it. The water was freezing cold. I shook violently. I wasn't sure if it was because of the water or terror or both. I felt like I was going to throw up.

Father sat down on the toilet seat across from the shower. He began doing something. I was too ignorant to know what he was doing. I closed my eyes and tried to force my brain to focus on something. It was so hard to find good thoughts. The New Order's POW training taught us to focus on small things rather than the current circumstances. This would aid in our survival. I felt so mortified. No one had ever done this to me, not even in the New Order. I had always managed to avoid this type of humiliating punishment. Recently escaping from the New Order, I had noticed that there were some physical changes taking place in my body. I didn't understand them either, but they made me feel even more embarrassed and seemed to cause my father to stare at me more.

Finally, the soap residue made me throw up. He just watched as I continued to vomit over and over in the shower. After a pause, he came over and turned off the water. I was so cold and scared that my teeth were chattering. Grabbing me by the arm, he whipped me around and started hitting me with his belt. It really stung on my cold skin.

"I'll beat every last bit of the dirt and vile out of you," he repeated over and over as he hit me.

I felt my knees begin to buckle under me. He let me slip to the floor of the shower.

"Clean up the mess in here," he ordered as he left the room. I was alone in my misery. I guess he returned to the living room. I could hear him fall onto the couch.

Whatever he had been doing earlier had made a mess on the floor. I cleaned up it up as quickly as possible and slipped into my room to find some clothes to put on. Once dressed, I crawled in bed with several blankets to try to get warm. I was still shaking. I felt sick, embarrassed, and hurt, but I was determined that he was not going to make me cry. I sat there hunched in a small little ball clutching the stuffed bunny Grandmother had given to me on my first birthday. She had kept it hidden during the time I'd been in the New Order. Somehow, the bunny had found its way into the bottom of the bag with my things from the caseworker. Now the bunny was my only concrete link to my life before the New Order, and with my grandparents. I wanted desperately to escape this living nightmare.

Vomiting sounds coming from the bathroom interrupted my thoughts.

From the sound of things, Mother was the one who was throwing up. After a short period of time, everything was quiet. I assumed she must have passed out. Father would leave her in the bathtub and let her sleep there all night in her own vomit.

Suddenly my bedroom door opened and slammed against the wall. I jumped and hit the back of my head on the wall. There was no such thing as privacy in this house. Father was always watching me in the bathroom and barging into my room for no reason. When he did, he would look at me with a look in his eyes that I didn't understand, and then leave.

"Come over here!" he ordered.

"What?" I groaned.

I stood and faced Father, but I kept my eyes diverted from him. I couldn't face him after the humiliation he had just put me through.

Father stood leaning against the wall with a beer bottle in hand.

Why is he barging into my room? First, he humiliates me in the bathroom, and now he's in my room. What is going on? I know I'll never have his approval since I'm not the son he wanted. I think my very presence pains him, so why is he here?

"I want to talk to you!" His words were slightly slurred.

I stared at him in confusion. I didn't know what to say.

What could he possibly want to talk to me about? After the bathroom incident, I would think that that would be enough for one day. Besides, he usually lets Mother do most of the discipline and beating.

He staggered into my room. He sat down on my disheveled bed.

Never let the enemy get behind you! My brain shouted the order. I turned around to face him.

"You look a mess! Don't you ever undress? Come over here!" He ordered. I stared at him as if I were seeing him for the first time.

I didn't understand why he wanted me to undress.

Why did men constantly want me to take my clothes off?

"Get over here and don't take all day doing it!" he ordered.

I inched slowly toward where he was sitting at the foot of my bed. As soon as I was within arm's reach, he grabbed me and yanked me over to him. He was stronger than I expected. He whipped me around and made me sit next to him.

He reeked of stale booze and cigarette smoke. I nearly gagged at the smell of him.

My training set every instinct on edge, and my brain raced as I tried to anticipate what he might have in mind, so that I could try to prepare myself.

"You're twelve years old and it's high time you learn the facts of life. As your father, it's my job to teach you. That military school sheltered you too much from reality." He set the beer bottle on the floor.

Every muscle in my body involuntarily stiffened. I tried to pull away, but he maintained a firm grasp on my wrist. With his free hand, he pulled a stack of pictures out of his pocket and handed them to me. I stared at the stack. I reached for the stack of pictures with my right hand. He let up the pressure on my left hand in order for me to use both hands to shuffle through the pictures.

"Take them!" he growled and twisted my arm, causing pain to shoot from my wrist to my elbow. "Look at them!"

I couldn't imagine what was so important about these pictures that he'd be so violent. I looked down at the pictures as I leafed through them. He grabbed my hair and pushed my head down farther to look at the pictures. I felt my stomach grow sick as each image registered in my brain. The pictures featured my parents in various unclothed poses together. My head spun with confusion. I couldn't comprehend what he was showing me.

This is bad! This is really bad!

He studied my expression and somehow realized through his drunken stupor that I did not comprehend the message that he wanted me to receive. He jerked the pictures out of my hand and shoved them clumsily back into his pocket. Thinking that was the end of it, I tried to stand up and pull free from his grasp. He yanked me back down on the bed.

My eyes met his. I searched his expression trying to understand what was going through his mind. His brown eyes were wild and hungry.

"It looks like I need to teach you more than I thought I did. I need to prepare you so that you'll be able to get married one day and please your husband. Can't have you living at home all your life, and unless you know what to do when you're married, a man would throw you right back to me."

My stomach knotted in terror. I wasn't sure what he was going to do, but my insides told me it wasn't going to be good. He stood to his feet, swaying a little, still grasping my arm. I tried making a break from him, but he flung me across the room. I hit the wall with a thud. Before I could react, he was upon me. He held me in place with his left forearm across my throat. I began to shake uncontrollably as I identified the various sounds he made with his clothing.

No! My brain screamed a silent cry.

Panic seized my insides. The reality of the pictures started to sink into my understanding. I tried to wrestle free. I didn't want him to do whatever it is he was doing with Mother in those pictures. It didn't look pleasant. I wasn't sure what it was, but I had a feeling it was wrong.

He grabbed me by the front of my shirt. I gasped for breath as the shirt collar began to cut off my air supply.

"Leave me alone!" I managed to say, catching some extra breath, but my words came out in a whisper.

"It's my duty as your father to teach you the facts of life and I am going to do just that," he said. He began to force me to do things that made me want to throw up. He loosened his hold slightly.

Taking advantage of the opportunity, I tried to break free. His expression flashed anger as he shoved me to the floor. Before I could roll away, things got worse. Panic drove me to fight harder.

"You let one word escape from your mouth, and you will find yourself in that juvenile detention cell. I can promise you that," he hissed.

There was no way anyone was ever going to lock me up again. I'd rather die first. Somehow Father must've known this was the only thing they had to keep me under their control.

He held me in place with his forearm. I had to hold onto his arm with both hands to keep it from choking me. I continued to shake uncontrollably.

What is happening? No one has ever done this to me before. This isn't right!

My brain continued to scream silently.

All I could hear were the screams inside my head as intense pain filled my being. Mercifully, my mind went blank and I passed out.

When I woke up, I found myself lying on the floor. I lifted my head slightly and looked around the room. Father was gone. A wave of nausea swept over me, forcing me to lay my head back down. The reality and violation of what my father had just done sickened me all the more. Trying to move, every muscle screamed in pain. I felt sick and dirty inside. I crawled over to a pile of clothes on the floor and found an old sock and cleaned myself as well as I could. I didn't want to go outside of my room and risk running into either parent.

What had happened to me? What had he done to me? Why did I hurt so much and feel so sick? Is Mother still passed out in the bathtub? She wouldn't believe me if I could tell her, nor would she even care.

Carefully moving over to the dresser, I fumbled to find some clean clothes that I pulled on as I gritted my teeth against the pain. After dressing, I curled up into the smallest ball I could make myself into on the bed. I wished I could become invisible. Something about all of this was wrong, but there was so much that I didn't know about because of the New Order's restrictions. I couldn't pinpoint what it was that was wrong. I felt a huge ache in my throat. I tried to swallow it down and bury it.

I could never tell anyone what just took place. Even without Father's threats, it would be too humiliating.

I wanted so badly to go to the kitchen and get a big knife and kill him, but I stayed in my room. I moved from the bed and curled up in a corner and just stayed there. I was so confused and scared.

Is there truly a God in Heaven that watches over us? Grandmother and Grandfather believed that. Did God see what happened here?

My face burned with shame at the thought of someone else knowing what happened. Father was very explicit about not telling anyone. Did that mean not to tell God as well?

God, what will I tell You about this if I could? I'm a refugee of the New Order and no one else will give me a chance, so why should you? How can I tell You about rages inside of me? How do I even admit this humiliation? It is all so ugly. My life continues to be stolen from me a piece at a time. I'm so confused.

God, what right do I have to say anything to You? Grandmother said that she was never alone because You were always with her. Does that mean You're not with me because I feel very alone? Are You even interested in me? You have so many that You have to look after. Day after day, my body is beaten and a part of me is broken. Do You know the terror that I face night after night at the thought of sleeping? Yet, I struggle on.

I can't tell you about what he did, but God, do You really know what happened? Do You hear me when I speak? Can I share this secret with You without getting into trouble? If You are there, how could You let this happen? Where are You, God?

Chapter - 12 - A Special Friend

Pain still pulsed through my body from the day before. I was thankful that the night was over. My mind had replayed the events of the day again and again. The rising of the sun was a welcomed sight, and it was the weekend. For that, I was thankful. My body still hurt from Father's attack on me in my room. I was glad that I didn't have to go to school. I don't think I could have faced anyone. I felt a sign was hanging around my neck telling everything that had happened. No matter what I did, nothing relieved the feelings of dirtiness and shame that covered me. My innocence revolted against me. Father had exploited my ignorance and used it to betray what little trust I had left.

Both parents left early to begin their day of drinking, so I had a brief period of time to myself. I could leave the house without them knowing that I was gone. Every place I looked around my room reminded me of the things that happened. The thing I needed was to get away from my room for a while. I had to escape the horror of the house. I opened the door and stepped outside and breathed the fresh, crisp, clean fall air. I painfully made my way to the woods. It was worth it to be in a place where I almost felt safe. It was an area in the middle of a tree cluster. The trees in this group grew so closely together that you could hide in the middle and be out of sight from anyone that might pass by.

I carefully squeezed between the trees and breathed a sigh of relief. I'd made it to my special place. I stretched out on the ground between the trees; I lay there staring up through the brightly colored leaves at the patches of blue sky. The details of the colors above me helped me focus on something else. Truly there must be some plan behind the origins of the world. Surely, such amazing colors didn't just happen on their own. It was in this place I could let myself be whatever I wanted. As I looked up, I watched the puffy white clouds move through the sky in their various shapes. One looked like a marshmallow; another resembled huge balls of cotton.

Can you touch the clouds? I wonder what they feel like? They look soft and squishy.

The white clouds on the beautiful blue sky covered me with a blanket of peace. I knew it was only temporary, but at least here I could find a piece of sanity.

Thoughts of the newly formed gang invaded my peacefulness. Planning the gang's activities would certainly complicate matters. As if all these things weren't enough to deal with, there was also the constant pain inside.

When the refugees arrived at school on Monday, we would enter it united. We would have a new purpose and that bothered me. I was still plagued with the idea that we were recreating the New Order, but I pushed those thoughts to the side and I returned to my revelry of the leaves and clouds.

I lost all track of time while there in my quiet spot. I noticed the shadows changed from one side of the trees to the other, I knew it was time to head for home. I pushed myself to my feet. Instantly, I could feel the stiffness from lying in one place too long. I slipped out of the woods and walked back to the house. I tried to walk as normally as possible, but each step was painful.

When I returned to the house, I noticed that Mother and Father were already home.

I guess they got tossed out of the bar.

I cautiously entered the kitchen. I wasn't sure what awaited me. Their unpredictability filled me with anxiety. I entered the kitchen through the back door. There sat both Mother and Father drinking and smoking. I braced myself for the tongue-lashing and possible beating for not being home when they were. The severity depended upon Mother's whim. If I were lucky, maybe she'd only yell at me instead of hitting me.

"Josephine!" Mother barked.

She never could say my name in a normal tone of voice. I was never sure if I was in trouble or not. I usually was. Stopping in my tracks, I cringed. I hated it when she called me that. I wished she would call me Joey. No one called me Josephine any more. I turned to look at her. I wanted to be prepared for any punches that came my way.

"Our friends, the Walkers, have a litter of puppies. They want to give you one," she stated. "Personally, I don't know why."

A puppy! She is telling me I can have a puppy? I can hardly believe my ears.

"They said if you wanted the dog you could come by this afternoon and pick one out. So, you may go get the dog now, just be home in time to fix dinner. Make sure you get a male!" she instructed.

I was out the door before she could finish her last syllable.

Why is she being nice to me? Either she knows what Father did to me and she is trying to make amends for it or she is planning on doing something to me.

I moved away from the house quickly because I was afraid that she would change her mind.

My feet felt lighter than air as I walked down the shoulder of the road. I couldn't believe it. This one happy thought made me forget all about the pain in my body. Yet, a thought in the back of my mind nagged in the shadows.

What would she expect me to do in return for this?

It was quite a shock that Mother announced that I could have a puppy. I'd wanted a puppy ever since I could remember but had given up all hope of ever having one. I never thought Mother would ever allow me to have anything that I wanted.

Now without any prompting, she tells me that I can have one. The only requirement at this point is to walk over to these people's house and pick out my very own puppy.

This one event made everything a little brighter. The prejudices, fears, and everything else dropped several paces behind in my mind. I continued walking and pulled my jacket up around my neck against the cold wind. The air almost felt cleansing as it blew against my body. I adjusted my baseball cap to block some of the dust from

111

flying into my face, and I continued walking. My mind pondered Mother's departing instructions.

"Be sure to get a male dog!"

Why is that such a big deal? Were they not all the same?

I still didn't understand the importance of Mother's order for a male dog, but knew that I needed to follow it. I arrived at the Walker's house and turned into their yard. I paused momentarily. I needed to decide where to go.

Should I go to the front door or to the back door?

It didn't look like the front door was used much. There was a build up of newspapers on the porch.

Finally, I decided that approaching the front door would be the best course of action. That way I couldn't get into trouble or accused of snooping around someone else's property. I walked up the steps to the front door of the house; I knocked on the door couple of times. My hands were cold from the wind and the rapping made my knuckles sting. As I stood there waiting, a thought caused a shiver of fear to run down my spine.

What if they didn't have any male dogs?

I shook off the thought. I didn't want to be disappointed one more time.

Before I could worry any further, a woman answered the door. I'd seen her with Mother. I wouldn't call her a friend but rather a drinking buddy of hers. I wasn't sure if Mother or Father had any friends.

The woman came to the door messy in her bathrobe and slippers. Her dark brown hair was sticking out in every direction. I wonder if she had still been in bed or just didn't get dressed until she was ready to go out drinking. I tried moving my mouth to speak, but the words wouldn't exit.

The woman studied me for several minutes through the screen door as I tried to tell her my reason for being there. I shifted from foot to foot hoping she didn't notice my discomfort. I hated having to speak to people.

Finally, the woman broke the silence.

"Are you going to stand there staring all day? I don't need anything you're selling," She snarled at me and then began to close the door.

I'm losing my puppy. I have to speak up.

"Wait!" I managed to shout.

The woman stared at me waiting for an explanation.

"My mother sent me here for one of the puppies!" I blurted out, hoping she wouldn't shut the door now that she knew why I'd come.

She stopped to think a moment and nodded her head.

"You're Benson's kid?" She asked in a softer voice.

I nodded.

"Follow the sidewalk around to the back. Meet me there. The dogs are in the backyard," she said with her gravelly voice.

I turned around and walked down the steps. The front door closed behind me. As I followed the sidewalk around to the back of the house, a wave of excitement filled me. The time was getting closer. Soon, I would have him, my very own puppy. When I arrived in the backyard, the woman was waiting for me. She puffed on her cigarette and looked bored.

"Mother said we needed a male puppy," I repeated to the woman Mother's instructions as I approached.

"Okay, there are two in there," I looked at her quizzically as she pointed to the puppies in a round fenced pen. There were more than two dogs in the pen, and so I wasn't really sure which two she was referring to.

"You stupid or something? How old are you?" The woman asked.

"Twelve, no thirteen!" I replied shakily. I forgot that I had a birthday recently. I was afraid that she wouldn't let me have my puppy because I couldn't tell the difference between the males and females."

"You should know the difference by now," she remarked giving me a strange look.

I shrugged.

"These are the two males." The woman bent over and grabbed two puppies by the scruff of the neck and held them up in front of me. "This is how you tell."

She dropped them back into the pen. One yipped as he hit the ground and rolled on his side. The other one landed on his feet and shook himself.

I didn't like how rough she handled them, and I felt I was responsible. If I'd known the difference, I wouldn't have needed to ask her and then she wouldn't have picked up the dogs that way.

I was determined to make it up to the one that went home with me. I bent down next to the pen and stuck my hand near the two dogs. The one that had landed on his feet noticed me and scampered over to me. The other one cowered on the other side of the pen. The first little guy toddled over to where I was kneeling next to the pen. He sniffed my fingers and then gave them a lick.

I guess he decided that I was okay because he began nudging my hand to pet him. The other male dog stopped his cowering and went romping on the other side of the pen. The first little guy's total focus was on me and that gave me a warm feeling inside. Someone, at least something, was interested in me. He was wagging his little tail so fast he couldn't stand in one place.

The pup continued to stay by me and kept nudging my hand wanting me to pet him some more. He craved attention. His brown and white fur was soft as silk. There was only a little bit of black coloring on him. His face looked like a little bandit because he had a black mask around his eyes, and he also had a pencil thin black stripe that went from his neck to his tail. He would be my own little bandit. I continued petting him. He'd stolen my heart.

"His mother was a collie and his father was an Alaskan malamute," the woman informed me.

I had forgotten she was still standing there. Maybe she felt she needed to give me his parentage to influence my decision. I didn't care. To me, this puppy and I were all there was in the world. I thought this little guy was terrific regardless of whom his parents were. I didn't need any persuasion.

"I'll take this one," I said as I lifted him out of the pen.

The woman nodded. Without further words, she returned to the house still puffing on her cigarette. I stood there in the backyard looking at my puppy. He was all mine. I couldn't wait for the two of us to really become friends. I would have my first true friend.

I took the wiggling bundle and started for home before anyone changed their minds. As we walked, I noticed he was shivering a lot from the cold wind. I held him closer to me hoping that my body heat would help keep him warm. I spoke to him as if I were speaking to another person.

"You're mine now! I hope that's okay with you. You seem to like me okay ... at least I hope you do," I said.

He continued shivering, and I felt sorry for him. I unzipped my jacket and shoved him inside it and zipped it back up tightly around the two of us. I felt him burrow down into the depths of my jacket for warmth. Between my jacket and body heat, I hoped he would keep warm. The only thing I could see was his little masked face sticking out. His brown eyes stared up at mine. He looked so trusting. I hoped I could prove myself worthy of his trust.

"You need a name." I informed him.

He managed to wiggle into a position where he could stick out his little pink tongue and lick my fingers. A smile crossed my face. I didn't smile often, but this little guy managed to find one inside of me. I believed he truly liked me. He didn't care anything about the New Order, the Underground, or anyone else. His attention was focused one hundred percent on me.

"What should we call you? What do you think about Bandit?" He wasn't impressed. "Doesn't suit you?.... How about Buddy?" He scrunched down further into my jacket making his head disappear completely.

"Guess not!" I thought about several names, but none of them seemed to fit. I started going through a list of television characters I'd seen while watching programs with Mother and Father.

"How about Chico?" He lifted his head and peeked out enough to lick my hand. "I guess that means you put your stamp of approval on it."

He looked up at me with his big brown eyes as though to say, "I like you!" I smiled and scratched his head as we continued homeward. I wished I could have been taking him to a better environment, but we would have to deal with it together. At least neither one of us would be alone.

No sooner had I opened the door, than the yelling began.

"It's about time you got back!" Mother shouted. She looked at the pouch in my jacket. "Is that him?

I nodded.

"Did you get a male?" she questioned.

"Yes!" I replied with exasperation wondering how many more times she'd bring that up.

"Remember that dog is your responsibility," Father added in a slurry tone.

As if they would take care of him. They couldn't even take care of themselves. They certainly didn't take care of me.

I couldn't even look in his direction. I responded by looking down at Chico, "I know!" I lost count as to how many times I'd answered the same questions. When the questions stopped, I assumed I was dismissed.

I carried Chico down the hallway to my room. He was still inside my jacket. I opened it and he crawled out and stepped onto the bed. He plopped down a couple times as he tried to walk on the spongy surface of the mattress. I giggled quietly. I lay on the bed next to him watching him explore his new world with wonder and found myself envying him. He still had his innocence.

Chapter - 13 - Don't Feel

"I feel so locked up inside," I told Chico as we lay on my bed. I put my head down near him so his soft fur rubbed my cheek. It made me feel good that Chico accepted me just the way I was. I didn't know how to change to make anyone else like me. The New Order shaped all my life's experiences. There was no changing it. The only hope I had now was to add other experiences to my life to balance the negative ones.

I stroked his head lightly. I gave Chico a big hug and held my only friend close to me. I could feel the beating of his heart against my chest. The feeling was reassuring that there is more to life than just sickening events.

He turned his head toward me and licked the tip of my nose. I giggled. Quickly stifling it for fear someone would hear it and demand to know why I was giggling. I was afraid they'd take him away just to be mean.

"No one understands," I told him. "I feel like my life is falling apart."

Chico listened to my words.

"It was horrible being a soldier. I don't think kids were meant to be soldiers. The New Order did so many awful things to us. There were times that I didn't think I would survive. We were forced to do things against our will. We were never given choices. They gave us an order to kill and we did. The thing is that we were so drugged and brainwashed that we don't know if we really killed anyone or if they just made us think we did. Chico, I watched others die. I

117

even watched a soldier under me kill herself. Pain and torture were their two biggest weapons to get inside our heads. They locked us in cages, constantly being threatened with death. I watched people held under water until they nearly died. They forced us to watch the torturing of others. It was horrible. Chico, I'm glad that you never had to see any of those things. I don't think I'll ever get them out of my head."

As I sat in my room with Chico, the house was quiet and I felt as if I never wanted to leave this place and time.

I don't belong in this world. Even belonging to the gang won't resolve the pain inside. The only thing it will do is provide protection from some of the bad things out there.

God, why won't You take me out of this mess?

"I wish this terrible pain inside would stop," I told Chico. "It hurts to live. It hurts to talk. It hurts to think. It hurts when I sleep, and it hurts when I'm awake. I wish I were invisible. I feel so crazy. Nothing relieves the pain," I complained to him.

He stared at me with his big brown eyes. I could swear that I detected an expression of sadness in them.

"Don't worry, I won't leave you," I assured him. I fell asleep snuggled close to Chico. Awaking the next morning, I quickly looked for him. A sense of relief washed over me knowing that Chico wasn't part of a dream. I gave him another big hug and again told him more of my secrets that were bottled inside.

I was jarred out of my complaining.

"Josephine!" Father bellowed.

They're up early this morning.

He was probably perched in his rocking chair in the living room. Cigarette butts surrounded his chair and beer cans. "Josephine!"

"Stay here Chico, stay!" I instructed him.

I was afraid that Mother and Father would hurt him the way they hurt me. He is such a little guy. I closed the door to keep him in my room. I walked to the living room and stood staring at the floor with my fists stuffed into my pockets. I hadn't been able to look at Father since he hurt me so deeply. The sight of him made me sick. If he noticed, he didn't let on.

"Go to the park and look for some bottles! I need money," he ordered.

I hated going to the City Park picking up bottles. Digging through the trashcans to find the bottles made my stomach turn. Then, I had to take them to the liquor store and cash them in. After that was done, I was to dutifully return home and bring him the bit of money. There was never a thank you. He just took the money and the two of them went out to buy more booze.

The city park was a dangerous place. Mother and Father ignored all of my pleas about not sending me there, even when I told them of the dangers. They dismissed them as false rumors and excuses not to go. Of course, if they bothered to pick up a newspaper, they would see that the park was not a safe place to go. A lot of drunks hung out there. It was a convenient place to get a bottle and sit behind the buildings and drink without the police arresting you for vagrancy. These drunks loved to harass the tourists that came to fish on the docks there. Young females were their primary targets.

Father sent me there at least once a week. So far, I had been fortunate in dodging the drunks and their advances and I had escaped any danger during the times I had to go there.

"Hey, honey! Come with me, I could teach you some good things!" I remember some of them calling out to me.

""Come party with us!" Others encouraged.

I wasn't sure what they wanted to do, but since Father's attack on me, I had a clearer picture of what they would probably do to me if they caught me. It frightened me to think about the possibilities that could happen by going to the park. Father didn't give me a choice. I felt like I was pressing my luck and unsure that I could escape if things got ugly.

I guess this is even further proof that I didn't matter to Mother and Father. They certainly weren't concerned for my safety!

I opened my mouth to protest.

"I don't want to hear any of your sass. You go and get those bottles and get them now! I can't believe you're afraid to go to the park after attending that military school," he ordered. His words stung like a slap in the face.

Frustration overwhelmed me. I wanted to hit or kick something. I left the house. I stood on the sidewalk for a few minutes trying to think of a plan. I didn't want to think about what could happen there. Maybe I could get in and out without being noticed.

It might be early enough in the day that I might miss them. Maybe they're still sleeping off their hangovers or cleaning themselves up in the public bathrooms.

I began walking slowly down the sidewalk. I hated to admit it, but I was scared to go anywhere near that park, especially in the early morning hours. Most of the sidewalks were vacant. Even if there were more people out, I doubted they'd come to the aid of one of the refugees.

The shops usually didn't open until around ten. Many had their lights on and you could see the shadows of the owners and employees scurrying around making preparations for the day's business.

Everything is safe and normal for them, a far cry from my world.

All too soon, I arrived at the park. Every muscle tightened as I felt a heightened sense of alert. My survival instincts were ignited. I didn't see anything or anyone stirring, so I stepped cautiously over to the first garbage can and I began to rummage for bottles. I usually didn't go too deep. It stunk, nearly making me gag.

Why would parents put their kids through this?

I hoped no one spotted me from the road. The humiliation of having to dig in the garbage cans was already more than I wanted to deal with.

I sifted through half eaten sandwiches, beer soaked cardboard boxes, and sticky candy. I was rewarded with finding a few returnable bottles. I plucked them from the can and placed them into a box I'd found near the park's entrance, I continued to the next can. The garbage cans were the main place to get the bottles. Once in a while you got lucky and found several on the ground, but that wasn't too often.

Before I reached the second can, someone grabbed me from behind. I dropped the box with the precious few bottles I'd found. The person put a grimy hand over my mouth and the other around my chest. He started dragging me backwards. I concentrated on trying to get my feet under me. I tried to throw him off of me, but he had too tight of a grip on me. The more I struggled, the angrier he became.

I became aware of a second guy joining us. At first I thought he might try to rescue me but then realized he was this drunk's partner. My worst fears of this place were coming true, and there was no one around to care. Even if I could have screamed for help, I knew no one would come to my rescue.

The smell of stale alcohol, cigarettes and urine filled my senses. I thought I was going to throw up there on the spot. They smelled worse than Mother, Father, and their drunken friends put together.

What am I going to do?

"Come on, darlin' let's go party together!" The one that was holding me whispered in my ear.

I fought even harder to break free. My mind was racing. I couldn't get my feet solidly under me enough to fight. The second guy helped pull me to the ground. They had dragged me out of sight of the entrance so that anyone passing the park couldn't see what they were doing.

The guy that was holding me flipped me over onto my back and sat on my stomach pinning my arms to the ground with his knees. He ripped the front of my shirt and started touching me. I tried to get myself free, but he was too heavy for me to move. The second guy wrestled to keep my wrists pinned to the ground

The first guy began to undress me. There was no doubt in my mind what their plans were. I kept squirming. The second guy released one of my wrists momentarily to strike me across the face. He was attempting to knock some of the fight out of me. I knew he had hit me, but I didn't feel the pain. After a few moments, I felt blood trickle down the side of my mouth.

The guy on top of me shifted his weight over me and rocked back slightly so he could adjust himself better. He was having a difficult time undoing my heavy belt. I seized the opportunity and twisted to free my arm. I punched whatever was in front of me. I don't know what I hit, but I heard a loud yelp and the first guy rolled off of me and onto his side. Whatever I hit caused him a great deal of pain. He was curled up in a little ball and crying.

A loud whistle from outside of the park sent the second guy running. I jumped to my feet and ran as fast as I could out of the park. My feet were pumping so hard. I didn't even feel them hitting the pavement, I was moving so fast. I didn't stop until I arrived at the house.

Mother and Father sitting in their usual places drinking as I entered the house. I wanted to try to slip quietly to my room, but with them sitting there I had no hope of it.

"You back already?" Mother yelled.

"Yes!" I managed to say between gasps of breath.

"What's the matter with you? Breathe like normal people!" she ordered.

That was easier said than done. She hadn't been the one running.

"I've been running," I panted.

Mother's eyes took in my ripped shirt. I could see her gaze move to my bleeding mouth and the big red welt on my face.

My entire body was shaking.

"What happened to you?" Mother demanded in a slurry voice.

She really didn't want to know my condition. I think she only wanted to know if I was able to get their money.

I tried to explain anyway, "I was in the park...."

They interrupted.

"Stop lying!" Father growled.

How could I be lying when I hadn't even said more than four words?

"Why didn't you stay out until you found some bottles?" Mother accused.

"I....I," was all I could get out before they started yelling again.

"You're lazy!" He growled.

"Look at you! Clothes ripped! You think we're made of money? I can't go out and buy you clothes all of the time!" Mother yelled.

Buy me clothes all of the time?

She hadn't purchased clothes for me since I came to live here. The only clothes that I had were the ones the social workers put in the paper sack when I arrived. What did she think I did; rip my own clothes so I could make up the story about the park? I guess they must think I hit myself in the face too.

I shook my head in disbelief but held my tongue.

While Mother was yelling about the clothes, Father staggered to his feet. Before I realized what he was going to do, he hit me with his fist. I didn't have a chance to duck. After his first punch, I dove for the floor and crunched up into the smallest ball I could become. He whipped off his belt and began using it on me. The sting of the blows made me wince, but I wouldn't cry or let him know how much it hurt. No matter how long and hard I was hit, I wouldn't show him or Mother that they were hurting me. I couldn't stop either of them from beating me, but I didn't have to react to the pain. I prayed he'd stop soon. I wasn't sure how long I could keep up the act.

Peeking between my fingers, I could see him begin to sway some from the exertion. I knew the end of the beating would be soon. The blows stopped and he staggered back to his chair flopping into it so that the springs creaked.

Both were quiet for the moment. I took that opportunity to move toward the hallway. I scrambled across the floor on my hands and knees. Reaching my room, I opened the door and slipped quickly inside. Chico must have heard the noise because he was standing at the door to meet me. Pushing him gently back, I shut the door. I crawled on the bed and stretched my aching body across the mattress. Chico jumped onto the bed and lay down beside me. He licked my face a few times and then settled next to me and stared at me, resting his head on my stomach.

The events of the park replayed in my mind. I felt like throwing up.

I had managed to protect my face and head from Father's blows but my arms stung from his belt. I reached up and gingerly touched the bruise on the side of my face. Pain shot through my cheek, I left it alone. My lip was swelling. It felt as if my entire body was covered with bruises and cuts.

God, are you listening? I'd really like to talk to You. I don't know if You're real or not. Grandmother and Grandfather said You were. I'm tired of being afraid. I feel like I'm sitting in a deep well. I can't get out. I'm trapped in this house of horrors. I ache. I want to stop time and get a rest from it all. Unfortunately, time continues to move on. God, I'm too tired to hold on. I'm not even sure I want to hold on. I don't see any way out of this misery. This aching part of me, what do I do with it? God, if You're real, have you abandoned me? I can't even pretend to feel You near. I can't pretend that I'm okay. All I can do is hold on. I guess all I can do is pray that this will all end soon and that I will find out that You're real and that You'll be there for me. If You are real, thank you for sending Chico. He's a good dog and a good friend.

Just as my heart began to finally return to a normal pace, a voice echoed through the house.

"Josephine!" Mother bellowed.

I hate it when she uses my given name. The New Order changed it. I am not Josephine any longer. Josephine was the little girl swinging from the tree swing with her grandfather in a world that was peaceful and wonderful. My given name reminds me of that little child. She can't ever be brought back.

I gritted my teeth.

Couldn't she leave me alone for once? Do I only exist to fulfill her needs?

Pain shot through my body as I shoved myself to my feet. I walked the best I could, trying not to show any type of pain. I returned to the living room, and I stood there awaiting her next command. This must be what the slaves felt like in some of the stuff we were reading about in history.

Mother was still in her chair by the front window looking like an army sentry. She let out a loud belch as I entered the room.

So appealing!

"Change the channel so I can watch my program!" She demanded.

She's less than ten feet from the television. You would think she could move that short distance to change it instead of summoning her personal slave from the other end of the house to come and change the stinking channel. She's so lazy! I'm amazed that she doesn't grow roots to that chair for as much as she plants herself in it when she's home.

Of course she assumed I knew which program she meant and that I had the channels memorized. Fortunately, she was a creature of habit and I knew what program was on at this time.

Mother's chair was the most comfortable one in the house, and I used it whenever she wasn't around. Father was slouching on the couch with a bottle of beer in his hand.

I guess he is afraid of exerting too much energy if he has to get up to change the television channels. Seems like there's something wrong with this scenario. It's not my fault Mother broke the remote control when she threw it across the room at Father, but as usual, I'm the one who has to stop everything I'm doing and come change the channel for them. Of course it doesn't matter that I might be studying and doing homework.

I pushed the channel selector on the box until the requested channel appeared.

She waited for me to get a half a dozen steps from the television before complaining again.

"I can't hear a thing. Turn it up louder!" She shouted.

I think she did that on purpose just to test my annoyance. Maybe she was looking for an excuse to hit me again. Mother continued to yell, even though I was in the same room with her not more than a dozen feet from her. I could assure her that I didn't have a hearing problem, but that would only have antagonized her.

I bit the inside of my lip and adjusted the volume. "Is that better?" I asked her trying to control the contempt in my voice.

"Listen, you little snot, don't go mouthing off to me!" she snapped.

I thought I had been rather civil. Good thing she couldn't read my mind.

If it hadn't required some effort on her part, I'm sure she'd have jumped to her feet, crossed the room, and belted me. I walked away before I said something that would inflict more pain on me. I got halfway down the hall when she summoned me to return a third time.

Why can't she decide all these things at once?

"The picture is snowy, fix the antenna!" she commanded.

If you paid the bills with the money you got from the welfare instead of using it for drinking, we wouldn't need an antenna. We could have some kind of decent connection. I overhear people at school talk about their cable television and other things that sound so cool.

I adjusted the antenna, but this time I didn't even try to hide the disgusted expression on my face.

"That's better!" she said, softening her tone slightly. She shifted her weight to the other side of the chair and settled back to watch her stupid programs. The irony was that she would probably fall asleep about ten or fifteen minutes into the show. The one good thing about this was that while she was occupied with the television, she would leave me alone.

Quickly and quietly exiting the room, I returned to the safety and solitude of my own room. Once safely back inside, I flung myself onto the bed and proceeded to punch the mattress and pillow repeatedly in frustration. I ignored the protests of my aching limbs. Chico sat next to the bed and watched.

I think he was reluctant to jump on the bed while I was hitting it.

One swing missed the pillow and struck the cast-iron head board. Pain shot through my fist and arm. I swallowed a yelp and rolled in agony around on the bed. Burying my head in a pillow, I tried to muffle my groans of pain. Chico jumped onto the bed and began to lick anything he could.

Exhaustion finally overtook me and I fell asleep. Once again the nightmares visited my dreams. I was watching the gun barrel aimed at my head. The click of the chamber made me sit up. My heart was pounding. I felt confused and disoriented. Chico nuzzled me. I realized it had been a nightmare.

Darkness was creeping in and the house was quiet. I moved slowly as to not make anything hurt worse than it already did. I removed my ripped shirt one and tossed it in the corner of my room. I put on my rust colored uniform shirt.

At some point, I need to get some clothes. The few that I had were either ripped or ruined.

Chico could use it as something to lie on if he wanted to.

Cracking the bedroom door, I stopped to listen. Silence! Opening the door a little further, I stopped and waited once again. Chico stayed behind me. I paused to peek into their room. They were asleep. Sometime after I had returned to my room, they must have awakened and moved from the living room to the bedroom.

Chico and I left through the back door. There was a chill in the air. We slipped through the woods and back roads trying not to be seen just in case there were any unfriendlies around. By the time we arrived at the gang's abandoned house, my stomach felt like a stone. My hands ached inside my jeans pockets from clenching them so tightly.

I was sorry that I suggested to the members that we try to come here every night in order to have some time to escape and plan.

My mind raced.

I had a nagging feeling that we were playing with fire having this many former members of the New Order gathering together. Our programming had been so complete; I had doubts about how long I would be able to control them.

The members were already there. I looked around the room at the expressions on their faces. Behind the excited front; they hid a world of pain screaming from within. They were all hurting and searching for a way to escape it. The activities of the gang might be one way to at least distract us from the pain.

"I scouted the restaurant," Willie reported. "It's a popular place for some of the guys that we think attacked Casey."

"Good job, Willie! I think this will be our first target. We will go in and make ourselves at home. The manager will probably try to throw us out again. Stand our ground!"

I think this is a safe enough activity, and hope that I am not wrong.

"I don't care if you want to be obnoxious to the manager and staff, just remember to stay alert for the townies," I instructed. "If we find any, we'll deal with them in the same way that they dealt with Casey. Only we won't need to use overwhelming odds. Are there any questions?"

They all shook their heads.

"Then let's go!" I ordered.

We left in pairs and regrouped on the street corner several blocks away. Chico remained close to my side as we walked. I made him walk on my left so that he wasn't close to the road. The gang was anxious to start building our reputation; especially after all of the abuse we'd taken from the townies. They were hungry for power. Looking for trouble was not really something I wanted to be a part of, but as the leader of the gang, I had to let them avenge Casey. Our very survival depended upon that. Once assembled, the group crossed the street. We entered the restaurant en mass. The manager watched us enter. He immediately began to perspire. The man was short and his belly pushed the buttons of his shirt out. He looked like he was aging before my eyes. This was the first time we had all entered a place at the same time.

We grabbed chairs from different places and moved them in the aisles so we could sit down close to each other. The few patrons that were there started gathering their belongings. I think they were going to leave. They appeared to not want to be in the middle of whatever might take place here.

Alex and Lindsey ordered a couple of sodas to share with the rest of us. Most of us didn't have much money, if any. I wasn't sure where they got their money and I didn't ask.

"Please leave!" the manager said nervously. He was just as prejudiced as the other townspeople. He already didn't like us and he didn't even know us. "And take that dog with you! We don't allow animals in here."

I had to admire the guy to some degree. He tried to act brave in front of us. I could see his hands shaking when he wiped the sweat from his face.

"The dog stays. He's with us," I announced.

The manager shook his head.

"I think they ordered a couple of sodas," Chris stated as he jerked his head in the direction of Alex and Lindsey.

"I reserve the right to refuse to serve anyone and I'm refusing to serve you," the manager stated, somehow managing to make his voice less shaky.

"We're customers," Willie replied.

"No, you're not! You can't be customers unless you are served here. I'm not serving you!" the manager said firmly.

"Hey, isn't that discrimination?" Jackie added.

Alex and Lindsey were both looking for some action. Angered by the manager's refusal to serve us, they started eyeing things that were on the tables.

The manager continued to mop the sweat from his brow. He retreated to a place behind the counter. I guess he felt safer with something between him and us. He never took his eyes off of us.

"Where's my soda?" Alex demanded.

The manager looked around at us. "Please, I don't want any trouble, but I would like you to leave." His tone was more apologetic.

Maybe he thinks we're going to bust up the place, or maybe he feels that if he serves us, he'll be in trouble with the other store managers. They all seem to have this pact to not allow any of the refugees into their places of business.

That was no excuse!

"We have as much right to be here as anybody else. We ordered a couple of sodas!" Lindsey complained.

I began to doubt that any of the guys we were looking for were going to show up. I felt like they should have been here by now, and I didn't want to agitate the manager to the point of calling the cops on us.

"Come on!" I commanded the group, feeling a twinge in my stomach for the manager. A part of me felt badly for the fear we were causing him.

I did not mind the group putting on a tough act, but I felt bad when the person's only crime was ignorance. It was a delicate balance that I had to perform. I had to put on a good show to keep the gang's respect, but at the same time use caution when it came to the townspeople.

The group looked to me eagerly. They appeared to want to be turned loose to have a little fun, but none of them questioned my orders. One by one they started moving toward the door. Casey knocked over a couple of chairs as we left.

The manager sighed audibly with relief as we exited his restaurant.

It was kind of fun to have the upper hand for once. A certain amount of intimidation is good for them. After all, it was payback to the townspeople for their prejudice.

We slowly made our way back across the street and hung out near the ice cream shop. There was always some group fighting with the town kids. We hid in the shadows. I didn't want us drawn into a fight that we weren't prepared for.

The gang liked watching the town kids pounding each other or anyone else they took a dislike to, especially the Indians. They hated the Indian kids almost as much as they hated us.

Many of the Indians lived in small shacks on the edge of town. The ones that lived there had moved from a reservation across the river. Perhaps they thought they'd have a better life here. I guess the town kids hated them because they were different too.

We hung out around the ice cream shop until almost everyone left, but there was still no sight of the guys that attacked Casey. The gang was getting antsy. They wanted action and they really didn't care who the action was against.

As a gang, we had begun to show ourselves. Word would spread and that was better than having to do anything. Individually, we were vulnerable to attacks from the townies. It remained to be seen how we'd be able to handle future threats.

Unfortunately, the most dangerous people were those that were under our own roofs and the gang members couldn't help each other there.

Chapter - 14 - Invitation for Trouble

One season flowed into another with little change in my living environment. Some of Father's resources for booze money were drying up. He desperately searched for additional money. Father decided he could rent our couch to one of his drinking buddies. We would take in a boarder. Our new boarder would live with us, pay rent, and buy some beer to share.

"This is Edward!" Father announced to me. "He's going to sleep on our couch, and we'll provide him meals."

Edward was in his forties. When he wasn't too drunk to show up for work, he made his living as a construction worker. His upper body was extremely muscular from the work. He had short jet black hair that he combed around the sides of his head and back to cover any balding spots. His brown eyes leered at me. I felt a chill run through me whenever he looked at me. I wasn't sure why, but he made me very uncomfortable.

"You'll be fixing Edward a plate at meal time along with ours." Father informed me.

Great! One more person to cook for and wait on.

Edward had been to the house on numerous occasions. He was one of my father's favorite drinking buddies. Edward loved the booze even more than Father and Mother. It seemed to be a perfect match for all of them. The whole situation smelled of trouble to me.

Chico was just about full-grown; I loved wrestling and playing with him. The distance from his head to the floor was nearly four feet now. I guess he probably weighed about eighty or ninety pounds.

His tail often hit some of Mother's knick-knacks, which made her angry. What was the big deal? She broke enough of them when she came home drunk.

"I think it's time you made a dog house for him outside. Big dogs don't belong in the house," she stated.

"Why? He's not in your way. He stays in my room and I like having him there."

"He belongs outside," she insisted.

"No! He isn't hurting anything," I countered.

"Your room smells like dog," she added.

I thought that is better than what their room smells like.

"I keep the door shut!" I defended. "Besides its not safe for him outside, someone might try to steal him."

He's my only friend!

She let the subject drop for the time, but I knew that we'd revisit it soon enough.

I left for school with Chico following. He was big enough to walk to school with me and wait for me on the front grass. Because of his size, no one bothered him. If anyone did try to approach him, he would scamper away and return when things were clear. He was a very intelligent dog.

Since the gang began making its presence known over the last six months, fewer people bothered us. I still wasn't comfortable with our activities. I tried to counter my negative feelings by reminding myself about the reasons we had formed the gang: protection, to have a sense of belonging, and to retaliate on the guys that had hurt Casey so badly.

We'd decided to wait on our revenge for Casey until we were working together as a team. Actually, I was a little afraid of going after the individuals. I'd hoped that the group would lose their thirst for vengeance. I guess I feared that if we went after the guys that hurt Casey, we would end up in more trouble than I wanted.

Whatever our intentions were at the beginning, we still had planted the seed of power within the individual members. Now, that seed was beginning to germinate. The more we hurt other people, the more the members became drunk with power. They believed power meant having other people scared of us. I noticed that some of the members were forcing the townies to give them stuff. It was obvious that some were also abusing the power we were obtaining. Yet, I wasn't sure how to stop it all.

My history teacher said in one of his lectures, "Nothing good ever comes from the misuse of power or from scaring and hurting people. Sooner or later those people will get tired of being scared and hurt and find a way to retaliate."

His words stuck with me knowing that is just what we did in the New Order and now in the gang.

The members were waiting on the street corner for me. We gathered a few blocks from the school so that we could arrive together. It provided a united front and struck fear into the hearts of all that saw us.

As we entered the school, the group divided. Lindsey, Casey, Alex, Bert, and I had history class together. Jackie, Willie, Gerry, Chris, and Billie had gym first period. Starting with the second semester, the principal tried to separate us to some degree; however, there was only two of each class for each grade so he had to let some of us be together. I was glad that I didn't have any classes alone. Now that the gang was building a reputation, it wasn't safe to be alone. Despite all of my reservations about the gang, it did give me a feeling of security.

I entered the classroom followed by four shadows. Each of us fell into a desk chair and slouched in our seats. We were learning quickly how to copy the others in our class. In some ways we still desperately wanted to fit in. We slouched in our seats with our feet propped upon the chair in front of us, trying to look tough.

Mr. Williams, our history teacher entered the room. He was a tall, muscular man in his forties. He had wavy brown hair that appeared to twist into a circle at the top of his head. His brown mustache was starting to show signs of graying. His deep, booming, baritone voice reminded me of one of the militia leaders.

"Everyone put your feet on the floor!" He commanded without looking up. The class continued their conversations, while he shuffled through some papers on his desk.

"Hey, Blondie, you want to go with me to get a coke after school?" Casey taunted the girl sitting next to him in a low voice.

He enjoyed teasing the girls, especially if he knew their boyfriends were in the same class. None of the girls would ever say yes to him, but he knew it made the boyfriends angry.

She flicked her head away from him causing her shoulder-length blonde hair to swish back and forth. She parted it in the middle and had it curled on the ends. She had makeup on, but it was much lighter than the caked makeup Mother used.

I don't think this particular girl had a boyfriend, or at least he wasn't in this class.

"Just leave me alone!" The girl said in a cutting tone. "Or I'll have some of my friends on the football team find you after school."

Maybe she did have a boyfriend. She at least knew guys on the football team.

I glanced over at the girl. Her expression clearly stated that this was no idle threat.

Now that I think about it, I did see her with several of the guys from the football squad standing around in the hallway between classes. If she followed through and got the football team after Casey, that would obligate the rest of us to defend Casey.

The thought of it all made my stomach hurt. It was bad enough we had to beat up the guys that hurt Casey to begin with. I really didn't want to go fight for the sake of fighting.

Why can't he leave well enough alone?

We already had enough trouble without stirring up more, but I knew that I couldn't pull the reins that hard on any of the gang or they would turn against me in a heartbeat. They liked the power too much. The gang wanted to rule the town if they could get away with it.

"Oh my!" Casey looked bored by her threat. "You've got me scared to death." He laughed. "I've seen war, baby! You think that your threats scare me? Think again!"

"Please leave me alone," she pleaded with both her soft voice and her deep blue eyes. "Be nice and just leave me alone."

That was a mistake.

Casey thrived on pleading like a shark after blood. I rolled my eyes and prayed that the teacher would take control of the class soon.

Casey grinned, "I don't know how to be nice. Why don't we get together and you can give me lessons?"

The girl's face turned crimson. "I wouldn't go out with you for a coke if I were dying in the desert and you were my only hope of rescue. As for learning to be nice, I don't think they can teach wild animals to be nice. Now leave me alone, you killer!"

"May I have your attention, please?" Mr. Williams demanded.

Finally, class was starting. Casey stopped taunting the girl. He shrugged and leaned back in his chair trying to act cool and unaffected.

The girl turned around at the rest of us with a pleading look. *What did she expect us to do?*

The rest of the school day passed slowly. Each class competed with the others to see which could be more boring. The teachers graded on the prejudice curve. It didn't seem to matter how well I thought I did on an assignment or a test, I never got anything higher than a "C-". I wasn't used to making such low grades.

School stinks!

Home was also getting worse. Several weeks after Edward moved in, significant changes began happening. Edward started making advances towards me. It was becoming harder and harder to avoid him.

One night Chico and I had gone to bed. Mother, Father, and Edward were at the local bar. I had to go to school the next day and the teachers didn't appreciate us sleeping in class. As it was, I didn't get much rest when I did sleep. Most of the time I had to will myself to sleep because the nightmares terrorized me each night.

… The Major ordered the training cuffs to be put on me. The training cuffs were like handcuffs only with bits of metal in them to cause more pain. The more you struggled, the more you ended up hurting yourself. I was led from the office to a wall behind the main compound. In the distance, I saw six armed youth soldiers. It was a firing squad. I remembered all of the movies that they forced us to watch of firing squads shooting people to death. The shooters took their position on a line about five feet away.

Holding my breath, I steeled myself for the inevitable. I didn't know what I'd done to merit this, but soon the pain of the New Order's tortured training would be over.

The Major gave the order, "Ready! Aim! Fire!"

Suddenly the night gave way to a burst of blinding light. Voices were shouting and carrying on. Through the fogginess of sleep, a light blinded me. Mother had flipped on the overhead lamp in my room. I was confused and disoriented.

Where am I?

Their riotous voices chased sleep from my brain.

I am in the house with Mother, Father, and Edward. They were announcing to me that they were home.

"Hey, anyone home?" Mother's voice bellowed and burst into a drunken laugh.

I quickly reached for Chico and put my hand on him to prevent him from barking at her. That would have been an immediate ticket to the outdoors for him.

"I'm trying to sleep," I growled back at her as I raised my head. "I have school tomorrow."

"Watch your tone!" Father rebuked. "You're talking to your mother."

Mother staggered out of the room, followed by Father. Edward lingered for a moment leering at me and chuckling. I squirmed with discomfort. He staggered after them to the living room.

I got out of bed, shut off the light, and closed the door again. My heart was still banging wildly in my chest. The nightmare ignited the memories of the firing squad. The guns were not loaded and all of them clicked on empty chambers. Even so, my legs had felt like rubber. I managed to stand straight and not flinch during the whole ordeal. I think the only thing I did was blink when the triggers were pulled. I earned my sergeant's stripes because of it.

What a way to be promoted!

Even with the door shut, I could hear them laughing and carrying on. After a series of crashes and bangs, the sweet sound of silence finally filled the air.

I wonder what pieces of furniture they broke this time. Of course they'll expect me to fix it, or I should say, require me to fix it. Maybe I'm destined for a career in furniture repair?

I chuckled to myself with the joke I'd made. Of course, I couldn't tell it to anyone, but at least it made me laugh a bit. Once in a while I managed to make a joke about the situation. According to my psychology textbook, it was a healthy way to deal with intense situations, and I certainly was in some very intense situations.

I crept to the door of my room and cracked it open. I heard them snoring from the next room. Relieved that they were finally asleep, I shut the door and climbed back into bed.

Sure, they're asleep while I'm wide-awake. Do they realize that I need to get up early in the morning for school, expected to be alert through classes, and understand the lessons being taught? Do they even care? Obviously, the answer is no.

My thoughts were suddenly interrupted as the door to my room slowly opened.

Instinctively, my body tensed.

Who was entering my room? I thought they were all passed out.

The moonlight allowed me to see a form moving through the darkness towards me. I was about to scramble to my feet when the figure lunged at me. The figure's hand shot out and covered my mouth shoving me backwards onto the bed.

How could he see so well? Who was it this time, Father or Edward?

The form's other hand began touching me. I tried to squirm free, but the hand's pressure on my jaw caused extreme pain whenever I tried to move. There was no place to hide. I was a kid stuck in a no-win situation. There was no such thing as privacy, I couldn't lock the doors to my room or even the bathroom to keep Edward and Father out. They came in whenever they pleased and did as they wanted. I was helpless to stop them.

I hate feeling helpless.

I knew the alcohol made them act crazy, but that didn't excuse them. As the frequency of "visits" increased, I became more afraid.

"Shh-hh!" A voice said.

It is Edward!

The Journey

I heard Chico growl and saw the moonlight glisten off of his teeth. He had no problem seeing the figure in the dark.

Even though Mother ordered me to keep Chico outside, I brought him in through the window whenever I was in my room.

Edward released his hold on me and backed away.

"Leave me alone!" I growled at him as he moved back toward the door.

He left without further incident.

I curled up next to Chico and hugged him for saving me this time. My entire body was trembling.

"Chico, what am I going to do? So many incidents like this keep happening. Why? Only you know the terror that I feel inside. These things are so wrong. What's wrong with me?"

Chico wiggled closer. I knew he understood. He was the only one that did.

"I feel so terrorized, invaded, humiliated, brutalized, and paralyzed to stop it." I mumbled to him.

Why are all of these things happening to me?

Exhaustion overtook me, and I fell back into a troubled sleep.

Little did I know what Edward had planned for the future…

Chapter - 15 - Welcome to my World

The sun's rays crept across the floor of my room until its warm fingers touched my cheek. I opened my eyes and saw Chico lying on my bed with his head on my stomach. He had been vigilantly standing watch over me through the night. Another day was dawning. Each day seemed a carbon copy of the day before. If it wasn't humiliation in school, it was activities with the gang, or violation, or abuse, and or neglect at home.

I rolled out of bed and stood. I felt groggy from the lack of rest, but I knew that getting up at dawn was the only way to have time to myself. It always gave me an opportunity to spend some quality time with Chico, and it gave me some time alone to try to regroup myself for facing the rest of the day.

I combed my hair with my fingers. The two of us moved silently out of my room and through the house. Opening the door, we slipped outside into the cool morning air. I closed the door quietly behind us. I loved to run with Chico in the morning before the grass drank the pellets of dew on its blades. It gave us a taste of freedom, and we greedily took advantage of it.

"Let's go down to our place by the creek today," I told Chico.

He trotted alongside of me. There was a certain way he held his tongue when he ran that made him look like he was grinning. That expression always made me laugh.

We arrived at our special place. I sat on the bank of the creek while Chico jumped in for a quick swim. The water was only about knee deep, but it was enough for him to splash around in.

I reached into the water and grabbed palms full of water and threw them on my head and in my face. I was all wet, but still felt dirty from Father and Edward's visits. We moved higher on the bank. I lay down and stared at the sky. Chico bounded out of the water and settled down next to me. I liked being able to talk to him about what was going on inside. No one else would listen, and I felt like I would explode if I couldn't talk to someone. Actually, I didn't know anyone else that I could trust to listen and believe me.

"Sometimes I just feel so sad and alone. Even the gang doesn't provide the companionship that I'd hoped for. I hurt so much inside. "You're the only one that I can share that with." I told him. "I feel like I've fallen into a deep dark pit and there's no way out."

Maybe it is all residual affects from the nightmares and Edward's appearances in my room. Then again, maybe it's just life itself.

"My stomach feels like it's tied in knots. I keep praying that things will get better, but they just seem to keep getting worse. I'm so exhausted."

Chico always seemed to sense my feelings and would move closer to me and lick my face. It was his way of comforting me.

Our freedom from reality would inevitably be interrupted by time. It was time to go to school. That meant I had to first meet with the gang members and go over any plans for the day.

Each day I hate this meeting even more. I don't want to be a part of this group any longer. I don't like the way we are becoming more and more daring and violent. I am quite sure that Grandmother and Grandfather would not be pleased with my involvement. Yet, I wasn't sure how to safely break away.

The thing that most people didn't seem to realize that we were scared too. I can't say that I wanted anyone to know this. Many of the members were afraid of everything just like me. Some of them may not have been afraid, or maybe they were just better at hiding it. Our tough act was to make the teachers, the kids, and anyone else think that we would hurt them. That's what gave us our power. When you're the one with the power, you can control your own fear a little better.

Now I am sounding like Jesse.

During and after school, the group often went looking for ways to exercise their power and dominance over someone else. The choice was either that or going home. When I went home, there was dinner to fix, dishes to wash, the house to clean, damage to repair from the night before, and staying clear of Father and Edward.

Since that first time Father entered my room to teach me his so-called lesson, he had repeated his lessons more times than I could count. I never knew where Mother was during these times. He enjoyed teaching his lessons to me. After he'd finished the lesson and humiliation for the day, he would beat me, calling me all types of names, and telling me everything was my fault for being so ignorant about meeting his needs.

His words cut me deep inside, but I need to act tough!

I didn't understand what I had done wrong. Why was it my fault? I wanted so badly for Father to accept me and like me, but I didn't like what he was doing to me. I knew that I'd never be the son he wanted, but I did everything I could to act like that son. On the few occasions that he went fishing, I volunteered to go with him even though I was afraid of him. I tried to show him that I could do anything a son could do. It seemed strange to so desperately want him to like me, especially after the awful things that he did to me, but I wanted so badly to be loved.

During dinner, sometimes I would watch baseball games with him, and tried to learn the statistics on the players so I could talk intelligently with him on the subject.

"Do you think we'll take the division this year?" I asked trying to talk to him.

"Shut up and watch the game or go to your room," he snapped.

That was our typical conversation; nothing I did seemed to win me any points with him.

Returning to the house, I headed straight for my room. There was a little time before I had to start dinner. I opened the window and let Chico in through the window and then lay on my bed pondering these things. At the age of thirteen, I felt like I had the weight of the world on my shoulders. The kids at school didn't seem to be this troubled.

"JOSEPHINE!" Father's deep voice bellowed.

He didn't often call for me. I jumped at the sound of it.

"Chico, stay!" I said as I got up from the bed and smoothed my clothes and hair. Father was nearly as critical as the Major had been in the New Order.

Opening the door, I stepped into the hallway. "Yes!" I responded to him.

"I need you to go with me to cash some checks," he stated.

I rolled my eyes, but was thankful that he couldn't see my expression from his vantage point, or he would have punched me. I hated going with him to cash checks.

This is wrong!

I'd overheard him tell Mother that there wasn't any money in the account. I guess that meant in some ways he was stealing the money from these people. I was afraid that the police would catch us both and put me in jail with him too.

He would force me to go into the store, purchase some small item, and ask if I could cash a check. The store clerk would then take the check. It would usually be written for ten or twenty dollars more than the item. The idea was to get the extra cash so he had money to buy more booze. He forced me to go because the clerks didn't question a kid with a parent's check. They assumed they were on an errand.

I dragged my feet as I followed him out the door.

"Stop slowing us down!" Father ordered.

We walked the several blocks to the store. I usually stayed a few paces behind him; he liked it better that way.

Maybe he is ashamed to be seen with me.

We arrived at the store, he sent me inside with the check.

"Buy a gallon of milk," he instructed. "The check is written for twenty dollars. Pay for the milk and bring me the change."

I nodded my understanding.

"Don't screw it up!" He added.

I've done this dozens of times. Why wouldn't I get it right this time?

He waited outside in front of the building next to the store. I went inside, got the milk, and paid for it with the check. The cashier held up the check and looked at it closely. I guess she decided it was okay to take it. She opened her register and counted out the money. I collected the change from her and exited the store as soon as possible. The moment I stepped outside, loud sirens grabbed my attention. Suddenly, police cars appeared from every direction at once.

What's going on?

The policemen jumped out of their cars with guns drawn, were crouching behind their car doors. I stopped dead in my track and nearly dropping the milk.

Who were they after?

"Put your hands up!" One of the cops ordered. My eyes followed the direction that the officers were all facing. They were talking to Father.

Father put his hands up.

"Turn around and put your hands against the building and step backwards!" The officer commanded.

One of the officers closest to Father holstered his gun and moved quickly towards him. He grabbed him roughly. In one fluid motion, the officer pulled an arm behind Father and cuffed it. I was dumbfounded as I watched. As soon as he was in handcuffs, the others put their guns away and moved towards him.

Leave it to the cops in this backwater town to do an over kill on the arrest.

An officer started patting Father down, searching him for weapons.

"Wait!" I shouted as I finally found my voice. I started pushing forward.

Policemen whirled around in my direction. His stern expression stopped me in my tracks.

"Where do you think you're going?" He demanded.

Once again losing my ability to speak, I pointed towards Father. He looked me over.

"What?" He asked.

"Where are you taking him?" I sputtered the words out.

"Sorry kid! He's going to jail. You go home now," he instructed.

When the officer finished his search another officer joined him and ushered Father to one of the police cars. He never even looked in my direction.

They pushed him into the backseat. Almost as quickly as it began, it was over, and they were all gone.

I was left standing on the street corner alone and confused.

The town's people were standing around on the sidewalk watching the police cars drive away.

I need to get away from here.

I ran home and slammed the milk down on the table.

"The police arrested Father," I blurted out to Mother and Edward.

"I guess it was just a matter of time." Edward replied. His voice didn't reflect any concern.

Confused, I stared at him.

Neither one of them seemed surprised or upset by the news.

I turned around and left the house without another word.

I need to go think about all of this.

I decided that the gang's basement was the best choice and began walking I jammed my hands into my pockets, and realized that I still had the change from the check. I guess I'd figure out what to do with that later.

Down deep inside I didn't feel like I was losing what little connectedness I had with the gang. Nothing seemed to be satisfying. It felt like a deep, hollow, emptiness in the midst of my soul that I couldn't even venture to examine. It was such a scary prospect. I decided to leave it unexplored. On my way to the basement, I ran into Bert. We nodded a hello but remained silent. With a quick glance around the area before entering the yard of our house, Bert and I crawled through the entrance to the basement.

I turned on the lanterns we had stolen and spotted a figure sprawled out on the broken couch. It wasn't that uncommon for one of the gang members to spend the night at the house or even an entire day there. At times it was too dangerous to be anywhere else.

We crossed over to the figure. It was Alex.

"Hi, Alex!" Bert said loudly, trying to wake him. "Alex!" He didn't move.

"Alex!" I echoed his name. He was unresponsive.

His face was pale. Bert and I exchanged glances not sure of what to do next.

"Do you think there's something wrong?" Bert asked me.

It was abnormal for any of the militia kids to be sick or at least let anyone know they were sick, so we weren't sure what to do. Alex appeared to be ill.

I took a deep breath and tried to think. I was reluctant to touch him, but my mind was shouting loud and clear that something wasn't quite right.

Moving my hand ever so slowly, I reached for Alex. When I touched his hand it was cool; Alex still didn't react. I shifted my fingers around to his wrist to feel for a pulse but I could barely feel a beat. Mustering a little more courage, I shook him and ducked in case he woke up swinging. Nothing happened. He didn't rouse.

Bert began to look around the couch for any clue as to what may have happened. She found a pill bottle just under the edge of the couch. Bert held it up for me to see. She looked from the bottle to Alex.

"Do you think he took these?" She asked, handing the bottle to me.

I took the bottle from her and inspected it, but the words on the label didn't mean anything to me. My mind flashed back to Bobby Matthews. He'd helped save Grandfather. After our escape, he began taking drugs. He claimed it minimized the internal pain he was feeling. Those same drugs caused his death.

Alex probably took the pills for the same reason Bobby did. I guess he thought they'd relieve his pain. In some ways, I didn't blame him.

"Look around! See if you can find any other clues!" I suggested. "I'll keep trying to rouse Alex."

She got down on her hands and knees and began crawling around on the sandy floor searching for anything. Almost as quickly as she began, she found a piece of paper lying next to Alex on the couch. Bert reached over and picked it up.

"I found a piece of paper." She said as she rose to her knees.

"What does it say?" I inquired.

"It says…" Bert tilted the paper so she could read it better in the dim lights of the basement. "It says, 'I can't take it anymore. There's too much pain! Please don't try to stop me!'"

After reading the note, she looked back at me.

"What do we do?" She asked, as her voice began to shake.

"We've got to get him out of here." I replied.

"We need to get him some help." Bert insisted.

"I know that! But we can't let the police and paramedics find him here. We've got to move him outside and away from this house." I stated.

Bert thought for a moment and then nodded in agreement.

"Let's pick him up and carry him out of here." I told Bert.

I grabbed Alex by his belt and one arm; I began to pull him off the couch. Bert quickly stepped up and grabbed his other side before Alex's weight tumbled me over, then we dragged him toward the opening of the basement.

"Wait here!" I said when we reached the doors. "I'll make sure no one else is out there."

Bert nodded. She held onto Alex. She faltered a little under his weight but was able to hold him upright. He was too heavy to set down on the floor and pick back up. Quickly, I opened the door and stuck my head out. I didn't see anyone around. I returned to Bert and Alex and she shifted some of his weight back to me. We dragged him out the basement door, through the yard, and onto the street.

I hope no one sees us.

We moved quickly carrying Alex to a corner several blocks away.

"This should be okay." I said panting. "Let's put him down here."

Bert and I lowered Alex to the ground and propped him up against a streetlight.

I ran to the nearest pay phone and called the police while Bert stayed with Alex. She was still trying to rouse him. I returned quickly. We stayed with him until we heard the sirens closing in. As the sirens drew near, the two of us ran for some nearby bushes and disappeared behind them.

When the ambulance arrived, the paramedics exited their vehicle and grabbed their gear. They knelt down next to Alex and made a quick examination. Since they couldn't revive him, they were forced to take him to the hospital. The paramedics put Alex on a stretcher and loaded him in the back of the ambulance. Then they took off with sirens wailing.

I wonder if Alex will make it. Perhaps if he doesn't, he won't need to face the suffering any longer. In many ways, I envy him. Perhaps he finally found the peace that we are all seeking.

Chapter - 16 - Still Captive

Father was sentenced to eighteen months in prison for passing bad checks and for tampering with the electricity. I guess that's what he did so he could watch the television even when the electric was turned off because he didn't pay the bills. It didn't seem very long before I noticed that Edward was no longer sleeping on the couch. He'd moved into the bedroom with Mother. I suppose Mother agreed to it. I wondered if it was her idea or his; it probably didn't matter. Wasn't she still married to Father? I didn't understand why she had done that.

I hope it means he will leave me alone.

My mind replayed the day Father was arrested. It seemed like they had a lot of police there. I guess they felt they had to bring so many policemen because they thought Father was dangerous since his kid was from the New Order.

Even though he's locked up, I still can't tell anyone what he did to me. I'd be too ashamed. I wonder if a secret has a lifespan?

"I need $5.00 for school tomorrow," I said to Mother as I entered the house.

"What for?" She demanded.

"I need it for a class trip," I replied to her.

"Don't have it!" She snapped.

"What do you mean you don't have it? You get money every month for me. You already don't buy clothes and other things that you're supposed to be getting for me, and now you won't even give me a lousy $5.00 for a school trip?" I exploded.

Mother jumped up from her chair and crossed the room faster than I'd seen her move.

I turned to make a run for it, but knew if she caught me things would be worse. Before I could think about what to do, she reached out and grabbed my hair, yanking me backwards. When she punched me along the side of the head it knocked me to the floor, then she grabbed the nearby broom and began hitting me with the stick across the back. I put my arms over my head to protect it as each blow stung, shooting fiery pains throughout my body.

Please God make her stop.

Finally, she stopped and walked back to her chair. I crawled on my hands and knees down the hallway. I arrived at my room and quickly opened the door, slipped through it and closed it behind me.

Chico was already in my room, since I forgot to close the screen earlier. He came over to me as I lay on the floor near the door. I reached over and hugged his neck. His soft fur was comforting.

I hate her. What gives her the right to hit me all of the time?

"Chico, I wish we could escape this horrible place, but there's no place to go and I don't have enough money to take care of us."

Pushing along, I made it to the bed. We crawled onto it. Chico licked some of the bruises on my arms. His soft, wet tongue felt soothing on the stinging areas of my flesh.

Lying there, I had one arm hugging Chico, and the other resting across my forehead. I had to think of some way to escape this, even if it was only temporary. Perhaps focusing on planning the activities of the gang would be a way of escape and possibly even settle some of the inner restlessness that I could feel stirring inside of me.

I knew the other gang members were itching to be turned loose on the town.

Maybe I should allow them to do some of the things they want to do.

When the gang formed, our purpose had been clear we needed the protection, the sense of belonging, and the strength that came in numbers. Now that the gang had begun its activities, our purpose seemed to have become muddied. I needed to find new ventures to challenge the members and to give some type of direction away from constant violence. One thing was true; if we continued escalating our activities, we would end up behind iron bars.

One of the tasks I attempted was shoplifting. As the leader, I felt as if I could violate some of the rules without penalty, so I didn't take anyone else with me. There was a local store that most of the gang members visited to obtain things we needed or wanted. We hadn't been taught that stealing was wrong. In fact, the militia leaders encouraged it when it would help the cause. They taught us that anything that furthered the cause was justifiable. Stealing had become a challenge to me. It was something that I'd do just to see if I could get away with it. Of course, most of the things that I took were small things that I needed because Mother refused to buy them or because I wanted them for entertainment. It also gave me a profitable way to vent some of my growing frustrations with normal society.

One of the drawbacks was that I was always terrified that I was going to get caught. Another was being overwhelmed by guilt. Something inside told me that the leaders were wrong and that stealing was also wrong, but right now, that didn't seem to matter.

I moved from the bed to the window and removed the screens and climbed out leaving him in the room.

"Chico, stay here and be quiet! We don't want Mother to make you go outside." I told him as I patted his head.

I made my way down the street cautiously, so that I could avoid any potential encounters with both townies and gang members. Once at the store, I glanced in the front windows. It was nearly empty. That was my first mistake. I entered and pretended to browse the shelves. Slowly making my way over to the baseball cards, I picked up several packages. After examining them, I faked interest in other things. I continued to browse items on the shelf as I walked slowly to the back of the store. I turned around the end of a counter. Quickly my hand slipped the cards into my jacket pocket. I left one package in the middle of the pots and pans acting as though I'd changed my mind, then I made my way for the door. The cards were probably worth less than a quarter per package, but the joy of something new, even if it was small, made it worth the risk. The fact was that I didn't have any money for anything unless I took it from Mother.

The front door was in sight. I focused on my exit and held my breath. Once outside, I began walking down the street. I heard the bells on the door of the store behind me; the manager was coming after me and hollering. Not wanting to look suspicious, I non-chalantly stopped. The store manager caught up to me and escorted me back into the store. Everything in me wanted to run away, but my feet felt glued in place.

Once inside the store, the manager pulled me over to a side aisle.

"I've watched you and your friends come marching in here day after day and walking out with my merchandise," he said in a gruff tone. His round face was turning red and his blue eyes were bulging behind his glasses. He stood only about two feet away from me. I felt very uncomfortable with him standing that close.

"Where are those baseball cards you took?" He demanded.

I tried to muster the most innocent looking expression and asked. "What cards?"

"Empty your pockets!" He ordered.

I pretended to empty the pockets while leaving the cards inside the lining of my jacket.

His face turned redder.

"Maria!" He called to the cashier. "I need you to search..."

The very moment he said those words, I panicked. I couldn't submit to a search. I saw what the police had done to Father. No one was ever supposed to touch me. I reached into my jacket pocket and into the lining, pulled out the packages of cards, and handed them to him.

My heart was pounding so hard in my chest that it echoed in my ears and my breathing was rapid.

He's going to have the police come, and I'll be joining Father in a cage.

To my surprise, he barked, "I should call the police and stop you and those kids that you hang around with from stealing me blind, The manager continued, You better go tell your buddies the next time any one of you tries this stunt again, I'll get you all locked up, and that's a promise! And unless you're with a parent, I don't even want you people in my store – you understand me? I nodded agreement.

He motioned to the door. I exited before he could change his mind. I ran out of the store as fast as my legs would carry me. I couldn't face the gang right now, so I went home. I climbed back into the window and hugged Chico. My entire body was shaking. I held him until the shaking stopped.

Exhausted from the day's activities, I knew I needed to get some sleep, but I was scared to sleep because of the dreams. It didn't seem very long before I woke up in terror. Beads of sweat rolled down my face as I lay there. I debated with myself whether or not it was worth an attempt to sleep any further. It did not seem to matter whether it was day or night, the memories of the past continued to invade and terrorize my mind. During the day I was plagued by flashbacks of the New Order's trauma, and it was nightmares throughout the night.

Against my better judgment, I tried to go to sleep. I needed some rest in order to be able to continue to function. I closed my eyes and consciously tried to control my breathing and eventually I drifted off to sleep.

… Sounds of laughter stirred the trees as they welcomed the streaks of sunlight. Higher and higher the swing flew. At age eleven, I thought I was flying. Grandfather could push me so high. Grandfather shouted words of encouragement to the little brown-haired girl on the swing. My laughter grew louder.

Suddenly there was a pounding on the door; uniformed soldiers broke into the house. They came to the yard and grabbed me. Grandfather made a move to stop them, but they waved their guns threatening to shoot him. I screamed as they dragged me from her home and threw me into a cage in the back of a truck. The door of the cage clanked shut...

I awoke with a start. My body was shaking and the sheets were saturated in sweat. I lay there staring at the ceiling trying to convince myself that this experience was over.

It was in the past. I no longer lived in the New Order. Violence was a monster that you could not face without being damaged in some manner, and I felt damaged beyond repair.

Why did these things continue to haunt me?

I wish I could live without being reminded daily about life while I was in the New Order. These memories were making me sick.

I glanced at the clock. There were still several hours left until dawn, but it seemed like more than a lifetime away.

When the panic finally released its grip on my rapidly beating heart, I was able to climb out of bed. I sat down at my desk and held my head in my hands.

There has to be something that I'm missing in learning to survive this thing called "freedom". I certainly don't feel free. Is there any place where I can truly be free?

All I find are places where everything that is good becomes consumed by something bad. Places where no light shines to give any relief. Places where most people would fear to go. This is the hell I live in.

Suddenly, I felt the need to get out of my room and out of this house. I needed a change of scenery. I decided to go to the gang's abandoned house.

With Chico at my side, we moved down the street. My mind continued to be invaded by pictures and memories from the New Order.

The scenes stubbornly refused to exit my mind. On occasion, it would seem like I could shove them aside, but then they would all come crashing down on me like a brick wall. It was times like those when the inner pain would become so intense in my stomach that I thought I would double over and die. Too many times I was sure that it was beyond my ability to tolerate.

I was so lost in these memories that I didn't even realize I'd walked to the basement of the gang's house. Once inside, I was overwhelmed by another wave of pain.

In complete frustration, I started punching the cinderblock wall of the basement. Chico sat down and waited for me to finish. There was not much else he could do. With each punch, pain shot through my fists and up my arms I was so overwhelmed by the frustration of the pain! Finally, my fists and arms hurt so badly, I couldn't deliver another blow. I sank to the floor in silence going from cradling my hands to hugging myself. At last, my brain had something else to focus on. A new pain; a self-inflicted pain, but one that I at least knew how to deal with. I could handle physical pain much better than this other kind. I rolled onto my side on the sand of the floor. Mercifully, I passed out from the extreme pain and total exhaustion.

I learned later that I hadn't been alone during my outburst. I had been so angry that I hadn't even noticed anyone else in the room. When I fell asleep, Bert had covered me with a ragged blanket and offered to stay with me when everyone else had to leave.

When the others had experienced similar outbursts in the past, one of the members would stay to watch over their compatriots. Each had experienced this accumulation of frustration that resulted in these types of outbursts. During the next few hours, the individual would experience further outbursts, nightmares, flashbacks, and other disturbing memories before we would be able to regain control. We really didn't know the first thing about comforting someone else. Once the overwhelming bout of flashbacks and nightmares finally subsided, I slipped into a restless sleep. After a few hours, I awoke with a start.

Where am I? Who's here? What happened?

I sat up quickly and looked around.

Casey was asleep on the couch and Bert was stretched out on the floor nearby. Chico was lying close to me.

How long have I been here? Why am I here?

The fog in my brain began to clear a little, and the pain in my arms and hands helped me remember what had happened.

It's hopeless! You could leave the New Order, but you can never escape their control. It is in the very blood feeding my brain. It eats away at me, and it will probably always be there. It's like a bomb ticking away in my head.

I wanted to scream, but I could not. The programming prohibited that. Everything was jumbled up inside and it felt as though a war was being waged inside. The pain inside was so intense. I felt like it was pushing me out of control.

I had to stop it.

It seemed that there was no escape unless you committed suicide like Alex, Charlie or Randy, or Bobby.

What else is there? How else could one escape?

God, are You there? I don't know why I kept trying to talk to You, yet Grandmother did and I hope maybe You'll listen to me one day if I'm good enough. Can you hear all the pain inside? How do I become free from this pain? There are no words to explain the terror I feel inside that threatens to overwhelm me. Inside, I feel as though I've grown small. Outside, I grow quieter. Why do I have to hurt? Why do people have to hurt other people? God, are You there and do You care? I feel so shattered inside. I want to know the Truth, but where do I find it? I feel so broken down inside by those who do not care; those who do not protect; and those who continue to hurt me.

God, I talk to You, but feel that I talk to the ceiling. I search for release, but find nothing but a tinge of something that prods me forward and doesn't let me give up. When my fists tried to shatter walls, I searched for release. My fists bleed and remind me of the blood that has already been shed by so many others and it scares me that I may become like them.

God, show me Your love as You showed it to Grandmother and Grandfather!

Chapter - 17 - Don't Tell

Chico and I left the basement and headed for home. My body ached both from the beating I'd given the walls and the one Mother had given me before that. I knew I'd better be home when Mother woke up or she'd beat me again. Mother would surely notice if I were not there. I didn't understand the big deal since she was never awake when I left for school. Nor did she seem to notice me unless she needed me to wait on her. I'd often wondered why Father and Mother even gave birth to me. Maybe I was an accident. At least that way I could tell myself there was a reason they didn't want me. I knew I was a further disappointment because I wasn't a son. Neither Mother nor Father wanted the responsibilities or demands of a baby. Some time after I was born, they gave me to my grandparents to raise. Now I was dumped back on them and they were told they had to take care of me. They were strangers to me. Maybe they felt the same way. Any way you look at it, I felt like a pawn in a life size chess game. I was in constant fear – one wrong move, and my life would be over.

I headed for my room, picking my way through the dark streets. At this hour it would be better to slip in through the window. I felt safe with Chico at my side. I knew he would protect me.

Since Edward had moved into Mother's room, I figured that Father probably would not be coming back to live with us even after he was released from jail. Everything was very confusing. Why would Mother trade Father for Edward? I wondered why these things were taking place. The one thing that was clear was that Mother expected me to treat him like a father.

The thought of accepting Edward as a father turned my stomach. My own father is bad enough. Edward is even worse.

Arriving at the house, I slipped the nails on the screen and quietly pushed open the window. Once the window was open, I shoved the screen through it, and then I hefted Chico up and through the window. As he climbed through and moved across the bed, I stepped up on the nearby sawhorse and pulled myself through the window. Taking the screen, I slipped it back into place and used my knife blade to slide the nails back into place to hold the screen. When I stopped to listen, I didn't hear any yelling or bellowing for me; I breathed a sigh of relief. We'd made it. I fell back on the bed.

I usually slept in my clothes it was a habit that carried over from the New Order. It helped one respond quicker when called to muster. Now living here with Mother, it made it more difficult for Father, Edward, and the others to violate me.

In many ways I was glad that Father was gone. I didn't like what he did to me. When he brought Edward to live with us, both of them took advantage of me. At least I was back to just one and the drunks. The drinking buddies that came to the house didn't always come to drink. They wanted to touch me and hurt me like Father had done. It didn't matter if I were in bed or under the bed or hiding in the closet. The challenge of finding me seemed to excite them. They sounded like hounds on a hunt. If I fought them, they liked it even more. I overheard one of them tell Edward they liked the challenge even if they weren't able to do what they wanted. At least with Father gone, that was one less to fight against.

My exhausted mind fell into a troubled sleep. Shadows of those men paraded through my nightmares.

Edward paid me regular nighttime visits. There didn't seem to be any way to escape. My brain refused to process the things that were happening. My brain refused to work and went numb. It was like it took a vacation and just shut down. My mind was beyond thinking and feeling.

The joy of growing up is twisted and stolen from me. I hate being a girl.

"You're lucky I'm teaching you these things instead of you learning them in some cheap hotel or the backseat of a car." Edward slurred his words as he looked at me with contempt.

What did he think I was going to do, go with any guy to do this? I don't think so. This isn't exactly my idea of fun.

That thought nearly caused me to vomit.

"Don't tell anyone!" He hissed at me. "If you do, I'll have your mother send you to jail." He left my room. I opened the closet door and Chico bounded out. He came running over to me, and then he ran to the bedroom door. He did this several times before I signaled for him to settle. I rolled off the bed and pulled my clothes back into place. Crawling in the corner, Chico joined me. My throat ached as I hugged him and my bunny, I began rocking back and forth. I fell into a fitful sleep there on the floor.

When I awoke, my body was stiff and sore. My legs throbbed. My stomach felt heavy and cold. All of the physical pain that Mother had inflicted upon me plus the pain I inflicted up on myself were nothing compared to all of these combined with Edward's brutal violation.

I feel so dirty and ashamed. Why are these things happening to me? Do all girls have to endure this?

When my brain finally began to function, I crawled out of the corner. Chico and I slipped noiselessly out of the house. The two of us began to run. Every stride brought a protest from my tortured body. I pushed on, picking up the pace. A couple of times I nearly doubled over from my stomach cramping. I pushed hard on my side with my fist and continued to run. I was off stride, but at least I could still run.

Why do they keep doing these things to me?

The physical pains won the battle and I slowed my pace. Eventually, I dropped down next to a tree. Pulling my knees to my chest, I hugged them close to me. Chico sat staring at me with his big brown eyes. I knew he could sense my turmoil and pain.

"Do you think I should have hit him?" I asked. "I really wanted to, but I was afraid he would make good on his threat to have me put in jail."

Chico let out a whine.

"We both know he wouldn't hesitate to have Mother put me in jail. You know that I'd go crazy in a cage. I really would! Besides, who would take care of you?" I spoke to him.

I reached over and scratched behind his ears. He always got the silliest look on his face when I did that. His goofy look made me laugh out loud.

I could talk to Chico about everything. He was the only one that would listen to me. No one else could ever know what was truly inside. Not to mention, I don't think anyone cared.

God, I'm only talking to You because I know Grandmother and Grandfather are with You. At least, that's where they said they would be when they died. Please let them know that I get so scared, so very scared of all the things that are happening to me. So many people want to hurt me and be mean to me. I'm so overwhelmed by memories from the militia. I feel so empty inside. I've got others who look to me for leadership, but I'm afraid that I will fail and make all of our lives worse. Besides I have a feeling You're probably not too happy with the gang activities. I'm scared of doing something wrong. Most of all, I'm scared of all these feelings inside of me that leave me feeling so small and shaking. The pain is so great and so scary. God, is there any way You can help me for their sake?

Chapter - 18 - Revenge War

Spring was pushing winter away. The trees were waking up from their slumber. All around me, life was springing to new life. It was such a contrast to my desire to die.

Why is it that everyone in this world hates me? I guess that is the only way to evaluate it. Nobody likes me! Not the teachers, not the other students, not the town people, and especially not my own parents. They won't even give me a chance. If they got to know me, would it be different?

Edward and his buddies continued their nightly visits, so I felt constantly tired from lack of sleep, and so depressed because I couldn't escape the constant violation.

After Mother and Edward had gone to bed and it was past the time Edward usually came to my room. I decided to slip out of the house and go to the gang's basement. I met up with Lindsey on my way to the basement. She walked on one side while Chico walked on the other.

Lindsey nodded her greeting.

I responded in kind.

We walked in silence. There wasn't much to say. Our relationship didn't extend beyond the gang, and aside from being their leader, I really didn't have much to talk about with any of them. We'd all been through the New Order training together. We'd all experienced the prejudice of the town's people, and I think we all lived in some type of abuse or neglect. Yet, these were not topics that we discussed with each other.

A sudden blast from a car horn made us jump. Turning in the direction of the sound, I saw a red sedan slowly circling the area. Lindsey and I stared at the vehicle as it crept along behind us.

"Looks like possible trouble," Lindsey said under her breath.

I glanced in the direction she pointed with her head.

"I think you're right," I said quietly.

"What do you think?" She asked.

"I think we should keep walking and don't look at them." I answered. "Maybe if we ignore them, they'll leave us alone."

I knew that would be unlikely.

"I'll keep my eye on them," Lindsey announced.

I have no desire to get into a fight. My entire body still hurt.

The car kept pace with us. Its windows were tinted so I couldn't tell how many occupants were in it. My anxiety was rising inside. Soon, we would need to decide whether to fight or flee.

"You think they're going to try anything?" She asked.

"I'm sure of it. Now be quiet!" I said through gritted teeth. "I'm trying to listen for any noise that may give us a hint of what they may be planning."

Lindsey's expression grew hard, but she remained silent. She knew the value of listening as much as any of the New Order soldiers did.

"Walk purposeful and with a lively pace." I suggested.

We increased our speed. The car matched us. A minute or two later, I heard the car's engine rev; then it sped around us and came to a screeching halt in front of us. The headlights nearly blinded us. As I lifted my hand to shield my eyes from the lights, I saw five townies exit the car and move toward us. From the way they were staggering, I guessed they'd been drinking. I knew that walk all too well from Mother and Father.

"Looks like five of them," I counted.

"Great!" Lindsey moaned. "Want to try to run for it?"

"It's too late for that now," I replied. "They're too close."

Under normal circumstances the odds of five to two wouldn't have been a problem for us, but I wasn't sure if they were armed or not. Chico's growls caught my attention. Make that five to three.

The situation scared me. I didn't want them to hurt me the way they hurt Casey.

I glanced at Lindsey and read the anxiousness on her face. She looked like an animal caught in a trap. I knew she was ready to defend herself.

We slowly backed against a nearby tree as the townies continued moving closer. Even at a distance, they smelled so heavily of whiskey that I nearly choked. This would be a good time for some additional gang members to show up. There's always safety in numbers.

I felt the blood drain from my face as the headlights reflected something shiny in their hands.

Knives! What a time to be unarmed!

I felt the anger rise inside.

How dare they come after us with knives! The little chickens!

I didn't have time to look at Lindsey to see if she'd seen the knives.

"Well comrades!" The townies' leader began. "Are you afraid of little ole' us? Is that why you're backing away?"

Actually, we were backing away to give us a strategic advantage of having a tree to cover our backs. Chico growled again.

"You better keep that mutt out of this or he's dead," The leader announced.

Not much of what the townies could have said or done would have cut me more than those words. A sharp pang of fear stabbed my heart. I wasn't afraid for me as much as I was afraid of the possibility of Chico getting injured or worse. Yet, Chico would protect me regardless of what I said.

"We're tired of you and your kind moving around town like you're something special. Let's see just how tough you really are." The leader continued.

"Yeah, we're tired of you acting like you own the place," one of the others added.

"I think you need to learn your place. You refugees are not our equals," the leader informed us. "We'd all be better off if you and your kind would just go back to where you came from."

No we're not your equals. If anything, we're superior.

"We've got all night to teach you two your place and then you can take that message to the rest of your comrades. Davey, let's put them in their place," another one of the group said.

They all laughed at the thought of what they were going to do to us.

Lindsey kept one eye on the townies and the other on me. She was waiting for instructions.

Our best chance is to possibly divide the group and get them to spread out. This might give us a fighting chance.

I jerked my head to the right. Lindsey understood and made a break for it. She took off running. It was a good strategy, but one of the townies on the end was able to catch her arm before she got too far. He twisted it behind her. Lindsey managed to break his hold, but was shoved back into the little circle they were forming around us. We were still trapped.

One of the townie's lurched forward and grabbed Lindsey. In the blink of an eye, two of them were attacking her. Chico grabbed one of them by the jacket and growled fiercely at the townie.

"Make that mutt let me go!" The kid cried out.

He wasn't having any luck freeing himself from Chico's hold on him. The two fighting Lindsey managed to knock her to the ground. They were throwing punches at her. I wanted to help her, but the other two kept me separated from her. From what I could see, she was giving them a good fight, but they were landing a number of significant punches.

At least they're not using the knives yet.

The leader and another townie launched themselves at me. I dodged aside, kneeing one of them in the groin. The other guy hit me along side of the head. My head felt like it would split open. I felt off balance, but managed to stay on my feet. I ducked in time to miss another punch to the head.

Meanwhile, Lindsey managed to get to her feet. At least she would have a better chance on her feet. The one kept trying to shake Chico off of him, but he wasn't having any luck.

A shout from Davey caused everyone to stop in their tracks and in mid punch. Without any clear explanation, the leader and three of the four others jumped into their car and sped off. I looked around and saw one of them lying on the ground, doubled up. The moonlight showed no movement from him.

Lindsey's eyes were huge. "I think I killed him!" She said in a strangled tone.

A dark pool was growing around the body. My stomach gave a violent jump and my blood turned to ice.

"What happened?" I questioned.

"I, I think I'm going to be sick," Lindsey said, her voice cracking.

"Go ahead," I said in my steadiest voice. "I won't look, and I won't tell the others." I turned my head and waited for Lindsey to finish throwing up.

This can't be happening! This can't be happening! This can't be...

"I really killed him, huh?" Lindsey asked after she'd finished.

I stood in beaten down silence staring at the motionless body. I didn't know what had happened. It appeared that the boy had hit his head on something when Lindsey hit him. The blood was pooling around his head. That moment seemed to be frozen in time.

"They're going to think I murdered him." Lindsey whined. Looking at her, I didn't see the hardened refugee of the New Order, but a frightened little girl. My heart ached for her. The grief I felt was echoed in the pained expression of the person I saw before me.

Chico batted me with his paw. The action caused my brain to resume functioning. I grabbed Lindsey by the collar and yanked her to her feet.

"We gotta get out of here. They won't associate us with this if they don't find us here. The police would never believe this was an accident. They wouldn't believe that we didn't start the conflict. They would think that the townies had another brawl with the Indians. The townies won't accuse us, because that would involve them as well. No one will say anything."

Lindsey was weak on her feet. I grabbed her elbow and steadied her. I was trembling,

"Run away! Go back to your house! The police will be coming on their patrol soon. Whatever you do, don't hook up with any other gang member tonight. Go directly home, don't let anyone see you slip into the house, get in bed and pretend you've been asleep all this time."

Lindsey nodded blankly. I took one more glance at the still form on the ground.

How many more were going to die before this nightmare would end?

I gave Lindsey a shove and we both began running away from the scene. Chico trotted at my heals. She ran in one direction, and I went in another. I would need to take my own advice and slip into the house unseen.

Please God, don't let him die!

Chapter - 19 - Flashbacks and Memories

Days had passed and I hadn't even heard any gossip about the boy from our encounter with the townies. Lindsey and the other members of the gang refrained from any activities. I was glad for the respite. As their leader, I could see the members abusing our reputation and power. We were proving that we really were the savages the townspeople believed us to be. This is the one thing that I was so afraid of happening from the beginning. I know I shouldn't have voted in favor of forming the group, but at the time, the choices seemed between bad and worse.

As I watched the members before and after our activities, I could see the hunger for more power in their eyes. I knew nothing good would come from it. We were nothing more than organized bullies, a group of thugs. Where was the respect in that? The one thing the gang did give each of us was a certain amount of acceptance that we were all so desperate for. At this point, we would have done anything to get that.

I ached so badly inside, I felt ill.

There has to be something to curb the pain. Why can't the pain go away?

I lay on the bed with Chico at my side. Even as I drifted off to sleep, I knew the pain would spark my nightmares.

… I found myself in a dark room; I couldn't see my fingers in front of my eyes. I groped along the wall to find each corner of the room. Measuring off the feet from one corner to the next, I was able to determine the size of my prison. After which, I lowered my body to the floor to conserve my strength. This was an important rule for survival. I rested for a short period. Time was lost in the darkness, so I wasn't sure of the amount that had passed. My mind recalled the war training films we'd been forced to watch. Terror started to creep in.

"Focus, I must stay focused!" I reminded myself. I couldn't let my fear control me or I wouldn't survive. I forced myself to move in order to investigate my surroundings for a possible escape. I couldn't remember why I felt so weak.

I rallied as much strength returning as I could and began to move around on my hands and knees feeling for possible loose floorboards or baseboards. I was searching for anything I could use to escape. There had to be something there, but there was nothing.

I slid back into a sitting position with my back against the wall. I could hear noises like bugs or rats that might also be living in that room. I felt my stomach turn a flip and again forced myself to wrestle the fear back. If I was going to survive, I had to stay focused.

I knew this was a test that the militia expected me to pass with flying colors, yet all of this matched the movies where they left you to rot and die in the darkness!

Determined that I wasn't going to be one of those that they found dead days later, I forced myself to grope around in the darkness, trying to ignore things that I felt crawling about. I was tempted to eat some of them my hunger was so severe, but since I didn't know what they were, I didn't need to eat something that would make me sick or poison me.

I think the last time I ate was over three days ago. I did have a canteen of very stale water, but felt like throwing up with every swallow.

Shaking my head, I pushed those thoughts out of my head. I needed to stay in control. I strained to hear any sound that might help me stay focused and oriented.

I crawled along through the blackness feel as though I'd gone blind. I moved forward groping along and searching for a way to escape. I crawled further and discovered a small passage I hadn't found during my first inspection. Maybe it was a maze, and I was really crawling in circles. I forced those thoughts from my head.

The darkness was stifling and I found myself gasping with each movement. I continued to struggle to find an exit in order to return to the camp and fulfill my mission. The loneliness of the dark pushed in upon me, I halted, hoping for an inspiration of direction, but felt there was none.

My instincts were all that I had to lean on, but my brain was becoming too foggy. Every muscle ached from the earlier days of torture. I was afraid to sleep because I wasn't sure who or what might come to visit. Distant screams and gunshots caused my heart to leap into my throat and pound in my head like a drum ...

I suddenly sat up in bed. It had been another nightmare. My head began to ache even more. Running for the bathroom, I just made it just in time to throw up in the toilet. After several very long minutes, I used the sink to pull myself to my feet. I splashed some cold water on my face. I saw glimpses of light through a break in the shades as I exited the bathroom. The dawn had arrived. Convinced that sleep would only bring additional nightmares, I decided to go out for a run. Chico and I slipped out of the house and started running across the field.

My feet were moving so fast I scarcely felt them touch the ground. I loved to run like this. It felt as though I were floating along. Running made the pain seem to temporarily drift away. Chico ran excitedly at my side. He loved running with me.

Through the gray mist of the morning, the dawn air was sweet to my flaring nostrils. I breathed deeply. A cool breeze rustled through the new leaves of the trees and cooled my perspiring brow. We continued to run on the hard dirt path. At this hour the sky had not completely given up the night, so they co-existed in a burst of oranges and reds shaded with black.

Chico panted with excitement as he trotted along. I could hear my heart beating in my ears in perfect synch with Chico's panting. As we ran, my pounding feet competed with the sounds of my heart. It amazed me that Chico's paws barely made a sound as they struck the ground. My spirit soared as the wind rushed past my ears as I urged my legs to move faster, my running feet fell into a rhythmic beat. Everything was in tune. It was these moments of running with Chico that gave me moments of blessed escape and respite.

Up, down, up, down, pick 'em up and put 'em down. Keep those feet moving! Eyes watching ahead for obstacles in the path. Up, down, up, down, pick 'em up and put 'em down.

All too soon, my respite ended. I had to slow my pace. My breath came in shorter bursts as I tired. With a final burst of energy, I threw myself on the ground in a tall patch of new grass. As I hit the grass, it was like flopping onto something spongy. Chico stopped and came over to lick my face in between his panting. His kisses always made me giggle, even if his doggie breath smelled bad.

I continued to gasp as I tried to catch my breath. These runs with him seemed to be the one pleasure in my life. I wasn't sure if that was a sad thing or a good thing. One thing they did do was to help me clear my head and lessen some of the internal turmoil, even if it was only temporary.

"It's a shame we can't run forever!" I mourned aloud.

Chico lay down next to me panting. His alertness caused his ears to twitch back and forth as various sounds caught his attention.

"Chico, you're the only one who understands me." I said haltingly, forcing myself to breathe normally.

He turned his black, masked face towards me and closed and opened his eyes.

"I don't know what to do anymore," I continued. "I can't tell anyone about what's happening at the house. I have to lie to the social workers when they come to see how things are at the house. Mother would certainly kill me if I told them how she beat me. I don't know what they would do if they found out about the other things that happen at the house. Add to that, there's no one who understands this constant pain."

Chico blinked again and let out a soft whine.

I love laying in the grass. I feel invisible. I don't have to worry about the town kids, Jesse Burrows, or even the other gang members. I can be my true self here.

I stared into the brightening sky. Soon the orange of the sun began to claim its dominance over the sky. As the sun pushed its way through the darkness, it turned the sky purple and yellow. Soon more colors surrounded the fiery ball.

Red fingers stretched across the darkness distorted by the shapes of passing clouds. As the fingers moved farther, shades of amber replaced more of the blackness. Quickly everywhere you looked, the darkness retreated and was replaced by blue, aqua, and white. The spectrum of color was beautiful.

I loved the sunrise. Its power to scatter the darkness mesmerized me. There were too many places that held darkness in my life. Too many memories involved the darkness.

I wish I could have some type of sunrise inside of me.

The sun was now above the horizon and began to stretch its warm arms toward the earth to embrace it. Both Chico and I felt the special warmth of its rays. Unfortunately, we couldn't remain in its warm and peaceful arms forever. I would have to face the gang's activities, school, and the family all too soon. But for this one moment, I felt special to be able to witness and experience again this miracle of nature.

"The sun must really love the earth to bring such a beautiful day to it," I remarked to Chico.

He leaned his head against my arm. I looked down at him and stroked his soft fur.

"I bet your mother protected you," I said to him.

Chico flicked his ears forward and looked at me.

"She probably would have torn a piece of flesh out of anyone or anything that would have messed with you or your siblings." I continued to pet him as I spoke.

He crawled closer to me. I rubbed his head and scratched behind his ears. He loved that.

"Before they arrested Father he was doing things to me that I would never tell anyone else. I understand now those things were bad. I can never tell anyone. Now Edward lives with us and he's doing the same things to me that Father did. Why do they do these things to me?" I asked him. "They all threaten to send me away and have me locked up if I tell. I can't let myself ever be caged again. Not just for me, but what would happen to you if I weren't here to take care of you?"

I hugged Chico tightly. He didn't seem to mind. "I feel so all alone inside." I buried my face in his fur.

Where are the people that are supposed to protect me? Don't I deserve to be protected too? Maybe I'm not considered someone who needs protecting. But I'm supposed to be a kid; don't you protect kids? Am I not worth protecting? Maybe I'm not worth anything! Am I not worth protecting because I don't fulfill some expectation of my parents?

The reality is that I am damaged for all time and nothing will ever change it. My only chance for survival is to make myself so hard inside that no one will ever be able to hurt me ever again. They might hurt me physically, but that would be as far as they could succeed.

I won't let myself feel anything.

"I really don't understand it. Mother acts as if I don't even exist. The only time she pays any attention to me is when she's yelling for me to wait on her or when she's hitting me. She slaps and punches me at every whim. Do you think that I'm that bad of a person?"

I paused. Chico leaned forward and licked my fingers.

"I guess you don't consider me bad, huh?" He gave me a little wag of the tail.

"Do you think other people love?" I shrugged to myself. "Maybe it's only for certain people that were never in the New Order. It's certainly not for me."

Sometimes I would lie there and create my own world....

A mom that would cook dinners and a dad that would be home instead of in prison. He would go to work every day and pay the bills so we could have a nice house with electricity and heat. And no one would ever have to experience the nightmare of the New Order or the terrible things that Father did to me or what Edward is still doing.

As I continued to lie in the grass hugging Chico, he seemed to let out timely whines and blinks. He is a true friend.

After a while, I stood to my feet, brushed myself off, and started to walk slowly towards home and return to my torturous reality. Chico stretched his paws and then he walked beside me. I scratched his head as we walked along.

As we neared, I noticed the car was at the house. Mom and Edward were home. I gulped.

Maybe they're asleep and I can sneak in.

When I peeked in the window, I saw Edward stretched out on the couch. He looked like he might be asleep, but I couldn't tell for sure. Mother was in the armchair watching the television.

I wonder who changes the channels for her when I'm not home?

I took a deep breath before I opened the door to the house. I knew things were going to get ugly fast. Chico slipped in ahead of me.

Mother looked at me. "Where have you been? And why is that dog in the house? He's too big to be indoors." She demanded. Chico ran to my room.

I stood there with my fists in my jean pockets and eyes downward. Eye contact at this distance was dangerous because it could enrage her all the more; however, if she moved closer, eye contact would be important to defend against her. A person's eyes betrayed their next action.

"I asked you where have you been? Don't you know what time it is? Saturdays are the days you're supposed to clean the entire house. Do I have to call the police to track you down?"

Mother's face turned red. I stood there wordlessly.

How can she call them? We never have enough money to afford a telephone!

"Come over here!" Mother ordered.

I didn't move.

"I told you to get over here, you little brat!" She bellowed. "Don't make me come over there after you."

I stood in my place. Chico was already in the bedroom. I didn't need him biting Mother because he was protecting me. I guessed Mother had started drinking early, or it was left over from last night. Her anger was always out of control when she had too much. It was the beginning of the month so they had the welfare check to binge on.

By this time, Edward had his eyes open and was sitting up.

"You heard your mother!" He echoed, his voice thick with booze.

I felt my own anger rising.

How dare he tell me what to do? He isn't Father. In my opinion, he doesn't belong here!

I bit the inside of my lip to keep from saying what I really thought. My fingernails dug into the palms of my hands inside my pockets.

Mother jumped to her feet and stomped over to me. I was familiar with this action. She took a swing at me. As her hand made contact with my head, I fell to the floor. Timing was everything in order to minimize the impact of the blow. Unfortunately, once on the ground I risked the danger of Mother deciding to kick.

Mother struck me a few more times on the head and arms and kicked me a few times in the legs. I tried to protect my head with my arms. The attack ended when Mother yanked me by the hair to my feet.

"Now clean this house!" She shoved me toward the hall closet.

Why bother cleaning it, you always trash it again?

I glared at her. I was determined that no one would ever break me. They may force me to comply, but they would not break me. I bit my tongue and put my fists back in my pockets to prevent me from doing something I would regret later. It wouldn't take much of an excuse for Mother to send me to that juvenile home. I was quite sure it was an empty threat, since the welfare money would stop if I were removed from the house, yet, I couldn't take the chance. After cleaning the house, I fixed the various broken objects and did whatever other chores she dreamed up.

That afternoon the gang members gathered in my front yard. They'd come by to play a little baseball. Since I lived on the edge of town, it was easier to come to my house to get our exercise. This way there was less risk of being harrassed by the townies. My house was also the only one with a yard big enough to play baseball. Baseball was a way to help us stay in shape and keep our reflexes sharp. We couldn't trust going to the ball fields in town or at the school.

Since Mother couldn't think of any more work for me to do, I was able to go outside to join the group in the yard. As I was exiting the house, a couple of Edward's drinking buddies entered. They were already drunk. The house would need to be cleaned again and more things would need to be fixed. That was a given!

The members split up into two teams. This left each team several players short, but it made the game more challenging. I was the captain for one team, and Bert was the captain for the other team. The teams were pretty evenly matched skill-wise. The game moved along without incident for several innings. The score volleyed back and forth; my team would gain a few runs and then Bert's.

"I want to try my special fastball," Billy stated. "I've been practicing it all week."

"I don't think that's a good idea this close to the house. Something could happen." I warned.

"You're too cautious over everything. I've got it under complete control." Billy wound up and threw the ball before I could protest further. Lindsey was at bat. Her expression was skeptical as she stood there waiting for the pitch. As the it approached the plate, she did a check swing and the bat made contact with the ball. Instead of it going straight onto the playing field, it took a strange angle away from the bat. I watched it fly at a ninety-degree angle from the bat toward the house. I cringed inside as I helplessly watched the ball. I closed my eyes.

Crash!

Opening one eye at a time, I saw a huge hole in the glass pane that once was our front window. The ball went through the window near the couch where Edward and the other drunks were sitting. I froze in place waiting for the verbal explosion that was sure to come.

A roar came from the house within seconds after the crash. "Josephine, get your butt in this house right now!" Mother's voice barked. The gang members scattered.

I glanced quickly around at the retreating forms.

So much for loyalty! Although, I can't say that I blame them. I'd run too, if I could.

Dragging my feet as I walked, I made my way towards the house. Mother was so drunk she couldn't even stand without falling back into the chair.

"I can explain!" I pleaded.

"Shut up!" She snapped. "What did you think you were doing out there? That ball nearly hit Edward...."

Most of the things she was yelling I couldn't understand. Nearly every other word, I did manage to make out as a curse word. She reached out and grabbed my arm and yanked me closer to her. I thought I'd throw up from the smell of alcohol that permeated from her. With her free hand, she started slapping and beating me on the head and arms. I ducked down and tried to stay low to minimize the impact of the blows, but it was difficult to do with her gripping my wrist. Finally, she must have exhausted herself because she stopped and released my wrist.

I felt even more humiliated curled up on the floor in front of those strangers in the house. When I was sure she had stopped, I slowly rolled over, rose to my feet and glared at her. If she saw the look, she didn't acknowledge it. I felt a certain rage of my own inside, but I bit my tongue to keep from expressing it.

Chico had stayed back in my room. I had signaled him to stay or he would have attacked Mother for hurting me. I attempted to retreat to my room before she got her second wind.

"Go take a shower! You're filthy," she ordered.

Did she need to say that in front of everyone?

My cheeks turned red with anger and embarrassment.

Turning on my heels, I headed for the bathroom. I hated taking a shower when they were home. Mother was always complaining that I used too much water. I undressed and climbed into the shower. I let the water flow over me to ease and caress my aching body. The water provided some means of comfort. I was furious with my mother and could probably have chewed through nails.

My heart leaped in my chest when I heard the bathroom door open.

Who is there? Why is anyone coming in?

Fear flared through me like a fire suddenly getting a burst of gasoline. I froze.

I heard the sound of a zipper and clothing rustling on the other side of the curtain. Suddenly, the shower curtain was yanked back and there stood Edward. His eyes looked like a hungry animal's. I used my hands to try to cover parts of my body but it was no use. He stood there completely unclothed and licking his lips. I gulped and tried to move further backwards wishing the wall would move back with me. There was no place to hide. Edward placed his fingers over his lips and hissed at me to be quiet.

I stared unblinkingly at his face. My body trembled.

Is he going to start attacking me in the shower now? Why in the shower?

"One word and you'll be put in jail," he whispered.

Sometimes I think jail would be better than this.

"Go away and leave me alone!" I protested.

I huddled further into the corner of the shower with the water beating down on the top of my head.

He stepped into the shower and moved toward me. My heart raced with fear and dread as he began running his hands over me. I closed my eyes and tried to take myself some place else.

No not again!

My mind cried out.

I hate being me! Why are you doing this?

"No one will believe you if you say anything! Besides, you know that you're going to like it."

I don't think so! This is not something I want.

I took a deep breath.

He covered my mouth with his. I felt ill at the smell of stale alcohol. I thought I was going to vomit. My brain shut down as soon as he started. It refused to comprehend anything more. When he was finished, he got out of the shower, dressed, and left the bathroom.

I just wanted the shower to wash me down the drain along with the water. I don't know how long I stood there in the water, but no amount of soap cleaned the dirtiness that I felt. The water turned cold, I was shaking even more.

Reluctantly, I turned off the water and dressed.

I want to die! Please let me die!

When I finally exited the bathroom, Mother, Edward, and another guy were all sitting in the living room like nothing had happened.

Mother yelled something about taking too long in the bathroom and using too much water. It would be my fault that the water bill would be high this month. I felt numb.

Is that all she cares about, the stupid water bill? Didn't she wonder where Edward went and why he was gone for so long? There's nothing else in that area of the house except the bathroom.

I went to my room and curled up on the bed in pain and humiliation with Chico at my side.

God, where were You? It seems to me that You leave when I needed You the most. I cry out but only hear silence echoing my cries back to me. No answer. No deliverance. When I lived with Grandmother, I diligently said my little prayers. Did they mean anything? Grandmother and Grandfather told me to trust You. They said You answered their prayers: so where were You when he came into the shower and hurt me? Where are You each night when Edward, and the others come to invade my soul and my body? Now, I admit I don't know how to ask You for anything. I don't know how to trust You. I know nothing about how to pray. I only know that Grandmother and Grandfather prayed to You, so I am willing to try to hold on somehow. Please God help me!

Chapter - 20 - To Survive

A breeze rustled through the leaves of the trees. They were fully dressed, as the days of spring passed by. The wild flowers were in bloom, dotting the fields with dabs of color. Chico and I lay in the grass looking up at the sky. The white clouds looked like floating marshmallows.

I wonder what it is like to touch them. Do they feel wispy like cotton? Or is there nothing there to touch?

"Chico, why can't anyone see what I'm like without the prejudice of being associated with the New Order? Outside I bear the marks of the New Order, yet inside I am someone different. I feel as though I am an actor in a drama that will never end. I play the part that I am forced to play in order that I might continue to survive, "but, there's no fooling you or myself about who I am," I rambled on to Chico.

When I look in the mirror, the person I see is someone that I don't even know. "I wonder if there will ever be a time when I can be the person I was meant to be? It would be so great if we could go back in time and I could end up being normal. The world I live in is foreign to me. It's probably not foreign to you, but for me, it's a world that will not accept me for who I am. It's a world that will not explain the rules to me. Why must we be ones who hide ourselves to conform? Why can't we all be the people we were meant to be? Live in peace?"

Chico watched me, listening to my every word. I always felt better when I talked to him. He paid such close attention and was really the only one that showed any type of love or acceptance.

In the middle of my confiding in Chico, I heard the snap of a twig. Quickly, I sat up startled by the noise. Chico's ears alerted at the same time. He heard something, too. At least it wasn't my over-active imagination. I scrambled to my feet and faced the direction of the sound and waited. My heart was hammering in my chest. It made it difficult to hear anything else. I held my breath, as I stood there ready to fight. Chico was on his feet and ready to charge the intruder.

Who was out here in these woods?

My mind flashed to the old man that I met in the woods a few years ago. He had locked me in a cage and wanted me to take off my clothes for him so he could look at me. I didn't understand why he had wanted that, but I was even glad to see Jesse Burrows that day. He rescued me from my captor.

"It's me, Bert!" I heard Bert's voice call from the woods.

I breathed a sigh of relief and walked around in small circles in the grass working to slow my heart rate. I continued to watch the tree line to be sure that it really was Bert. Soon she emerged. After a few minutes, I sat down. Chico sat near my leg. He assumed his protective posture.

"What are you doing sneaking up on me like that?" I chided. "How did you find this place?"

"What are you doing out here without another gang member present?" Bert countered. "You're breaking your own rules."

Technically Jackie made that rule.

"If it's my rule, then I can break it," I retorted. "Besides, Chico is all I need. He and I like to watch the sunrise. Not to mention, the woods are a lot friendlier than most other places around here."

"You've got a point there!" Bert agreed.

"Why are you here without another gang member?" I questioned suspiciously.

"I wanted to talk to you without the other members around," Bert answered. She sat down in the grass near me.

That is rather odd. This is a first for any of the members. They mostly keep things to themselves.

"What's up?" I asked.

She glanced around the area to make sure we were alone.

"I wanted to let you know some of the things that Jackie has been doing when you're not around." Bert continued.

Her words quickly got my attention and peeked my curiosity.

"What's been going on?" I asked hoping I didn't sound worried.

"She's been raising questions and planting doubts in the other member's minds about your loyalty to us. She asks questions why you're not going on some of our activities, even though you've given your okay. She says that you're setting us up to be caught. She's even approached me. I guess she doesn't think I'd come to you, or maybe she doesn't care if I tell you."

"That's nuts! She's the one that suggested I be put in charge," I protested.

"I know! And now she's undermining you," Bert replied.

I reached over and stroked Chico's soft fur.

The truth is I couldn't bear the violence that the gang was drifting towards. Little by little, I was leaving more and more of the mission activities to be carried out by Billy as my second. I also knew, that I was losing control over them. I could no longer control them from becoming more violent. I didn't want any part of it. I'd had my fill in the New Order. I didn't want any more, especially since now it was our choice.

"I hadn't heard anything." I responded, I could feel my anxiety rising.

"They're making sure you don't get wind of it. I believe most of the members are still quite loyal to you. They're mostly listening, but the thing is they are listening instead of shrugging her off. I felt you needed to know what you were up against. I'm not sure where this is all going to lead," Bert stated.

"Thanks for the information." I replied absently.

"What are you going to do?" Bert asked eagerly.

It was like she wanted to be a part of putting Jackie in her place. I knew that I couldn't challenge Jackie openly because that would force the gang members to choose sides, and that could be disastrous. I was quite sure that Jackie wouldn't have any reservations on the subject when the time came. It wouldn't bother her to make them choose sides.

This whole situation was not good. My instincts were sounding off in my head. Bobby had warned me before he died that Jackie was possibly trouble.

I wonder how he knew.

Bert's news confirmed Bobby's suspicions. The whole ordeal bothered me. I knew Jackie was bad news, but I was confused as to why she pushed for me to be the leader and now was undermining my leadership.

Has she been setting me up? Or is it just because I wasn't participating in the violent tirades?

"If I were you, I'd watch my back," Bert added. "Maybe you should try to make yourself seen more by the members. You know, hang out at the house more, go with us on some of the activities."

I nodded but remained silent. I didn't want to be more involved with their activities.

If I could, I'd quit today! I don't want to be the leader of this group – they've become hoodlums. I don't even want to be a member. If I knew how to get out without causing more trouble for myself, I'd be out today.

Yet, a part of me knew I needed them. They were my only link to a world that was familiar to me. I felt I couldn't abandon them even if it meant a chance that Jackie's stabbing me in the back.

My instincts were delivering a different message; one said that my participation in the gang's violence would lead everyone into more trouble and possibly even our own death.

I don't want to die that way!

Chapter - 21 - Mistaken Plan

The gang members sat quietly in their respective places in the basement. The last time I'd been here with the entire group present was prior to our baseball game a month earlier. I hadn't wanted to face any of them because I didn't want anyone seeing proof that Mother had beaten me again. I know they probably saw the bruises when we were at school, but nothing was said. For the past month, Billy had been leading the gang members. I'd heard that many of their activities were becoming more violent. Billy had gone against my expressed instructions about the type of activities they were to be participating in. I wasn't sure what to do to counter him.

The bruises from Mother's beating last month were all faded now and Edward's attacks buried deep inside so I didn't have to think about them. None of the gang members spoke of the baseball incident, and I had no plan to bring it up. The gang members sat in silence. As I glanced around the room, I saw most of them focused on something on the floor, or their hands or feet. I wondered what they were thinking about.

Perhaps they are missing Alex. Maybe they are wondering the same thing I am, how did I get myself into this.

Billy disrupted the quietness. "I think we should hit those guys that got Casey for a second time. We promised two-fold pay back. We've only hit them once. We owe them another hit. One that they'll never forget."

I remember the vow that anyone messing with us would receive two-fold payback.

"I think the townies now realize that we are a force to be reckoned with. We're no longer sitting back and taking their attacks without pay back." He added.

I shot a look in Billy's direction. His face remained expressionless, but I could see a certain coldness developing in his features.

I looked from him to the others and saw them all nod in agreement.

Billy continued, "We go after the group that attacked Casey again. We make a challenge for them to meet us in open combat. None of this hitting from the shadows this time. They meet us face to face. We should meet them in a place where it won't be easy to run away."

"What if they refuse to meet us?" Casey asked. His voice sounded cold with the hunger for revenge.

"If they refuse, we broadcast it to the entire school that they're chickens. If they accept, we fight them on the same field where they attacked Casey. That area is fenced in and the gates are locked at night. That will also keep anyone out who might decide to help them."

"I wouldn't put it past them to bring weapons," Jackie added.

"Good thought!" Billy remarked. "We should be ready for that, right?"

He looked directly at me. I knew he was challenging my authority as the leader. Billy was my second in command. His statement was proof that he was tired of being second. He wanted my position as leader.

As far as I am concerned, he can have it. But, I think he wants to take it by a show of force against me, and that I can't allow.

Everyone was looking at me.

"Definitely!" I answered. "We can't afford to be caught unprepared."

I knew as soon as I said the words that I wanted to take them back. I would probably regret giving my approval. However, it would be foolish to face the townies without some type of weapons available to us. They had no honor, and they would do whatever they could to beat us.

A cheer went up from the group when they heard they could bring weapons. Fighting was in our blood and programmed into our minds, yet for me there was something very unappealing about it. My stomach turned in knots at the thought of what could possibly happen.

I knew this fight of revenge would be the major hurdle to establishing our domination over the school and possibly the town. I wasn't naïve to the amount of risk and danger associated with it. Either side could have a renegade that would escalate matters to the point of someone being killed. I wanted no part of killing any longer. It was hard enough when Lindsey accidentally pushed that kid, and he hit his head. He nearly died. If he had died, no one would believe it was self-defense. That fight wasn't even planned on our part.

There was always the possibility that someone would hear the noise from the field and call the police. We'd all end up in jail. That would be a fate worse than death.

"We need to do a lot of planning before we meet them in this type of fight." I announced. "Billy, since this was your suggestion, you will be in charge of setting it up with the group. Be sure that you have the same guys that attacked Casey. Remember to emphasize to them that we want a skin for skin fight. No weapons! Be very clear about the rules with them!" I informed him.

I hope that will help keep it under control, but I am not even sure that Billy will tell them. Fights have a way of getting out of control without any warning. In the back of my mind I guess that weapons will probably be used, and that scares me. I only hope that it will be for posturing rather than for killing.

"Casey, you and Bert scout the times when there is no one at the field. Also, find out when the police patrol the area." I ordered.

"No problem!" they replied in unison.

"Willie and Jackie, you're in charge of planning our entry and exit. I want at least two possible strategies for each."

"You got it!" they answered.

"Chris and Gerry, you're in charge of what is acceptable in the weapons area. I want us all carrying the same stuff." I instructed.

"We're on it!" they joined together.

"Does anyone have any questions about what you're expected to do?" I asked, looking around the room.

There were headshakes all around.

"This meeting is adjourned. You'll be notified when our next official meeting will take place. That will be after Billy has made contact. At that point, we'll get together and share our findings and detail our strategy," I stated.

The members nodded.

"You're dismissed!" I stated.

They left two by two at various intervals. We never left in larger groups so as not to attract attention.

Why did I let them push me into this?

I didn't like what we were planning, but I also knew that in this situation, I couldn't show weakness to the members or I'd be the one to die. A sixth sense was telling me that conspiracy was growing and I needed to watch my step. It was a no-win situation for me. I stop the fight, and I'm at the mercy of my own compatriots who have been programmed to be ruthless; or we fight and turn a massive destructive force loose. Either way I felt trapped. I was scared that disaster sat crouched waiting for its prey.

Chapter - 22 - The New Order Lives on

Billy stopped me in the school cafeteria a few days later. My mind was a whirl from Mother's news about Father getting out of prison soon.

I wondered what that meant. Would he try to come live with us again? Probably not, since Mother had said that she never wanted him back.

I wonder what it means for me. I hope he doesn't want to see me. I don't want to see him.

"Hey, Boss! You listening?" Billy questioned.

"Yeah!" I replied absent-mindedly.

My eyes focused on him. His eyes were cold and filled with anticipation.

"It's all set for 11:30 tonight," he stated. "It's perfect timing, since we're starting spring break. By the time we return to school, none of the school officials will be interested in investigating the fight."

That soon? Maybe it is better not to have a lot of time to think about it. I do like his point about spring break.

"Spread the word to the others to meet at 10:00 p.m. in the house," I replied.

He nodded and walked on.

I was quite sure that Mother and Edward would be asleep or passed out by then. They started drinking early today. It shouldn't be a problem to slip out of the house undetected. Edward wouldn't be paying me a visit if he were passed out.

The day dragged on. My mind was a million miles away from my school subjects. Fears of every size, shape, and kind paraded through my brain. I couldn't shake the nagging sensation that something would go wrong. I didn't know what, but I felt something terrible was going to happen.

After school, I went home and quickly did my chores. As soon as I possibly could, I disappeared into my room and paced around. Chico lay in the middle of the floor and watched me. I wanted this night to be over.

Darkness crept in through the windows. The time was getting closer.

At this rate, I'll wear myself out before I even get to the fight.

I forced myself to lay down on the bed and relax. Chico followed me with one bound, nearly knocking me out of the single bed.

Ruffling his fur, I playfully scolded him; "You're getting too big to be leaping like that. One of these days you're going to knock me right off the bed!" I said, chuckling at him.

It felt good to laugh a little, even if it was only for a few moments. It helped break the tension.

I continued petting Chico and trying to force my mind to think about our special times together. Anything to pass the hours.

The time finally arrived.

"Chico, you're going to stay here. I don't want you anywhere near the fighting out there. You could get hurt and I'd never forgive myself," I informed him.

He looked at me with his big brown eyes. I could swear he looked hurt that I wasn't going to take him.

"Sorry, pal. Not this time," I said sadly.

After slipping out of bedroom window, I secured the screen so Chico couldn't follow me. I walked slowly with my hands jammed in my pockets. When I arrived at the basement of the abandoned house. The other members of the gang were already there.

"What's did the rest of you find out?" I asked.

"No one is at the field after dark. There are no night games scheduled, so the field should be deserted." Bert reported, and Casey nodded.

"Entry and Exit?" I asked Willie and Jackie.

"The gates are locked with a chain and padlock access to the field is either by scaling the fence or by crawling under it." Jackie stated.

"There's a broken section of the fence by the bushes that allows you to crawl under it. I'd recommend that be the alternative exit since it is a slower way out." Casey added.

"Okay!" I said. "Chris and Gerry?"

"We all have knives with a chain connected to our belts and we can use our heavy belts. Our shirts cover everything. We think that should be sufficient to deal with them." Chris answered for both of them.

To aid in our defense, we wore our heavier flannel shirts over sweatshirts, providing extra padding to cushion the punches. I wasn't sure if I was sweating from so many clothes or from nerves. It was time. After crawling out of the abandoned house's basement, we took up position down the block.

A few stars dotted the sky casting just enough light to make visible the outline of shadows. As soon as everyone was together, we formed a staggered line that looked more like a small "V" rather than a line. The militia had taught us this formation was more defensible than being in a straight line.

I led the way with Billy at my side. The others fanned out behind us. As we walked, most of us had our thumbs hooked in our pants' pockets. This allowed us not only to look tough, but it kept our hands near the knives and chains. We walked slowly toward the playground. Rushing would have used up too much energy.

My muscles began to tense and my breathing became quicker. As we moved closer to the field I glanced around at the others and could see their tense expressions. It was the programmed training within us.

My stomach knotted. Fear tried to crowd into my thoughts, but there was no place for it in combat. Fear was pushed aside, and I forced myself to stay focused on the event of the night. Whether we wanted to admit it or not, we were marching into battle. We spread out against the chain link fence that surrounded the field. We began climbing it hand over hand. I could feel the cold metal wire bite into my hands and squish my toes together. One by one we topped the fence and jumped the six feet to the ground. After everyone was inside of the fence, we formed two staggered lines. The only thing left to do now was to wait for the town kids to show up.

I hope they don't come. I don't want this fight. I had my fill of fighting in the militia. Though I may want to die, I don't want it to be at their hands!

Casey stood a few steps apart from the group. His job was look out. I glanced to my left and to my right at my troops, checking their readiness. I really did feel like we had stepped back into the New Order and they were my troops preparing for battle. My mind flashed to the multitude of times I stood in similar situations as an officer in the New Order.

Casey's voice jerked me back to the present. "Here they come!"

I followed Casey's gaze. In the dim glow of the streetlights, I was able to make out ten dark figures approaching. Silently, their group climbed the opposite side of the fence.

I kept my eyes on them, knowing that my people were doing the same thing. When the townies landed on the inside of the fence, they turned to face us. They formed one straight line. It wasn't good battle strategy in my opinion, but they weren't trained for battle like we were. We stood there facing each other, hands hooked over the buckle of our belts and feet slightly apart.

Both groups stood there staring at each other for what seemed to be an eternity. Maybe they didn't want to do this any more than I did. Yards separated the two groups as we stood there assessing each other. I really preferred to have been any other place than standing here on this field tonight. John, one of the guys from my history class, stepped forward. He, evidently, was their leader for the night.

"Did the militia whores let their babies out of the house tonight?" John smirked.

The others with him began laughing, but even their laughter couldn't disguise their obvious tension. It sounded more like a tension release laugh. I wanted to go for his throat at the insult, but I knew I had to exercise control. Our training kept us from blindly rushing in. We knew that insulting a person's heritage was one way of pushing your opponent into attacking blindly and prematurely thus giving you the advantage.

"Steady!" I spoke softly to my people trying to keep them from falling for the trick.

"Why don't all of you just go back to your own kind? We don't want any monsters around here!" another of their group chided.

"Monsters?" Casey exploded. "You're the monsters coming after us six and seven against one. He broke ranks and charged forward.

"Casey!" I yelled.

He ignored me and headed for the nearest one of the townies he could reach and hit him.

I knew he was a walking time bomb from the time that they beat him so badly.

Casey was on the kid before anyone knew what had happened. I stood there stunned. This was not the way I had envisioned this battle starting.

It's begun! And there is nothing I can do now to stop it.

"I'll show you who's a baby!" Casey shouted through gritted teeth. "I bet you all aren't so tough now that the odds are closer to being even!"

We can't leave Casey out there alone against them.

"Move out!" I ordered. "Go!"

Each of the gang members went after the closest townie. Soon we were paired up with the town's kids. I had two of them to deal with. Together they managed to knock me to the ground. Quickly, I was able to spring to my feet and drop kick their laughing leader in the chest. He fell backwards, hitting the ground with a thud. This gave me the opportunity to whirl around and punch the other guy in the face. He hit the chain-linked fence hard. I regained solid footing and was ready by the time the leader sprang to his feet. He charged me. I could see the rage in his eyes. His anger blinded him and made it easy for me to step aside. As he went flying by me, I swung my arms like a baseball bat, catching him under the chin and flipping him onto his back onto the asphalt. That knocked the breath out of him.

I yanked the other one off the fence. He was still in a daze. I hit him again before he had the opportunity to fully recover.

I'll show him what it means to be afraid, just like they did to Casey.

I could feel my thoughts being controlled by the programming, and I didn't know how to stop it. I was afraid of what I would do under this influence. No time to think about it.

I grabbed and hit the second repeatedly until he cowered near the fence with his hands over his head. I managed to stop myself from beating him into unconsciousness.

Stopping to look around and catch my breath, I could see that each of the gang members was holding his own. They were fighting as the trained soldiers they were. The townies' leader proved to be a little tougher than I'd first anticipated. While my attention was diverted, he hit me in the chest with his knee and knocked the wind out of me. I dropped to my knees and doubled over. He lunged for me. I rolled to the left to avoid his kick at my head. I managed to get to my feet while working to regain normal breathing. I was determined not to be caught off guard again. He lunged again. I grabbed his right wrist and yanked it up and back as hard as I could. He screamed in pain and slipped to his knees. Not wishing to inflict more pain than was necessary, I let him go. He crumpled to the ground. I turned to step away from him.

"Boss!" Gerry shouted. I was startled to hear someone use the title the gang used for me. I turned quickly in the direction of the call and saw a flash of light out of the corner of my eye. Whatever it was, the object was coming directly towards me. By ducking, I was able to block the charging figure. He rammed into me. I had been able to brace myself, so the guy hit me and then ricocheted backward, falling to the pavement with a yelp.

It was then that my brain registered that the shiny object I'd seen from the corner of my eye was a knife.

They plan to escalate this beyond fists! I'm glad that we planned on this happening, but on the other hand this could make things very bad.

Looking around, I could tell by the gleam from the streetlights that all of the townies had their knives drawn.

"Use whatever necessary!" was my curt order to the gang.

I can't leave them defenseless. I don't want to be responsible for any of them dying on my watch.

The gang pulled their knives in one swooping motion. I pulled my knife. Satisfied that we were at least able to defend ourselves, I turned my attention back to John and his buddy. Before I could do that, I heard footsteps charging from behind me. I whipped around with my knife drawn. John stopped abruptly. His expression registered shock.

I don't think they were prepared for us being armed as well.

We stood there staring at each other. Knives drawn, we danced around.

My heart was racing so fast I thought it would quit from overuse. The posturing continued. Their leader and I both waved our knives in the air, jumping forward and backwards. I prayed that neither group really wanted to use their weapons. Maybe the knives would scare one side or the other into retreating. Raising my hands, I was able to block an attack that John aimed at my face. He was serious about using his knife to inflict damage. A police siren caught my attention. It split the sounds of the night and I shuddered with fear. Someone must have heard the fighting and called the police. Turning in the direction of the noise, I brought my hands down in a swift, slashing motion. I hadn't realized that John was so close to me. I heard the sickening sound of cloth and flesh rip as the razor sharp knife came down. He screamed as the knife made contact with his flesh. Turning quickly, I saw blood oozing through the tear in his shirt from his shoulder to his belt. He crumbled to the ground clutching his chest.

The worst scenario happened. The nagging feeling I have been feeling all night has shown its ugly face.

Staring in horror, my eyes moved between his body on the ground and the bloody knife in my fist. John's screams made everyone freeze in place like statues. Both sides stood staring at the fallen boy. I don't think either side expected to draw blood.

"Let's get out of here!" someone shouted. I wasn't sure which side sounded the retreat, but both sides ran for their sides of the fence and quickly climbed over. The sirens grew louder and the sound jarred me out of my state of shock. I turned to join the members at the fence, but I took one last look at the helpless boy lying on the ground, writhing in pain.

My mind screamed at me to get out of there.

This has to be a bad dream...
I didn't mean to hurt him. Honest! Please let him be okay.
I tried to plead with some invisible force.

I can't let the police catch me here. If they catch me, I'm liable to get the electric chair or something. Or worse yet, they'll lock me in a cage. Had I let myself be bullied into allowing this revenge? Or was it just my own pride as a leader... I have to run!

Finally, my brain was able to get the message to my feet. I turned to the fence and gripped the links and began to climb. I reached the top quickly, swung myself over and dropped to the ground. When I looked around, I saw that everyone else had scattered. John and his friend were the only two still inside the fence.

No one was supposed to be hurt like that! They were only supposed to be beaten up.

My brain kept repeating this as if it needed to convince some part of me.

I need to run! I need to get out of here!

I ran through the night as fast as my feet would carry me. I covered my escape by turning on every back road that I could find.

How can I be this stupid? How could I have let myself be drawn into giving my approval for this fight? Why didn't I listen to my instincts?

I wasn't sure how far I'd run or even where I was, but the sound of the sirens had faded away. Slowing my pace to a fast walk, I finally recognized a street sign that allowed me to get my bearings. Soon, I reached the backyard of our house. After removing the screen, I swung myself through the open window and landed on the bed. Sweat was pouring down my face and back. I collapsed on the bed in exhaustion. My entire body trembled.

The events of the night continued replaying in my head. They were joined by other memories from the New Order. I noticed that my clothes were covered with dirt, blood, and sweat, and quickly jumped up and changed. I ditched the clothes in the back of my closet for the time being and climbed back into bed.

Chico climbed up on the bed and lay next to me. The house was silent. Everyone in the house was sound asleep or passed out. I hoped they didn't know I'd been out tonight. At least I'd have an alibi in case anyone came looking for me. I lay in bed staring at the ceiling.

Please don't die, you stinking townie. We were only supposed to beat you up, not kill you! Please don't die! I can't live with myself if I killed you. No one was supposed to be killed. Why did any of us have to bring weapons?

Exhaustion overtook my body, and I fell into a troubled sleep.

... Charlie came into my dreams as she had so many nights before. She was wearing her fatigues, but the clothes were all bloody. There was a large hole in her head. She whispered something that I couldn't hear. She wanted me to come closer. I struggled against my inclination to run and leaned close to her face. Charlie whispered one word: "Why?"...

Chapter - 23 - All Alone

The rising sun chased the remaining nightmares back into their corners. I woke up in a cold sweat, still trembling. My brain felt clouded and foggy. After climbing out of bed, I patted down my clothes, trying to straighten them from their slept-in state. As I looked in the mirror, all I could see was the kid lying on the ground with blood seeping through his shirt. I shook my head to try to clear the memories from it.

Last night things were too out of control.

It was suppose to be a fistfight that was all. It never should have escalated to weapons not to mention someone being injured or possibly killed. Especially by me.

I can see now that I won't be able to keep the gang members under control much longer. They've tasted blood. They're going to want more. I need a plan.

For now, I'm going to lay as low as possible until after spring break. If nothing happens in the way of retribution for last night, I will quit the gang the next time we all meet. I want out before I reach a point of no return. It is going to be dangerous to quit. I wish I could find another way out. For my own sanity and conscience, I can't continue in the brutality that my grandfather died to get me out of!

The guilt of knowing that I could have ended another person's life was weighing heavily upon me. I knew it was influencing my judgment. There was no escaping the fact that unless I quit the gang, I would be dragged down a path that I didn't want to go down. I needed to separate myself from them as much as possible.

I made a bad decision to go along with forming this gang to begin with. I should have stood up to Jackie, and not taken the easy road. We put ourselves back on the same road the Underground had rescued us from. Remembering my grandfather and his sacrifice, I can't disgrace him any longer by staying in it.

The thought of facing the members to tell them I was leaving made me shiver. We had decided in the beginning that no one be allowed to quit without disastrous consequences. My mind began imagining all types of things that the members might do to me.

Maybe that was Jackie's plan all along? I was the "best and brightest" of the New Order, and that may not have set well with her. She pushed the gang in a direction that she knew I wouldn't want to continue on and then eliminate me. That would give her considerable respect in the eyes of the members.

If I quit, I'll be opening myself up to several battle fronts: the gang, the townies, and Jesse. And if that isn't enough, I will have no refuge away from the abuse at the house.

I feel trapped in a no man's land.

Despite all my fears, a voice deep within assured me this was the right thing to do. I knew I needed to get out of the gang before something worse happened. For Grandmother and Grandfather, I was determined not to continue on the paths I'd been on. I knew it would be difficult, but it's the right thing to do. Life would be Chico and me against the rest of the world.

Spring break lasted nine days for us. I had that long to figure out my plan for quitting the gang and getting out of the basement alive. Once outside, I would be in fate's hands.

I couldn't decide if whether the nine days flew by or dragged on. It depended on the time of day. I didn't want to associate with any of the gang until I had my strategies in place. This forced me to stay around the house. Mother had no problem finding things for me to do.

Every night, I joined Mother and Edward to watch the evening news.

"Why are you suddenly interested in the news?" she barked at me one day.

I want to see if there is any word about John. I still don't know if he is alive or dead. I need to know if the police are investigating and if they have any leads.

"School project," I mumbled.

Each broadcast sent my heart racing, but there was nothing. In many ways I was glad, but in other ways, I needed to know if he was alive. I picked up the neighbor's newspaper whenever I could and flipped through the pages. There was nothing about the fight or about John's fate. I guess tne authorities didn't think it was worthy of the news.

Whenever possible, Chico and I would go for runs and spend time at our special place. Where I could talk to him about my fears. He sat and listened as he always did. If I didn't have him, I don't know what I would have done. Maybe just kill myself and make the world a better place. After I'd talk awhile, we would just sit in quietness enjoying the spring air and watch the clouds sail by. The sounds of the birds and crickets took my mind off the horrible scene of that night. My thoughts drifted back to that terrible scene on the field.

Maybe I really am a savage. All of the townspeople seem to think that's what we are. Maybe they're right. After all, I may have killed a kid. I didn't have orders from the New Order or anything. I was there of my own choice. I'm no better than Jesse.

Today's newspaper had a small story about two rival groups of kids fighting at the school. The article said police were investigating, but were not receiving any cooperation from the public. It didn't say anything about John except that he had been stabbed. I knew that the townies weren't talking because they didn't want to incriminate themselves. Without any leads, they let it fall through the cracks.

The days passed and the time approached to face the gang members. I dreaded that moment. The last day of spring break was my target date to make my announcement. As the day drew closer, I grew more and more anxious. The day finally arrived and I felt sick.

Moving through the house and out the door, I headed for the gang's basement. I knew sooner or later, they would all show up. Going there now and waiting for them would give me the advantage of staking out an appropriate place to make my announcement and plotting an escape route.

Chico and I walked toward the basement. On our way, we met Bert.

"Hi! Where have you been hiding?" She said.

"Get word to the other members to come to the house for a meeting!" I ordered without answering her question.

She nodded and went to find the others.

I went to the house and waited for them to arrive. I was glad I'd brought Chico along. He would help protect me. I knew I'd be safe at least in the short term. None of the members would attempt to tangle with him.

We arrived at the basement and crawled inside together. To my surprise, everyone, except Bert, was already there. I guess they'd been spending most of their time hanging out here in order to avoid being in their own homes.

I nodded to them as Chico and I entered. We took the best spot for the easiest escape. Silence hung in the air. I didn't want to speak until Bert arrived. My hands were sweating and my heart raced as I waited. Finally, Bert arrived at the house. She looked around and saw that everyone was there. She took a seat near the couch.

"I'm glad to see you," Bert said to the others. Her voice was filled with relief. "When I couldn't find you, I thought the cops might have gotten you."

They shook their heads and smirked.

I asked, "Anyone know about the kid that was hurt?"

"Heard that he's going to be okay. It was a flesh wound. I also heard that the cops are questioning him, but he's not talking," Jackie reported.

A wave of relief washed over me. It was the first good news I'd heard the whole week.

"Why do we care whether or not he's okay?" Chris demanded.

"Because we don't need to be hung with a murder charge!" I snapped back.

Chris retreated to a place on the other side of the basement. The rest sat in stunned silence and stared at me in disbelief. They hadn't heard that tone of voice from me in a long time.

I guess they weren't expecting me to be so defensive of the enemy.

I cleared my throat. My stomach was in knots. I prayed I'd be able to keep my breakfast in place when I opened my mouth.

"You might think I'm a coward for what I'm about to say, but it is one that I feel I need to make. As of this moment, I am resigning as your leader and quitting the gang. You can think whatever you want to me. Remember one thing, a coward would not come to face you with such an announcement as I have. Whatever you say, it will not change my decision. We have become the very thing that we escaped from. I believe it is wrong. We were rescued to be free from that life, and we have no right to recreate it here. People risked their lives to get us to safety. I feel we owe it to them to do our best, and I don't think violence is a part of that."

Even in the dim light of the basement, I could make out their stunned expressions. They had no idea that I would do such a thing.

"I can't continue as your leader or participate in your activities. I don't feel the obsession for violence that our path is dragging us down. Currently, the things we have done make us no better than those who commanded us in the New Order," I explained.

"Why not, that's what everyone expects from us," Casey interrupted.

"Maybe, but now the choice is ours. No one is forcing us to commit violence. I believe we were meant for a different path. One that will change their prejudices," I continued.

"I woke up this morning wondering if I was alive or dead. My head pounded with every beat of my heart. I decided that I didn't need to add to the crap that the New Order did to me by continuing their activities here. All the junk we rallied around about power and being in control is nothing more than an illusion. The real power is already inside each of us. Even in the New Order the feelings of power were a mere illusion. What we didn't see then and are not seeing now is that true power is being able to control your own destiny by the choices we make in the present. You get real power over your life by making good choices and doing the right thing each day." I paused to let my words sink in. "That's all I have to say. Now I am going to walk out of here, and you are going to stay right where you are," I informed them.

I began moving towards the door with Chico close to me.

"You're abandoning us!" Lindsey protested as I passed her.

"Call it what you will. I am not changing my mind. Whether you all continue this way or not is your own choice. Make Billy will be your leader if you want. My only request from you is that you leave me alone."

"In your dreams!" Willie growled.

"You better grow eyes in the back of your head, Benson, because you've just made yourself a whole lot of new enemies. Powerful ones!" Jackie smirked.

Sometimes I'd just like to smack that smirk right off of her face, especially now!

"Just remember, when those townies come after you, we'll be cheering for them," Chris stated. "And if they don't get you, maybe Jesse and his group will get you, or maybe we'll get you! Anyway you look at it, you've got some powerful enemies, and I hope whoever gets you eliminates your cowardly carcass."

I decided not to respond any more to their comments. Chico bared his teeth at them as a parting gesture. Quickly moving out of the basement door, we raced away from the house. No one moved as long as we were inside. Once outside, I don't know what they did. We took a different route than usual in case anyone decided to follow us. I was too afraid to look back to see if anyone was running after us; I couldn't risk breaking my stride, especially if they were coming.

It seemed all too easy to quit the gang. My instincts told me that it wasn't over by any means. I hated the thought of possibly moving again, but this was one time that I really wanted to move far away from here! I wanted to be in a different state far away from any of my former compatriots as possible. I knew better than anyone some of the things that they were capable of. As long as I lived in this area, there would be no such thing as safety for me.

I would have loved to find a place to hide out forever. It would be just Chico and me and a feeling of peace and safety. But for the time being, that was not to be.

I would be at risk no matter what the circumstances. My battles were now to be on multiple fronts. Add to that, Mother forced me to do the laundry, the shopping, and other errands outside the house providing ample vulnerability. Each time I leave the house, I would be at risk. There would be no place that truly was safe.

I truly am alone!

Chapter - 24 - Time to Die?

Even though I knew it was risky, I needed my morning walk with Chico and to spend time in our special place. I longed for my moments of escape. The fog was rolling in off of the river; hanging so low to the ground it made visibility difficult even for walking. We lived about ten blocks from the river, but the fog here was thick as soup. The river ran past the City Park and stretched the length of the town. It was the boundary that kept most of the Indians on their reservation. I hated feeling blinded by the fog, especially knowing that I could be a probable target of anyone. It felt like everyone was my enemy. A drizzle sprayed everything. My clothes were soggy and clung to me. All of these circumstances put me in a very foul mood. Even spending time in our place didn't help. The weather prevented me from enjoying the colors and beauty of nature.

Returning to the house, I ran into Mother.

"Josephine! Go look for bottles!" She ordered. "We want to go out tonight. This time bring back all of the money, not saving any for yourself."

"I always bring back all of the money," I lied. "You expect me to go out in this mess? I won't be able to see a bottle unless I fell over it." I snapped back. My mood was so nasty I didn't much care what she did to me.

"It wasn't too nasty for you to go out into it early this morning to wherever it is that you go. No more argument out of you. Get moving and find some bottles!" she commanded.

I knew I'd never hear the end of it until I went. The weather was so nasty I decided to not take Chico out into it again. I didn't want him to get sick. I had to protect my friend. If he got sick, Mother wouldn't pay any vet bills for him. At least if I got sick; the welfare would pay for me.

The spitting drizzle hit me in the face as I stepped outside into the soup-like fog.

No one in their right mind would be out in this mess.

The fact that I couldn't see beyond arm's reach made me feel uneasy. I knew the gang would probably come after me at some point. They had to. The rules we established demanded that they obey for honor's sake. The only question left to answer was when would they make their move? I guess there was one more question: what would they do to me when they did come? My only hope was to be on guard every moment and not underestimate them.

Moving along cautiously, I froze at every snap of a twig and squinted into the fog for signs of movement.

It must be an animal!

When I was sure there was nothing, I continued walking. Anxiety filled my being.

In the blink of an eye, a violent push knocked me off my feet. My face hit the sidewalk, and I tasted a mixture of gravel and blood. An enormous pain flooded my body. I was angry that I'd been hit. I couldn't decide if I was more disgusted with me, or whoever was attacking me. I'd let my defenses down. I was stupid enough to believe no one would come after me in this weather.

I scrambled to my hands and knees trying to prepare myself for the next assault, but the fog made it difficult to see my assailants or how many of them there might be.

"Hit her again!" a voice insisted out of the murk.

It was Jackie's. So, the gang was out, and they were my attackers.

What an idiot I am! I should have known. This mistake might end up being fatal. I wonder what they have in store for me now.

The fog was too thick to see the hands come from behind and lift me by the hair. They pulled my head back until I felt an electric pain run down my spine. I struggled to get to my feet, but it was impossible. I tried punching at my captors but only connected with air.

Before I could react, someone grabbed my arm and yanked it behind me. I tried to wrestle free. Now I heard other voices. They pulled me to my feet and shoved me ahead of them down the street. My feet searched for the ground. Panic's icy fingers gripped my insides. My head was pounding so loudly I couldn't think.

"You all are making a big mistake!" I tried to say, but the words came out in a gasping whisper.

"You're the one who made the mistake by leaving," a voice responded. "We chose you as our leader. You failed us. Failure must be punished, and it must be punished severely."

After a moment, I recognized the voice of Billy. He must be their new leader. At least, I assumed he'd become their leader. He sounded like he was reciting the New Order's rules.

"You abandoned your compatriots," he continued. "We vowed to be banded together for life and you broke your word."

"Is that what this is about? Abandonment?" I gasped out the words.

"No," he barked. "It's about making you an example. You know the penalty for desertion."

"This is not the New Order," I retorted.

"Shut up!" he snapped.

Suddenly, someone slapped a piece of duct tape over my mouth. They had such a tight grip on my arm and hair, I could barely move, and now I couldn't speak.

They must be taking me back to the basement.

I wanted to cry, out, but the tape made it impossible. I also knew no one would come to my aid if I could call out. More importantly, I couldn't show any sign of weakness to them. It would be like putting blood before sharks.

I wanted to try to reason with them, but terror gripped my insides and silenced my tongue as the tape sealed my words. Limping along blindly in the fog, I assumed they were leading me to the basement. The person with a fist of my hair let it go as the one that had my arm shoved me to my knees. Another hand grabbed my hair and pulled me through the entrance of the basement. Before I cleared the opening someone shoved me flat on the ground. With their knee in my back, they yanked both arms behind me and taped my wrists together. Once my hands were secured, the knee was lifted. I was then dragged across the floor to the other side of the basement. Between the drizzle, the dirt and the blood trickling in my eyes, I couldn't focus on anyone's face. I was once again in the shelter where I had spent so many hours sitting with my compatriots who were injured or just needed someone to watch over them. There was a certain irony about it all.

Before I had an opportunity to think, two members quickly blind-folded me. I guessed they didn't want to make eye contact with me.

What are they planning on doing to me? Whatever it is, I think the end result could be death. They've killed before, and they have a thirst for it. If I die, what will happen to Chico? Mother certainly wouldn't care for him. I don't think she'd miss me, but he wouldn't understand if I didn't come back for him!

My heart ached for him. I was glad that I hadn't brought him with me. There's no telling what the gang would have done to him in order to hurt me.

Time stood still. I listened to my former compatriots laugh and talk in muffled voices. Laughter was a new concept. I hadn't heard them laugh often.

They left me sitting against the cold cinder block wall to commune with my imagination and pain. This was a much-used tactic in the New Order: leave an enemy prisoner bound and gagged, cutting off as many of their senses as possible. Their mind then goes into hyper drive. This way your mind begins torturing you long before your captors do.

I forced myself to control my imagination. Forcing my mind to focus on the layout of the basement; I tried to place a person with each voice. I was losing the battle with my brain.

What are they going to do to me? The possibilities are beyond counting. Memories from the nightmarish training films ran through my mind.

With all of my training, I didn't think I'd survive whatever they had in store for me. It was somewhat ironic that I would be tormented at the hands of my own compatriots. Actually, that thought felt like I'd been stabbed in the heart.

I listened to the voices around me. Their words had begun to slur.

Were they drinking? When did they start drinking? How did they get the stuff? Someone probably stole it from their parents.

If they were drinking, there was no telling what they would be capable of. I was acutely aware of what alcohol did to one's judgment.

Stay focused! Fear will only make the situation worse.

If I could talk them out of whatever they were planning for me, that would be the best solution, but with the duct tape on my mouth, I had no chance.

I can't allow this situation to control me.

Pretending to be still, I prayed that they would think that I was asleep, and that they'd be content just to have me as a captive.

While I was contemplating the possibilities, someone grabbed me by the hair and pulled me away from the wall. My head ached from so many of them pulling my hair. A booted foot shoved me forward and I landed face first on the sandy floor. I was helpless to do anything. Sand flew up into my nose and scratched the inside. I tried to blow it out but it didn't help much. With my hands bound, I couldn't protect myself.

"What shall we do first?" Jackie asked the group.

"She thinks she's too good to be with us any longer. She used us, now we should use her," a husky voice slurred. The voice sounded like Billy's.

It was then that my worst nightmare began.

I'd rather face demoralization at the hands of Father or Edward, or the beatings by Mother. I'd even prefer the townies over these former members of the New Order.

A chill run throughout my being.

Before I could dwell on the thought for very long, several members were pulling and ripping my clothing off of me.

God, please help me! Don't let this happen!

The first step in punishment was to humiliate and dehumanize the offender, and this was the quickest way to accomplish it. I was left exposed before them all.

The sound of a hammer striking metal captured my attention. I was too afraid to imagine what they were planning to do with the stakes. Someone yanked my legs apart. They tied my ankles to the stakes, forcing them as far apart as they could be pulled. Others sat me up long enough to untie my hands. They pulled me back down and I hit the floor hard. My hands were tied to another set of spikes. I was so stretched that every muscle screamed in pain. My stomach knotted and my heart raced. I thought I was going to be sick. It was clear what they planned to do. They were going to act out the sexual abuse they'd been experiencing. This was their opportunity to hurt someone the way they'd been hurt. I was so petrified that breathing was nearly impossible.

One of the guys crawled on top of me. His body was hot, almost burning. His hands were rough and violent as he tore at me. My mind shut down and refused to register anything more.

Soon other members of the gang were on top of me. I felt teeth biting me. I tried to twist away, but my action was rewarded by a slap across the face. My breathing turned into panting. I couldn't control anything. My own body betrayed me.

Please let me die! This can't be happening to me. I was their commanding officer, their leader. I am not the enemy. Please God make it stop!

A few of the members were giving me a verbal description of what they were going to do to me next, things that were malicious and grotesque. They were set on humiliating me. They were all laughing at my humiliation and violation. Pain overwhelmed me. As I faded into darkness, I thought I would never wake again.

Feeling a chill, I awoke and was disappointed to still be alive. The blindfold was still in place. They still had me tied to the spikes. I was repulsed at the thought of the entire gang seeing me naked and vulnerable. I couldn't think straight. Everything was wrong. My muscles were cramped and spasming. I was horribly alone.

They kept on touching and doing horrible things to me. They didn't want sex from me: they only wanted to humiliate and violate me beyond description. My mind once again shut down and my body went numb. My brain mercifully disconnected me completely from the situation, and I had no idea how long these things continued.

The next time I awoke it was to the smell of fresh air. I felt the warmth of the sun on my face. Blades of grass tickled my skin. I was outside. The gang had let me live.

How did I get out here? Why am I out here?

I didn't know who had put me out here or why. My hands were loosed I reached up and removed the tape and blindfold. Every movement brought excruciating pain to every part of my body. Whoever my savior had been, they had left some old clothing nearby that I could use to cover my nakedness. My arms and legs didn't move as I wanted them too, but somehow I was able to get into the clothing and crawl on my hands and knees for a few feet. My head was pulsating to the rhythm of my heart. I had experienced the true animal behavior that the New Order had instilled deep within us. Exhaustion overtook me and I rolled back under the bushes.

I must be alive if I am in this much pain. Someone must have convinced the gang members to let me live. They should have killed me. No one quits and lives. Yet, I am still alive.

I drifted off to sleep. When I awoke, I couldn't decide if I was alive or dead. All I felt was pain.

I crawled out from under the bushes and staggered to my feet. My knees were rubbery under me as I took a few steps, and I stumbled into a passing stranger. They gave me a look of disgust and shoved me off of them. I grabbed a post to prevent myself from falling to the ground.

"Get off of me you lousy drunk!" the stranger snapped.

Life was going on around me as if nothing of significance had happened. It felt like an eternity before I finally managed to stagger home.

My legs were raw and full of dried blood. I don't know how I got home, but somehow I had managed. Hoisting myself through the window, I rolled onto the bed. As I moved through my room and toward the bathroom, I decided to shower off the feeling of filth from the night before. I was thankful that no one was awake in the house. Mother would demand an explanation as to why I didn't bring her any money from the bottles. She wouldn't care about anything else. I stood in the shower letting the water wash over me.

My whole body ached. It seemed the only places on my body that didn't have a bruise, a cut, or a burn were the palms of my hands and the bottoms of my feet. After the water turned cold, I somehow managed to towel myself off and put on some clothes. I staggered back to my room. My head was a whirl.

My body betrayed me.

As I closed the door behind me, my strength gave out and my knees buckled. I was too tired to make an effort to catch myself from falling. I crumpled across the bed in unbelievable pain. The gang had proved how well they'd been trained. The things they had done to me left me feeling vulnerable, open, betrayed, and violated. The things they'd done were things they'd learned since they'd been freed from the New Order. It was a mix of militia doctrine with the practice of freedom.

Betrayal had become a basic theme in my life. What hurt more than anything else was knowing that the compatriots were the ones who had brutalized me. I wonder if they all participated. I know some did it just so they wouldn't be viewed as being on my side and possibly having to face the same thing.

God, please let me die!

Chapter - 25 - Don't Feel

Sounds of Mother and Edward's shouting and yelling at each other aroused me from my sleep. My brain refused to focus. I drifted in and out of wakefulness. Even lying still, my body hurt. I wanted to find a place to crawl into and die, but it hurt too much to move.

Mustering as much strength as I was capable of for the moment, I lifted my hand slightly in a feeble attempt to find Chico. He was in his usual place at my side on the bed. My hand fell back down and rested on his soft, silky fur. I wiggled my fingers in his coat. Petting him was always a comfort to me.

From the sound of Mother and Edward's voices, I could tell they'd been out drinking last night while my life hung in the balances. I guess they found some money from someplace.

Of course, what did they care, as long as those welfare checks kept rolling in?

Their voices grew louder, making it harder for me to fade back into my restless sleep. I could hear them calling each other horrible names. Their arguments always followed the same pattern. Soon their words would graduate to swearing and cursing. They would climax with an ear shattering crash, and my name would be bellowed throughout the house.

My body protested as I forced myself to sit up, preparing for the inevitable. The room was spinning. I couldn't hurry as quickly as I knew they expected. At least I would be prepared to respond to their yelling. If I moved too slowly for their judgment, it would mean a beating from them. At this point, I didn't care. I was hurting so much already, what would more pain matter?

The body has only a certain threshold for pain and after you reach that, you don't feel any more pain. When the room finally stopped spinning, I stood to my feet. It took every bit of concentration to put one foot in front of the other. I leaned against the wall by the door waiting for Mother to summon me.

Their voices continued to rise. I wonder how much of their yelling the neighbors could hear?

Crash!

Now what did they break?

"Josephine!" Mother screamed.

There was my cue. Opening the door, I entered the hallway and moved slowly into the living room. Even with all my training to be superior, I felt very small inside when I faced her.

This was just another one of those routines in my daily existence that I couldn't change and had to live with until I could find a reasonable way out. I couldn't say that living here with them was any better than living in the horror of the New Order. Possibly it was worse. I stole a glance at Mother; her face was dark red with fury and rage. I had no idea what she was so angry about. As I looked at her, the hairs on the back of my neck stood up.

Please God, make me disappear!

"Come over here!" Mother ordered. "Where were you last night?"

Why did she care where I was? Did she need the television volume adjusted? Or maybe she and Edward had friends over that were looking for a good time, and I wasn't here for them to play with?

I believed they were selling me to their drunken friends. The drunks would pay and then have the thrill of trying to succeed with me, no refunds if they weren't successful. For as often as I was being violated, I didn't think their accepting money for the chance was too much of a stretch.

I took a few steps towards her but stopped out of her reach.

"I said come over here!" she gestured with her hand for me to move to a spot directly in front of her.

Cautiously, I moved to the spot. No sooner had I stepped forward than I was met with a slap across the face. Instinctively, I did my drop and cover routine. She couldn't hit me as hard when I was curled up on the floor. After about half a dozen blows, she stopped.

I peeked through my hands to see if it was safe to move. She'd returned to her chair with her eyes glued on the television. Rolling over, I moved out of her reach, climbed to my feet and returned to my room.

Was that all she summoned me for?

Walking back to my sanctuary, my mind drifted on the bits and pieces of things that I could remember from last night. The thoughts made me feel sick inside.

I feel so empty. I feel as if the gang took everything that was left of me. There is nothing left. Nothing except Chico.

I entered my room, and returned to the bed. I didn't feel well. I lay there trying to focus my thoughts while staring at the ceiling.

"Whatever happened to the days when I knew no pain?" I wondered aloud.

I can't find any pleasant memories from the days of living with my grandparents. The New Order did a good job of erasing those from our minds. I can't stand being in this house any longer. I need the peacefulness of my special place.

I grabbed my jacket and waved for Chico to come along. We walked slowly down the hallway, through the kitchen and to the door.

"Why is that dog in the house again?"

"Where are you going?" Mother shouted.

"I'm taking Chico for a walk!" I snapped.

I was out of the house before she could say another word. Closing the door behind me, I walked slowly down the pathway to our special place. I wanted to run, but my body was too weak. Chico walked at my side, matching my slow pace. I just wanted to get to our special place and rest in peace. At least I still had this one place left for me to feel safe.

As we walked, from somewhere in my mind, thoughts of Rachel crept in my mind. I hadn't thought about her in a long, long time. She once told me she'd overcome the programming and had escaped the New Order's captivity of her mind. At the time, I didn't want to hear what she had to say. Now I wished I knew where she was so she could tell me how she did it.

I need to find her. She can help me be free. How can I find her? Where would I start looking? She'd been the only person since this whole nightmare began that was kind to me. She even tried to share her hope in God with me. I need to find her. Only where do I begin?

The first time I met Rachel, she had assisted in freeing me from Major Doyle's torture chamber. Rachel had argued with other members of the Underground to accept me. At the time of our initial meeting, I hadn't trusted her. Trust was completely against the New Order's indoctrination. She'd tried to let me know she had some understanding of what I'd experienced. I wasn't ready to hear it. Rachel had been captured in the same violent manner as all of us had been and taken to the New Order's compound. However, The Underground Movement helped her escape shortly after. Though she too had experienced the cruelty, drugs, and brainwashing, the short amount of time she was exposed to it allowed her to recover more quickly.

I remember I used Rachel as a shield to escape, and she still was kind to me.

The thought of what I'd done to her made me shudder. I had to find her, if for no other reason than to apologize to her.

I need to talk to her. Maybe she can help me to make some sense of life. Maybe I can even find that person inside that Rachel said was still there. The one that the New Order tried to do away with. I need to find something to make me feel good again something to get rid of this never ending pain inside.

Maybe it's fruitless.

Perhaps I'm dreaming because life will never be like that again.

But maybe it's okay to dream.

It hurt too much to think. As we approached my special place, I felt very dizzy. Weakness washed over me. The world was spinning out of control. The last thing I remember was Chico barking at me as I hit the ground. Everything went black.

I awoke in a very sterile looking place. The room's paint was chipped and cracking. There were no windows and no clocks.

I wasn't sure where I was or how I'd gotten there, wherever "there" was.

Was I in the hospital?

I looked around for Chico, but he was gone. I panicked.

Where is he? If anything happens to him, I'll never forgive myself!

I tried to get out of bed, but my head started whirling again. I lay back down. My thoughts were confused and jumbled. One thing I managed to focus on was Chico.

I need to find him. I can't let anyone hurt him. I am his protector.

Exhaustion tried pushing me back into unconsciousness, but I was afraid to sleep. My first responsibility was to escape this place, but I didn't have the strength. Exhaustion won.

The sound of a door being unlocked and opened woke me. I opened my eyes and looked at the door. There, standing in the entrance, was Rachel. I lay there with my mouth open as I watched her walk into the room.

I must be dreaming. I am certain I'd never see her again. I'd been thinking about her, and here she stands.

I stared at her in shock. My mouth refused to form any words.

A silence hung in the air as we each studied the other. She looked older than her nineteen years. Maybe it was because of the pressure of her work with the Underground. Her blonde hair was still shoulder length and her blue eyes were brighter than anyone's I'd ever seen.

The silence made me very uncomfortable. Finally, I managed to find enough of my voice to croak out a question, "Where's Chico?"

"He's fine. He's being kept in another room. He's very protective of you, so for the safety of those that are here, we felt it was best to keep him in another room."

I didn't like the idea of Chico being separated from me, but I did understand her point. "Do you still go by Joey or have you gone back to Josephine?" Rachel asked.

"Joey I've gotten kind of used to it," I said hoarsely.

"Maybe you'd fit in better if you went by Josephine," she suggested as she pulled a folding chair over to the bed.

I shot her an angry look. She got the message and changed the subject.

"I got the feeling from your expression when I walked in the door that you may have at least been thinking about me," she continued moving the chair as she spoke.

This time I looked at her with a puzzled expression.

"I guess the more appropriate statement would be, I thought you might be looking for me. I'd been having some of my people keep a watch on you to see how you were fitting in around the town. I know its not the easiest place to be accepted." She said. "So, am I right about you wanting to see me?"

"Yes!" I responded. For some reason, I couldn't get my voice above a hoarse whisper.

"Why were you thinking about me?" she questioned. "The last time we were together you made it perfectly clear that you wanted nothing to do with me, my beliefs, or trying to find the peace within. Has something changed?"

She maintained a stern countenance. I felt my face flush as I remembered the awful things I'd said to her. Now face to face with her I wasn't quite sure how to say what was on my mind. I'd rehearsed my speech a dozen times in my head before but now the words were gone.

I weakly nodded my response to her question.

Her countenance softened slightly.

"You seem to have made some enemies," she stated.

I nodded slowly.

"I know about the gang and their activities. I also heard that you recently quit the gang after some trouble. That took some courage on your part." She paused a moment before continuing. "That's why when some of our people found you unconscious on a trail in the woods, they brought you here. I assume your present condition is the price you paid for leaving the gang."

"Yes!" I whispered.

"After they brought you here, we had one of our doctors check you over," she paused for a moment to study my reaction.

I felt extreme fear that a terrible secret had been exposed. I started shaking at the thought of someone touching me.

"The doctor reported that in addition to some pretty bad bruises and cuts on your legs; you have some badly bruised ribs, as well as evidence of severe sexual assault. Did you want to talk about what happened?" She asked.

I shook my head and realized that moving my head was a mistake. It pounded in protest. I couldn't tell her about the things that happened. I was too embarrassed

"You know the best thing is to talk about these things,"... she pressed.

"No!" I croaked. My face burned with embarrassment.

"Okay, then let's try a different subject. Why did you want to see me?" She asked again.

"I - I – I," self-conscious at my stuttering, I cleared my throat and swallowed the lump that suddenly forced its way into it. "I'm tired of hurting so much inside." I managed to say. "You said you could tell me how to stop the pain."

My eyes shifted to the ceiling. Asking for anything was totally against all of the programming. My brain was chastising me for saying that much.

"I see; and you believe that I have the answers?" she continued. Her voice maintained a skeptical tone.

I nodded slightly. I need to try to remember not to move my head.

Why is she asking so many questions?

"Joey, the pain you are feeling is the conflict between the New Order's programming and what you know to be right, in other words your conscience. You're fighting against it because you're not used to it being active. Your conscience is what separated you from all of the others. Yet, you're fighting it because you feel it will make you unable to survive if you let your feelings be expressed. The New Order still has you enslaved. Even though your body is in free territory, your mind is still locked into the New Order's brainwashing and programming," she stated.

I stared at her trying to stay focused.

"Joey, the only thing that can free you from the mental prison you're in is God," she continued.

I felt my eyes widen in surprise.

"God?" I asked.

I remember all of the times that I prayed to Him asking Him to stop the horror, but He never did. How could God be the answer?

"Yes, God!" she emphasized. "He's the only One that can truly help you through this pain. We can be His instruments and demonstrate His love and care. But, ultimately, you will have to face what has happened to you, allow the emotions and feelings to be a part of your life, and then let God give you peace. Your first step is accepting God's free gift to you."

"Gift? Nobody gives me gifts," I stated flatly.

"God did! He gave you the best Gift before you were born. He allowed His son, Jesus Christ, to die on a cross to pay the penalty for your sin and mine. He offers that gift to you freely. You don't have to be good enough or brave enough," she said with conviction in her voice, "you just need to receive it."

I stared at her in disbelief.

"I want to help you. As a Christian, it is my job to help provide an environment that is protective and supportive to help you on this healing journey. Yes your body needs healing, but even more than that you need to let God heal your mind. However, you can't even begin to heal without the Great Physician, and that is God."

I raised my eyes to meet hers and stared. "You're saying I have to deal with these things you call emotions and feelings? I barely know what they are, and you know they are against the law."

She shook her head. "Emotions and feelings are what make us human. It is the New Order that tried to pervert something that is good and healthy. I know they tried to steal your humanity but it is still there. If it weren't, you wouldn't be here searching for me. Without feelings, you couldn't love that dog of yours, and I know you love him."

I looked at her with a confused expression. I hadn't thought about my relationship with Chico as 'love'.

"Yes, I did say the word 'love'. You may have a difficult time accepting that you can love, but it is obvious because the first question you asked me was about your dog.

I continued staring at her as I tried to comprehend.

"What the New Order did to you and the others was, and is, horrific!" she stressed. "No one should ever have to face those things."

"God doesn't want me!" I replied. "If He did He would stop all of this stuff that's happening to me."

"What stuff?"

I shook my head. I couldn't tell her. I was too embarrassed.

"Do you mean the sexual abuse?" She questioned.

I couldn't reply or even look at her.

"You've been sexually abused by others?" She pressed. "I know that you have been."

My face burned with embarrassment. I think she sensed the topic was too uncomfortable for me. She let that part drop.

"You blame God for not helping you!" She stated rather than asking me. "I thought the same thing about God in the beginning, especially when I had to face the painful memories of what the New Order did to me and the things they forced me to do. I know I was only there a short time, but that was long enough for them. Even after you accept God's free gift, there will be battles to fight in your mind and painful memories to work through. It will all take time. It is a one step at a time process. There is no instant cure, but at least with God in your life you would have Someone to help you through those difficult times. You wouldn't have that lonely, empty feeling inside."

Was she seeing inside of me?

"I can tell by the expression on your face you need some time to process the things I've said," she stated. "Do you have questions that I can answer?"

"I hurt so badly inside, I can't even ask God or anyone else for help. Not to mention it's against the law to seek help," I protested.

I didn't want to tell her about my attempts at praying. I didn't want her to think I was too dumb or too stupid to pray.

"That's the New Order's programming talking," Rachel nodded. "I've been where you are now. Only I wasn't brainwashed as long as you were and I didn't have as much of the other abuse as you've had. I do know it will take time."

"God will never forgive me for the things I've done," I objected.

"You are not and were not responsible for any of those things," she tried to explain. "You didn't have any choice. You are not accountable for the things that happened to you, and any choices that you were forced to make were between bad and worse. The only choices that you are responsible for are those that you make for yourself in the present."

"There's not enough of my former self to salvage any more," I said with resignment. "You know, they shoot horses for less. What you don't know or may have forgotten is that they programmed a self-destruct button inside all of us. It's only a matter of time until the bomb goes off and then there won't be anything left."

"You said there wasn't enough left of the person you were to save. You're wrong! That person is still there. She's only hiding inside of you. You have to grab hold of and hold onto the hope that someone will find that person, but you have to help them. Maybe it will be me, or maybe it will be someone else. It will be your choice as to who you let past the walls. Seize onto that thread of humanity, which can pull you back into a normal life! Find that hope! The New Order's programming is not flawless. You will eventually find someone you trust enough to help lift you from this self-imprisonment. You can heal from this! You can find the truth! Just the same as I did," Rachel's reply was filled with so much hope, it struck a chord somewhere deep inside me. Her ability to thwart each of my arguments made me wonder if there was truth in what she was perhaps I was not a savage after all.

Rachel stood up; she leaned over and touched my hand. The programming in my head screamed 'Don't Touch!' Yet, for whatever reason I didn't pull away. Her touch gave me a warm feeling inside; I didn't know for sure what the feeling was, but it seemed okay.

A few tears began to flow down my face.

Why now? I'm not supposed to cry. It's wrong!

My brain protested, but they continued to come.

Rachel gave me a hug. It was the first real hug I'd had since before the nightmare of the New Order. I couldn't hug her back. I felt like a baby. I looked up in alarm, and quickly dried my face on my sleeve.

"It's okay! Those tears prove to me and should prove to you, that the they didn't take everything from you," Rachel said in a soft reassuring tone. "A heart that cannot feel pain cannot feel joy either. Let your heart feel the pain and let it all out. The tears are a start. They are the release valve on the pain."

I shook my head.

"I'll let you rest. We'll talk more later." She said with a smile.

I was afraid to let her to leave. I didn't want the moment to end. For the first time, there seemed to be a revived sense of hope within, but my brain refused to comprehend anything more. Rachel hugged me again, and I drifted off to sleep.

Chapter - 26 - Lost Opportunity

When I awoke again, my head still felt foggy.

Where am I? Am I dreaming? Did I really find Rachel? Why I am so disoriented?

The brain fog began to lift a little. I realized that seeing Rachel had not been a dream. Pangs of fear seized my stomach as memories of our meeting replayed in my mind.

She touched me! Why did I let her touch me? Why did I let her hug me? She saw me cry. Those things are strictly forbidden. I wasn't supposed to trust anyone to allow them to get that close. I have to find Chico and get out of here.

Mother would be furious that I wasn't there to wait on her. There's no question a beating awaited me at home. I had no idea how long I'd been gone.

I need Rachel. I need to talk to her more. Our conversation yesterday awoke something deep inside of me. Something that I thought was lost forever.

Gently pushing myself up, I paused a moment to make sure my head wouldn't spin. Convinced that it was better, I slid gingerly to the edge of the bed. My entire body protested at the movement. I was still raw and bruised.

I inched closer to the edge of the bed. No sooner had my feet touched the floor than the door swung open. Two large, burley young members of the Underground entered and stood blocking the door.

How did they know?

I glanced at them and then at the ceiling. There in the corner was a surveillance camera. They were watching me.

That's how they knew. Why are they watching me? Why are they charging into my room the minute my feet touched the floor? For all they knew, I might be heading for the bathroom. What is going on?

I froze in place and stared at them. They stood with their gaze fixed straight ahead.

"Where's Rachel?" My question broke the silence.

They stood like mute statues. Their manner was very intimidating. I still decided to test them. I pulled myself to my feet. As I stood there leaning against the bed my legs felt like rubber.

"We suggest you return to bed," one of them said in a flat voice. His eyes were emotionless.

"Am I a prisoner here?" I demanded.

My weakened condition prevented me from making a run. I think they sensed it and that's why they didn't force me back into bed.

"No! You're our guest," the other insisted.

"Guest?" I looked from one to the other, skeptically. "Since when do you spy on a guest or have guards rush the door of a guest?"

"We protect our people. You've been a threat to us in the past. We're not taking any chances this time," The guard replied.

"Where's Rachel?" I repeated my demand.

"That's none of your concern. You endangered her once before, and we're not going to let you do it again."

My heart sank. I felt sick inside. My sixth sense told me something was wrong.

There is something they are not telling me.

As I stood there, I felt dizzy. I sat down on the bed and lay back on the pillows. I tried to make it look like compliance rather than weakness. When the guards were satisfied with my obedience, they turned and left the room. I drifted back into the darkness of sleep.

Too many hours of my relatively short life have been in the darkness enduring one form of abuse or another. Escaping the New Order had not brought an escape from the terror of the darkness.

I awoke with a start. I glanced around the room trying not to move. I didn't want them to see that I was awake yet. The camera's red light shown in the dimly lit room. They were still watching.

Without a clock or windows, I couldn't determine how long I'd been asleep or how long I'd been there. When I sat up, I felt stronger than before. My head was clearer now. Moving to the edge of the bed brought the two guards back into the room.

"Where's Rachel?" I repeated my question with more authority in my voice.

Again I was met with stony stares. This time I was able to move quicker.

"We recommend that you return to the bed," the guard repeated. He sounded like a recording.

I spotted my boots near the foot of the bed. I walked over to them and sat down in the nearby chair. I pulled them on and was on my feet quickly. The guards didn't move.

"If I'm not your prisoner, then you have no right to keep me here. As a guest, I'm free to stay or leave. I choose to leave. Return my dog to me, and I'll be on my way," I said matter-of-factly.

"I don't think so!" He replied.

Before he could finish his statement, I grabbed his partner and shoved him to the floor. After I elbowed the other guard in the gut, I reached for the door handle. These two men were back on their feet quickly; they were trained better than I had anticipated. One spun me away from the door, while the other kicked my feet out from under me, and I landed hard on my already bruised knees. Pain shot through my legs. My head began spinning again. I felt a boot in the middle of my back shoving me to the floor. My face hit the floor hard. I was pinned.

Now what?

"Why are you so interested in the whereabouts of Rachel?" a new voice demanded. "Are you going to take her hostage as you attempt to escape again?"

I wasn't sure who had joined our little group, but I was reluctant to speak.

"Answer me!" He demanded while the boot pressed harder into my back.

"No, I only want to talk to Rachel. She and I were having a conversation yesterday. I want to continue speaking with her," I managed to say between gasps for breath.

Normally I would not have answered, but it seemed to be a harmless question, and I wanted to prevent any more pain.

"A conversation? My information was that she was interrogating you," the voice responded with a note of surprise.

"Do you always interrogate your guests?" I hissed.

"We do when the guest is or has been a threat to our organization. You are considered both," the voice growled.

"I want to talk to Rachel. I demand to speak to her," I insisted.

"You are in no position to make demands," he responded

I squirmed and tried to wrestle myself free from the boot holding me in place. I could hear mumbling voices and then realized that at least one of the guards had on an earpiece for communication. I figured someone was watching these proceedings and now had some orders for them. I only hoped that the orders didn't involve another beating. I was quite sure that my poor body couldn't take any more bruises.

The mumbling stopped and the weight of the foot lifted from my back. One guard pulled my arms behind me and bound my wrists while the other yanked me to a kneeling position by pulling me up by my collar and belt. With my hands securely bound, the guards hoisted me to my feet by grabbing me under the arms. The door was opened, and I was escorted through it. The guards had to practically carry me. All the strength I'd felt earlier quickly drained away, especially after wrestling with the guards.

Where are they taking me now?

The guards dragged me down a long corridor to a door at the end. We paused long enough for one of them to knock. A buzzer sounded, and the door was pushed open. There sat a man behind a large desk with a monitor on the side. I assumed he must have been the voice in the earpiece.

"Put her in the chair!" he ordered the guards.

The guards sat me down in a chair, and they exited the room.

I sat there staring at the little man. He was older than most of the members of the Underground that I had met up to this point. His round, chubby face, and large overhanging belly told me that he probably didn't do much fieldwork. The buttons on his shirt were straining from the pressure. He moved around to the front of his desk and stared at me. I met his eyes with defiance.

"You are worse than a bad penny!" he began.

I wasn't sure what that meant, but it didn't sound like a compliment.

"Once we rescued you from the New Order, you were supposed to blend in to society. We didn't expect to have to continue to bail you out of problems only to have you defiantly work against us," he continued.

"I did what I was trained to do. You worked with Rachel. You should be familiar with what we are programmed to do. Besides, you left us without showing us how to fit in," I complained back.

He ignored my complaints and asked, "Why are you making inquiries about Rachel and the Underground? Your questions make a number of our people nervous, especially since you took Rachel hostage during your escape attempt the last time we rescued you."

I sat mutely.

What does he want me to say?

His stern expression softened slightly. "You're Josephine Benson. You were forcibly removed from the home of your grandparents and brainwashed by the New Order. We helped you escape after they had sentenced you to death for sparing the life of your grandfather. Your confused mind didn't know whom to trust, and you fought us, which nearly cost us a number of people. Later, your grandfather was shot and killed by a bullet from a member of the radical faction of our Underground bent on killing you. Actually there were probably a number of radicals at that rally that wanted to kill you. Your reputation of being the New Order's 'best and brightest' frightened a lot of our people"

My head jerked to look at him more closely. I was surprised that he knew so much about me.

"Surprised?" he quipped as if he was reading my mind.

I couldn't respond. It was against every trained instinct to do so.

"So, I think under the circumstances, you will understand why we're suspicious as to your constant questions about the whereabouts of Rachel," he continued. "She is one of our best operatives. I worked with her personally to help her to overcome the problems that she faced after her escape from the New Order. One thing she did remind us about frequently was that we were not doing anything to help those that we rescued. For that, I apologize."

I stared at him. I wasn't sure what to say.

He helped Rachel? He knew Grandfather?

"Now tell me, why do you want to know where she is?" He repeated his question in a softer tone.

Something in his eyes touched me inside. "You knew my grandfather?" I managed to choke out the words.

"Yes. He was a good man. I know that he loved you a great deal. That is why we have been so patient with you."

Leaning against his desk, he stood there with his hands folded in front of him. He maintained eye contact with me.

"I want to know where Rachel is so we can continue our conversation." I said as I struggled against the restraints.

"Sooner or later you're going to need to stop struggling," he said. "You're going to need to trust someone."

I studied the man.

"Why can't you believe that Rachel visited me yesterday, and that we talked?" I questioned.

"She didn't say anything about talking with you," the man replied. "And we're skeptical about your true motives after what you did to her the last time."

"I told you that I was doing what I was trained to do." I paused. "You speak of trust; yet, here I sit with my hands bound behind me. If you want me to trust someone, then maybe a demonstration of trust on your part might be in order. Release my hands! These restraints are cutting off my circulation."

He moved his right hand and rubbed it across his face. As he held his chin in his hand, he thought for a long moment, and then he stepped forward.

His movement startled me, and I ducked. I wasn't sure if he was going to strike me or not.

What is he going to do?

He moved behind my chair and eased me forward enough to reach the restraints around my wrists. Suddenly I felt my arms separate in freedom. He gently touched my shoulder and pulled me back against the chair. Sauntering back to the front of his desk he resumed leaning up against it.

"Okay?" he asked. "I've taken the first step. Now it's your turn. Why are you asking for Rachel?"

Surprised by his act of trust, I felt an ache creep into my throat. "As I said, she and I visited yesterday. At least I think it was yesterday. I'm a little confused about how much time has passed. Rachel said that she would help me. She said she'd be back. I haven't seen her since."

The sound of my pounding heart was deafening in my ears. Memories of the Militia's training raced through my head. I'd already broken the rules of captivity by speaking at all. My own mind became my enemy. Fear ate at my insides as I sat there staring at this man who held my fate in his hands. I fought with my brain to maintain focus. I had to stay alert and be prepared for whatever might happen.

The man stared back at me, probably wondering if he could believe me. After several minutes, he nodded. He turned and walked behind his desk and sat down.

He cleared his throat and spoke, "I know Rachel went to see you. I wasn't sure what she spoke with you about. She had led most of our people to believe that she was interrogating you, but I knew Rachel has a special spot in her heart for you and would like to help you in any way that she can. I needed you to tell me why she went to see you to test you. I had to know if you were going to hurt her again."

The man shuffled some papers on his desk until he found the folder that he was searching for. As he opened it, he laid it flat on his desk.

"I have a report here that I am going to share with you because I believe what you've said. I also know that any compromise to our organization in the past was done under the influence of the New Order's programming of your mind. Your grandfather believed you to be a person of integrity. It is this integrity that I am going to rely on now by sharing this report with you."

My stomach knotted. I had a feeling he was about to tell me bad news.

"After Rachel visited with you, we had to send her into the New Order's headquarters to rescue several young people scheduled for execution. We wanted to try to get them out of there before Major Doyle had a chance to kill them. One of these was an undercover operative for us.

"Somehow, Rachel was captured shortly after she crossed into their territory. We believe we were fed false information. The New Order had been anxious to recapture Rachel. Major Doyle has wanted to get her back ever since we freed her, the same, as he wants you back. He became especially interested in getting her back after she began working for us to help others escape.

"The report we have is from a second operative we sent in with Rachel. We'll call her 'Pat'. You will forgive me if I do not use the real names of our under cover operatives."

I nodded my understanding.

"Rachel was brought before Major Doyle for interrogation. It was only the two of them in his office. He planned on torturing her to get information about our Underground operation. She would then be put on a public trial, humiliated and made an example of. It was already determined she would be charged with treason and then executed. Many of our people wanted to go in to rescue her, but without a clear idea of what we'd be facing, we couldn't risk losing anyone else. Rachel knew the risks before she went back into their territory," he continued.

"Pat found one of the tunnels that led into a secret passage inside the Major's office, so she was able to hear and witness all that took place."

I remember those passages. Grandfather and I hid in one for days waiting for someone to come to help us to freedom.

"Major Doyle circled around and around Rachel trying to intimidate her. She stared straight ahead and never flinched."

She too was trained well.

"According to Pat, the fact that Major Doyle could not intimidate Rachel angered him. In frustration, he grabbed a knife from his boot. Pat wasn't sure what he planned to do with it, but his eyes were eager to inflict pain. Maybe he'd hoped that she would beg him for mercy. Anger overpowered his emotionless front, and he lunged for Rachel. She spun to the side. As he tried to follow her, he tripped. His momentum caused him to fall face first onto the floor. He tried to break his fall by putting both arms out, but he still hit the floor with his arms under him. Rachel froze in place not knowing what to do. She stood there staring and waiting for him to get up. Pat assumed Rachel viewed this as some type of trick to force her to move closer to him. After several minutes of him just laying there and not moving, Rachel cautiously inched towards him. She stopped after each step and watched him.

"It seemed like he may have been playing dead. Rachel crept closer. When she was close to him, she used the toe of her boot to nudge his head. He didn't move. Standing perfectly still, she watched him to see if she could detect any breathing. There was none. Using her foot, she turned his body over and jumped back out of reach. Rachel's hand flew to her mouth to stifle a scream. A dark pool of red was spreading across his uniform jacket. Major Doyle had fallen on his own knife, stabbing himself in the heart."

Is he telling me that Major Doyle is dead?

"Pat's report continues. She said that Rachel stood looking at the body of the one who was ready to execute her. He was laying there dead. Her life had been spared."

A sense of relief washed over me, but there was still a nagging feeling that there was more to the story.

"The one that caused so many so much pain ended up stumbling and dying by his own hand. It all seems very ironic, and in some ways poetic," the man added

Somehow the death of Major Doyle seemed just. The treacherous was killed with his own treachery.

"Pat was ready to come out of her hiding place and lead Rachel out of there. They would be able to complete their mission and return here. Before Pat could move, she heard someone approaching the Major's office. Pat stayed in her hiding place.

"One of the Major's aides entered. He quickly took in the scene. We guess that he assumed Rachel had killed the Major. He immediately pulled his pistol and shot Rachel on the spot. She died instantly."

I gasped in horror.

Rachel is dead! Why? Why did she need to die? She cared. She was going to help me.

"Knowing Rachel cared about you, I thought you should know, but I must ask that you keep this information to yourself," he concluded.

He closed the file and looked at me.

I nodded.

I couldn't believe it. Rachel was dead!

He waited a few moments to let the news sink in before he spoke again. "I'm going to summon the guards. They will put the restraints back on temporarily. They will also blindfold you. I apologize for these precautions. I will instruct them to return you and your dog to the spot where they found you, at which point you'd be free to go. The restraints and blindfold are necessary because we can't afford to take any chances on our operation being compromised. Even with the death of Major Doyle, we still need to be cautious. I'm sure that someone will step in to take his place. Do you understand?"

I nodded absently.

The guards came in, and they bound and blindfolded me. I was in such a daze, nothing seemed to register after the man's words, "She died instantly!"

Without Rachel's help what chance did I have? Why God? Why did You let her die? She said she would help me. Why do You take everyone away who cares about me?

Chapter - 27 - Nothing Left?

Why? Why do so many bad things happen to me? What did I do wrong? My last hope died with Rachel. Why does God take away the people that possibly could help me? Rachel was such a good person. Why did God have to take her? I am trying to find answers about Him, and yet He takes away someone that could help. It's not fair! Grandmother said that God is loving; yet, He took them and now Rachel. Am I so bad that I don't deserve to find help?

The death of Rachel made my stomach hurt. In the New Order, I watched other people die and it didn't bother me, now the thought of someone dying makes me ill. What's happening to me? Am I becoming weak like Jesse predicted?

I felt a deep emptiness inside, a longing for someone who might understand. At the very least I needed someone who would care enough to help me through this pain even if they didn't fully understand it. Rachel's words replayed in my mind. 'You will eventually find someone you trust enough to help lift you from this self-imprisonment.' It was entirely possible that she might have been the one to help me move past all of this mess. Instead, I end up being abandoned once again. It's almost like anyone that tries to help me will end up dead or disappear.

Maybe I'm not meant to be on this earth. Maybe someone made a mistake and I ended up being trapped in the middle of it. Maybe the others were right when they said, once you are in the New Order; it sucks the heart and life out of you until there is nothing left.

I lay in my bed. If Mother had missed me the past couple of days, she gave no indication.

That's peculiar!

Maybe she drank so much that she ended up being passed out for several days. It wouldn't be the first time. I watched the shadows creep across the floor of my room. I was exhausted and in pain both emotionally and physically.

Before I was able to reach too deep of a sleep, my mind flashed to the image of Charlie.

… Her face was bloody. She was wearing a dress rather than her militia uniform. Her mother scooped her into her arms. The blood began dripping onto her mother's shoulder. I tried to warn Charlie's mother that she was being covered in blood, but the words would not come out. Finally, I managed to make a groan that took every bit of strength I had. Her mother turned toward me. Her mother's face was covered with blood as well …

When I awoke, I was drenched with cold sweat and shaking. I clutched the blanket closer too me. It took me a few moments to realize I was in my room.

The nightmares have been my constant companion since I was in the New Order's militia, but they seemed to be getting progressively worse. Sometimes they're so bad that I usually am afraid to go to sleep.

Why can't I get this stuff out of my mind?

Maybe it is a residual affect of their brainwashing and programming. The militia didn't consider us human. We were forced to become their robots. It doesn't feel so good to be a piece of property; Property has no feelings.

If I'm property, why do I hurt so badly? It hurts so much.

Suicide had become a constant obsession. I had developed a plan about how to kill myself so that I wouldn't leave a mess for who ever found me. I would take enough of Mother's sleeping pills to do the job. As I thought about it, that seemed to be a wimpy way out. I had a knife that I could use to slit my wrists, but that would make a mess. It would serve Mother right to be left with a mess. I also wasn't sure about how painful that would be. I guess my plan wasn't completely clear yet, but I was still working on it. I knew I wanted to die and the time had to be soon. I just couldn't deal with this inner pain any longer. It would be in the early evening after Mother and Edward had left for their night of drinking. That way there would be no one to find me for hours. There would be no way anyone could save me.

I wonder if they would even feel bad that I was gone.

I'd get to the point of deciding to follow through with my plan, but I would always chicken out in the end. Somehow, somewhere there had to be a better answer to all of this. Somehow I knew deep down inside that suicide was not the answer.

Besides, who would take care of Chico?

I needed to take a walk to clear my head. I hoped if I'd stay in the woods, no one would see me. It was still dangerous for me to venture out, but I couldn't stay in the house forever either. I needed to go to my special place and have some time to think.

"Come on Chico!" I called. He came bounding off the bed along side of me.

I was still hurting so it would be a slow walk rather than the fast run that we both enjoyed so much. I took a deep breath and exited the house. The air smelled fresh and clean. Only a couple of months, and it would be summer.

It would be a lonely summer this year. There would be no baseball games with the gang members. The only place I could go was to my special place in the woods. There would be no other people. It would be just Chico and me.

As we walked, I noticed the white, puffy clouds had so many different patterns and shapes. They dotted the deep blue sky making a beautiful painted canvas. All of the beauty and orderliness couldn't have happened by some random chance like the New Order told us.

How could the New Order say there is no God in Heaven with such magnificent work above their heads? With everything so perfect and beautiful, how could God have made such a mistake in me?

I'd been away from the militia for about three years. It was long enough to understand that my life was not the same as other peoples'. Most people didn't even come close to following the teachings of the New Order. Yet, those rules remained stuck in my head. Their programming scrambled my brains, and I had no clue as to how to unscramble them. It was like trying to get a broken egg back into its shell.

God, I just don't understand why You would take away the one person that I was willing to listen to. A person who could explain some of the mystery. I grow tired with the question, 'Why?' I'm exhausted with the question, 'Where are You?' I'm so tired of the pain, the sadness, and the confusion, the feelings inside that I don't understand. I want to turn to You as my grandparents said that I could, but instead I run in fear. Are You really big enough to protect me from all of the pain, the sadness, and the confusion? Can You truly help me understand? Can I allow You near me without You hating me? Without You hurting me? When I think of how Grandmother called You 'Father', I cringe inside, remembering the pain and violation Father inflicted upon me. Can You really teach, soothe, comfort, and heal?

I needed to pull myself out of this mood. Looking over at Chico, I decided that the best way to get some temporary relief from the pain would be to wrestle and play with him. It would distract me from these depressing thoughts.

Chico was romping around in the grass. I loved to watch him play. When I was with him, I felt different. When I was with him, there was a certain lightness within, something that I couldn't remember feeling at any other time. It was my respite in time, like a bubble surrounding us and forcing all of the memories of the New Order and the gang out of my mind. It was the closest I ever got to feeling what one might have called "normal". I wished that we could remain in this bubble forever, but that was neither possible nor practical.

Chapter - 28 - Pain of Feeling

Somehow I managed to survive the rest of the school year without further meetings with the gang or attacks by the townies. I overheard many rumors about the trouble the gang members were causing. When I watched the news, I learned that many of them were true. Billy had led the gang into a major fight where they killed some of the kids. The police arrested a couple of the members. While they were in jail, some of them committed suicide. I could understand why they would do that. I knew that being locked in a cage would have driven me over the edge to suicide. Even though I paid a horrific price for quitting, I was glad to be free of them. There were feelings of remorse, however; I wondered if I had remained their leader whether or not they'd have gotten into that kind of trouble.

Summer vacation arrived. In the fall, I would be entering high school.

Would that be any different than junior high school? There would be many of the same kids there. Perhaps going to high school would cause them to mature a little. I doubted it, but it was a thought.

Nothing else changed much. Each night I had to deal with Edward and his drinking buddies. After they were gone or passed out, I would fall into a nightmare filled sleep. Why couldn't I be free of all these things?

Every night I'd see the soldiers come to take me away. From that moment on, my life as I knew it ceased. I could hear the screams of the other kids. I'd relive the bombing training. One of the worst was reliving the day Charlie ran away and then, with a pistol in her hand, killed herself right before my eyes. Why did she have to do it on my watch and in front of me? Day after day there were new horrors and torture. Time became meaningless for us while we were in the New Order. Somehow I had survived these actual events, only to relive them in my memory and nightmares every night.

As I lay there half awake with the horror of the New Order lurking in the corners of my brain, I suddenly felt hands touching me. I shook the remnants of the nightmares from my mind.

"No!" I protested.

Edward ignored me and continued to push himself on me. I punched him and scratched at his face. Pieces of flesh embedded themselves under my fingernails. He jumped back, giving me just enough room to slide out from under his grasp and slip under the bed. Before I was completely under the bed, he grabbed my hair and pulled me back toward him. I whirled and slapped his face.

"Leave me alone!" I ordered. I guess because I was getting older, I was also getting bolder.

After I kicked him in the knee, he released me to reach for his aching leg. I made my escape. I ran for the front door and bounded down the steps to the outside. I scampered under the porch into a back corner that no one could reach without crawling under there with me. I curled up as small as I could. My body shook. As I rocked back and forth, I worked at trying to slow my racing heart.

I no longer felt grown up. My heart ached for someone to take me into their arms and hold me close and tell me that everything was going to be okay. I convinced myself that was a dream that happened only to other people but not to me.

Chico crawled under the porch with me. Mother forced him to stay outside now. She said he was too big to stay in the house. I built him a nice house and I wished I could stay there with him. He crawled in as close to me as he could. I reached for him and held him tightly.

"Why?" I whispered to him. "Why does he keep doing this to me? I hate living here! I hate living at all! Why? Why would someone expose their own flesh and blood to all of this? Why? Why? Why?"

I felt my throat begin to ache and my eyes begin to burn. Life was so cruel and memory a curse.

I must have fallen asleep there. The next thing I remember was Mother's voice echoing through the neighborhood.

"JOSEPHINE!" Mother bellowed my name.

I swore people in the next state could hear her. The sun was up now. I crawled out from under the porch, and brushed the loose dirt from my clothes. I didn't want Mother knowing my secret place so I hurried away from its entrance. My muscles were stiff from being outside for hours. I left Chico at the door. Mother and Edward were both sitting in the living room. Edward's face had huge red scratches across his cheek. I expected that I was going to be beaten for attacking him. Mother wouldn't believe me if I told her the truth. Maybe she was summoning me to change the television channels or some other stupid thing like that. When I entered the room, the television was off.

"What?" I snapped. Even though I knew this would possibly set her off, I didn't care. Standing there with feet apart and hands jammed into my pockets, I waited for her to make her requests known.

"We're moving!" Mother announced.

"What?" I blurted out in shock.

"I said we're moving. You deaf or something?" she snapped. "Edward's got some buddies of his that are going to help load up their truck. We'll load up our car and that should take care of everything."

I had prayed that we would move, but there was something about Mother's tone that felt wrong.

"Where are we moving?" I asked.

"Just a few miles on the other side of town." She replied.

That was still in the same school district. This move wouldn't solve my problems with the gang members or the townies. I started to ask why we were moving but I knew the answer. They didn't pay the rent again.

I walked away to begin packing my room. "One more thing - that dog of yours isn't coming with us. The new place doesn't allow animals," she added in the same matter-of-fact tone.

My head snapped up with a look of shock.

"No! You can't!" I shouted. "We can't leave him behind. He won't understand why we're abandoning him. He's my friend," my protests turned into a whine.

"It's only a stupid dog!" Mother stated without understanding.

You can't take the last good thing away from me. God, why would You allow this? You took Rachel away just after I found her again, and now I'm losing my only friend. God, why do You hate me?

"The neighbors will take care of him," Edward added. The look on his face told a different story. I didn't trust him any further than I could throw him. I think he talked Mother into a place that didn't take animals to spite me.

"Why can't we take him?" I argued. "Why couldn't we find a place that accepts pets?"

"Houses don't grow on trees. We have to take what we can afford," Mother countered.

We probably can't afford the place we're moving to since you don't pay the rent. Besides, we wouldn't need to be moving if you stopped using the rent and food money to buy booze.

"We can't leave him! Why are you taking him away from me?" I demanded.

"Go get your stuff together!" Mother ordered. "Edward will take care of tying the dog up so that he doesn't follow us."

"No! I'm not leaving him behind." I shouted back at her.

Mother flew into a rage. She was on me in the blink of an eye. Her first blow caught me across the mouth. I tasted blood. Before I could duck, she landed several more punches to my head. She finally stopped hitting me.

"Now, go pack your room, and not another word about that dog. I'm sorry I ever let you get him," she bellowed as she moved back to her chair.

I slowly stood up. My feet felt like they had lead weights on them as I slowly plodded to my room. I felt tears filling my eyes. I quickly wiped them away with my sleeve. I didn't want Mother to see them.

The rest of the day was a whirl. The house was packed up and loaded into the vehicles. It all seemed was so surreal.

Once the last items were loaded on the truck, I went to say goodbye to Chico. I knelt next to him and hugged him tightly. When I buried my face into his soft brown fur, I didn't want to let go. I didn't know what to do. My heart felt like it was breaking into pieces.

"JOSEPHINE! We don't have all day!" Mother bellowed. "We need to get going."

I ignored her. I would probably pay for it later, but I didn't care. This was my best friend.

What does she know about friends?

I continued hugging him tightly. My heart ached. It was like someone was ripping a huge hole in me. Lifting my head, I looked into those kind brown eyes that seemed to understand everything I said to him.

How could she demand that I leave my friend behind? It wasn't fair.

I stroked the silky fur that comforted me so many times in the past.

Who would comfort me now? Who would I talk to? Who would be my friend?

My mind pictured the way we would run like lightning through the woods and then roll into the tall grass. I'd miss wrestling with him. But I would especially miss having him to talk to. He gave me something that I haven't had since before the New Order invaded my life, with the possible exception of Rachel.

"Josephine, get in this car right this minute! Leave that stupid dog!" she screamed.

"I'm not finished saying goodbye." My voice wavered as I spoke.

Now the entire neighborhood knew what was going on.

Edward headed in my direction. Before he could grab me, I reluctantly pulled myself away from Chico, my true friend. He remained sitting in the front yard. I walked backwards a few feet. I lunged back at Chico and hugged him again.

"Now Josephine!" Mother yelled from the car.

Edward was about to grab my shirt collar. I ducked away from his outstretched hand and slowly walked towards the car dragging my feet. I couldn't take my eyes off of Chico.

He isn't on a leash. I thought Edward was going to tie him up.

I couldn't find my voice to mention his oversight. Mother got out of the car and stomped over to where I was slowly walking. She grabbed me by the collar and shoved me. I still couldn't take my eyes off of my friend.

He can't understand why I'm leaving. I don't even understand.

Mother pushed me into the backseat of the car. I hit my head as I sailed through the rear door onto the back seat. She slammed the car door behind me. Scrambling to my knees, I turned around to stare out the back window. Edward got into the driver's seat. Mother took her place and slammed the door, and we began to move. As the car exited the driveway, Chico must have known he was being left behind.

He began running and barking after the car. He wanted to be with me as much as I wanted him. We drove down the dirt road. I could only stare at my friend. I held my hand out and touched the glass of the back window.

Go back! Don't run after us! Please go back!

My heart ached as I watched him run after us. Fear gripped every part of my being as I watched him continue following us. It was as if I knew what was about to happen. A few tears escaped before I managed to bite my tongue to stop them.

The car pulled onto a major road, and Chico continued running after us.

I could hardly breathe as I watched him run after us.

I was instantly afraid. A car came speeding behind us. The driver of the car didn't see Chico run out onto the road. The sound of brakes squealing was mixed with a thud. It was too late. My hand flew to my mouth as I saw Chico's brown and white body thrown into the air. I couldn't muffle the scream when he crashed back onto the pavement. That car hit my only friend in the world.

Edward slammed on the brakes when I screamed, "STOP THE CAR!"

As the car slowed, I jumped out of the car and raced to him. I ran down the road as fast as I could; I had to reach my faithful friend. I couldn't let him be alone. Finally, I arrived at the spot where he lay and slid to the ground. Gently picking him up, I cradled his bruised and bleeding body in my arms, I buried my face into his blood-matted fur. We were in the middle of the traffic lane. Cars came to a standstill around the scene.

When I realized we were in the street, I tenderly lifted Chico and we moved to the shoulder of the road. I sat in the gravel holding him tightly to my heart. Never had I felt such pain inside.

Oh, God! Please, don't let him die! Please, don't let my only friend die!

I lifted my head and could see Chico looking up at me with his big brown eyes, and he weakly licked my hand. His breathing became slower and more labored. In a few short moments, he closed his eyes and his stopped breathing.

I guess licking my hand was his way of saying goodbye. After all, that was his greeting when we met.

"NO!" I heard my voice scream. "NO! NO! NO! Not my only friend! Please, God, don't take Chico! If you're going to take him, take me too!"

I rocked my dead friend as I had done so often in life with his head cradled in my arms. I held him with my face buried into his fur and felt tears running down my face.

My only friend in the entire world is dead! Life is so unfair! Why? He was always there for me. Why can't I help him now? He accepted me just the way I was. He is the only one that ever understood the things that happened to me. Now he's gone! Why? God, take me too!

My face burned.

How could the world be so cruel? Haven't I experienced enough cruelty at its hands for one lifetime? What have I done so wrong that I have to be continually punished in this way?

Just then, Edward grabbed me by my shirt collar and yanked me to my feet. He forced me to drop Chico. His limp body fell to the ground with a sickening thud. I fought against his grasp. Edward shook me and shoved me towards the car. I broke free and stopped just out of his reach to watch what he was going to do.

"It's a dumb animal!" he yelled back at me.

I charged him ready to fight him. I didn't care anymore. He punched me in the stomach, and I crumpled to the ground. Edward went to the trunk of the car and took a garbage bag out. He held in one hand and walked over to Chico's body. He picked my friend up by the collar and shoved him into the bag. Edward added a few rocks that were nearby and tied the bag shut. He heaved it into the nearby canal.

I jumped to my feet still gasping for breath and raced for the canal.

"NO--------OOO!" I shouted. I took a running leap and tried to jump in after the bag, but Edward grabbed me in mid air. I struggled against him to free myself, but he held me by the belt and hair. He dragged me back to the car; I kicked and screamed the entire distance. I would have freed myself once he released me at the car, but Mother began slapping me. When I ducked, Edward shoved me into the car and drove off.

"It's just a dumb animal," she echoed Edward's words. "If I knew you were going to get so attached to the thing, I never would have let you get the dog in the first place."

I want my Chico! I want to hold him again. The pain inside was so great that I hadn't even felt Mother slapping me.

I want the world to stop and notice that someone great has just died. My best friend is dead!

Chapter - 29 - One Makes a Difference

The hot summer days dragged on. Our new house was smaller than the last one. It made it difficult to find places for all of the Mother's junk. My room was even smaller and more difficult to secretly slip out of at night. To make it all worse, the place and the neighborhood were even dumpier than the last place.

For this trash heap, my best friend died. There is such a hollowness inside, like someone carved a huge hole inside of me.

Nothing had meaning. In my opinion, this was a wasted move.

My best friend died only because Mother and Edward were too lazy to pay the rent.

I missed Chico so much. There were times that I couldn't stand the pain inside. Each day I spent time standing in the kitchen staring at the collection of cooking knives and thinking about how much it would hurt to kill myself with one of them. Would cutting myself enough to kill myself hurt as much as a regular cut? What would it be like to die? Would anyone even miss me if I were dead? Would Edward throw me in a ditch, too?

We moved again before school started. Summer finally drifted away and autumn slipped in as September arrived. I would be fourteen soon and starting high school. I couldn't wait for the years to pass until my sixteenth birthday. At least that one would be recognized by the state. I would be able to finally drive legally. I would then be the master of my own fate instead of being at the mercy of a drunk driver. Those times I was stuck riding with Mother and a drunken Edward were so terrifying I usually sat on the floor of the backseat so I didn't have to see death coming.

The change from junior high school to high school wasn't much different. The problems were still there. Even after three years, it was as if the townies still viewed me as if I were from a different planet. There was also danger from the remaining gang members.

One thing in its favor was that the high school had a nicer building and it was all on one floor. Having everything on one floor made it much easier for me to find my way around to my classes.

I hated school in general, hated the other students, and the teachers. I was tired of them judging me before I'd a chance to prove myself. But since I hated being home even more, I guessed between the two, I'd have rather been in school.

One day during the summer there was a knock on the door to the house.

"Josephine, answer the door!" Mother commanded from the living room.

I shuffled down the hallway with thumbs hooked in my jean pockets.

It's probably more of their drinking buddies.

When I opened the door, there stood an elderly man and woman. They both appeared to be in their sixties. The man was about six foot tall, thin, and balding. The woman had brown-hair, about five feet five inches tall, and overweight.

I stared at them. The only people that ever came to visit us were either drunks or caseworkers.

They stared back at me. Something about them seemed familiar, but I wasn't sure what.

"You must be Josephine!" The man said.

How did he know my name?

"May we come in?" The woman asked.

"Who's at the door?" Mother bellowed.

"I don't know. They're asking to come in. It's a man and woman that know my name." I shouted back to Mother.

"We're your grandparents." The woman replied.

I felt my eyes grow wide with surprise and suspicion.

Grandparents?

I stepped back and let them enter just as Mother yelled, "Don't let them in!"

Too late, they were already coming through the door. They walked directly to the living room.

"Elizabeth, that's no way to act!" The woman said to Mother.

I hung back watching. I'd been able to move into a position where I could see everyone's face.

I didn't know I had more grandparents. The only ones I could remember were the ones that raised me.

"This is my house and I decide who can come in." Mother argued.

The man and the woman took a quick glance around the house and shook their heads slightly. The expressions seemed to be that of disappointment with the trashiness of the house. I'd have to agree with them there. This place was a dump.

"What are you doing here?" Mother demanded, "and how did you find us?"

"We felt it was time that you let us get to know our granddaughter. After all, she's almost fourteen years old now. You've kept us out of her life all these years. We thought we could at least be part of her life now." The woman responded to Mother in a gentle tone. "Besides, we're your parents and we want to have contact with our daughter."

"Since when?" Mother scoffed.

"I know that things haven't always been the best between us, but there's no reason we can't have a relationship now," the man added.

"You just want to take the kid." Mother accused. "Well, she's not going anyplace. The welfare pays for her to stay here and she takes care of the house. Besides, you don't want any dealings with her; she's a troublemaker and hoodlum. She's not someone you want for a granddaughter."

Mother's words made my insides hurt.

Turning away from Mother, the couple focused their attention on me.

"I'm your Grandma Menkin," the woman introduced herself. She motioned to the man. "This is your Grandpa Menkin."

I stood staring at them. So, these were Mother's parents. Since coming to live with Mother, I'd heard them mentioned in arguments between Mother and Father, but didn't know anything about them.

"We'd like to get to know you and for you to get to know us," Grandpa Menkin added.

They seemed a bit uncomfortable and struggled to find the right words to say to me. It didn't help that Mother sat on her chair giving them hateful looks.

"We're sorry that we couldn't be part of your life earlier. There were circumstances beyond our control," the Grandma Menkin said, giving Mother a stern glance.

"Will you let us be your grandparents now?" Grandpa Menkin asked.

What am I suppose to say? What kind of a question is that? If they are Mother's parents, that made them my grandparents whether I liked it or not.

I stood there with my hands in my pockets and stared at the floor. I couldn't look at them.

Why now? Why did they want to be a part of my life now? Where were they? Why didn't they help Grandmother and Grandfather rescue me from the New Order? So many questions and no answers.

An awkward silence hung in the air. I shifted from foot to foot in discomfort. The couple looked puzzled at my lack of response.

"She doesn't want anything to do with you!" Mother broke the silence.

The woman gave her a nasty glance.

"I think she's afraid to respond," the man stated to Mother. "It would help if you were more supportive of us getting to know our granddaughter."

"Why don't you let us take her out to get an ice cream sundae and spend a little time together? We'll bring her back in a couple of hours," the woman suggested.

"No!" Mother bellowed. "Now get out before I throw you out!"

The expression on the couple's face turned very sad.

Turning to me, "we're sorry, Josephine! We really do care and would like to get to know you better."

"Joey!" I stated, managing to find my voice.

A look of surprise registered on their faces, but they nodded.

"Joey!" They said together. "We'll be back to try again later. Okay?"

They didn't wait for an answer. The two of them walked to the door and let themselves out. I stared after them. I didn't know what to think or feel.

Here were two people that said they cared about me and wanted to spend time with me. I couldn't understand why. I was even more confused by Mother's refusal to let me go with them for a few hours. Since Mother didn't seem to like me around except to do the chores around the house.

After they were gone, I looked at Mother.

"You stay away from them!" She ordered.

"Why?" I asked boldly.

"Don't give me any of your lip! Just do what I tell you and stay away from them. They'll only cause trouble for us. Now go to your room!" She commanded.

I happily retreated to my room.

I think she means that they'll cause trouble for her if they were to find out some of the things that go on here. My mind raced with thoughts about these two new family members that entered my life.

Could they be the answer to so many prayers? Maybe...Maybe not!

The rest of the summer dragged by. There were no further visits from my new grandparents.

Did they really mean that they would try again?

I still wanted to die so badly. The pain inside felt like it would consume me. At least now that school was starting, that would be something to distract me a little and to get me out of the house.

My feet felt like lead as I walked to school. Everything seemed to be drudgery. I found my way to my first class, English. At least it was a subject that I was beginning to like. My favorite parts were reading books and creative writing because both let me escape into other worlds. I usually read war stories and westerns or wrote about them. I liked the action. I looked at my watch and noticed there were still a couple of minutes until the bell rang. I didn't want to go into the classroom immediately. I didn't need the townies or any of the remaining gang members picking on me. I moved into the shadows of a nearby door jam and practiced being invisible.

A couple of seconds before the class bell rang; I emerged from my hiding spot and entered the room. Shuffling into the room with my thumbs hooked in my pockets, I worked on looking tough and cool. It was the only way I knew to cope with this new environment. I was alone and needed to be sure that I didn't appear vulnerable. Inside, I felt more like a scared little kid.

Rumor had it that this teacher was some kind of a religious fanatic. I'd never met a fanatic before. I wondered what they are like. I wasn't sure I knew what one was, but I knew it didn't sound like a complement.

Moving toward the back of the room, I found a desk near the windows. I wanted to be as far away from everyone as I possibly could, including the teacher. Most teachers took an instant dislike to me, and I didn't like them. I think they shared stories in the Teacher's Lounge about me. I moved toward the seat that I wanted. Another kid was already sitting there, when she saw me, she got up and moved to another seat. I took the vacated seat.

As I slouched down into the seat, I put my feet up on the desk in front of me and covered my eyes with the brim of my baseball cap.

When Mrs. Smith entered the room. She stood before us and smiled. Her smile was the most genuine one I'd ever seen. Her voice was soft and kind. I think she was the first teacher that both smiled and sounded kind. The way she spoke captured my attention. I took my index finger and pushed the bill of my cap up slightly to see her face better.

Mrs. Smith was middle-aged and about five-foot, five inches tall. Her graying curly golden hair was cut short, and her eyes sparkled like Christmas bulbs reflecting the light of a fire.

I've never seen anyone's eyes sparkle. How did she do that?

I shifted uncomfortably in my seat.

It's an act! It has to be! No one's eyes sparkle.

At least that is what I tried to convince myself to believe. While I was sitting there contemplating the mystery that was Mrs. Smith, I saw her walk toward my side of the room. She stopped in front of my desk. Seeing her so close up made me feel awkward and uncomfortable. Anxiety made my heart beat faster.

I looked around the room in desperation, but everyone was pretending to be looking straight ahead. I was afraid to make eye contact with teachers. I felt if I did they would see inside of me. Just in this short period of time, I knew she was different from anyone that I'd ever met, possibly with the exception of Rachel.

"Hello!" she spoke to me, keeping that same soft voice.

I looked up and briefly met her eyes. Genuine warmth radiated from her. It was something that I didn't understand, and it made me feel very uncomfortable.

Why is she speaking to me? Why isn't she yelling at me when she speaks like everyone else before her?

"You're one of the kids that they rescued from the New Order, aren't you?" she asked.

That was a first! No one ever bothered to ask me anything, especially that question. I wonder how she knew that. My hair is longer, and I'm not wearing the New Order uniform. I wonder what it is that lets a stranger know that I came from the New Order?

Not knowing what to do, I let myself respond in anger. I shoved my hat back so she could see my face.

"Yeah! What about it?" I blurted angrily.

I wasn't sure where she was going with the question, and I didn't want her to think that she was going to take me that easily. I'd been through too much at the hands of teachers and knew better than to trust anyone especially someone that came across as being nice this early on. I didn't want to speak to her in such a tone, but I was afraid. I didn't understand someone like her, and I couldn't let anyone see fear in me. I didn't like the way her presence made me feel inside. Wishing she'd go back to the front of the room and leave me alone, I sank lower in my seat. I felt like the center of attention.

"I'm glad you're in my class," she said with a smile.

I nearly fell out of my seat. No one had ever said that to me before.

I think she sensed my discomfort at the attention. Mrs. Smith nodded and walked back to the front of the room. She continued speaking in the same soft, gentle tone.

She's a fake!

I went to my special place in the woods. Even though it was cold being outside in the wind, it was better than being in school. I wasn't used to anyone, especially an adult, being kind and gentle. The New Order's programming replaced the memories of my grandparents' actions too completely.

Am I getting soft or something? Letting a teacher get to me that way! I must be soft in the head.

Too much experience had taught me to be suspicious, but at the same time I was a little curious. I needed to discover what made her tick, and then I could expose her as a fake.

No one smiles that much. No one can really be as genuine as she sounds. She's putting on an act and I'm going to figure out what her deal is. I'll find her weakness! I'm the best! So I should be successful.

I decided the way to proceed would be to feign compliance. Something about her reached beyond my walls of survival, and it was difficult to shake it off. Even though I told myself I would be watching Mrs. Smith to expose her, I also had a strong desire to feel accepted by her. This ambiguity puzzled me. All I knew is that I couldn't explain the longing inside of me that was awakened in her presence.

In some ways Mrs. Smith reminded me of Grandmother, but there was something that made her even more different. She was different from anyone I'd ever met. She was even gentler sounding than Rachel. I knew it might be wishful thinking, but maybe Mrs. Smith could be the one that held the key to finding some way out of to my nightmarish world?

Chapter - 30 - Emptiness Within

The majestic autumn sun rose in the eastern sky spreading its warm rays across all nature and gently caressing every creature under its touch. The morning sky was blue with small wisps of white clouds scattered about. Soon, the sun would be taking its long deserved rest for the winter, but for now it shared its warmth with the creatures below. With the rising of the sun, everything seemed at peace -- everything except me. With the dawn of a new day came a renewal of the inner turmoil and pain that was a permanent part of my young life.

Allowing my mind to focus on some of the beauty of nature helped me to escape from some of the constant internal pain.

It wasn't long before the warmth of the September sun turned into intense heat. The sun was truly making its autumn performance a good one. Indian summer was upon us with its intense sunshine beating down on my head. It made me feel a little dizzy. Perspiration dripped down my face and body, making my clothing cling to me. I needed to find some shade and take some time to understand my purpose and why I exist. I thought I knew when Chico was alive. I existed to care for him and to learn from him. Without him, what was the purpose of living? He was the only one who really needed or wanted me.

I'd been in high school for a couple of weeks now. One thing that kept me going was my intrigue with Mrs. Smith. She was so different from anyone that I'd ever met. Rachel was close, but since I've been able to spend more time with Mrs. Smith, I'd gotten to know her better. Every word that proceeded from her mouth was filled with genuine kindness. I hadn't heard her utter a cross word yet, even when some of the other students acted up. There was a radiance about her that overflowed and touched those around her. She was truly a mystery to me. In my fifteen years of life, she truly stood out from everyone else that I'd ever met.

What makes her tick? Why is she so nice to me? What makes her different?

Mrs. Smith entered the building as I was staring at the way the sunrays played through nature's painted leaves of the trees.

"Hi Joey!" She greeted me with her warm smile.

"Hi!"

She looked in the direction where my attention was focused.

"Isn't God's handiwork beautiful?" She stated in a reverential tone.

I turned toward her and saw the sparkle in her eyes.

"I'm so glad God has blessed us with such beauty and eyes to enjoy it," she said.

Her speech was always filled with references to God and His goodness. It was a lot like Grandmother and Grandfather from what little I can remember of that time when I lived with them.

"You look very sad! Is there something wrong?" she asked with sincerity.

"I miss my dog, Chico. A few months ago a car hit and killed him. On days like today, he and I would romp and play in the grass." I answered in a very low voice.

I couldn't say much more about him without inviting that painful ache into my throat.

She squeezed my shoulder and we walked down the hallway to her classroom. I guess she sensed that Chico was a painful subject.

For some reason, I found her easier to talk to than most people. Yet, I didn't want to tell her about some of the things that happened at the house. I'm sure if she knew she wouldn't like me any more. I was certain those things were in some way my fault. They took place so often, so I must be doing something wrong.

"Joey, you sound like you have an emptiness within. God is the only one that can fill it," Mrs. Smith stated.

I shrugged.

How can God love me? I'm nobody!

"What's preventing you from reaching out to God?" She asked.

The question caught me by surprise. I could not bring myself to describe all the things that haunted me from the New Order, from living with Mother and Edward, all the times that I tried to pray to God but felt that my words bounced off the ceiling. How could I explain all of those things to her? I couldn't.

Instead of answering, I just shrugged again.

Mrs. Smith gave an understanding nod. She certainly was the first person other than Rachel that wanted to spend some time with me, listening and caring, but I couldn't express the feelings that I had buried deep inside.

I sensed that she knew that I was hurting, but she didn't quite know how to help.

"What if I go visit your mother and explain to her that you need to have a professional counselor to talk to and help you through these things you've got locked up inside of you?"

"NO! That wouldn't be a good idea. Mother would be very angry with me if she even knew that I'd said anything to you. Please don't go to see her!" I begged.

"Okay! I'll respect your wishes," she sighed.

"I'm sure you miss your dog a great deal." Mrs. Smith continued. "Even though you feel bad, are you taking care of you?"

I wasn't sure what she meant so I shrugged.

"I mean that many times when people are very sad, they don't eat properly or care for themselves. Are you eating?"

I shook my head. I would make dinner for Mother and Edward and then act like I was eating in the kitchen, but stared out the window instead. The thought of food made me sick.

"You can't stop eating. I don't think Chico would want you to not take care of yourself. You need to be eating regularly so that you don't make yourself sick. You also need to be getting some exercise, and generally taking care of your day-to-day needs. That would help with some of the sad feelings," she paused to wait for a response.

The ache in my throat prevented me from saying anything. I stared at the floor. I was sure that if she looked into my eyes that she would be able to see everything inside of me.

When she realized that I wasn't going to say anything, she continued. "Would you promise me that you'll eat a little something for each meal?"

I looked up at her for a moment and saw the concern in her eyes and nodded again.

She paused to think for a few moments.

"I have just the thing for you to get some exercise. The school is starting a girls' varsity basketball team. You look athletic, I bet you would be a good player."

I looked up at her again and stared at her in disbelief.

"No one's going to want me on a basketball team here," I said flatly.

"Sure they will! You try out and see if they don't put you on the team. I think some of the bad feelings between the refugees and the other kids are fading now that both groups are getting older and perhaps becoming use to each other. I'll talk to the coach to get you signed up. Okay?"

After a few seconds, I nodded reluctantly, but I still wasn't too sure about it.

"I know that eating and getting some good exercise will help you," she said with satisfaction.

"Okay, I guess," I replied.

I wonder why she cares.

"There's a few minute before the first bell. Let me go see if I can talk to the coach."

Mrs. Smith left me alone in her room for a few minutes. I was glad for the time to work on stuffing the ache in my throat back behind its walls.

Nothing seemed to fill the void left by Chico's death. I still want to die so I could be with him. I missed Chico like I never thought I could miss anyone. There is such a sadness and deep ache inside that I thought it would rip me apart.

She returned just before class.

"It's all set!" She exclaimed. "You need to report to the gym immediately after school. The coach will give you instructions from there. Okay?"

That was fast!

I nodded my understanding. The bell rang and I took my seat for class to begin.

As the day passed, I had a difficult time concentrating on my subjects.

I can't believe I agreed to try out for the basketball team. This would put me in front of the entire school body.

By the time the last bell of the day rang, my stomach was tied in knots. My hands were clammy with sweat by the time I arrived at the gym.

The coach spotted me and waved me over to the group of girls standing around him. He took us into the locker room and assigned us each a locker and passed out our practice uniforms.

"We'll be practicing everyday after school for ninety minutes, except on game days." He announced.

All of the girls shook their heads with understanding.

"Okay! Run ten laps around the gym and we'll call it a day."

He blew his whistle and we began running.

This was a lot different than running in the fields. I'd never worried about pacing myself before. After the third or fourth lap, I was tired. My shins were hurting from running on the hard floor. Soon I was bringing up the rear of the pack. Before we were finished, the other girls had passed me. I left when they did even though I was only on lap eight. My lungs felt like they were going to explode.

This is going to take some getting use to!

The rest of the team headed for the locker room to take a shower. I decided to leave instead. The cool fall air felt good as I stepped outside of the stuffy gymnasium.

I still had a little time before Mother would be expecting me. So, I headed for my secret place.

At least my secret place was still close enough for me to go to from the new house. I was able to find a safe route to the tight cluster of trees that Chico and I used to go to for solitude after one of our runs. Somehow by coming here, I hoped I could feel closer to him, and maybe not miss him so much. It made me sick to think of him in that plastic garbage bag somewhere at the bottom of the canal.

I still could kill Edward for doing that to my best friend! I truly believe he left Chico unleashed so he would be hit by a car and no one would need to care for him. It was a way for them to get rid of Chico, and probably punish me for fighting his advances. Perhaps to punish me for some misdeed they dreamed up.

I wiggled in between the trees. It was a little tight, I guess because I was growing up that it fit in to the small opening. As soon as I was inside my safe place, I stretched out on the grass. The soft grass felt good to my tired body after that workout with the basketball team.

I stared up at the blue sky lying back in the soft grass.

"Why?" I muttered out loud. "Why did you have to take him? Haven't I suffered enough down here without losing the dearest thing to me? What do I have left? You could have let me die too. I don't think I can go on without him."

I don't know if I was praying or just rambling. My brain was too exhausted to think. Every part of me screamed for some rest. Despite all of my weariness, I fought against sleep. I didn't want the monsters of my nightmares to visit me here. Despite my attempts, however fatigue over took me, and my eyes closed for a brief moment. My mind started playing the familiar nightmare track.

The crack of a stick in the distance brought me immediately to consciousness.

Who can it be? Is it Jesse? No one knows about this place except for me. Maybe it's just an animal.

The hair on the back of my neck prickled. I tried to think of all the things it could be, without letting my imagination get out of control.

Something isn't right. What's out there?

I peeked through the small opening. I swiveled around looking out of each of the openings. I peered into the shadows straining to see the source of the noise.

I listened and hoped that I could get some bearing on the direction of the sound, but there was only silence. Every muscle was tensed with anticipation.

As I watched my mind, my mind wandered onto other things. There was no question that I was angry with God for taking away everyone that I even thought remotely cared about me: my grandparents, Rachel, and now Chico, and possibly my new grandparents. Perhaps this God was a very selfish being. He left me alone to face trauma after trauma while taking away everyone that could help me through them, but then there was Mrs. Smith. Where did she fit into all of this? I might not know a lot about the way things are here, but I had discovered that it shouldn't hurt to be a child. I look around at the other kids, and they don't seem to be suffering or in pain.

Another sharp cracking noise stopped my thoughts. I stared through the openings of my hiding place once again. Not more than ten feet from me stood the most beautiful deer that I'd ever seen. I to watched the deer. He was beautiful. His antlers were large and sharp.

Definitely not one to tangle with.

His light brown fur reminded me of Chico's. Suddenly, my mind went back to that day, and I watched Chico die in my arms again. While my mind replayed Chico's death, the deer scampered off deeper into the woods. I was sad to see him go.

That was the first deer I'd seen here. I wonder why it came now.

It was time to start for home. After squeezing out of my hiding place, I headed for the house. I was glad my classes ended early. It gave me more time to spend time to be away from the house and the horrors that were all around me there.

I looked back at the spot where the deer disappeared and wished I could be free like him.

Chapter - 31 - Unsweet Sixteen

Time moved on.
It's hard to believe that today is my sixteenth birthday.

I had heard some of the other students refer to this special land-mark as 'sweet sixteen' that sounded like it might be something nice. I wonder what made it sweet.

I should have known better than to allow myself to buy into the idea that anything could be sweet for me. The one thing that I was looking forward to the most was getting my driver's license. It would be the end of the rides of terror. I couldn't wait to get my license.

Unfortunately, my birthday fell on a Saturday this year. My learner's permit expired today so I couldn't legally drive until I went to the license place on Monday. I didn't have the escape that school provided. I hoped against all hope that something would make this day special.

"Josephine!" Mother summoned me from the other end of the house.

Much to my surprise, instead of being perched in her chair, she had her coat on and was headed out the door with Edward at her heels. It was early for them to be up and about.

"We'll be back around three, then we can have cake and ice cream to celebrate your birthday." Mother spoke in a soft tone. I don't think I can remember her ever speaking to me in such a nice way.

"Okay!" I replied, allowing a bit of a smile to cross my face.

She is actually going to have something special for my birthday! This is a first! Does she look at the sixteenth birthday as special too?

Maybe I shouldn't get my hopes up too much, since she's never told me the truth in all of the years that I've known her. Yet, I can't help myself. Her gentle manner was infectious.

"We're going out shopping for a few hours. We'll pick up a birthday cake and some ice cream on our way home then we'll celebrate. What kind of cake would you like?" Mother asked.

I can't believe it! She is actually carrying on a conversation with me. Have I reached an age when I finally mattered to her?

"Chocolate with vanilla icing," I answered.

If she noticed the shock on my face, she didn't say anything.

"What kind of ice cream?"

"Okay!" She said.

"I think vanilla would go good with it," I replied. "Maybe we could invite Grandma and Grandpa Menkin to join us?"

Her face darkened. "No! That would not be a good idea!"

I followed them to the door and stepped out onto the porch. The got into the car and Edward backed the old Falcon out of the driveway. I watched it bump its way down the little dirt road that led to the main highway, and then it disappeared.

I breathed a sigh of relief. With them out shopping, I would have most of the day to myself without being summoned at every whim. That alone made the day a special.

My thoughts wandered to Grandma and Grandpa Menkin. I wonder why Mother doesn't want me to get to know her parents. Each time they try to visit, Mother is meaner to them than she is to me. That was very confusing to me. I quickly shook the puzzling thoughts out of my head so they wouldn't ruin my special day.

I enjoyed watching my television programs while stretched out on the couch relaxing. The hours passed way too fast. When I looked up at the clock, it was after three o'clock. I looked out the window. There was no sight of the Falcon. The day grew later.

Why am I so stupid and naïve to believe what she said? She's never done anything for my birthday in the past. Why would she start now? And why would I even allow myself to believe that she would?

Four o'clock came and went, followed by five o'clock. The realization that they had lied to me again hit me like a punch in the stomach. At six o'clock, I slammed my fist into the door jam in frustration. The physical pain was a short-term distraction from the circumstances. Finally, I spotted the Falcon bumping down the dirt road about six thirty. I waited until they pulled into the driveway before I stepped outside.

Why did she say all those things to me before they left? Why do they do these things to me? Was this just another one of her games to torment me? Why am I so stupid to believe her?

A part of me still hoped that she did have a cake and ice cream in the car even though they were over three hours late. All questions about whether or not they were drunk were settled when Edward parked the car halfway onto the sidewalk. I walked around to Mother's side of the car.

"Where's my cake?" I asked as she opened her door.

"A cake? Why did I need to buy a cake?" Mother slurred.

Her words felt like a knife ripping through my heart. I starred at her in disappointment.

How could she forget that it was my birthday, especially after the conversation we had this morning?

They both nearly fell out of the car as they climbed out and staggered their way into the house. I followed them. Mother and Edward headed straight for their room where an argument erupted.

I ran to my room and began pounding the mattress with my fists in frustration.

One of the most important birthdays of my life and my own mother can't even remember it.

I beat the bed until I was to exhausted to lift my arm one more time. I sulked in misery staring at the shadows on the wall. I lay there fighting back any possible thought of tears. I wouldn't give Mother the satisfaction of making me cry.

"Josephine!" Mother's voice echoed.

I wiped my face in my hands in case there were any tears that escaped. I wouldn't give her the satisfaction of knowing how upset she'd made me. Mother was now in the living room sitting on her perch. Edward was still in the bedroom. I thought he might be already passed out.

"I need you to go get milk and bread for breakfast," she stated. "Here's the car keys."

I stared at her in disbelief and was speechless.

"Did you hear what I said?" She repeated in her drunken slur.

"I heard you!" I snapped. "I just can't believe what you're asking me to do. You know that I don't have a license until after I pass my driver's test on Monday. Do you want to ruin my chance to get my license?"

"You have a learner's permit," she retorted.

"Yeah, a learner's permit that is expired. Besides, that requires a licensed driver to be in the front seat with me," I explained.

"You'll do just fine. Just take back roads. No one will ever know," she said without concern.

"You're asking me to break the law. If I get caught, I'll never get my license," I complained.

"You're always so dramatic. Just take the car and go get what I told you," she insisted.

I looked towards the bedroom.

Mother guessed what I was thinking, "he's in no shape to drive. Don't even say it!" She said as if she were reading my mind. "No more arguing. Go!"

"It's against the law!" I shouted back.

"Go!" She yelled and tried to take a swing at me. I ducked in time for her to miss me.

I figured that I had no choice but to go. I was afraid to find out what she'd do if I refused, the possible consequences to me. Reluctantly, I took the keys and walked out to the car. I opened the driver's door and was slapped in the face with the overwhelming smell of booze and who knows what. I got in and quickly rolled down the windows.

Please God; don't let anything go wrong. I don't think I can survive without getting my license. I need that license; I can't deal with having to ride with drunk drivers any longer.

I put the key into the ignition and started the engine. I took a deep breath and backed out of the driveway. I swung the car around onto the dirt road. My hands gripped the wheel so hard that they began cramping. I just knew something would go wrong. As I came to a complete stop at the end of our dirt road, I patiently waited for the traffic to clear before pulling onto the main road. My heart was beating so loudly that I couldn't hear anything else. The road was clear. I pressed a little more on the gas pedal, and began the journey. I kept one eye on the speedometer to make sure I didn't go over the speed limit. Suddenly, my heart leaped into my throat. When I glanced in the rearview mirror, a police car was right behind me.

He didn't have his flashing lights or siren on, but terror gripped every fiber of my being nonetheless. I continued driving. Finally, I reached my turn to get off the main highway. From this point, I could take the back roads the rest of the way to the store. After I made the turn, I quickly looked in my mirror. The police officer continued driving straight on the highway.

I breathed a sigh of relief and continued driving. The car began making a clunking sound.

Great! That's all I need is car trouble.

The stress of driving without the proper license, the police following me, and now the car making noises made me feel as though I couldn't go any further. Much to my surprise, I realized I was on the road that led to Mrs. Smith's house. At least I think it was the right road. I'd only been to her house once.

She had a very nice house. I had no idea that people could live in such lovely houses. One day she'd driven me home from school when the weather was bad. She didn't want me walking while it was thundering and lightening out. I was afraid of Mother's reaction if she knew I'd gotten a ride home, so I asked her to stop a few blocks from our house. I figured Mother would never know.

Just hang in there! I think it is only a few more blocks to her house. I'm sure she'll help me.

Those few blocks seemed like forever. Finally, I spotted her house; at least I think it was her house. I pulled the car onto the gravel shoulder next to her garage. I turned the engine off and leaned my head on the steering wheel. I was having difficult time breathing. Mrs. Smith was outside working in her flowerbeds.

It is the right house.

Mrs. Smith looked up when she heard the car. I guess she recognized me, and noticed my head resting on the steering wheel.

"Are you okay?" she asked. Her voice was filled with concern.

I shook my head.

"What's wrong?"

I launched into my tale. The words tumbled out of my mouth so fast, I wasn't even sure she could understood what I was saying. I started with the fact that it was my birthday and how Mother had ruined it by getting drunk and making empty promises. I finished the story with Mother's requiring me to drive without a valid license and now the car was making a clunking noise.

"Don't you worry! We'll take care of this," she said assuredly as she patted my shoulder.

I looked up from the steering wheel and wondered how she was going to make everything work out.

She walked into the house and a few minutes later came out with her daughter.

"Joey, you remember my daughter, Ann?

"I nodded. We'd met the one time I visited her house.

"Ann will drive your car. You'll ride with me. We'll go to the store and get the things your mother wanted you to buy, and then we'll take you home. Okay?"

I nodded. I was unable to find my voice since that aching lump lodged itself in my throat again. A wave of relief washed over me knowing she was going to help me.

We went to the store. As I got out of the car, my legs felt like rubber. I was shaking all over as I walked around the store gathering the items Mother wanted.

After getting the things at the store, we all drove to the house. Ann followed us to the house. We all got out.

"The car didn't make any noises. Hopefully, its okay now," Ann said and handed me the keys.

"Thank you!" I said softly.

Mrs. Smith patted my shoulder again.

"I'll be okay," she said in a comforting tone.

I shrugged.

"Just remember, you did the right thing! When you do the right thing, no one can take that away from you. No matter what else may happen," she said as she got into her car. Ann got in on the passenger side.

I watched them drive away. I was so relieved she'd been home and willing to help me that I didn't even mind her touching my arm. I was afraid to go into the house for fear of Mother's reaction to Mrs. Smith being here.

I'd seen Mother sitting in her chair in front of the window as we'd driven into the yard. I knew she'd seen everything. I entered the house carrying the bread and milk.

"Who was that?" Mother demanded.

"Mrs. Smith. She's one of my teachers from school," I explained.

"Why was she driving you home?" Mother questioned accusingly.

"I was driving to the store and the car started making funny noises. I got scared so I stopped the car near her house. She offered to have her daughter drive the car. She took me to the store, and we came home." I answered.

"Why did you go to her house?" Mother continued.

"She lives on the back roads. The car started making noises and I didn't know what to do," I explained.

"I don't like people knowing our business," Mother complained. "You stay away from that woman and stop spreading tales!"

"I didn't spread any tales." I shot back. I was glad I was out of her reach and she was too drunk to come after me.

Why did Mother want me to stay away from everyone that wanted to be nice to me? She didn't want me around her own mother and father, and now Mrs. Smith. Why did she think I was telling everyone about her business?

I moved towards the kitchen to put away the milk and bread. Mother tried to push herself up from her chair and take a swing at me, but she was so drunk she fell back into the chair. After putting the groceries away, I retreated to my room. I didn't want to give her any targets to punch. There I resumed my pounding of the mattress.

I was so frustrated. I didn't understand any of Mother's suspicions, and she didn't even care that she ruined my birthday.

She doesn't care about me. She doesn't care that it's my birthday. Why doesn't she care about me? Why doesn't she want anyone else to care about me? What did I do wrong that makes her hate me so much?

Exhausted, I stopped pounding on the mattress and lay there with my face buried in the pillow. My heart ached as if it would break into a thousand pieces. A lump lodged itself in my throat. I felt so empty and so alone. The pain was even more unbearable. I wanted to die.

Chico, why can't I be with you? If I were with you, I wouldn't hurt so much.

I was startled by the sound of gravel crunching under a car's wheels and stopping in front of our house.

I rolled over and peeked out the window. Much to my surprise, I saw Mrs. Smith getting out of her car and walking towards our front door. I quickly pushed myself off the bed and ran to answer the door. I knew Mother wouldn't answer it. Besides, I didn't want Mother to be nasty to Mrs. Smith.

Opening the door, there stood Mrs. Smith holding a birthday cake.

I stared at the cake and then looked up at her.

"Why?" I worked to find my voice to say that much.

People didn't do nice things for me. Why is she being nice to me?

"I thought you could use this," she said and handed me the cake. "Happy Birthday!"

"Thank you!" The words stumbled out of my mouth. My voice wavered.

Before she left, Mrs. Smith gave me a big hug. I glanced nervously toward the house. The gesture reached beyond my inner walls, so I didn't even mind her hugging me. In fact, it was rather nice.

Her words were some of the sweetest words I'd heard in a long, long time. I think Grandmother and Grandfather probably said them to me before the days of the New Order, but I couldn't remember anymore. Why would anyone be this kind to me?

Chapter - 32 - Random Kindness

The days had grown steadily colder. As I stared out of the window, I caught sight of the first snowflakes of the year. Each one was so delicate as it daintily drifted down from the clouds. It was hard to imagine that all of those millions of snowflakes were each uniquely designed. They were here one day and gone the next. Yet, their beauty was special.

I remembered the winter days when Chico and I would play in the snow. Sometimes we'd romp around and knock each other down. Other times I'd throw snowballs into the air and he'd catch them in his mouth and eat them. It would always make me laugh.

A smile crossed my face as I remembered the fun we had together. A deep ache followed, I missed him so much.

Today was early dismissal from school for the members of the basketball team. We had a home game today. I was just too happy to be getting out of class early. At the sound of the bell, I quickly walked to the locker room and put on my uniform. I wasn't too wild about wearing shorts and a short-sleeved shirt, but I told myself that it was only for a couple of hours. It still made me very uncomfortable.

The noise of the crowd drifted back into the locker room. Several of my teammates were peeking of the door to see if any family or friends were there to watch them play. I sat on the bench and waited for the time for us to run out onto the court and warm up. I knew no one would be there to see me play. Mother wasn't even happy that I played on the team. She never explained why, even when I questioned her on several occasions. When she threatened to hit me and force me to quit the team if I didn't shut up, I stopped asking.

The buzzer sounded and we ran out onto the court while the home crowd cheered us.

"Go Joey Go!" I heard a booming voice over the noise of the crowd shout.

I stopped in my tracks. The girl behind me almost fell over me, and the ball thrown my way ended up hitting me in the chest. I looked around searching for the source of the voice.

There in the middle of the home team bleachers sat Grandma and Grandpa Menkin and Mrs. Smith. I blinked to make sure that I wasn't seeing things. When I opened my eyes, they were still there. They'd come to see me play.

No one's come to any of my games before.

I snapped out of my daze and began my warm-ups with the rest of the team. Even though I hadn't played basketball before joining the team, I managed to learn the needed skills to play on the team. The coach didn't put me on the starting team, but he did usually give me some playing time during each game.

I hope he let's me play tonight.

The whistle blew and each team went to their respective benches to huddle up for the last minute pep talk from the coach. The starters took their places for the tip off, and I took my place on the bench. Periodically, I glanced over my shoulder to see Mrs. Smith, Grandma and Grandpa. Whenever we made eye contact, they waved at me. It felt good to have people in the audience waiting to see me play.

"Benson in for 42!" The coach shouted over the din of the crowd.

He called my name! He was letting me play in front of people that were there specifically to see me play. My heart raced with excitement.

I moved to the score table to check in and waited for the buzzer to signal me into the game. It sounded, and I was on the court. The couple of minutes that I was able to play during this quarter, I ended up being fouled. The referee handed me the basketball.

"One and one!" He announced and blew his whistle.

Both teams were lined up on the key waiting for me to take my first shot. I took a deep breath and looked at the basket in front of me. My hands were sweating as I bounced the ball a couple of times.

I prepared to take my shot. I wanted to make a good show in front of my cheering section. The ball left my fingertips and sailed through the air. It hit the rim and circled it. I held my breath as I waited. At the last second, the ball tipped into the basket.

I made it!

The referee handed me the ball for my second shot.

"Hurray Joey!" I heard three voices shouting over the crowd.

The teams lined up again waiting for me to take my second shot. I swallowed hard as I looked at the basket. It looked further away this time. I threw the ball into the air. I watched it sail through the air and missed the basket. The teams jumped for the rebound. One of ours grabbed it on the rebound and made the shot. The coach buzzed someone else in for me. I walked back to the bench.

At least I made one basket.

I was put into the game a couple more times but didn't have any other opportunities to shoot the ball. The game ended with us winning. After the game, I hurried to the locker room to change. When I game out, my cheering section stood waiting for me.

They greeted me with smiles.

"Hi Joey!" Grandma Menkin said. "I'm so glad that we were able to come see you play today."

I didn't know what to say so I gave her a slight smile.

"You played a good game," Mrs. Smith stated.

I shrugged and replied, "I didn't get to play much."

"We're very proud of you!" Grandpa Menkin added, ignoring my comment.

"I gather you all have met?" I asked.

"Yes, we met your teacher right before the game." Grandma confirmed.

"Why don't we all go out for ice cream before you go home?" Grandpa suggested.

"I'd love to, but I need to be getting home to grade some papers. You three should go ahead," Mrs. Smith encouraged.

I wonder if she somehow got word to them about my game.

"I'll see you tomorrow," Mrs. Smith said. "I am very proud of you playing on the team."

She beamed as she patted me on the shoulder.

"It was nice meeting the both of you," she added.

"It's been nice meeting you as well," Grandma replied and Grandpa nodded.

Mrs. Smith walked away leaving the three of us standing near the bleachers.

Words failed to describe my feelings. I had three people in the crowd actually cheering for me.

I went with Grandma and Grandpa for ice cream, and they took me home.

"Drop me off here," I told them.

They looked back at me, and then nodded their understanding.

"We wish it could be different," Grandma said sadly.

I moved my head up and down.

"In the mean time, know that we do love you," Grandma stated matter-of-factly.

I got out of the car and watched them drive away. I felt very warm and special inside.

Chapter - 33 - The Sun Rises

High school days turned into months and the months became years. With Mrs. Smith's influence, I took more interest in my classes and became an honor student.

"I'm so proud of you, the way you've really been applying yourself," Mrs. Smith said.

I beamed inside and looked for things I could do to please her. I was starved for the praise.

I ranked fourteenth in my class of over two hundred. I couldn't believe it.

"Joey, you've come along way despite the circumstances that have hindered you most of your life," she said with a note of pride in her voice.

Graduation was nearly upon me and soon I would be free from Mother, Edward, the drunks, and the remaining townies that still hadn't gotten over the fact I was a refugee from the New Order.

Soon Mother wouldn't be able to use her constant threat of having me declared an unruly minor. I would be free from her tyranny. My life would finally be my own. Graduation would be my opportunity to escape from the never-ending nightmare I lived. I could leave all of my problems behind.

I arrived at school early as had become my habit over the years. I enjoyed getting out of the house as early as I could. It reminded me of the times Chico and I would leave for our early morning runs.

Most of the time I arrived at school before Mrs. Smith. I usually stood by the front doors and watched for her car. I enjoyed being her teacher's aide, and discovering how much I liked helping people. We'd walk together to her room, and I'd help her get ready for her morning classes.

"Hi, Joey, how are you doing?" she greeted me with her warm smile.

I shrugged. Mrs. Smith nodded. Over the years she'd gotten used to my shrugs. For me, it was easier to shrug than to try and find the right words to say. Most of the time I felt my words didn't come out right. I'd taken to writing down my thoughts, and found I had a special talent for writing. As I wrote, the words would flow onto the paper. Sometimes they'd come so fast, my hand had difficulty keeping pace. I discovered that if I wrote my thoughts and questions in a letter, it was easier to communicate with Mrs. Smith.

We entered her room and I took a seat at a table near her desk. It had been a rough night with the drunks attempting their attacks on me and Mother's beating. The drunks would do nasty things to hurt me when they couldn't get what they wanted. I think Mother was jealous of Mrs. Smith. Anytime I mentioned her name at the house, Mother snapped back with unkind remarks. Mother seemed to be jealous of everyone who befriended me. Was she afraid that I'd learn what it was like to have someone be kind to me?

Mrs. Smith moved around to her desk and began pulling papers out of her briefcase. She must have been grading them at home.

It must be rough being a teacher having to grade papers and do work at home in addition to a full day at school with thirty kids for each of the seven classes you have to teach!

I enjoyed having this time in the morning with Mrs. Smith. It usually was just the two of us, and it gave me an opportunity to have someone to talk to. Actually she'd read the letter I'd written the night before and comment on it. I was better able to explain in my notes my frustrations with Mother.

One of Mother's favorite things to do to torment me was to say I could go some place, and then she'd change her mind on a whim. At the last minute she'd make up some stupid reason that didn't make any sense, and I'd be stuck in the house with them. What made it even more frustrating was Mother forced me to pay for the privilege of being allowed out of the house, but she'd change her mind and still keep the money.

I worked hard to earn a little money. The school had a special work program that allowed kids of welfare families to work in some of the community offices. It was nice being able to work to earn a little money. I tried to save every penny that I could by putting it in a bank account. Unfortunately, Mother would go to the bank and make withdrawals on my account whenever she felt like it. Since I was a minor, the bank allowed her to do that.

As I watched Mrs. Smith, the same sincerity that exuded from her the day I met her still intrigued me. I studied her expressions as she read my latest letter. While she read, my mind wandered various subjects we'd talked about before.

Mrs. Smith looked up from the letter.

"I know things are rough for you at home, but one thing never changes and that is God loves you. He loves you more than anyone can imagine. He wants to be there with you through all of the things you face here."

I can't imagine since I am not sure anymore what it really means to be loved.

"The Bible says, 'God so loved the world, that He gave His only begotten Son that whosoever believeth on Him should not perish but have everlasting life.' Joey, this means that God loves you. It means that if you were the only person on this earth that needed to be saved, He still would have sent Jesus to die for you. That's how important you are to Him."

Me, important?

I gave a nervous chuckle.

"I'm not important to anyone."

She smiled at me with that same warm, loving smile that she gave me the first day that I had met her. Mrs. Smith didn't justify my statement of being unimportant with a response.

"Joey, let me share with you some other verses. The Bible says that we are all sinners. 'For all have sinned and come short of the glory of God.' This means that I'm a sinner. You're a sinner. We are all sinners. Do you understand that you are a sinner? Do you know that you've done things that are wrong?"

Remembering the things they had forced us to do in the New Order, I cringed. My mind shifted to the gang activities that I participated in and those that I had allowed. Add to that the stealing, lying, and other things that I did to survive. All of those things were wrong.

I guess that means that I've done things that were wrong.

"Would you agree that you're a sinner? You've done things that are wrong?" she asked again.

I nodded. A choking lump formed in my throat, and I was afraid to speak.

"Because we're all sinners, the Bible says we deserve death. We know this because the Bible says, 'For the wages of sin is death.' This means the payment for sin is death, not just physical death, but spiritual death. Eternal separation from God in a place of fire, prepared for the devil and his angels. I know you know what physical death is, but you may not understand spiritual death. Spiritual death is separation from God. That means we are separated from God forever. This paints a very dark picture of our future if God left His plan there."

I nodded to let her know I was listening.

"He didn't leave it there. The rest of that verse says, 'but the gift of God is eternal life through our Lord Jesus Christ.' God has given us a special gift and that gift is eternal life. It means we don't have to face this spiritual death that sin requires. God sent His only Son to die on the cross for our sins so that we wouldn't have to pay the price for our sin. Jesus Christ paid the price for my sin and for your sin," she continued.

I stared at my fingers in silence.

"The Bible goes on to say, 'But as many as received him, to them gave He power to become the sons of God, even to them that believe on His name.' This means that we receive Jesus Christ as one receives a gift. Has anyone ever given you a gift?"

I nodded, remembering the cake that she had brought me on my sixteenth birthday.

"Did you accept the gift or did you refuse it?"

"I took it," I mumbled to her, not quite sure why she was asking the question.

"You took it that means you accepted it. That's the same with the gift of God. You have to accept it. God gives you the choice."

She paused and looked at me. I refused to make direct eye contact with her. I knew if I did she would see inside of me.

The silence became painful. I could hear the minutes ticking by on the clock. I didn't know what to say or what she wanted me to say.

I guess she sensed that I wasn't processing all the things that she'd said.

Thankfully, the bell rang and Mrs. Smith let the conversation stop there.

Other kids poured into the room.

I was relieved that the conversation had ended. It made me feel strange inside. My throat ached and my chest felt tight.

As the day progressed, the conversation with Mrs. Smith replayed in my head. I didn't like the way it made me feel. Yet, when classes ended for the day, I returned to her room. Knowing she might continue our earlier conversation.

I'm not sure if I'm a glutton for punishment, or just hungry to be around her kindness.

I sat down in a desk and waited for the last student to leave. I continued thinking.

Her voice startled me out of my thoughts, and it seemed she had a different topic to discuss with me this afternoon.

I was relieved.

"Joey, I've been wanting to ask you if you've thought about what you're going to do after graduation. I assume, by the things you've told me, that you're not planning on living with your Mother."

I shook my head in agreement. I didn't know what I'd do or where I'd go. I just wanted out of there.

"Have you thought about going to college after you graduate?" Mrs. Smith asked. "You certainly are bright enough to make it in college. In fact, I think it would be a waste for you not to go."

I nodded, and then added, "I would love to go to college, but I'm afraid. I don't know where I'd go to college, or how to pay for it. I don't have any good clothes or other stuff for going to college."

Mrs. Smith met my eyes, which was not an easy task since I was usually too embarrassed to make eye contact with anyone.

She pulled a large envelope out of her brief case and laid it on the desk in front of me.

"I picked this up in the office. It's an application to the government for grant money. The money is designated for students like yourself who can't afford to go to college."

My eyes grew big with surprise.

Could it be true? Is there a chance that I could rise above Mother and Father's lifestyle and go to college?

I picked up the papers and held them gently as if they were gold.

"A number of our young people from church are attending a Christian college in Tennessee. You might consider going there. The school has a work program. If you could get the grant and get on their work program, you'd have enough money to pay for college," she explained. "It won't be easy working your way through college, but you'd be able to go to college. With a degree, there's no limit to what you could become."

I stared in disbelief. It all seemed so overwhelming.

Can this all be happening?

A Christian college. I was still in shock over the possibility of being able to go to college at all; not to mention a Christian one. I'd heard that they were stricter than other types of schools. Since I've grown up with so much structure from the New Order -- that still influenced every part of my life -- that I am afraid of the sudden loss of it and not knowing how to handle it.

I'd been attending church with Mrs. Smith for a couple of years. That was thanks to Mother's parents. A few days after the basketball game, they came to visit Mother again. Mother had let them come into the house this time, but she still yelled at them.

"Elizabeth, we think you should allow Joey to go to church. It's not like she's asking to go to nightclubs. It's church!" Grandma tried to reason.

"No!" Mother stated firmly.

"Elizabeth, you're not being reasonable why don't you want her going to church." Grandma continued pushing.

Mother didn't have an answer.

"If she wants to go to church, you should let her," Grandpa added.

"Why does it matter to you that she wants to go to church?" Grandma asked.

"Why are you taking her side?" Mother countered.

"It's not a matter of sides. I'm stating the facts. She would like to go to this church and there's no good reason you can give for her not to go." Grandma continued. "She could be out doing things that are a lot worse than that."

Mother didn't say anything further.

The conversation ended and Grandma had won. I would be allowed to go to Mrs. Smith's church. Mother was so angry with them for siding with me.

"You've said your piece and gotten your way, now why don't you leave?" Mother barked.

"Okay, we'll go, but on one condition. You don't take this out on your daughter after we leave." Grandpa said firmly.

After they left, I thought for sure Mother would beat me, but she didn't.

For whatever reason, Mother did follow their advice.

"Don't get the idea that you can go running to them every time you want to get your way. You can go to your church, but it will cost you. You will pay ten dollars per week for the privilege of going. Do you understand?" She announced.

I was afraid that if I said 'no', she'd refuse to let me go and all of our hard work would be useless.

"You're working. You can afford it."

"But ..." the words escaped.

She slapped me across the face.

"Now don't go running to tell your grandparents that I hit you, or you'll get much worse and you'll never go that church. Remember, I'm still your mother," she snapped.

Yes, I was working part time at the local library. I was trying to save that money so I could go to college. I would need to buy clothes, supplies, and books with that money. That didn't seem to matter to her.

The next day in school, I gave Mrs. Smith a note telling about what had happed about attending church.

"I'm glad your mother decided to let you come. I think you will meet some new friends and learn a lot about our precious Saviour. I'll pick you up and bring you home," she responded.

"How can I save for college if she keeps stealing my money?" I complained to Mrs. Smith.

"God will take care of your needs. You need to trust in Him," she replied. "I also have an idea, at least to protect the money you're putting in the bank. Why don't I go with you to another bank, co-sign the card, and keep the deposit book? That way you could deposit your check there and your mother couldn't get to the money. This way you'd be able to save some of your money. I'm afraid I can't stop the weekly charge for being allowed to go to church, but God will honor your faithfulness."

I nodded my understanding. I didn't know why she took so much time to help me and even going out of her way. She truly was different from most people I knew.

What makes her do nice things like this?

The days were clicking down. I could actually count the days until graduation. I never thought I'd make it through these years in public school, but somehow I did. I felt a wave of sadness when I thought about the rest of the gang members. They didn't make it.

My job at the library would end once I graduated. Mother refused to pay for anything. Besides, I needed something to keep me out of the house. Every moment I spent at her house, I could feel the pain seeping out through the walls and creeping as a fog to overtake me back into the darkness of the suicidal thoughts.

Graduation day finally arrived. It was a beautiful sunny day as they held our commencement services outside. Truly, the warm arms of the sun were reaching down and embracing me for a job well done. A feeling of pride welled up inside as they called my name.

"Josephine Benson," the principal called.

I walked across the platform and the principal extended his hand to shake mine.

"Congratulations!" He said and handed me my diploma.

That special piece of paper was the key to my future.

I wish Grandmother and Grandfather could be here to see it. They would truly be proud.

Mother and Edward were at the graduation. They were actually sober for once. Grandma and Grandpa Menkin were there too. Mother had relented some and allowed them to see me a few times. It felt good to be able to invite them. Father did not come to my graduation. I guess part of that was because I didn't send him an invitation.

I was amazed Mother and Edward came, but perhaps they wanted to be a part of the spotlight and play the part of the "good parents".

As part of my graduation, I was able to have an open house. Mother made me pay for it myself, but it was nice to have the people I had met at Mrs. Smith's church come over and wish me well. It was the first time that I had so many wishing me well. Many of them gave me money towards college.

Before graduation, I received a letter informing me of my acceptance at the Christian University. The school was located over seven hundred miles away. I also received notice that the government was going to give me a full grant. That was enough to pay for two-thirds of my school bill.

"Joey, you'll need to reapply for this grant every year for them to continue to pay."

"Okay!" I replied.

I also received a letter from the school accepting me on their work scholarship program. That would pay for the remainder of my tuition. It was hard to believe that everything worked out for me to go to college.

I was so overwhelmed by all of the good things that were happening.

Maybe there really is a God who cares about me!

Chapter - 34 - Step Forward

I was able to get a job working in a factory for the summer to help earn additional money to buy some of the things I would need for college. I needed almost everything since Mother hadn't used the welfare money to buy me the things she was supposed to. Working in the factory wasn't hard, though, it was a way to be out of the house. That experience taught me that I didn't want to spend my entire life working in a factory.

Whenever possible, I would stop after work at Mrs. Smith's house and spend a few minutes before I headed back to Mother. This gave me a much-needed boost to brighten my day before having to deal with Mother and Edward.

One afternoon, while I was visiting Mrs. Smith a siren for the fire department went off. Just as quickly as the siren sounded, I dropped to the floor.

… I was in the New Order's militia training. I covered my head waiting for the live shells to explode around me.

"Take cover!" I ordered my unit.

The bombs exploded, I crawled to the nearest corner and huddled there. The bombs were shaking everything and the body parts were flying through the air. I sat there shaking and hugging myself.

I didn't knew I was safe in Mrs. Smith's house.

I heard a soft a gentle voice telling me between the bombs, "it's okay," but the explosions continued.

"Get command on the radio set!" I barked an order…

When the sirens faded, my mind finally began to refocus. Mrs. Smith was speaking in her soft, gentle voice. I could finally distinguish that it was her." Joey! It's okay! You're safe!"

Drops of sweat were rolling off my forehead. I'd been terrified. An awkward silence followed while I scrambled to my feet. A wave of dizziness swept over me. Mrs. Smith reached out to steady me. I was disoriented and embarrassed.

"I'm sorry!" I apologized.

She's never going to want me to come over again after this.

"It's okay," Mrs. Smith said in her soothing tone of voice.

And somehow, I believed her.

In the middle of the summer, instead of being excited with anticipation of leaving and embarking on a new life, I was depressed. It was as bad as the times when I wanted to die. One thing that added to it all was a message I received about Bert. She decided to end her pain by jumping into the river and allowing the current to drown her. She was one of the only gang members left. Of all of them, I had been closest to her; yet, I hadn't spoken since the gang's brutal attack on me. The one member I hadn't heard anything about was Jackie. It was almost like she'd disappeared into thin air. No one seemed to know what happened to her.

Maybe she really was a spy and she returned to the New Order? Or maybe the New Order moved her to another area where the Underground was taking refugees, and she was assigned to find away to annihilate them the same way she did most of the ones in my area. I guess I'll never know. I knew I couldn't underestimate her. She might still have a grudge against me. My mind wandered back to the others.

Will I be the next to die? How can anyone live with so much pain inside? Will I be able to leave the pain here when I go to college?

The pain and depression were so overwhelming that I spent every free moment in my room lying in bed. I didn't know why I was feeling so bad inside. Everything seemed so dark, but I had so much to look forward to.

Now that school was out, I felt very alone. I couldn't see Mrs. Smith as often. I tried to stop by after work, but I couldn't go every day because Mother kept a tight watch on my schedule. I wanted to write to her, but when she would write back, Mother took my mail and read it first.

Even with the bright summer days, I felt as if the sun never came out. I sensed an enormous weight on me. It was a huge effort to get out of bed in the morning. I had trouble making myself eat, and I couldn't fall asleep. When I did sleep, nightmares invaded my dreams. I thought about stealing some of Mother's booze to try and dull the pain, but I decided that was merely a short-term escape. I couldn't focus enough to read or watch television. I would just lie in bed with the covers over my head and pray I would die.

I was surprised that I felt so bad knowing that I only had a couple of months until I would be free. Maybe it was hearing about Bert that scared me into a tailspin. Maybe I was afraid to look forward to going to college too much for fear that it wouldn't happen. Maybe I was afraid that something would go wrong, and I'd be stuck here forever.

I hated myself and feared that I would forever feel this way. I didn't have to kill myself with pills or a knife; the life I was living was a slow suicide. It seemed the harder I tried to pull myself out of the depression the farther I slipped into it. It was like quicksand. I was thinking about suicide almost constantly. I had slipped into Mother's room once and found her Valium, but when it came time to swallow the pills, I couldn't do it. Ironically, I was too afraid of dying.

I managed to bury the emptiness deep enough in order to attempt a normal life. When the pain would come to the surface, I would push it back down again. I could handle physical pain any day; it was the emotional pain that was so unbearable. That pain that felt like it went to the depths of my soul. There was no escape. I felt trapped in my own body.

I couldn't help but think about all of the kids in the New Order Militia like Charlie and Bobby that I knew didn't make it. Even if they escaped physically, they couldn't escape mentally. Eventually, they couldn't deal with the pain any longer and ended their lives. There was Terry. And Alex. And now Bert.

I could have continued the list, but forced my mind away from it.

I'm incompetent! I'm bad! I'm a failure! I've let people down! I've done horrible things!

There were questions too.

What is wrong with me? Where is my life heading? What am I going to do with myself? What does all this mean? Why would they even want me at that college?

There was always one answer that kept repeating itself.

I don't know.

I would have given anything to free myself from the dark world that I'd been living in. My outward circumstances were scheduled to change in just a few weeks, but I was afraid to allow myself to hope. Somehow, I felt as though something would happen, and I wouldn't be allowed to go.

The inward desolation, the emptiness, the programming, and brainwashing would all have their final triumph. No one ever won this battle. No one escaped. We were all on a death sentence. It was just a matter of time until it was carried out.

I don't like to remember the events, because I'm too ashamed. Each memory lowers my head to my chest in shame. I feel worthless and ugly. I beg of myself reasons why I didn't resist more. Even when I know that I was helpless and unable to stop the gradual debasement of my soul, I long to believe I didn't succumb.

How do you miss something you've never had? Can I grieve a loss of something I don't even know what it's like to have? There's a pain that wells deep within that aches and hurts so deeply. The pain is all too real and it never seems to leave.

Will I ever be anything more than damaged property? I need to know! I need to be strong! I need to hang on! I need to try to make it to college!

Chapter - 35 - Echoes of Darkness

The summer sun heated the days until the air became stifling. Every leaf stood perfectly still in the breezeless day. The only noises to be heard were the buzzing of the fans coming from the living room. Mother refused to allow me to have a fan in my room. She said it took too much electricity. Sweat poured down my entire body making me feel even worse.

"If you'd wear something besides jeans and a long-sleeved shirt, you'd feel cooler," Mother ridiculed.

"They have nothing to do with whether or not air is stirring or not." I retorted.

I retreated to my room to prevent further argument and a possible blow from her.

Depression continued to be my companion. Maybe if I could just go to college now, I could lose this dark shadow.

I gave up on trying to take a nap. I attempted reading some of the books Mrs. Smith loaned me. My brain was so foggy that I couldn't concentrate and found myself re-reading the same words repeatedly. I threw the book on the floor in frustration.

Sitting cross-legged on the bed, I rested my chin in my hands and stared. The shadows were beginning to grow longer. Maybe a breeze will visit after the sun goes to sleep. Images from the New Order and from the gang flashed through my brain like a slide show.

Am I losing my mind?

Secretly, I tucked away into the far corners of my mind a hope that everything would be new once I leave here. Things would be different; all of the darkness and torment would stay behind. That thought was only thing that spurred me to keep on going day after day. Yet, I was afraid to allow hope to grow too much since I'd been disappointed far too many times.

Dinner passed and I returned to the solitude of my room. Eventually, I heard Mother and Edward go to bed. I continued to sit in the middle of the bed and stare at the darkness.

Still sitting there in the early morning hours, I decided to skip work for the day. I just couldn't muster the energy to pretend that all was well and put in a day at work in that hot factory. Yet, I couldn't stay home. Mother would have too many questions about why I didn't go to work. Not to mention she would find some additional chores for me to do. I needed a distraction. An idea popped in my mind. I remembered Grandma and Grandpa Menkin didn't live too far from us. Maybe I could go visit them. I knew if Mother found out, she'd beat me.

As the sun yawned in the morning sky, I readied myself for work. I left the house at my regular time and began walking the few blocks to the nearby pay phone. We didn't have a phone since Mother never paid the bill for it.

Fishing the appropriate coins out of my pocket, I put them in the phone. Grandma had slipped me her phone number to me one day when she visited. Dialing the number, I waited as the phone rang. I hoped I wasn't calling too early. My hands were sweaty as I gripped the receiver waiting for someone to answer. I wasn't sure what Grandma or Grandpa would think of this unexpected request to visit. Finally, someone answered the phone.

"Hello!" Grandma's familiar voice answered.

"Hi, Grandma!"

"Hi, Joey," she replied with a smile in her voice. "What can I do for you?"

She didn't sound sleepy.

"I hope I didn't wake you," I said apologetically.

"No, we've been up since dawn," she said sweetly.

"I don't feel much like going to work today. Would it be okay if I come to visit you?" I stated without explanation.

"Why certainly!" she answered without hesitation. "I gather your mother doesn't know you're coming?"

"If she knew I were even calling you, things would not be too well for me," I replied. "It will take me a couple of hours to walk there, so I'll see you then."

"Nonsense! You don't need to walk. We'll come pick you up in town," Grandma insisted.

"I don't want to be a bother," I replied.

"It's no bother. We'll be there in about thirty minutes," Grandma announced.

"Are you sure?" I asked skeptically. "I really don't want to be a bother or anything."

"Joey, you are not a bother. Besides, we've missed most of your growing up, I'm excited that you want to come and visit with us. We want to spend every minute we possibly can with you. We'll pick you up," she said.

"Are you sure its not a bother?" I asked again.

"Joey!" she said in a firm tone.

"Okay! But I don't want to wait in town. I'll start walking from here and meet you on the way," I offered.

I am afraid of being alone on the streets of town. I'm never sure who might still be around looking for me. There is still a number of threats, like Jesse. Perhaps after the death of the Major, he decided to give up the chase since there would be no one to give him any special rewards for bringing me back as a trophy. But, I can't assume anything.

"Okay! We'll see you soon!" she said. The phone went silent.

I hung up the phone, stuffed my hands into my pockets, and began walking.

I had to walk through the streets of town to meet Grandma and Grandpa. I looked around at the flashing neon signs on the stores around me. They advertise cures for everything from being a financial success to losing weight, even to telling the future.

Too bad they couldn't offer a light for the darkness and pain inside. But there is no flashing light advertising an end or cure for this nightmarish darkness and pain that engulfs my world.

291

As I looked around at the few people beginning to stir, I wondered what thoughts they were thinking. They were walking and talking, but it was as if they were not speaking at all or as if I'd become deaf. I couldn't understand the voices of their world. I still felt as though I were from a different planet. I truly prayed that when I arrived in college, things would be completely different. I hoped it would really be the wonderful place that Mrs. Smith and some of the others at the church described.

What language must I speak to make people listen and understand me? What words must I say to let them know that I am locked in a prison of social darkness? What must I do to get them to build bridges from their side, so we can meet half way? Are there others like me? What will it take to make them shed their prejudice and accept people that were not exactly the same as them? I don't know the answers to those questions. I'm not sure if it will ever happen. It is as if no one can disturb the darkness that has become my world.

I remember Rachel's words that she spoke to me years ago. "The bad memories won't stop until you give each one of them the attention that the little girl of you inside is demanding that they receive. You have kept them stuffed inside of you too long, and you need to free them from their compartments. Instead of fighting the memories, why not try to give them attention? Take them out and look at them. Write about them if necessary. I know it is painful, but the child inside you was not able to feel the pain when they occurred, and now she's searching for a way to release her pain. That's the only way you can become emotionally healthy. These memories will not stop until you give them your attention. I know this from my own experience. Joey will be tormented until you deal with them the correct away. Keep in mind that little child inside is still YOU! You need to stop and allow yourself to think about the memory, allow yourself to FEEL what you should have felt as a child. Don't push the memories from your conscious mind. Don't get angry with them. From what I've seen, when you begin to have a flashback or a memory, you try to stop it or push it back, but you can't keep doing that forever. God loves you! Let God into your life, and He will help you through all of this, if you let Him," she would say.

Rachel's words repeated, "You must be willing to start the journey and find your own unique way through it. You must be willing to hurt, cry, endure, and forgive. Forgive those that hurt you. Forgiveness is only possible through God's grace. You have to be willing to ask Him to show you the way to forgiveness - and He will, but it will be through your journey. This journey is a procession. It doesn't happen all at once. Remember, you don't have to take this journey alone. God will provide others to help you along the way. These people will travel with you through various parts of it. Above all, God will be with you. Of course you're going to fall and have set backs, but remember you're HUMAN! Humans need relationships. Those militia people were brainwashing us into animals. You were able to keep your humanity and you're going to WIN!"

It is so hard to believe her words.

God, I wish the wounds weren't so deep. I didn't know that when all of those people hurt me that my life was shattered into so many pieces. I hoped the pain wouldn't last this long. Why, God? When I felt it at first, I thought I was strong enough to make it stop. I hoped that being away from the New Order would make the nightmares stop. Instead, I keep stepping forward into more pain. Why can't I be healed from these things now? Why is there more suffering? How do I pick up the pieces and keep going? God are you listening to me?

Before long, Grandma and Grandpa pulled up along side of me. Grandma got out of the car and let me get into the front seat. She knew that I get car sick in the back seat, so she was willing to switch so I could ride comfortably.

Mother would never do that for me. Why was she so much kinder than Mother?

"I'm so glad that you called us," Grandma said. "We're looking forward to spending the day with you."

I nodded politely. We rode the rest of the way in silence. I stared out the window at the passing scenery. Arriving at their house, we exited the car and went inside. Their house was so much nicer than Mother's. Entering the house, I was afraid to sit on the furniture for fear that it was only for show.

"Sit down, make yourself comfortable!" Grandma encouraged.

I wasn't sure what it meant to make yourself comfortable at someone's house, but I did sit down in a big overstuffed chair.

They sat down on the couch across from me.

"Do you want anything to eat or drink?" Grandma offered.

I don't know if she noticed the surprised look on my face, if she did, she didn't say anything. She sure wasn't anything like Mother!

"We are so sorry that we haven't been a part of your life until now. Your mother refused to let us," Grandma started to explain. "She's extremely jealous of sharing you with anyone. You've probably realized that by now. I think she's afraid that if you form a relationship with anyone that you might tell them her secrets, and she's afraid of that."

I looked at her in surprise and amazement.

How did they know what went on at the house? How much did they know?

"Yes, we know that there are things going on there that you can't talk about. I wish we could have done something, but we never had any proof. We even offered to have you come live with us after your Grandmother and Grandfather Benson died, but your mother would have nothing to do with the idea," she continued. "Even your father fought us on it. We didn't understand why they were so against it when they had left you with your father's parents."

I couldn't believe the things that she was telling me. They had actually wanted me from the very beginning.

Someone really wanted me?

If Mother had allowed me to live here, all of the other horrific things wouldn't have happened. I wonder why Mother wouldn't let me come? It wasn't any secret that she never wanted me.

They talked a little more about their desires to have a relationship with me. It was obvious that they didn't know what they had done wrong as parents to have Mother end up being so cruel. While they talked about Mother and their desires to have me live with them, I remained silent. I really didn't know what to say to them.

"Well, enough of that! Let's enjoy the time we have together," Grandma changed the subject.

The remainder of our time together was spent talking about college and the things that I liked to do. They were trying very hard to get me to talk to them.

I didn't know how to explain the good feeling that I had just knowing that they had wanted me during those teenage years after the escape from the New Order.

I wonder what things would've been like? That's a question that probably could never be answered. One thing for sure, I probably wouldn't have had to fight off Father, Edward, and the other drunks; nor would I have been treated like a slave and beaten by Mother at every whim. Who knows, I might not have needed to be a part of the gang.

Time flew. Before I knew it, it was lunchtime.

Grandma fixed sandwiches for us. We had a peaceful lunch together sitting at a real table. Mother's kitchen table was loaded with junk. It felt funny not having to fix the meal and wait on them. I didn't even need to worry about a fight breaking out and making a run for the bedroom and diving under the bed in order to finish eating out of the line of fire.

"Would you like to go anywhere or do anything special? We could go see a movie or something," Grandpa suggested.

I shook my head. It was nice being able to relax and not feel that the threat of an attack by Edward or one of the drunks or a beating by Mother.

"I'd rather just stay here and relax," I said.

They nodded their understanding.

The afternoon, we watched the boats go by from their sun porch. It was a nice respite for me from all that was going on inside, from the nightmares, the pain, and all of the things that tormented me. The water was so blue and peaceful.

Grandma and Grandpa Menkin are very nice people. I wonder how Mother turned out so opposite from them.

As quitting time at the factory approached, I knew I would need to be leaving soon. It was sad to see the day come to an end. I wished it could go on indefinitely. They drove me back to a spot near the house, and I walked the rest of the way.

"We'll try to be available for you as much as we possibly can," Grandpa said.

"Call us any time day or night," Grandma instructed. "We'll be here as soon as we can whenever you need us."

"We're so proud of you! You've overcome so much and now you're going to college." Grandpa said as they prepared to drive away.

Her parting words made me smile inside. It was a bright spot that I was able to hang onto as I returned to my world of darkness.

Chapter - 36 - Wanted, One Childhood

One adult wishes to acquire childhood experiences. The childhood must include toys and a demonstration of how to use such items. Also, this childhood must include time to play, to pretend, and to explore with the innocence of a child without fear of condemnation. This childhood must include at least one warm, loving parent who is not afraid to show affection.

Childhood also must include being held and comforted not only when there is a hurt, but also simply because they are loved. This adult wishes to acquire childhood as soon as possible. Those who are able to supply such a childhood, please make contact as quickly as possible.

I wrote this ad one day while I was on my lunch break at the factory. I was watching a group of children playing together. I wished it could be as easy as running a want ad to acquire the loss of a childhood. What would the reader think? Would they think that the author was crazy or that perhaps it was a joke? After all, everyone has a childhood, don't they? Besides no one advertises for a childhood. I guess most people don't realize, how much is lost when a child grows up in the shadow of abuse and fear. As I thought about going to college soon, I realized how much of my life had pieces missing. I felt as though I was missing something very vital. It was a loss that could never be retrieved.

How will I be able to relate to the other students lacking such an important part of my life?

Turmoil and pain stirred within me as I looked around at the playing children. I could see the sparkle in the eyes of the little boys and girls as they ran into the arms of their loving parents at the end of playtime. As I watched, the deep ache inside grew more intense, but I quickly shoved it down deeper. This was not the time or place to deal with this. There was nothing else to do, but to ignore these feelings with hopes of being protected from them. I hope God really does hear me when I pray.

God, I stand before you as one in deep sorrow and grief, my innocence was stolen, my trust was betrayed, and my sexuality confused. I'm in deep pain because of a childhood that gave no opportunity to explore, no sense of awe and wonder, and no sweet curiosity. My teen years have had no gradual unfolding, no tender discovering, no choices of whom I will love, and no knowledge of how to love appropriately. I'm sad because of an adulthood obtained through trauma and pain, from loss and neglect. I continue to suffer long past the days of the infliction. Will college be what brings it all to an end? God, when will the pain end?

Chapter - 37 - New Life?

The hot August sun beat down on its subjects without mercy. It was especially hot in the old sedan Mother and Edward were taking me to college in. I'd been surprised they planned to take me. I thought I'd have to take a bus or something. Maybe she was afraid that if she didn't, Mrs. Smith or her parents would and then she'd look bad. Edward enlisted the help of his brother and his brother's girlfriend to take us. Nothing like being stuffed in a sardine can in the hottest part of summer heading south.

I carried the last of the suitcases out to the trunk of the car. The day had finally arrived. I was on my way to college. The seeds of excitement were germinating inside of me. Yet, I was afraid to show too much enthusiasm. I didn't want to face Mother's wrath, not on this very special day.

"What are you doing, taking everything you own?" Mother demanded.

"I don't know what I will need when I'm there," I replied.

The reality is that I don't want to leave anything for her to sell for booze. Besides, I don't have that many belongings.

I'm almost there. I don't ever have to put up with any of her abuse again. I can be my own person. I will now make the choices that will affect which way my life's path will follow.

The car was finally loaded. The five of us piled into the small car, and we were on our way. I sat sandwiched between Edward and his brother's girlfriend in the back seat. Between the heat, being stuffed in the back seat feeling ill, I was in a very foul mood and sick.

Mother kept up a constant monologue of complaints during every mile we traveled. I was relieved when we stopped for the night. It felt good to stretch my legs and breath fresh air. Since most of the three hundred and fifty miles, I had to balance my feet on the hump in the middle of the back seat.

We spent the night in a motel. The room only had one bed so I had to sleep on a roll away cot they brought to the room. It was lumpy and very uncomfortable. Between the lumpiness of the cot and the fear of being in the same room with Edward, I didn't sleep much.

The morning light was a welcomed sight. It took Mother forever to get ready. I anxiously paced outside of the room. I wanted to be on our way. Finally, she was ready to go, and we were back on the road. The car ride was a repeat of yesterday.

After seven hundred miles of driving, and listening to Mother complain during every one of them, we pulled into the place that would be my new home. It took us two days to drive the distance, but we were finally here. The car stopped at my assigned dorm. One of the girls let us in. Edward actually did carry my things into the dorm room.

After we unpacked the car, they drove me to the center of campus and dropped me off. I was now standing on the sidewalks of a college. Mother and Edward had left me there without so much as a "take care of yourself". Maybe in some ways that was better. It would have been out of character for them to do more than that.

Now that I was here I finally allowed myself to breathe. The anxiety slowly gave way to guarded relief as the realization that I had made it registered in my brain. I was here! I was going to college!

Me, of all people!

It had been a long hard struggle to get this far. It had taken all of the courage that I could muster and a lot of hard work. I was standing on the walkways of a real college campus. Something that neither of my parents had done, Mother hadn't even finished high school.

I imagine that Grandmother and Grandfather would be very proud of this moment. Grandma and Grandpa Menkin told me they were proud of me for making it to college. Those are words that I haven't heard much in my life. They are nice words, 'I'm proud of you!'

Walking along the sidewalk, I breathed the fresh air of freedom. It smelled sweet. I began exploring the campus and locating the important places, like the dining hall, the student center, and the laundry. Though it didn't look like the college campuses that I'd seen pictures of, it still was the most beautiful place I'd ever seen.

The girl that let us into the dorm told me that I needed to go to the Dean of Women's Office and fill out some type of paperwork and get a key to the dorm. She gave me directions. I found the office without difficulty.

So far, so good!

As I entered the office, I met the Assistant Dean of Women.

"Hi!" I said as I entered the office. "I'm a new student."

The woman behind the desk looked up from her papers. She appeared to be in her twenties, with long-blonde hair that was curled in the front. Her green eyes were cold and very expression.

The sight of her struck fear in my heart, and I wasn't sure why. I blinked in surprise. She certainly didn't seem friendly, and not at all like any of the Christian people I'd met back home. I tried not to show how afraid I'd become. I maintained eye contact with her. I didn't want her to think I was intimidated even though I was.

"You are inappropriately dressed for being out on campus," she informed me.

"I'm sorry! I didn't know!" I gulped.

I hope this mistake doesn't mean that she's going to send me home!

I choked back the threat of tears. Somehow I didn't think that would make things any better. I certainly wasn't starting off on the right foot.

"Don't let it happen again!" she said sternly. "Fill out these papers! You'll be sharing a room with two other girls, and an additional four in the upstairs of the house dorm."

I nodded my understanding.

"Here's a booklet explaining the Code of Conduct on campus. You're expected to read it. You will be tested on it during Orientation. Here this is a schedule of the dining hall hours. Do you know where your dorm is located?"

"Yes!" I replied.

"Here's the key, if you lose it, there's a $5.00 replacement fee," she informed me.

"Okay!"

"Good! Welcome to College!" Her voice didn't reflect the meaning of the words.

"Thank you!" I said as I turned and exited the office.

Walking back to my dorm, there were a few other students milling around campus now. I noticed that at least most of my clothes were similar, so at least I'd fit in that way. Mrs. Smith had helped me pick out some of them. I didn't think that any of them had heard of the New Order. So, perhaps I would be free from that stigma as well. I returned to my dorm room. Entering the room, I was greeted by my new roommates.

"Hi, I'm Sally!" One of the girls introduced herself. She was tall with shoulder length blonde hair. Sally had taken the top bunk. It appeared she had unpacked her things and was relaxing and reading a book on her bed.

It looked like the Code of Conduct booklet like I'd just received.

"I'm Gina!" the second girl announced. She was shorter, maybe five foot tall with short black hair and thick glasses. She was on the chubby side and when she smiled, she closed her eyes for some reason. Gina was moving around the room putting things away.

When we'd been here to drop off my few things, I had staked out the single bed for myself. I wasn't sure how I'd feel sleeping on a top bunk or even a lower bunk with someone above me. I thought that it might set me up for nightmares and that certainly wouldn't make a very good impression on my roommates.

Both girls seemed nice enough. This would be a learning experience in itself since I'd never had to share a room with anyone before. Even in the New Order, we had cubby like areas that we didn't share.

"Are you on work scholarship too? Sally asked me.

"Yeah!" I replied. "Where are you working?"

"Dining hall!"

"Same here!" I replied. At least I'd have someone that I knew working there. "Any idea what we'll be doing?"

"I heard that we have to wait on twenty students each meal. We set the tables, serve the meals, and clean up afterwards. We go to classes around the meals," Sally said knowingly.

I nodded.

"Are you both freshmen?" I asked.

They nodded.

I guess that means we will all be learning together.

The three of us sat on our beds and talked about where we were from and what we planned to major in.

As time went on, I learned the three typical questions that every college student asks when you meet them are: What's your name? Where are you from? What are you planning on majoring in?

To my surprise, all three of us were majoring in Education. Sally and Gina were interested in Elementary Education, while I was more interested in Secondary Education. I didn't think I would be very good with little kids.

We shared a little about ourselves. The questions directed to me, I answered as vaguely as possible.

Sally was from the Midwest, same as me. Gina was from the South. Listening to her talk, there was no question about that.

I got the impression that Sally came from a rough life too. She didn't go into much detail, but she did say that she lived with foster parents prior to coming to college. I wasn't sure what foster parents were, but I'd look it up next chance I had.

Gina, on the other hand, seemed to have a life that was much more pampered. When I first returned to the dorm, her mother was there making her bed and helping her unpack. I noticed in my walking about the other dorms that this seemed to be more the norm than not. Many parents stayed with their sons and daughters to help them get settled before leaving. When they did leave, there were often tearful goodbyes before the parents finally left. Watching such scenes left me feeling a little empty inside. I didn't see any one else being left on the curbside while their parents drove away without so much as a look backwards.

Why did I have to miss out on all these things?

I unpacked my clothes into the dresser drawers that were designated as mine, and put away the few other things that I'd brought.

God, please let everything go well here. I finally escaped the horrific home life. Please let me make Grandmother and Grandfather as well as Grandma and Grandpa Menkin proud of me.

Chapter - 38 - New Hope?

W hen I left for college, I truly believed that moving seven hundred miles away would leave all of my problems behind me. It wasn't very long before I discovered that the problems followed me. I could never escape myself. I realized that though the external circumstances changed, you couldn't escape your true self. Maybe its the little child within that Rachel told me about. She's the one searching for peace and freedom from all the emotional baggage.

One thing a new location did do was generate a new hope within. That prospect did give me a spring in my step, a smile on my face and a pseudo-joy. Unfortunately, I couldn't hold onto the newness of being here. Soon the daily activities pushed me into a regular routine and the newness wore off. The inner pain came surging back dragging its companion, depression, with it.

I am here! I am a college student. Why isn't that enough?

Sometimes I did manage to rekindle some of the excitement; then I would need to need to pinch myself to be sure that it wasn't all a dream.

College life was filled with new experiences. Sharing a room with two other girls was one of the first things. They each had different habits from me. I liked to listen to music before going to bed, Sally liked to read, and Gina liked to stay up late. Gina's habit was difficult for Sally and I, since we had to get up early to serve breakfast each morning. As I observed my roommates, I realized there were so many things that I still didn't know or understand. There were things about living in society and about being a girl that I didn't. Things like how often to bathe; how many times you could wear clothes before they needed to be washed; washing out pantyhose on a daily basis, and so many other things. There were so many unanswered questions. I wasn't sure how to find the answers. One thing I did discover was that my ignorance was not going to be tolerated for very long.

God, I just want people who will love me for myself!

God, I want to know who I am and know that I am worth something!

The girls all seemed confidant about who they were and a sense of self-worth, something I longed for every day.

Not to mention they knew and mastered those day-to-day activities associated with normal society. More than once, one of my roommates became short tempered with me for not following proper hygiene. I didn't know how often one was to shower or wash their clothes. Mother was always so concerned about me using too much water, and then there was the fear of Edward. Unfortunately, the girls did not understand, nor could I explain my ignorance. They thought I was being lazy and hard to get along with, so they reported me to the Dean of Women.

The Dean sent me a message to come to her office. I arrived at the Dean's office and was immediately ushered in. She motioned me to a chair and I sat down. She was a woman in her forties with short dark hair. Her expression was sterner than her Assistant's. Neither of them acted like the Christians I knew from Mrs. Smith's church. I was scared.

God, please don't let them kick me out!

"There have been complaints about you," she began immediately.

She listed the complaints and I felt my face flush with embarrassment. The things she was talking about were ones that were very personal and I'd never had anyone even mention them to me.

"These things need to be taken care of immediately. You may go," she said dismissively.

She gave me no opportunity to explain. There was no discussion or instruction about how to fix the situation; only that I needed to remedy it. Leaving her office, I became very upset and frustrated. I didn't have a clue as to where to begin. I didn't have the money to wash clothes more than once a month.

I thought Christians were understanding and accepting people

I suddenly felt very much alone and very disappointed. So far, these people seemed as prejudice as the townspeople had been. Where is the kindness, the love, and concern I'd come to expect from Christians. Why weren't they caring like Mrs. Smith?

Returning to my dorm, I went directly to my room and lay on the bed facing the wall and hugging my bunny. I felt very depressed. My thoughts drifted back to the things that I'd survived to be here.

Basically, my entire life has been consumed in search for acceptance. I had tasted it with my friendship with Mrs. Smith. My expectations were that coming to a Christian College would give me a feast of acceptance, and they would patiently teach me the things that I didn't know. Weren't Christians supposed to be known for their love?

From the very beginning, I have felt that I had to perform special acts or conform to a list of rules to be -- at the very least -- approved of. Acceptance was always conditional, and I never seemed to meet the conditions at home or any place else. Mrs. Smith and Rachel were the only ones to show me any acceptance, but I still felt that I needed to protect my inner self from possible contact. I didn't want to be hurt any more. I didn't know how to trust anyone to truly know my real self. I usually tried to act in such a way so that people would accept me. I sought their approval, but wasn't the truly me. I did what people expected me to do in order to gain some form of acceptance. This usually meant I needed to conform according to their plans. I did this with everyone for fear of rejection; everyone except my dog, Chico.

The years that Chico and I were together were the most precious time of my life. Because our relationship was so special, I felt as though I could tell Chico everything, and he would understand. He never sat in judgment of me, nor did he think I was strange or weird because I thought certain things or acted a certain way. Even though he couldn't talk back, he was still the best friend that I've ever had.

It has been my longing for many years now that a person or a group of people would accept me, but people are funny creatures. They want acceptance, but they are afraid to give it in return. They want someone to love them, but they are afraid to love anyone. And above all, most people are afraid to accept or love another who is different. I am different. I think differently from many people. I think very deeply, and consequently feel very deeply. My thoughts and feelings often reach a depth that most people are afraid to allow themselves to touch because of the risk of them finding out things about themselves that they would rather not know. Why can't I just find …

"Hi!" A voice broke through my thoughts.

I turned over on the bed and looked into the face of a girl I hadn't met yet.

"Hi!" I replied as I pushed myself into a sitting position.

There stood before me one of the girls from the room next door.

"My name is Bea. I'm the senior dorm monitor. It's my job to make sure that all of the girls in the dorm get settled. I'm also here to help with any problems they may be having. I apologize that I haven't had the chance to meet you until now."

Bea was a little older than the rest of us. My two roommates as well as myself were in our teens, but she was in her mid-twenties. She was shorter than me and was a little heavy, Bea she dressed like most of the college girls, with a polyester skirt and cotton blouse. Her blonde hair was cut short but not like the haircuts we had in the New Order.

"How are you doing?" Bea asked.

"Okay," I gave the answer that I thought she wanted to hear. There was no way I was going to tell this person what had just taken place in the Dean of Women's office. Maybe she already knew. Maybe she was one who had complained. I didn't trust her or anyone else at this point.

"You seem to be getting settled into the routine here okay?" Bea asked.

I nodded.

"Good! Well, I just wanted to introduce myself and see how things were going," she said. Her smile was infectious. I couldn't help but smile back at her.

"If there's anything you need or if you want to talk don't hesitate to ask," she said.

Bea went on to meet the other girls. There were a total of about seven of us in this particular dorm. We lived in what they called the "old" dorms. Basically, the old dorms were houses that the school had purchased and converted all of the rooms into bedrooms. They didn't have enough room in the regular dorms for all of the students that were enrolled. Personally, I liked the house dorms better than the regular ones. I'd walked into one and there were too many girls to suit me.

For the time being, I let the visit to the Dean's office slip to the back of my mind. I got ready for bed early and went to sleep without speaking to anyone else in the dorm.

My typical day started by getting up before the sun and going to the dining hall. There I set up two tables with ten places each and served breakfast to twenty hungry students, who were not very understanding if they didn't get everything they wanted. This involved running back and forth from my tables to the kitchen for refills. You had to move fast, the kitchen tended to run out of some of the more popular entrées. When that happened, you had some very unhappy people at your table that took their frustrations out on you.

Once breakfast ended, I cleaned up the mess that the twenty people left. It wasn't much different than cleaning up after Mother and Edward, only there were more of them. You had to be fast or you'd end up being late for your first class.

Often times, I was so tired by the time I got to class; I had difficulty staying awake. The classes opened with prayer and a short talk about God. Mid morning we were required to go to chapel. This was in addition to all of the services of the church throughout the week.

I didn't like being forced to go to services. I had paid Mother to let me go to services back home but now that they were required I hated going. The messages often used many of the same words Mrs. Smith and Rachel read to me from their Bibles.

After chapel, there was another class and then the rush to serve lunch. Once lunch was finished, I had to clean up my tables and rush off to the afternoon classes. Fortunately, I had a short break between my afternoon classes and serving supper. After cleanup, there was homework and then bed.

As the days went by, I became more and more aware that my problems followed me. It wasn't the new start that I had hoped for. I felt the pain inside grow stronger day by day.

Time moved quickly following the same routine. Soon there were mid terms and then finals for the semester. I'd survived the first semester. I worked overtime at being observant of the things the other girls did and tried to copy them. I hadn't heard anymore from the Dean of Women. I figured no news was good news. Despite all of the frustrations, I managed to pass all of my classes. I'd completed my first semester as a college freshman. That brought a bit of satisfaction.

I still was scared that they'd find some reason to kick me out. After so many months of continued preaching and teaching from the Bible, I was becoming more and more uncomfortable in the services. When the Bible was read, I felt an increasing pain in my chest. After the service, I felt very depressed. It was different from the other pain I felt inside. I wasn't sure what this pain was, but I didn't like it. I wondered if there was something physically wrong with me.

The second semester began and the pain continued to increase.

One day I looked up from my book and Bea was standing in the doorway to my room.

"Hi!" she said and smiled.

"Hi!" I replied.

Why is she here? Who complained now?

"How are things going?" she asked.

"Okay!" I replied automatically.

"Pardon my saying so, but you don't seem to be okay," she observed.

"What do you mean?" I answered with surprise in my voice.

Why would she care? Am I in trouble?

"I mean for the past several months you seem rather troubled. Is there anything I can do?" Bea continued.

I stared at her in surprise.

Is it obvious? No one has asked me that question since I've been here. Why would anyone want to do something for me? What is in it for her?

I managed to shake my head. The ache in my throat began again.

"You look like you could use someone to talk to. I'd like to help if I could. Perhaps we should talk further," she pressed.

"I don't think so! You've done your job; you've shown your interest in me. Now, go on and check on someone else!" I snapped. But something about her made me soften, "I'm sorry, I don't mean to be rude, but I'm not use to having anyone interested in what's going on with me."

"I understand," she said. "I still think we need to talk."

"Talk about what?"

"Let's continue this conversation in a place with a little more privacy," she said.

Why do we need to continue this conversation in privacy? What is it that she wants to say to me? Does she know something that I don"t?

I lived in fear of someone telling me that I didn't fit in and that I would have to leave this special place. This conversation was fanning the fires of that fear.

But if I say no, what will she think of me? Will it make things worse? Will she report me as being uncooperative if I don't go with her?

"Okay," I replied hesitantly.

"Come with me!" she said.

I followed her through our kitchen area. We passed the other room.

Where are we going?

We stopped at the room that had been designated as the storage room. She stopped in front of the door, unlocked and opened it. Bea motioned me inside. Fear and anxiety began to rise from the pit of my stomach.

Is this some kind of a trap? Who is waiting inside? Is someone in there to hurt me?

I pushed the thoughts from my brain. I had to stop thinking of everyone in the light of the gang members.

After all these are Christians.

I entered the room. She motioned me to a place across the room from the door.

"Have a seat!" she said.

"I'd rather sit here on the floor by the door," I choked out the words through the growing ache.

"It's better if you sit over there." Her tone of voice was a little firmer.

I moved inside the room and took a seat on someone's footlocker on the far side of the room. My heart ached with fear as I watched her close the door.

"That's better!" She said as she took a seat on a box near the door. "Is there something that is bothering you? You seem rather down, and I felt impressed that I should talk to you."

"I'm okay," I insisted.

Being the center of attention increased my anxiety. Impressed by who? Why did she say that she felt like she should talk to me? Where did such a feeling come from?

"Your name is Josephine, right?" Bea asked.

"I go by Joey," I replied.

She nodded." Do you like it here?" she inquired.

"Yes, very much so!" I replied.

Why is she asking me if I like it here? Is she planning on telling me I can't stay?

She smiled tenderly. "I'm glad to hear that. A lot of girls come here and find it doesn't measure up to their expectations."

"I like it just fine!" I said, not wanting to tell her about the issues I'd had with the Dean of Women. Maybe she already knew.

"Good, I'm glad to hear that! How's working in the dining hall?" she continued to question.

"It's fine!" I replied not wishing to give too much information.

What is with all of these questions?

"Joey, you say you like it here; that you like your job," she started.

"Yes!" I interrupted her.

"Yet, in the times that I've seen you working, or here in the dorm, you appear to be very unhappy," she observed.

I shrugged, not knowing how to respond. Silence rested in the air.

I wonder why she's not saying anything...I wish she would say something.

Finally she broke the silence, "what kind of a church did you come from

Why does she want to know all these things? How do you describe a church?

"It was a church and I liked it very much. There were a lot of people there who helped me and made it possible for me to be here," I said.

She smiled. "I like hearing good things like that!"

Another silence hung in the air. Each one seemed longer than the previous.

"Joey, I feel very impressed to ask you a very important question," Bea began.

I stared at her confused.

What is she going to ask me next? Why does she feel impressed to do it and by whom?

"Have you ever accepted Jesus Christ as your personal Savior?" She asked.

Where did that question come from?

My mind remembered the conversations I had with Rachel and later with Mrs. Smith. Each of them talked to me about Jesus and shown me verses in the Bible about Him, but I don't think I ever accepted Him.

I know Mrs. Smith tried to explain that to me, but I don't think I know what that means. I am afraid to admit that I don't know what she means.

I felt Bea studying me.

A wave of fear swept over me. The thought occurred to me that if I hadn't accepted this Jesus that she'd tell the school authorities, and I'd be expelled. It was a requirement you had to answer on the application. I copied a story I read to answer that question. When I attended Mrs. Smith's church, I'd act like everyone else so I guess they all thought I was a Christian.

I know I need to find some type of an answer quickly. I needed an answer that wouldn't get me thrown out of school. No matter what, I had to stay. I didn't want them to send me back to Mother's.

"I don't know," I answered. It was the only thing I could think of. It was at least non-committal.

Bea pulled out her Bible. I didn't see her bring a Bible into the room with us. She opened it and began sharing with me some of the same verses that I'd heard from Rachel and from Mrs. Smith. My heart felt like lead inside.

The more she talked, the more I ached inside. I don't know how long we were in the room, but in many ways I wanted out and yet, I wanted to hear more.

"Do you believe that we are all sinners?" she asked.

I thought about all the good things I'd done with Mrs. Smith. Before I could answer, Bea read, "'...all our righteousness are as filthy rags...' That means, even the good things we've done are like filthy rags in God's sight."

I nodded.

"The Bible says that because of our sin, we are under a death sentence," she continued. "I'm sure that you've heard the verse, 'For God so loved the world that He gave His only begotten Son, that whosoever believeth in Him should not perish but have everlasting life.'"

I nodded again. It was the only thing I could do. Every time I thought of an objection or an excuse, she'd read a verse that would shoot it out of the water. It was happening so frequently it became rather creepy.

"Joey, God loves you so much that He sent His Son Jesus to die on the cross for your sin. If you were the only person on this earth that needed to be saved, He would still have sent Jesus to die for you."

I did a double take as I looked at her. Mrs. Smith had said the same thing to me, but what was really weird was I'd been thinking about how to dodge her next question.

Who is telling her my thoughts?

God loves you so much He gave His Son to die for you," she said. "The Bible says in John 15:13, 'that greater love hath no man than this, that a man lay down his life for his friends.'"

My mind flashed to Grandfather diving in front of me to take the bullet meant for me. He gave his life for me.

Someone else loved me that much?

My chest hurt even more.

"Joey, God wants to save you. He wants to make you His child. It doesn't matter what you've done. God loves you more than anyone else ever could. You can become His child as easily as accepting a gift. Salvation is a free gift."

I remembered Mrs. Smith's example of the cake on my sixteenth birthday.

Bea closed the Bible and looked at me.

"Joey, after all Jesus has done for you, do you want to accept Jesus Christ as your personal Savior?" She asked me.

I knew this was the thing I needed. It was the thing I'd been searching for to fill the emptiness inside.

I nodded. We prayed together and I accepted Jesus Christ as my personal Savior in that storage room. A wave of peace flowed over me. It was something I had never experienced before in my entire life. I felt peaceful inside for the first time in my life.

God really does love me.

Chapter - 39 - Heart Changes

The very next Sunday I walked the aisle of the church and made my public profession of faith in Jesus Christ. I was letting everyone know that I now wanted to be identified with Christ. My excitement of realizing that God was now living inside of me and that He wanted to show me just how much He loved me. A major fear loomed in the back of my mind. I knew I had lied on my application for school. This fear continued to grow larger and larger until I felt consumed by it. I just know that the school would expel me for lying.

That fear ate away at me until mustered the courage to face the fear head on. Rather than waiting for them to discover this fact, I decided to take action. I made an appointment with the head of the school, tell him what I had done, and let the chips fall. Would I be forgiven this misdeed; or would I be expelled without apology?

I arrived in his office and anxiously took a seat and waited. My entire body was shaking. The secretary told me I could go in. I walked into the office on rubbery legs.

The head of the school stood as I entered the room. He was an elderly man in his seventies. He had white hair and was balding. His face was genuinely pleasant and had a warm, friendly handshake. Motioning me to a seat, I sat down. I was relieved to sit. He took his seat behind his desk. His soft blue eyes made eye contact with me.

"What can I do for you?" he asked.

"I wanted to let you know that I lied on my application for acceptance to school. I wasn't saved when I came here." I blurted the words out so quickly that I thought they'd trip over each other.

He sat back in his chair.

Here comes the fireworks!

I prepared myself for a tongue-lashing.

I felt my stomach tie in knots as I waited for him to break the silence. He continued making eye contact and appeared to be deep in thought. Maybe he was analyzing me.

Finally, he broke the silence, "are you saved now?"

"Yes sir!" I replied quickly. I had to force myself to not jump to attention and salute. This was a common practice in the New Order when asked a direct question by a superior. My fingers gripped the arms of the chair and I remained seated.

"That's wonderful!" he said with a sincere smile.

Did I hear him correctly?

I think I started to breathe again.

"Do you love the Lord?" He asked.

"Yes sir!" I replied immediately.

His warm smile never wavered.

"I appreciate you coming in and telling me. All I ask is that you continue to grow in your new life in Christ and let God control your life."

"Thank you, sir!" I responded.

"God bless you!" he said.

With that he stood, shook my hand, and I was sent on my way.

Relief flooded my brain. I felt like I'd been lifted out of the deep, dark pit that I'd spent most of my life in.

The sky was bluer and the grass was greener than I'd ever seen them. It was like seeing God's creation through new eyes. Words fail me when I try to describe those days that followed my accepting Christ as my Savior. It was truly the mountain top experience that most people refer to it as. My heart felt lighter, my feet had a spring in my step and I felt a strong desire to read God's Word and learn more about Him and the wonderful things He had done for me. I was hungry to discover His plan for me.

I'd like to say that everything that was wrong was better, but it didn't work that way. Yes, I had the joy of the Lord, but I was still bound by the fleshly existence. It wasn't an instant cure for all that was wrong. It was however, a realization that I didn't even need to feel alone again. God promised to be with me always.

I arrived at work and looked around the cafeteria at all of the people. They were huddled together in small groups nibbling on their lunches and talking about things of no importance. Conversations that I still didn't know how to participate in, since small talk was not something I knew very little about.

What would it be like to belong? Even as a Christian, I still don't feel like I fit in with the other Christians.

As time went on, I was able to make some friends, but for one reason or another the friendships never lasted very long. The remainder of my years in college were mostly uneventful. I continued taking classes, even took classes that weren't part of my curriculum. I wasn't in a hurry to graduate. I did want to become a teacher like Mrs. Smith. I didn't know what I really wanted to do when I graduated, I decided to learn as many different things as I could. School was a much better place to be instead of the house with Mother and Edward. My summers were spent as a camp counselor, and school holiday I'd go home with different individuals. This way I get to travel and see things I hadn't seen before. It also was a good excuse not to go home as often.

After six years, graduation day arrived. I had made it! I not only went to college, but now I was going to graduate from college. I felt like I truly accomplished something important in my life.

Who would have thought? Me, a former refugee of the New Order and a former gang leader; A kid who was unwanted and didn't belong anywhere. Me, a kid from the wrong side of the tracks was graduating from a Christian University!

Chapter - 40 - My Journey

I'd like to say that everything is now wonderful in my life since becoming a Christian. The truth is that life will always be a series of hurdles. In my case, I need to deal with the past hurdles while still moving through the present. I still am working to overcome so many traumatic events in my life. One day, I sat down and wrote this poem to describe my situation.

My Journey

I am on a journey. One that has many ups and downs.
It is a journey from the shattered to the whole
The breaking took place a long time ago when I was small.
My life was torn from me. I became not my own. Choices were
    forced upon me.
And I lost all that makes childhood sweet and innocent.

The little child within found a safe place to hide inside
Surrounding myself with thick walls to block out the hurt
My trust was stolen, and so I was very much alone
No one was there to protect me; no one was there to help me
Too scared, I could not tell.

*Time passed and I grew up, and then was left to pick up the pieces,
    to find myself and survive.*
*As I tried to pick up the pieces, I discovered my hands could not
    grasp them.*
How could I go on with so many pieces of me scattered about?
I limped on into adulthood, learning to pretend all was well.

No one cared that it was an act.
*I soon found that on this journey, I could not continue with the
    missing pieces*
*My brittle walls could not contain all the hurt that was my
    companion.*
It could change with life, but I didn't know how to continue.
My childhood refuge was too small for the adult me.
I despaired that no one cared and I felt doomed.

Quit, I could not. With the darkest hour of my soul upon me
*There was one that came along side and said I will not
    abandon you*
*We will walk this journey together. We will shine the light into the
    darkness.*
*My guide patiently waited as I allowed her through the walls
    of my sanctuary*
*She exuded an aura of care and concern and I began to rebuild
    some trust.*

*My journey is from shatteredness to wholeness. It has many ups
    and many downs.*
*My guide is there to cheer me on when I fall, and to share her hope
    for me to rest upon.*
*With the fresh wounds and scars knitted to my heart, to my being,
    I know that my guide*
*Will not abandon me and so we travel on shining the light into
    the darkness.*
*Until my journey reaches freedom so that I might at last stretch
    my wings and fly.*

Epilogue

Thirty years have passed since the day I left Mother's house and the abuse ended. I wish I could say that time heals all wounds, but the truth is that it does not. Time can create new memories for your mind to dwell on instead of the painful ones, but learning to dwell on those takes a lot of discipline and reprogramming of your mind. This is a process that doesn't happen overnight. It is truly a journey. I still live with the constant emotional pain, but I am learning ways and techniques of dealing with it through counseling and very supportive friends. As time goes on, I do feel like there is hope. Why? Because I can see, little by little, that I am making progress.

The first hurdle that I faced was coming to grips with the fact that none of the abuse that happened to me was my fault. I still fall back into that rut and think that somehow it must have been, but then my support system comes to my rescue and reminds me of the facts. My abusers took so much from me in those years, but it is my choice to not let them take anything more from me. I don't have to be afraid of facing that type of abuse ever again. From this point on, my life is based on the choices that I make.

Life is a journey for every person on earth. For some of us it is harder than others because of the rough start we got. But with each step forward, we can move beyond the control of those horrific memories and regain a sense of happiness and balance in our lives. The choice is now mine and it is now yours. We have the choice to play, to love, to enjoy the beauties of life around us.

The nightmares still come, and I often become very depressed. The flashbacks often are so intense at times that I have a hard time knowing if the events are really happening now or not. It is like a wall inside of me that prevents me from letting out all of the emotional pain, not to mention experiencing those emotions it is a very scary prospect.

There are days that I don't feel like I can take another step forward, but that's when my friends come along side and encourage me and cheer me to keep moving forward. They remind me of their love for me and above all they remind me of God's love for me.

I don't know the answer to the question of why all this happened to me, but I do know that it has shaped me into the person that I am today. Somewhere between the therapy and openly talking about the events, I can truly say that the New Order and those that abused me have lost their ability to destroy me. I'm back in control of my life. It's worth repeating: I am the one who makes the choices in my life.

It's been a long dark night, but I'm on the journey to the daylight, and I keep moving forward. It is my desire that by sharing my journey with you, that you will be encouraged to begin your journey toward wholeness.

Today, I bow my head and say a prayer for all those who have been abused in any way - those that have died and those who must continue to deal with the pain. Prayers for peace within. Prayers that awareness will win out and not one more individual will have to face the horrors of abuse in their lives. For me, the silence is now broken. And by speaking out, I pray that people will never let this happen to anyone again.

Living Tapestry

by Susan Kaye Behm

A lie, a moment of anger or fear, a timely pat on the back
all spin into threads.

As each experience molds and shapes our lives
It causes these threads to weave a tapestry.

This cloth is then colored and sewn in many different shapes
portraying our finite character.

Many times we chasten ourselves and have regrets
for things that may bring shame to our faces.

Our choices at times may be poor,
and we may desire to change our past.

But if we begin to pull on these threads,
the fabric of our very being will unravel.

With each deed performed and every choice made
we must weave a tapestry of beauty and not shame.

Note: Though I would not have chosen to be abused and wouldn't have chosen to live with nightmares and flashbacks; if I were to start pulling these threads out of my life, I would change the person that I am today.

Too many people have tried to change me. I choose today to love myself for who I am. I will not allow others to unravel me any longer. I love myself enough to sew new and beautiful threads into the tapestry of my life. Make your tapestry beautiful ... see what you can become.

The Author's Healing Journey:

Essential Keys to Healing

We use keys for many things in our daily lives: car keys, and house keys; and office keys, and miscellaneous other keys. Without which we would be lost. In our healing journey, these keys summarize our purpose. Using these keys is what keeps us moving forward even through the midst of intense pain and other obstacles. The keys to healing are Faith, Hope, and Love.

The first essential key that we must have is **Faith**. The dictionary defines **Faith** as "the confident belief in the truth, value, or trustworthiness of a person, idea, or a thing".

It is a hard road we travel, but that is what makes us survivors. It is this key of faith that continues to unlock the obstacles before us, so that we can continue to move forward. During all of the years of humiliation, torture, violation, and abuse, somewhere deep inside of me, there was a seed of faith that kept me going and believing that there was more to life than this.

At the time, we may not have recognized it as the key of Faith. But it was this very key that kept us going as we were forced to endure the constant abuse. We somehow managed to hold onto our humanity though our abusers tried to steal it from us. It was this

Faith that we held onto because something in our character would not let us give up.

Once we escaped our abusive circumstances, we still needed to keep a firm grip on the key of Faith in order to unlock our inward prison and be able, at some point, to reach for the telephone to make an appointment with a mental health professional and admit that we needed help to overcome the horrors that we experienced. Many of us agonized over whether or not we had the courage to make that call. For me, it wasn't until I began having panic attacks, flashbacks, and nightmares and nearly became homebound before I understood and admitted that I needed help. With a firm grasp on the key of Faith, I had to will myself to go and show up for the appointment with the therapist and then somehow find the words to explain why I was sitting in her office. I had to use this key to unlock some of the doors within in me to learn to trust the therapist. It was the key of Faith that kept me moving forward and helped me believe that she could help me through these experiences.

Through therapy, I learned what Mahatma Gandhi meant when he said, "You must not lose faith in humanity. Humanity is an ocean; if a few drops of the ocean are dirty, the ocean does not become dirty." This means that not every person was of the same caliber as my abusers.

As you and I move through our abuse to our healing, we use the key of Faith to unlock the many obstacles that face us. It takes courage to face the pain and the memories that are stirred up through therapy.

While we hold the key of Faith firmly, we reach out and grasp the second key **Hope**!

Hope is defined as "looking forward with confidence or expectation; a wish or desire accompanied by confident expectation of its fulfillment".

With the key of Hope, we look forward with confidence that we will overcome much of the damage that our abuse has done to our lives. That's what motivates us to continue working in therapy even though it is hard and often unpleasant.

Don't let anyone tell you that therapy is not hard work. It is some of the hardest work that we shall ever do. Releasing our feelings and emotions from their hiding places is often a very scary experience, but it is an absolutely necessary one in order to move us towards becoming whole. One of the first things we feel as we begin to unlock the doors of our hearts and minds is a deep pain that wells up inside of us; that deep, dark, black pain that makes us feel like we are being turned inside out. That huge pain that tries to push us into hopelessness and despair. You might compare this experience to that of a burn victim. Each time they go in for treatment, they have to endure excruciating pain in order to continue taking steps toward becoming healthy. I believe that is what we endure each time we work through therapy until we can strip away those things from our abuse that has bound us.

Even when we fall, we must firmly grasp the keys of Faith and Hope and get up again believing that there is a life worth living. Hold onto those keys and never give up. By allowing these keys to open the doors within our hearts and minds, we demonstrate to our abusers that they have not won. Hope renews our stamina to keep on going.

In the course of time, the key of hope helps me to retrain my thinking and to accept the things that have happened and to realize that I am not the sum of my abuse.

The key of Hope unlocks the door of new beginnings: These new beginnings bring the satisfaction and purpose that we lacked during our years of abuse. I have often wondered what possible purpose all of the torture and abuse could have. I know I have often questioned the reasons for all of the abuse. I firmly believe that God can use some the nightmare that I survived.

I believe that when we stop and evaluate our talents and then allow them to intersect with the needs of the people around us, we will find that purpose. It is not important what that purpose is. It **IS** important that we have one.

One purpose I have found for myself is the deep conviction I have to raise awareness that Ritual Abuse exists. We cannot make people care until they are aware. It wasn't until I fully took hold of the Key of Hope that I began to learn how to reach out to others that are hurting and to share with them that they are not alone. As I reached out to others, I found that I grew and I moved further down the road towards healing and am becoming a more complete person.

I have survived another day and I live this day facing only the **<u>NOW</u>** of life. Training ourselves to stay in the present, we become better equipped to cope with the abuse of the past. A quote that I feel is appropriate for this point is by Dr. Robert Schuler, Jr. from the Hour of Power stated, "The past is history, and tomorrow is still a mystery, today is our gift, and that is why we call it the present."

I believe the third essential key to healing and the most powerful of the three keys is the Key of **Love**. "Love builds bridges where there were none." As abuse survivors, we may feel like we are stranded on an island alone with no one knowing how to reach us. Most people cannot even begin to fathom the things we have suffered and continue to suffer. This key of love helped me reach across the chasms and build the bridges that began to bypass and create some holes in the emotional prison walls that I had built through the years. By wielding the Key of Love, I continued to learn about building relationships and that I was not alone-and neither are you. As we move on our journey with the Key of Love in our hand, we begin to learn how to trust. Through the assistance of fellow survivors, a trusted therapist, and supportive friends and family, these walls of seclusion are slowly decaying, and we discover the true power of this third key. This is crucial to our healing. It has been proven from various studies that love is the one power that is strong enough to overcome the power of the brainwashing and programming that we have endured and returns our humanity to us. We need the support of others. It is this key that also opens the door to a new way of thinking. As we unlock the doors before us we learn to love and care for ourselves as someone worthy to be loved. We learn that it is okay to allow others to help and sustain us on our journey. Grasping this key firmly helps us to unlock the chains that keep us from those things that are rightfully ours: the freedom from abuse; the freedom to love and be loved; the freedom to overcome the past.

If we are to move forward in our healing journey, we must grab hold of all three of these keys and wield them as needed. At times, we may stumble and fall and possibly drop a key from time to time. When that happens to me, I feel overwhelmed by the pain, discouraged, and depressed and that I'll never recover. Be aware that we all move on this journey at our own pace.

I encourage each of you to reach out and firmly grasp these keys of **Faith, Hope**, and **Love.** They are essential to our healing and freedom from our abusive past. **LOVE HEALS**.

Dale Carnegie said, "Most of the important things in the world have been accomplished by people who have kept on trying when there seemed to be no hope at all."

Orison Swett Marden that said, "The golden opportunity you are seeking is within yourself. It is not in your environment; it is not in luck or chance, or solely in the help of others; it is within you."

Individually we must make the decision to begin our healing journey and grasp the keys. You and I deserve all the support that we need to move us from being a victim to being a survivor and beyond that to become a victor. Take the keys and hold them firmly within your heart and hands.

Faith to step forward regardless of the pain you face;

Hope that this nightmare will not last forever; and

Love that will build you up and support you along the healing journey.

These keys will give each of us the strength and courage to start and continue on the healing journey; moving step-by-step, even when it feels like one step forward and three steps backwards. Take hold of these keys: Faith, Hope and Love.

As survivors, we can be voices of encouragement to other survivors and continue to work to raise awareness. Our journey is hard, but we can make it. I encourage you to reach out and grasp these Essential Keys and move forward on your healing journey.

God bless you!

The Romans' Road to Heaven

The Bible tells us in Romans that:

As it is written, There is none righteous, no, not one: Romans 3:10

For all have sinned and come short of the glory of God; Romans 3:23

For the wages of sin is death... Romans 6:23

But God commendeth his love toward us, in that, while we were yet sinners, Christ died for us. Romans 5:8

...the gift of God is eternal life through Jesus Christ our Lord. Romans 6:23

That if thou shalt confess with thy mouth the Lord Jesus, and shalt believe in thine heart that God hath raised him from the dead. Thou shalt be saved. For with the heart man believeth unto righteousness; and with the mouth confession is made unto salvation. Romans 10:9,10

For whosoever shall call upon the name of the Lord shall be saved. Romans 10:13

God tells us in the Bible that we have all sinned, and the payment for our sin is death (both physical and spiritual). God has provided the payment for our sin in the shed blood of his only begotten Son, Jesus Christ, on the cross. If you are to have eternal life in heaven, you must:

Admit to God that you are a sinner: **Repent** (turn away from sin) and **believe** with your heart that Jesus died for your sins and rose again; Ask God to forgive your sins and **invite** Him to be your Lord and Savior.

For God so loved the world, that He gave His only begotten Son, that whosoever believeth in Him should not perish, but have everlasting life. John 3:16

Now, with your heart, pray a prayer like this:

"Dear Lord, I know I have sinned. I am sorry and turn away from my sin. I believe you died for my sins and rose the third day. I now ask You, Jesus, to come into my heart and forgive my sins and be my Lord and Savior. Thank You, Jesus, for saving my soul. Amen!"

Appendix - A

Definition of Terms

(Statistics were gathered from the Rape,
Abuse and Incest National Network (RAINN)

Definition of Rape

RAPE is forced sexual intercourse, including both psychological coercion and physical force. Forced sexual intercourse means vaginal, anal or oral penetration by the offender(s). This category includes incidents where the penetration is from a foreign object such as a bottle. This definition includes attempted rapes, male and female victims, and heterosexual and homosexual rape.

Definition of Sexual Assault

SEXUAL ASSAULT includes a wide range of victimizations, distinct from rape or attempted rape. These crimes include completed or attempted attacks generally involving unwanted sexual contact between the victim and offender. Sexual assaults may or may not involve force and include such things as grabbing or fondling. Sexual assault also includes verbal threats.

- Every two minutes, somewhere in America, someone is sexually assaulted.

- One out of every six American women have been the victims of an attempted or a completed rape in their lifetime.
- In 2002, seven out of eight rape victims were female.
- In 2002, one in eight rape victims were male.

Definition of Sexual Abuse

Sexual abuse can be defined as any experience during childhood or adolescence which involves inappropriate sexual attention by another person (usually an adult, but sometimes an older child, teenager, or even playmate the same-aged. This attention might involve:

- Sexualized language, and or touching,
- Being forced to perform manual or oral sex on another person,
- Oral, vaginal, or anal penetration,
- Exposure to sexual behavior or to pornography.

The behavior may be forced, coerced, or even willingly engaged in by the survivor, but is understood as abusive because a child cannot truly give free consent. Any activity that a person feels violates her or his boundaries may fall within the realm of sexual abuse.

Definition of Incest

Incest is any sexual behavior imposed on the child by a family member, including extended family members and even teachers or clergy. Sexual contacts may include a variety of verbal and/or physical behaviors; penetration is not necessary for the experience to be called incest.

<u>Definition of Ritual Abuse</u>

Ritual abuse-torture is intentionally planned and organized by family and/or non-family brutal group ritualism:

- acts of human evil that terrify and horrify;
- acts of pedophilic, physical, sexualized, and mind-spirit tortures;
- acts that can include modern day slavery (pornography, trafficking, sexualized
- labour-intensive exploitation;
- acts that cause life-threatening torment;
- acts that distorts beliefs and values, thoughts, emotions, perceptions, behaviours, and world-view of the victimized person;
- dehumanizing and despiritualizing acts that have the capacity to destroy the personality of the infant, toddler, child, youth or "captive" adult victim; actions of a co-culture that can be inter-connected regionally, nationality, internationally, and transnationally; and, criminal acts that are a violation of the victimized person's human rights.

Appendix - B

Helpful websites for support and information

Survivors of Rape & Sexual Assault:

http://www.Ephesians.org
http://www.rainn.org
http://www.voices-action.org_
http://sexualabusesurvivors.com
http://www.alltheseyears.net
http://www.dancinginthedarkness.com
http://www.sandf.org
http://www.survivingtothriving.org

Information about Flashbacks and Ritual Abuse:

http://www.healthyplace.com/communities/abuse/safeline/
flashbacks.htm
http://members.aol.com/smartnews/index2.html
http://www.ritualabusetorture.org/index.htm
http://www.mental-health-matters.com/articles/article.
php?artID=154

Information on Anxiety and Panic

http://www.anxietypanic.com/
http://www.anxieties.com/

Survivors of Abuse:

http://www.soc-um.org/survivors/index.html
http://www.victimsnolonger.org.uk/
http://www.ascasupport.org/
http://www.latebloomerpublishing.com/abuse_incest.htm

Miscellaneous other Mental Health Sites:

http://www.mental-health-today.com/index.htm
http://www.emofree.com/
http://www.urnotalone.org/

Online Support Groups:

http://www.urnotalone.org/
http://www.survivors-treehouse.net
http://www.thereisocdhope.com/
http://www.angelsurvive.com

Printed in the United States
50394LVS00006B/1-87